New World Orders in Contemporary Children's Literature

Also by Clare Bradford:

GENRE IN PERSPECTIVE: A Whole Language Approach

READING RACE: Aboriginality in Australian Children's Literature

UNSETTLING NARRATIVES: Postcolonial Readings of Children's Literature

WRITING THE AUSTRALIAN CHILD: Texts and Contexts in Fictions for Children (*edited*)

Also by Kerry Mallan:

CHILDREN AS STORYTELLERS

IN THE PICTURE: Perspectives on Picture Book Art and Artists

LAUGH LINES: Exploring Humour in Children's Literature

PERFORMING BODIES: Narrative, Representation, and Children's Storytelling

SERIOUSLY PLAYFUL: Genre, Performance and Text (*co-edited with Sharyn Pearce*)

YOUTH CULTURES: Texts, Images, and Identities (*co-edited with Sharyn Pearce*)

Also by John Stephens:

LANGUAGE AND IDEOLOGY IN CHILDREN'S FICTION

WAYS OF BEING MALE: Representing Masculinities in Children's Literature and Film (*edited*)

LITERATURE, LANGUAGE AND CHANGE: From Chaucer to the Present (*co-authored with Ruth Waterhouse*)

By Robyn McCallum and John Stephens:

RETELLING STORIES, FRAMING CULTURE: Traditional Story and Metanarratives in Children's Literature

Also by Robyn McCallum:

IDEOLOGIES OF IDENTITY IN ADOLESCENT FICTION: The Dialogic Construction of Subjectivity

New World Orders in Contemporary Children's Literature

Utopian Transformations

Clare Bradford, Kerry Mallan, John Stephens & Robyn McCallum

palgrave
macmillan

First published 2008 by
PALGRAVE MACMILLAN
Houndmills, Basingstoke, Hampshire RG21 6XS and
175 Fifth Avenue, New York, N.Y. 10010
Companies and representatives throughout the world

PALGRAVE MACMILLAN is the global academic imprint of the Palgrave Macmillan division of St. Martin's Press, LLC and of Palgrave Macmillan Ltd. Macmillan® is a registered trademark in the United States, United Kingdom and other countries. Palgrave is a registered trademark in the European Union and other countries.

ISBN-13: 978–0–230–02005–4 hardback
ISBN-10: 0–230–02005–4   hardback

This book is printed on paper suitable for recycling and made from fully managed and sustained forest sources. Logging, pulping and manufacturing processes are expected to conform to the environmental regulations of the country of origin.

A catalogue record for this book is available from the British Library.

A catalog record for this book is available from the Library of Congress.

Printed and bound in Great Britain by
CPI Antony Rowe, Chippenham and Eastbourne

Contents

Acknowledgements

We would like to thank our research assistants, Margaret Aitken, Elizabeth Braithwaite, Victoria Flanagan, and Geraldine Massey, for their interest and support. We acknowledge the contribution of the Australian Research Council, which provided funding to the project of which this book is an outcome.

1

A New World Order or a New Dark Age?

This is the dawn of the ending
It's the time of a new world order
This is a new beginning.

Gamma Ray, *No World Order*, 2001

The phrase 'a new world order' has been used by politicians from the early years of the twentieth century to describe the new political dawning, the end of the old warring world, and a new beginning. Woodrow Wilson is credited with being the first US president to proclaim the optimism of a 'new world order' at the end of the First World War, 'the war to end all wars'. Again at the end of the Cold War, other leaders (Prime Minister Rajiv Gandhi, President Mikhail Gorbachev, and President George H. W. Bush) spoke of a new world order, and outlined their various visions for a world shaped by tolerance, human rights, superpower cooperation, north-south alliance, and an end of military conflicts. By the time of the attacks on the Twin Towers and the Pentagon on September 11, 2001, 'new world order' rhetoric had been replaced by other concepts: 'globalisation', 'end of history', 'clash of civilisations', and 'the war on terrorism'.

As we write this introduction in July 2006, we watch daily news reports of the escalation of conflict in the Middle East, where bombings of Lebanon and Israel have left many children, families, and citizens dead, injured, homeless, and traumatised. The era of the new dawn brings fear, insecurity, and pain. While a new dark age might well be upon us, our intention throughout this book is to examine how texts written and produced for children and young people imagine future world orders, how they respond to current and past world crises, and the kinds of utopian dreamings they offer their audiences. These are dangerous

1

times, but they are also times of possibility. As Zygmunt Bauman puts it:

> To measure the life 'as it is' by a life as it should be (that is, a life imagined to be different from the life known, and particularly a life that is better and would be preferable to the life known) is a defining, constitutive feature of humanity.
>
> (Bauman, 2002b, p. 222)

Within popular and political discourses, the term 'utopian' is often taken to refer to unrealistic imaginings of improved world orders which when tested against the realpolitik of pragmatism collapse into ineffectuality. We argue, on the contrary, that utopian thinking both draws upon and generates ideas capable of influencing cultural, economic, and political practices. For utopianism incorporates what Lyman Tower Sargent refers to as 'social dreaming', the complex of 'dreams and nightmares that concern the ways in which groups of people arrange their lives and which usually envision a radically different society than the one in which the dreamers live' (1994, p. 3). Utopian thought thus informs social, political and cultural practices: it enables processes whereby intentional communities determine material practices; it shapes visions for improved world orders; and it pervades cultural production (including film, artwork, fiction, and drama) which engages with utopian and dystopian ideas.

Our aim in this book is to focus on contemporary children's texts, a field of cultural production highly responsive to social change and to global politics, and crucially implicated in shaping the values of children and young people. We locate our examination of these texts in relation to utopian studies and critical theory, calling on the concept of 'transformative utopianism' to suggest that utopian and dystopian tropes carry out important social, cultural, and political work by challenging and reformulating ideas about power and identity, community, the body, spatio-temporal change, and ecology. Children's literature is marked by a pervasive commitment to social practice, and particularly to representing or interrogating those social practices deemed worthy of preservation, cultivation, or augmentation, and those deemed to be in need of reconceiving or discarding (see Stephens, 1992a). An outcome of this commitment, in both the literature itself and the critical discourses which serve the literature, is a pervasive impulse towards what can be termed 'transformative utopianism'. This concept is realised as fictional imaginings of transformed world orders and employs utopian/dystopian themes and motifs which propose new social and political arrangements (Parrinder, 2001). In Shaun Tan's picture book *The Lost Thing* (2000), from which we borrow an image for the cover of this book, a small boy discovers a 'lost thing', a large red object, a hybrid figure with mechanoid, animal and human features, which is 'out of place' in the boy's world, where order and uniformity find expression in linear directions and monolithic forms. The utopian world shown in our cover image is a space of freedom, in which posthuman figures engage in purposeful play. Debra Dudek describes this space as one in which 'the beings are animal and machine and human and organic and musical instrument. They are grounded yet they fly. They are caged but have wings' (2005, p. 63). When the boy protagonist leaves the once lost (but now found) thing in this space and returns to his neat, orderly world, he nevertheless retains a consciousness of utopian possibilities where things '[don't] quite fit' (Tan, 2000). It is through its advocacy of difference and its refusal of closure that *The Lost Thing* proposes a transformed world order, one which reaches beyond a fear of the unknown to embrace new ways of being.

In a way similar to fiction, film produced for children and youth audiences serves both a socialising and a political function by representing and communicating the subjectivity of children and young people. By privileging the point of view of a young person, film offers visual and narrative pleasures, but, like literature, film is not an innocent medium devoid of ideology. Thus, by extending our focus texts to include film — animated and live action — we consider how a transformative utopianism operates through both the narrative and the body of the child who is the subject of the narrative. By paying attention to the child-subject, we attempt to understand how adults produce projections of children as citizens in the making. Our attention to the different layers of story and their significances offers ways of reading the social critiques they imply and the alternative futures they construct.

Within the interdisciplinary field of utopian studies, formulations and discussions of utopia draw upon the practices and theories of philosophy, sociology, history, political science, and cultural and literary studies to consider ideas, social movements, and cultural production. Our work, too, is interdisciplinary in scope, incorporating utopian studies, cultural geography, literary theory, and environmental and socio-political studies in its approach to literary and filmic texts.

Transformative utopianism

The notion of transformative utopianism forms the conceptual framework of this book because of its pertinence for analysis of the ways utopian themes are deployed in children's texts. Transformative utopianism is a construct we have selected as an alternative to other theorisations of utopian literature, which tend to be grounded in a particular theory or political philosophy (e.g. socialism, liberalism, feminism). For our purposes, transformative utopianism offers a number of narrative and theoretical possibilities.

Utopia must be transformative if it is to imagine a better world than the one that readers/audiences currently know. However, as Lucy Sargisson notes, 'utopian transformation doesn't have to be located in the future, in a far-distant hope for a better place. Rather, it can be part of transformation in the now' (Levitas and Sargisson, 2003, p. 17). Hence, our selection of texts includes those that do not necessarily conform to the traditional utopian genre. Many nevertheless contain what Moylan (2003, p. 2) sees as crucial to critical utopias, 'an emancipatory utopian imagination' which breaks away from the restrictions of the traditional utopia while preserving these texts' ability to challenge and resist dominant ideologies and social practices. In our critique of the transformative utopian potential in children's texts, we consider to what extent the narratives resist 'stasis and uniformity' (Beauchamp, 1998, p. 223) and authoritarian systems of control, which characterised earlier utopian models and interpretations, prevalent in both child and adult utopian writing.

David Harvey's Marxist framework displaces these traditional models with the notion of 'dialectical utopia'. His formulation of a 'dialectical utopia' and a 'spatio-temporal utopia' introduces the notion of spatio-temporal change and provides a space for the interplay between individuals and the environment and an understanding that social change is attainable. Harvey's work provides a useful resource for our conceptualising of transformation, rather than stasis, as a textual element of literary and filmic utopias and an ever-present condition of today's world. As Harvey observes, free-market utopianism, expressed in the spread of globalised capital, has resulted in 'geopolitical struggles' (2000, p. 178) which reinforce and exacerbate distinctions between populations more or less advantaged by the supposedly free play of market forces. To counter these illusory utopian orders, which depend upon institutional and political control for their maintenance, Harvey postulates more transformative visions of utopias. The novel, he says, has now become 'the primary site for the exploration of utopian sentiments and sensibilities' (2000, p. 189), its representations of spatiality taking multiple forms which include feminist, anarchist, religious, and ecologically informed varieties of the 'good place' of utopia. In many of the texts we consider, spatiality is a site of struggle over competing visions of social and political orders. Nor do these texts generally adduce narrative resolutions where utopian visions are enshrined in spatiality, achieved once and for all; rather, as in the closure of Lois Lowry's *Messenger* (2004), where a community returns to the utopian ideals of its original foundation, this apparently utopian resolution is contingent upon a continuous struggle against the reassertion of dystopian tendencies on the part of its inhabitants.

Further theoretical direction to our analysis is found in Richard Rorty's pragmatic liberalism (1989), which argues, firstly that social change is implied and advocated by processes of redescription — that is, the evolution of new vocabularies which impart new significances to things, or at times shift the meaning of key words, and secondly, that social formations, language and identity are contingent. Redescription enables the reformulation of social institutions and practices, of how they develop, of the effects they produce, and of the issues to which they give form. It thereby invites a critical discourse analysis of the extensive dystopian elements in children's literature. In positing the virtues of a critical pedagogy (with its utopian visions), Henry Giroux too puts language at the centre of those imaginings of a different and more just world which are crucial to transformative utopianism. Giroux's proposal of a 'language of critique and possibility' (2000, p. 694), like Rorty's utopian project, suggests a way in which our analysis will move from theoretical and conceptual concerns to consider their pragmatic and pedagogical implications and possibilities.

In summary, our formulation of transformative utopianism provides for a focus on the variety of forms and ideological positions which characterise children's texts, rather than driving our analysis towards definitions which fall back on static notions of utopian and dystopian forms and elements. In examining these texts, we consider the extent to which they promote and advocate transformative possibilities, either through constructions of fantastic or realistic worlds (both utopias and anti-utopias) or implied through negative example (as in the many dystopian narratives produced since 1988). Far from assuming that utopian texts are progressive and liberatory in regard to the ideological systems which inform them, we are interested in tracking the extent to which contemporary texts reinscribe conservative views and values embedded within narrative and discoursal features and naturalised because accepted as given. Our use of the term 'transformative utopianism' is based on the assumption that works of fiction employ utopian and dystopian themes and motifs in a way that has a transformative purpose: that is, they propose or imply new social and political arrangements by imagining transformed world orders.

The better worlds envisaged in utopian thinking project both liberation and constraint. Frances Bartowski succinctly labels such narratives 'tales of disabling and enabling conditions of desire' (1989, p. 4), and this concept is especially pertinent to children's texts, since to grasp what children's texts propose about values, politics, and social practices is to see what they envisage as desirable possibilities for the world. There exist clear contrasts between texts informed by alarm and pessimism about political conflict, war and environmental degradation (see Mallan, 2001), and utopian rhetoric which reinvokes Romantic formulations of an innocent child. The concept of transformative utopianism identifies the intellectual ground implicitly underlying most political and social inflections in children's fiction. Further, it transcends the interpretation of works written specifically within the genre of literary utopias because it has a wider application in the examination of the utopian impulse in children's literature and its associated critical discourses.

Utopianism and contemporary contexts

As Bartowski has pointed out, utopian writing and thought 'would seem to chart certain moments or ruptures in Western social history — those times when utopian desires/projective longings are driven by both hope and fear, those times particularly marked by anticipation and anxiety' (1989, p. 7). The texts we consider, produced between 1988 and 2006, derive from just such a time and play out many of the concerns of adults as they give shape to children's imagined anxieties and desires. In particular, the events of September 11 and their aftermath in world politics have sharpened cultural unease about children's perceptions of the worlds in which they live, and the futures which they imagine.

The engagement of children's literature with social practices was arguably pushed in a new direction by the various upheavals set in train at the end of the 1980s and which continued beyond the end of the millennium. Children's texts have reflected and responded to historical moments such as: the end of the Cold War in 1986–1987; the disintegration of the Soviet Empire in 1989, with related consequences such as the outbreak of civil war in Bosnia in 1992; the Persian Gulf War of 1990–1991; and the formal end to apartheid in South Africa in 1990. These events have prompted shifts in the social and political discourses of the fiction; for example, disaster literature, originating as a cold-war phenomenon in children's literature, has changed its focus over the past decades from nuclear holocaust (1960s–1980s), to pollution, greenhouse gases, and global warming (1980s–1990s), to (post-)apocalyptic scenarios (1990s–2000s) (see Stephens, 1992b; Bradford, 2003b; Braithwaite, 2005; Free, 2006). The timeline of this book (1988–2006) is framed by the contrast between the 'openness' of Glasnost and the more closed system of surveillance, power, and control which invokes utopian visions in the rhetorics of 'the new world order' and 'the war against terror'. In films targeted at child and youth audiences, a similar trajectory of disaster is reflected as filmmakers respond to shifting global political, environmental, and social agendas, and predict future scenarios. To grasp what these films propose in terms of the contexts of our times is to see what adults regard as desirable possibilities or cautionary tales in the face of an uncertain and complex future.

A noticeable feature in contemporary political and popular discourses is a distrust of history and a rejection of the idea that knowledge of the past can be a regenerative and productive force. For instance, the lessons of European imperialism — such as the enduring and mainly negative effects of colonisation upon Indigenous peoples — do not serve as warnings as to the long-term consequences of the hegemonic and expansionist directions of neocolonial politics. Samuel P. Huntington's view that the future of global politics inevitably involves a 'clash of civilisations' between the West and the East arises from his tendency to reduce both West and East to a single scale of values, much as Orientalism depends on a monolithic view of the East in order to construct the West as the standard by which cultures are judged. Since September 11, 2001, Huntington's thesis has been taken up in discourses of the 'war on terrorism' and in Bush's formulation of the 'axis of evil'. It is often the case in the field of children's literature that texts for children lead in new directions while the existing critical paradigms lag considerably (see Stephens, 2000). This is particularly the case in contemporary texts which address the politics of globalisation and neocolonialism. Our approach, then, is to locate children's texts as an object of theoretical and critical analysis within the broader domains of democracy, social justice, politics, and struggle.

Transforming the present

Our project of identifying and analysing utopian elements in contemporary texts has proceeded from a wide sampling of narratives for children and youth and across a range of text types including contemporary realism, historical fiction, speculative fiction, film, and picture books. From this body of texts we have chosen symptomatic works, treating these in relation to the key concerns we have identified. Rather than engaging in an encyclopaedic account of utopian tropes in children's texts, our approach is to model theorised readings which may then inform further explorations of utopian and dystopian tropes as they relate to the cultural and political contexts of texts.

Over the course of this project we have come to understand that utopian narratives are, more than anything else, concerned with the present, and with the values, politics and social practices conveyed in these texts as desirable possibilities for a transformed world order. Viewed in the broadest terms, their subject is that of society itself: the political systems, the networks of power and resistance, and the discoursal regimes, which constrain and enable identity-formation.

Focusing on English language fictions drawn from Canada, the United States, Great Britain, Australia, and New Zealand, and a small selection of films from the United States, Japan, and Iran, the following chapters address in various ways the transformative potential of these texts for realising utopian possibilities. This broad canvassing of children's texts and the transdisciplinary approach we take in our discussions highlight the largely untapped resource of children's literature and film to utopian studies. While we engage with the general topic of utopia, we also consider dystopian and anti-utopian genres and tropes as necessary elements to non-traditional utopian models and critiques. In an aim to unsettle any complacency about the innocence and benignity of children's texts, we actively challenge assumptions (our own and others) and scrutinise the explicit and implicit discourses that invariably shape the politicising and socialising agendas and subtexts of the narratives.

In the next chapter, 'New Dialogues: Children's Texts, New World Orders and Transformative Possibilities', we offer an overview of the range of genres, forms, and narrative strategies by which children's texts engage with contemporary political and social discourses. Drawing on a selection of texts discussed throughout the book, we explore the question: 'What forms does the dialogue between children's texts and new world orders take?'

From this overarching narrative framework, the focus then shifts to a number of textual readings, beginning with 'Masters, Slaves, and Entrepreneurs: Globalised Utopias and New World Order(ing)s'. This chapter considers the impact of globalisation on the lives of young protagonists as they inhabit global/local spaces that characterise the shifting social and technological landscapes of new global world orders. By examining a diverse range of films and fictional texts, we consider how these new global 'utopias/dystopias' reinscribe social hierarchies requiring young people to be creative, resilient, and flexible in order to survive times marked by consumerism, globalisation, new technologies, and international conflict.

In 'The Lure of the Lost Paradise: Postcolonial Utopias' we contend that formulations of nationhood in contemporary societies whose histories are marked by experiences of colonisation (e.g. Canada, America, and Australia) are inevitably shaped by collective memory and imagination. In this chapter we focus on treatments of utopian spaces in the narratives and consider how these texts attempt to position readers using strategies such as the powerful trope of 'a lost paradise' which induces a strategic forgetfulness of past atrocities, or, by contrast, utilising processes of remembering by envisioning new modes of collaboration and engagement that address the dysfunctional relations of colonialism.

In 'Nature Versus Culture: Reading Ecocritically' we examine a number of environmental utopian fictions to argue children's texts remain 'environmentally informed' rather than 'ecocritical' in that the fictions are constrained by a pervasive commitment to maturation narratives (exemplified by the *bildungsroman* genre). This environmental approach ensures that any environmental literature remains anthropocentric in emphasis, rather than engaging with biocentrism or 'deep ecology', a way of thinking which rejects the anthropocentric assumption that human beings are special within the world-order, and which replaces it with a biocentric or 'life-centred' attitude.

Chapter 6, focusing on imagined communities in children's texts, argues that in contrast to the general tendency in literature to locate utopian communities out of time and space, providing models of peaceful and productive societies, a noticeable trend in children's literature since 1990 is that the utopian imaginings of ideal communities have been largely supplanted by dystopian visions of dysfunctional, regressive, and often violent societies whose deficiencies nevertheless open up a space for utopia, in that by negative example they gesture towards transformed world orders. This chapter considers the narrative strategies through which dystopian texts advocate and critique models of community and of human behaviour, focusing on children as catalysts for social change and/or reform, and as being subjected to social engineering and manipulation as members of cults or fundamentalist communities.

In 'Ties that Bind: Reconceptualising Home and Family' we shift focus from community to family and home, and consider how late modernity has seen many children growing up in post-traditional and risk societies. Characteristic of this development is that traditional notions of family and home are changing in ways that see many families fragmented or its members function independently of familial structures and support, often relying on other associations or networks for economic, emotional, and functional security. In our selected texts, we examine the ties that bind families and the reimagined configurations imagined across a range of dystopian children's fiction and film.

The final chapter, 'The Struggle to be Human in a Posthuman world' takes us back to the lyrics of our opening epigraph: 'It's the time of a new world order/This is a new beginning' in that we turn from the human subject to the posthuman. In examining how children's literature responds to the idea of the posthuman, we argue that children's texts access four areas most commonly linked to the posthuman: robotics and artificial intelligence; biological interventions into the human — cloning, genetic manipulation, 'test-tube' creations of human life; cybernetic interventions that either modify the human body or fashion artificial life in its evolutionary image; and information technology. These scientific and technological developments have impacted on how we think about the world, how we make sense of our experience, and, most significantly perhaps, how we think about ourselves as human beings, in other words, what it means to be human in a world in which traditional conceptualisations of being 'human' have been increasingly problematised and rendered inadequate.

2
Children's Texts, New World Orders and Transformative Possibilities

> The failure, if failure it was, is only in how your father's dream of a happy, useful community was carried out. The failure was not in your father's dream.
>
> Whelan, *Fruitlands*, 2002, p. 116

> America has no empire to extend or utopia to establish. We wish for others only what we wish for ourselves — safety from violence, the rewards of liberty, and the hope for a better life.
>
> George W. Bush, at 2002 Graduation Exercise of the United States Military Academy, West Point, New York 1 June 2002

The changing global politics we pointed to in Chapter 1 call for a thorough examination of the rhetoric of utopian imaginings and speculations in children's texts, and of the ways in which these texts participate in what Ruth Levitas has termed 'the education of desire' (1990, pp. 7–8), especially in so far as they mediate ways of regarding the world and offer shape to children's anxieties and aspirations. In this chapter, therefore, we will consider the variety of themes and narrative forms in which the concept of 'new world orders' and 'transformative utopianism' are brought into conjunction. Representations of utopian societies are virtually non-existent in children's literature, where such representations swiftly disclose themselves as critical utopias (rejecting utopia as blueprint while preserving it as dream — see Moylan, 1986, p. 10). Gloria Whelan's *Fruitlands* (2002) or William Nicholson's *The Wind Singer* (2000) are notable examples of narratives in which communities ordered and orchestrated ostensibly for the good of all members are revealed, through the perceptions of young enquiring minds, to be repressive patriarchies organised to serve the self-interests of those in control.

What makes the depiction of utopia problematic in fiction for younger readers is its need to engage with the concerns that both authors and critics concur are the dominant problems and concerns of adolescence. The common node is the production of subjectivities: adolescent fiction is pivotally preoccupied with the formation of subjectivity — that is, the development of notions of selfhood. Fictions are typically concerned with existential questions like: who am I, why am I here, where am I going, and what does it all mean? They construct narratives of personal growth or maturation, stories about relationships between the self and others and between individuals and society. And in their preoccupation with personal growth, maturation, and the development of concepts of selfhood, adolescent novels frequently reflect complex ideas about subjectivity — or selfhood — in terms of personal concerns, intrafamily concerns, and interpersonal concerns (see McCallum, 2006, p. 217). A child protagonist is bound to rebel against the high level of conformity demanded by a utopian society. The imbrication of unfolding story events with narratives of growth thus shapes any quasi-utopian closures such narratives may aspire to, and subjectivity may be narrowly conceived as a point of destination rather than a constant process of self-production. Where some narratives may exploit the subject's alienation from society by exploring the competing desires between the child/adolescent protagonist and the utopian project, others might appear to offer transformed subjectivities but in effect redescribe desire so that it conforms to existing socio-cultural codes and modes of expression.

Further, while it is plausible to distinguish between utopia and dystopia as distinct adult genres, the dialogue between children's texts and new world orders is conducted by means of the genres which prevail in childhood texts and cultures, within which, as we argued in Chapter 1, utopia or dystopia appear rather as tropes, modes, themes, or settings than as genres. During the Cold War era, the interest of authors of children's literature in the capacity of human beings to transform the world was dominated by dystopian 'disaster' narratives, but by the end of the twentieth century the field had expanded to include narratives reflecting the different assumptions about the world following the enormous geo-political shifts set in train at the end of the 1980s. Children's literature now often functions with a sharpened awareness that literature and society are interpreted, if not shaped, by major concepts in cultural theory, some of which deeply challenge the liberal humanist assumptions which underpinned children's literature during the Cold War. An attempt to find narrative modes with which to address these concepts has led to a substantial increase in a self-conscious and critical deployment of utopian themes and motifs, along with the obvious and predictable shift in the represented dystopias of disaster fiction to a focus on environmental crisis and ecological collapse.

The end of the Cold War thus marked a sharp turning point in the representation of dystopias in children's literature, because the most overt form of dystopia, the post-disaster narrative depicting a world devastated by nuclear warfare (see Stephens, 1992b), abruptly became passé. This essentially Cold War formula can be attributed to the mutual assured destruction (MAD) doctrine articulated in the 1960s, and thence was introduced to children's literature in the later part of the decade by John Christopher's trilogy, *The Tripods* (1967–1968). While other forms of catastrophe underpinned end-of-the-world scenarios in both adult and children's literatures, the idea that a nuclear war would produce such a disastrous radioactive fallout that the world would subsequently sustain little or no human life constituted the dominant catalyst for the imagined disaster for about two decades of children's literature. The shift in the 1990s to other catalysts — extreme environmental degradation caused by self-serving capitalism, as in Louise Lawrence's politically charged *The Disinherited* (1994),[1] or a disease pandemic, as in Jean Ure's *Come Lucky April* (1992; a.k.a. *After the Plague*) — can be seen as a direct consequence of the effective disappearance of the MAD doctrine from public discourse (even though it still exists today as military policy, and attempts to develop more feasible versions of it remain the Pentagon's largest budget item).

Because its settings are inevitably somewhere in the future, post-disaster fiction has consistently depicted the present as history and uses this temporal relationship as a strategy to foreground dystopian tendencies in present societies: overt examples are the history classroom essays and the staged debates about the meaning of the past in *Come Lucky April*; the use of artefacts familiar in our culture, such as mobile phones, as personal ornaments in the steampunk society of Reeve's *A Darkling Plain*; or, in the same novel, the activating of the ancient 'Orbital Defence Initiative (ODIN)', in an allusion to various US so-called 'star wars' defence schemes of the late twentieth and early twenty-first centuries.[2]

One of the obvious challenges posed by such constructed historical perspectives, then, is to suggest that the ideological systems of the past (i.e. our present) have lost their explanatory force — in terms of their social (including gender), political, ethical, and religious institutions and practices. But is it all of these, just some of them, or a different configuration? A strength of *Come Lucky April* is that it calls them all into question, even if it has no ready alternatives to offer; this is also partly why it plays with a conventional ending which most post-disaster novels are apt to employ (including Ure's own *Plague 99*) — 'boy-and-girl on their way to a new, utopian beginning'. The structure informing this type of ending, through which personal outcomes can stand for larger political outcomes, often underpins the texts we examine in this study because of their dependence on narratives of personal development or because books for younger readers see the parallel as a constructive metonymic substitution. *Come Lucky April* pulls back from that substitution when April is given the opportunity to go away with Daniel, but chooses the harder route and higher moral action in deciding to stay in order to try to change her dystopian community. A question raised by such an ending is whether unexpected directions in the close are more generally used in 'new world order' interrogations to destabilise teleologies.

New directions in post-disaster narratives

The newly dominant emphases on ecology and biology are likely to have a longer life span than nuclear holocaust narratives. The pandemic scenario gains plausibility from recent experience: the twenty-first century has already endured two potential pandemics — first, the major epidemic of severe acute respiratory syndrome (SARS) in 2002–2003, which gave us future-dystopian images of the citizens of large cities wearing protective face masks; and second, recurrent outbreaks of Avian flu H5N1 in the decade since 1997, and the propensity of the virus to mutate, prompts medical scientists to suggest that a pandemic will occur whenever the virus mutates into a form which can be transmitted from one human to another. The result may be far more deaths than the millions caused by the 'Spanish flu' pandemic of 1918. Such a prospect is not directly attributable to the global changes of the late 1980s, but can be linked with globalisation in terms of world travel and the roles which fiction might attribute to multinational pharmaceutical companies. The way has been recently marked out in adult fiction by *The Constant Gardener* (2004), John Le Carré's brilliant exploration of the dark side of capitalism within the new world order — specifically, the complicity of the international pharmaceutical industry in African illness and poverty.

Ecological issues are even more acutely evident, in that even though there are recently some signs that major world powers are preparing to become more proactive on environmental issues and hence to begin to confront the economic demands of rampant capitalism, there is little prospect of reversing ecological damage within present lifetimes. Indeed, the Report released by the Intergovernmental Panel on Climate Change on 2 February 2007 (Working Group I: scientific aspects of the climate system and climate change) concluded that global warming and rises in sea levels would continue for centuries, because the process has already begun. In that changes to human practice implemented now will have little or no impact in current lifetimes, and politicians will before long begin to talk down the present sense of urgency, it will be imperative that futuristic scenarios keep reminding audiences that they are responsible for the future. Post-disaster fiction already incorporates a significant focus on the human causes of future calamities, and this will necessarily continue. Lawrence's *The Disinherited*, for example, is a projection, from a particular perspective, of the social impact of the economic policies of Britain's Government under Margaret Thatcher (social reforms which favoured the middle class over the working class; the decline of heavy industry; the destruction of mining communities). By the end of the decade, with the British economy flourishing, such projections seemed wide off the mark, but have been reasserted as a characteristic of post-Cold War globalisation in one of the most significant explorations of dystopian themes published in the early twenty-first century — Philip Reeve's account of a world ravaged by 'municipal Darwinism' in the *Hungry Cities* tetralogy (2001–2006). Municipal Darwinism, elevated to a necessary ideology with quasi-religious status, is embodied in *A Darkling Plain* (2006) by the predatory Wolf Kobold, whose icon is 'an eight-armed image of the Thatcher, all-devouring goddess of unfettered Municipal Darwinism' (p. 153). Wolf defines his creed as follows:

> As soon as you start helping others, or relying on others to help you, you give away your own freedom. They [the big cities] have forgotten the simple, beautiful act which should lie at the heart of our civilization: a great city chasing and eating a lesser one. That is Municipal Darwinism. A perfect expression of the true nature of the world; that the fittest survive.
>
> (p. 155)

Using an eclectic, postmodern and often very comedic mode, Reeve links much of the action of his story to a military and ideological struggle between the dystopian capitalism of the traction cities and the dystopian deep ecology of the Green Storm, an Asian federation devoted not just to keeping the traction cities out of their central Asian stronghold but also to making the world green again. Frequent references to arte-facts from the past (a version of 'our' present) underline the extent to which Reeve is hybridising the genre by exploiting the frequent overlap between post-disaster narratives and other post-apocalyptic narratives dealing with dystopian societies eking out an existence on a ruined Earth (e.g., the metonymic function of rubbish dumps as settings, as in, among others, Melvin Burgess's *The Baby and Fly Pie* (1992)). The West–East conflict which constitutes the global setting for Reeve's tetralogy is traced to 'The Sixty Minute War' fought between the American Empire and Greater China, which left both countries uninhabitable. Intertex-tually, it glances in two directions. First, it evokes the *Mutual Assured Destruction* doctrine of the Cold War era, and especially Ronald Regan's 1983 'Strategic Defense Initiative' — the space-based, missile defence program popularly known as 'Star Wars' which threatened to destroy the delicate balance of *MAD*. Second, the grounding of Reeve's imagined West–East conflict in deep ideological and cultural differences points once more to the 'Clash of Civilisations' doctrine, of which the tetralogy is deeply sceptical.

Agency, society and new world orders

Both thematically and structurally, children's texts seek ways to engage with such major ideas and explore their impact upon individual subjectivities. Tom Moylan (1986, p. 11) has argued that by the 1970s critical utopian texts had embraced opposition to 'the emerging system of transnational corporations and post-industrial production and ideo-logical structures,' that they reflected a radical politics focused on 'autonomy and justice for humanity and nature,' and that they were infused with 'the politics of autonomy, democratic socialism, ecology, and especially feminism.' Two decades after Moylan made these obser-vations, the position he then identified resonates strongly with the transformative utopianism informing texts for children and young adults, and with the versions of subjectivity which validate that position. A transformative utopian vision will challenge hegemonic structures of political power and totalising ideologies by revealing the ways in which human needs and agency are restrained by existing institutional, social, and cultural arrangements. (We are hence using *agency* here in the broad sense that discourse may represent action that transcends its material context; that is, an individual psyche may be attributed with a capacity for either self-alteration or remaking the world in contrast to society's propensity to represent itself as always already instituted, thereby denying the possibility of creative action to individuals.) A transformative utopian vision will explore a character's human aspirations to gain the agency which might make it possible to attain his or her desires, and seek to define some notion of optimal practice in terms of social formations, gender relations, and economic and ecological sustainability. Finally, a transformative utopian fiction will build in some notion of attainability. In books for younger readers this might take the form of simple optimism, or it might fall back on some sense of a humanistic propensity towards goodness and other-regardingness even within a permanently flawed world, as underlies Reeve's tetralogy and a range of works such as Ure's *Come Lucky April* (1992) or Nicholson's *The Wind Singer* (2000), and realist narratives such as Norma Howe's zany *The Adventures of Blue Avenger* (1999), Joan Bauer's *Rules of the Road* (1998), or M. T. Anderson's *Burger Wuss* (1999).

A dominant preoccupation of much adolescent fiction is with how notions of identity are formed within specific contexts and shaped by larger social structures and processes. Thus, the school, peer group, family, and various cultural institutions frequently have important metonymic functions within adolescent fictions. Any one individual will typically occupy various subject positions within society; these are determined by gender, age, class, ethnicity, and so on. And these various positionings shape an individual's sense of identity, though often in contradictory ways. An issue that recurs across a wide cross-section of the texts we discuss in this book is the question of how far human beings are responsible for their own actions, and in what ways they might be deprived of this responsibility, and this issue is deeply imbricated with representations of utopia and dystopia as contrastive systems of surveillance and control. An imagined utopia is grounded in the idea of a world different from the world of everyday experience; this different world answers to a desire for a better life, but is perhaps only possible as the ending of a narrative, as in, say, Monica Hughes's *The Other Place* (1999) or Reeve's *A Darkling Plain*. Texts which begin in a putative utopian setting — Whelan's *Fruitlands* or Nicholson's *The Wind Singer*, for example — are rather about the erosion or shattering of the 'dream of a happy, useful community', as the epigraph to this chapter phrases it.

Fruitlands, a historical fiction about 11-year-old Louisa May Alcott's experiences of a would-be utopian community, is of particular interest not only because it is one of three historical fictions on this topic published between 2000 and 2002 (see Mills, 2005) but also because it exemplifies how a recent utopian/dystopian narrative about the past can implicitly reflect post-Cold War attitudes. Claudia Mills postulates that interest in the story could be prompted by 'the general boom in spinoffs on literary classics' or an urge 'to revisit the idealism of an earlier time' in reaction to 'recent financial and political scandals' (p. 257), although she concludes that the answer is probably 'simply ... fascination with the subject'. Indeed, the sense of a crisis in political morality was already widespread in the United States in the 1970s, so it seems difficult to attribute an interest in a nineteenth-century utopian movement to this cause. We would prefer to put the question in a different way, and ask how the representation of the story is impacted upon — in production and reception — by how notions of new world orders had evolved over the previous ten years or so. *Fruitlands* is overtly about a failed utopia, an attempt to realise one of the recurrent metaphors of American political and social rhetoric, the city built on a hill:[3]

> All I see is a large old house on a hill with acres of woods and meadow ... Father sees what the future will bring ... As he stood there telling us of his dream for Fruitlands, I was sure that others hearing of our way of life will be eager to join us. We shall build cottages for them on the hill.
>
> (pp. 8–9)

Whelan's strategy in this novel is to tell her story by juxtaposing entries from the two diaries Louisa keeps: one (as cited above) to be read by her parents, the other, private diary, to be used to express her more acerbic view of the utopian experiment. The utopian theme is thus explored in a mode common in children's literature since the late 1980s, a dialogue between first person narrators in which events or incidents may be narrated twice and hence an interrogative mode established by contrasting points of view. Because Louisa is (self-)presented as fallible, impulsive, and often thoughtless, the doubled perspective highlights the potential or actual fallibility of the narration, and hence constitutes a dialogue between ideals and actualities.

The failed utopia implicitly connects with the idea, and possible exhaustion of the idea, of American exceptionalism (see Kammen, 1993), which is always evoked by the 'city on a hill' metaphor. The concept also contributes to anti-American sentiments elsewhere in the world, and it is no accident that two of the most significant of recent futuristic dystopian narratives in young adult (YA) fiction — Reeve's *Hungry Cities* tetralogy and Jan Mark's brilliant *Useful Idiots* (2004) — both envisage the erasure of the United States as a world power: as an uninhabited wasteland ('the Dead Continent') in Reeve (*Predator's Gold*, p. 8); as fragmented into 'dozens of dissociated states' in Mark (2004, p. 191). As the dialogical structure of *Fruitlands* unfolds the difference between ideals and everyday failures, it both looks back to an earlier, idealistic version of American exceptionalism and enacts its limitations: Fruitlands/America offers hope for humanity, grounded in comity — a balance of community and individual interests governed by personal and economic freedom. Its strengths — and weaknesses — are its geographical isolation, and the strong religious influence which affirms its moral superiority. Fruitlands fails, however, because it is a patriarchal, authoritarian community: this is indicated by the official diary's record of the steady departure (or expulsion) of community members, which Louisa attributes to the overbearingness of their leaders, Charles Lane and her father.

Individuality and conformity

Fruitlands exemplifies one of the key tensions in new world order narratives, the tension between individual subject position and the ideology of a society built on surveillance, conformity, and repression. Some of the central concerns of children's and YA literature are embodied here, and the extent to which they are endemic concerns can be seen from a comparison with a very different work, Jan Mark's *Useful Idiots*. Both novels express a familiar bundle of personal concerns. In *Fruitlands*, Louisa shows concern about the body, especially her appearance in the clothes designed by Charles Lane (which, she suggests, reveal that he is a misogynist); she has a deep need to have and maintain a private space, a desire both recorded in and embodied by her secret diary; and she demonstrates a regard for justice both in immediate family relationships and in the wider social world of the Fruitlands community — her diaries record a sequence of events in which she challenges Mr Lane's authority and is accordingly chastised. The novel's opening sentence, 'We are all going to be made perfect' (2002, p. 3), offers an instant meeting of utopianism and identity politics: if subjectivity is culturally constructed, performative, incomplete, always in process, always fragmentary, and transitional, a would-be utopian community can be expected to channel subjective becoming within narrow parameters — being 'made perfect' presupposes a particular concept of perfection.

Whelan has used the idea of Louisa's secret diary to problematise utopian subjectivity. By the second entry, Louisa already articulates two sources of tension: first, a tension between community participation and the desire 'to hide away and just be myself' (p. 11); second, a tension between essential subjectivity and the intersubjectively formed self ('Being with other people nudges me first one way and then another until I hardly recognise myself' [pp. 11–12]). These tensions between a self and the expectations of the utopian community which seeks to shape that self in specific ways are, not unsurprisingly, similar to the tensions experienced by a subject in a futuristic dystopian society. In principle, conceptions of the subject are a key marker of difference between utopia and dystopia, but representations of that difference will pivot qualitatively on the capacity of the representation to enable a sense of subjective agency.

Increasingly, societies in the twenty-first century are consenting to higher levels of pervasive surveillance, now also as a component of the 'war against terrorism'. Surveillance is already an issue in contemporary fiction,[4] since it may be deemed an intrusion of privacy, a direct limitation of agency and even a breach of civil liberties, but interest in it can be expected to intensify further. In a utopian society, of course, surveillance would not be a threat because no one would need to conceal an action, although such an assumption presupposes that the social structure is moral and just, and challenges to its precepts are redundant. Foucault argued in his discussion of the concept of a panopticon that a major effect of surveillance is to induce 'a state of conscious and permanent visibility that assures the automatic functioning of power' such that the subjects themselves become the bearers of surveillance (see Foucault, 1995, pp. 195–228).[5] Unlike modern surveillance, which is predominantly electronic, surveillance is evident in *Fruitlands* in ways reminiscent of a Foucauldian reading: members of the community have limited private space; Louisa's official diary is subject to parental perusal, so while she declares in her first entry that 'Father says that a journal is the way to come to know yourself, and it is only by knowing yourself that you are free to become yourself' (p. 5), that self is masked and effectively mendacious; William, the son of Charles Lane, reports to his father on the other children's behaviour; and Louisa struggles between the interiorised values of the community and her own impulses and inclinations. Tellingly, an entry in her secret diary for *2 July 1843* begins, *Father was right! I need others to guide me* (p. 30), and goes on to recount how, during a solitary ramble, she accepted forbidden food (cake) from a neighbouring farm. Few readers will fault her for this, or for the parallel entry in the official diary which implies merit rather than blame 'I took a long walk this afternoon by myself. When I returned,

I made hollyhock dolls for Abby May' (p. 30), and the perspective of a modern, more individualistic society will readily identify the fallibility, self-interest, and misogyny of the community's patriarchal leaders as a factor in the failure of the utopian experiment.

In the futuristic world of *Useful Idiots*, attenuated subjectivities are the consequence of biological homogenisation and dystopian surveillance. The novel's dystopian setting, in 2255 CE, is posited on a new world order whereby geological and political changes have largely erased the British Isles as an independent entity. First, a substantial rise in sea level which has drowned some of Europe's major cities ('St Petersburg, Venice, London, Stockholm' [p. 185]) has reduced the former United Kingdom to a small island group now named 'the Rhine Delta Islands'. Second, the European Union has become a monolith resolutely opposed to any ethnic or national distinctions. Third, the Union has used genetic engineering and medical intervention to produce an utterly homogenous European race. Authorities are consequently deeply hostile to historical studies, especially archaeology, which seem to be too interested in ethnic differences. The metanarrative, however, valorises local, cultural distinctiveness, in so far as the identity politics of the novel revolve around a young archaeologist's contacts with a small population of Aboriginal people, known as the 'Inglish', who live on a self-governing reservation. Like much dystopian fiction, the transformative impulse here lies in a conservative perspective on cultural change: acknowledging that subjectivity is culturally produced, the narrative privileges the local and the distinctive over the global and homogenised. Thus the principal character, Merrick Korda, whose grandparents were Inglish who had chosen to assimilate, is entirely nondescript: that nobody seems to recognise him functions as a metonym for the erasure of subjectivity.

Useful Idiots employs a narrative strategy that has been widely used in children's and adolescent fiction for at least the last half century — a third person narration which restricts knowledge of events and motivations to whatever a single character focaliser (the principal character) is able to discover or understand. Character development is thus determined by the character's cognitive processing of his or her experiences. The notion of a 'useful idiot' is pertinent here, because it pivots on a gap between ideology and political actualities,[6] and impacts significantly on the question of agency — can a person have subjective agency if her/his actions are deluded and result in a negative consequence? The impact of a dystopian society upon such characters is then perceived as a mixture of practices that are internalised without question until the characters find themselves in conflict with society and thus needing to rethink social values. Surveillance again offers a good example. When Merrick is taken to the Inglish village and left at the mayor's house, he is surprised that the house is unlocked and appears to lack any surveillance system:

> Half-consciously he examined the door frame, the masonry surrounding it, the little overhanging brow of a porch, but he could find no evidence of surveillance. Either they really did have none or it was so sophisticated that it surpassed anything he had ever encountered.
>
> It was not a subject to which he had ever given much thought until now, when he was so conscious of its absence ... Aboriginals on their own land were free to conduct their own affairs in their own way. If they chose to exist without centralized surveillance then they were presumably free to do that too. But what had they paid for that choice; had they all chosen?
>
> (p. 159)

The representation of Merrick's cognitive processes here demands close reader attention. There are some obvious cues that he is doing something unaccustomed, but which is connected with naturalised mental assumptions — *half-consciously*; *not a subject to which he had ever given much thought* — and this might alert readers to two key elements of the passage. First, the contrast between what is there and not there foregrounds the distinctive, archaic architecture of the cottage, which Merrick, having by this point got over his surprise at these buildings, is now beginning to assimilate. Readers, of course, recognise the style as a form of everydayness. Second, Merrick assumes that centralised surveillance is a cultural norm and that to repudiate it and thus have 'no record of who goes in and out' (p. 157) must put a society at some indeterminate risk. His assumption is, to an extent, shocking, because it simultaneously reverses what twenty-first century readers assume is the norm — that consensual surveillance may be a necessary evil — and compels readers to reflect on the extent to which they, like Merrick, take surveillance for granted.[7] The strongly evident individual differences of the Inglish are thus only superficially attributable to their rejection of twenty-third century genetic engineering, but more deeply laid in conservation of culture. In restricting the dissemination of the information technology which underpins and constitutes surveillance, they are asserting nationalism, for, as Frederick Buell contends, 'information technology has been one of the most exuberant sites for reconstruction of an official national culture for postnational circumstances' (1998, p. 565; and see Chapter 3, for further discussion). Briease, the Inglish village, is not a utopia, however — it is a version of a world with which readers are familiar, after all. It is, however, the place in which Merrick suffers the deepest betrayal in his quest to prove a dark history of exploitation of the Inglish.

Strangers in a strange land: strategies of defamiliarisation

In sending her principal character from the dystopian new world of twenty-third century Europe into an isolated village, almost inaccessible to outsiders, where many twentieth-century cultural practices had been preserved, Mark drew upon a common strategy of utopian fictions, whereby a stranger from another society (usually a version of 'ours') visits a utopian society and then his or her discoveries about it and reactions to it are recorded. The form — essentially a defamiliarisation strategy — is used in many children's texts, although Mark has used a variant in which the traveller visits a version of the everyday world familiar to readers. A comparably effective use of the strategy occurs in the *Doctor Who* episode 'The Rise of the Cybermen' (*Doctor Who*, Second Series, 2006), in which The Doctor and his companions find themselves in the London of a parallel universe, where whole populations are controlled through EarPods (small devices attached to the ear, whose sinister function is masked by the mass of data, including jokes, fed through them, and their propensity to become a fashion accessory). This 'other' London is a nightmare version of Earth's possible new world order.

The chief effect of the 'stranger in a strange land' strategy as realised in *Useful Idiots* is that the dialogic relationship between contrasting social formations highlights the possibility that contemporary society already has dystopian propensities, and that a new world order which might develop from it may be a dystopia masked as a utopia. The outcome is a 'critical dystopia', an alternative society worse than the one we know but which contains some possibility of transformation into a better society, or at least contains some possibility of escape for the principal characters. A critical dystopia 'self-reflexively takes on the present system and offers not only astute critiques of the order of things but also explorations of the oppositional spaces and possibilities from which the next round of political activism can derive imaginative sustenance and inspiration' (Moylan, 2000, p. xv). In *Useful Idiots* transformation, escape, and oppositional space lie in a recuperation of the past, not in a repudiation of the past nor in a resistance to change. Thus at the otherwise bleak ending of the novel, Merrick is depicted walking out of the fens both cured of 'trust' and singing an old nonsense ballad, *Nottamun Town,*[8] which has somehow welled up from his memory — one of several 'scraps of fragments, songs, Inglish songs, long suppressed' (p. 396) rising up from his childhood contact with Inglish grandparents or from a deeper racial memory. Angry, puzzled, a little bemused, no longer a useful idiot, he returns to his society now as an interrogative subject and with a sense of the past as felt experience.

Both 'the stranger in a strange land' narrative strategy and formal dialogic structure are used to particular effect in Jean Ure's *Come Lucky April* (1992) and Peter Dickinson's *Shadow of a Hero* (1994). *Come Lucky April* depicts two communities which have evolved in isolation after the eradication of most humans through a mysterious plague. On the one hand, there is a strictly matriarchal society in Croydon, once a borough in Outer London, which is the setting for most of the novel; on the other, a strictly patriarchal community in Cornwall. The narrative form of the novel — third person narration variously focalised by a member from each community — ensures a dialogic structure and interrogation of fixed assumptions. An immediate effect of setting the story in the matriarchal Croydon community is to replicate that process of presenting a radically different form of social organisation as viewed from a more or less familiar position, and to do so in such a way as to interrogate both sets of social values. In Chapter 6 we will discuss this feminist dystopia more fully.

Another important issue for reading this novel is the uses it makes of the process of telling and interpreting history. A description of a late-twentieth century society from the ideological perspective of a very different society convinced that it represents an optimal new world order forces readers to consider the possibilities that either they themselves inhabit a dystopia or their world has the potential to become dystopian. The attempts to account for the present in terms of the past in *Come Lucky April* constitute a struggle between rival narrations, both of which may be partial. 'What really happened' in history is thus shown to be susceptible to ideological shaping; both the Croydon and Cornwall communities perpetrate, and are victims of, such shaping. Historical narration is driven by a demand that sequences of real events be assessed as to their significance as elements of a moral drama (see White, 1987), and this demand can be aligned with the construction of imagined different outcomes as utopian or dystopian.

The attitudes and outcomes discernible in *Come Lucky April* have their foundation and meaning in some ideological presuppositions which existed generally in the social thought of twentieth-century Western cultures. These presuppositions tend to stand out prominently in this example because of its futuristic setting and structure as a dialogue between utopian and dystopian concepts. While such ideologies are aspects of social forms and apparatuses, and are only secondarily involved with questions of morality, they are nevertheless commonly thought about as moral issues. In pointing to them here we are not suggesting a value judgement about them — individuals will (or will not) subscribe to variously different versions of them — but rather wish to suggest that the possibility of imagining a better society will be preconditioned by a text's unaddressed ideological presuppositions. In other words, Ure's dystopian satire is conditioned by an assumption that a better world will need to be based on the best versions of present day ideologies, and this is perhaps why the book seems to offer few specific answers to the questions it raises.

The 'stranger in a strange land' strategy employed by Ure and Mark is given a powerful political nuance in Peter Dickinson's *Shadow of a Hero*, perhaps the most significant response in children's literature to the collapse of Communist Europe at the end of the Cold War. In dealing with the extreme political and social disorder that occurred in the Balkans following the end of communist hegemony, the novel acutely raises the question whether the new world order ushered in at the end of the 1980s is not indeed a new dark age.

Shadow of a Hero is the story of 13-year-old Letta, who was born in England and has grown up there, and an imaginary Eastern European country, Varina, the homeland of Letta's family. Varina has no political status, but consists of three provinces, one each in Rumania, Bulgaria, and Serbia. With the collapse of the Eastern European communist hegemony in 1989, the Varinians see an opportunity to become an independent country once again. Through alternating chapters, the author juxtaposes the stories of two wars of emancipation led by two Varinian heroes with the same name — Restaur Vax. The first led a nineteenth-century campaign against their Turkish conquerors, and the other, Letta's grandfather, the last prime minister of an independent Varina, is the figure-head for his country's aspiration to regain independent statehood. Involved in a terrorist plot by her older brother, Letta must make important decisions which will affect the future of Varina.

Letta inhabits two cultures, without belonging entirely to either, but remains determined to preserve her Varinian cultural heritage. Varina, however, is a special form of dystopia, both as a place and an idea: Letta cannot effectively return to Varina because there is in effect nowhere to return to as Varinians can only exist in a state of permanent exile, even in their homeland. The dystopian condition of statelessness, implying an endemic lack of subjective agency, is precisely summed up in a conversation between Letta and her grandfather about identity and political engagement:

> [Letta:] 'Momma's much Englisher than I'll ever be. You can't tell me what I'm going to be, not even you, Grandad. I'm going to choose for myself. Poppa isn't English, really.'
>
> 'No, but nor is he Varinian any longer. He is an exile, a citizen of Exilia. There is no country he can ever call home.'
>
> (Dickinson, 1994, p. 34)

Dickinson's strategy in this novel is to construct a form of 'faction', primarily a strategy in realist or historical utopian/dystopian fictions — both of which genres are invoked here. The modern story is a plausible account of what is most feared by composite states (and which Mark was to pick up subsequently in *Useful Idiots*; see also the discussion of *Turtles Can Fly* in Chapter 3), the aspiration of national minorities to independent statehood. Dickinson constructs a language (both formal and demotic), a literature, and a complex cultural tradition to validate this aspiration. The nineteenth-century story is authenticated by numerous footnotes, again of a factive kind, which discuss places, history, artefacts, and international contacts. These footnotes are often humorously self-deconstructing, as when in the chapter 'The English Milord' (pp. 49–51) the note comments: 'In one version of this legend the Milord is identified as Milord Byroñ. Byron, though sympathetic to the Varinian cause (cf. letter to Hobhouse 19 February 1822), did not in fact at any time visit Varina.' Despite (or because of) its scholarly seriousness, the note is in effect a delightful spoof, (mis-)appropriating Byron's support for Greek independence from Turkey and his friendship with Hobhouse in support of a non-existent cause.

The contrapuntal relationship between the alternating narratives is, needless to say, a pointer to the thematic significance of the novel. A revolution is in part inspired by a utopian dream to constitute a social and political fabric expressive of the essence of a people, renewing their language, traditions and customs: 'In Varina everything was new. This was the beginning of a new world, before rules, before problems, before disasters. It was alarming and exciting too, and somehow, Letta felt, pure' (p. 104). Subjugation, exile and diaspora are, reasonably, attributes of dystopia. The legendary stories, however, are ideology driven archetypes: as Letta's grandfather tells her, 'In the Legends all bishops are Bishop Pango, all heroes are Restaur or Lash the Golden, all enemies are Turks ... The world is a simple place, in legends' (p. 14). He has experienced this effect personally, because Varinians associate his own name, Restaur Vax, with heroism, and have expected him to live up to it. Ultimately, Varina itself exists only as a name, but a name with powerful associations for people who cling to it.

As the Legends are reproduced by Letta's reading of them, she expresses increasing dismay at how stories which celebrate great deeds also disclose an underlying horror — a history of manipulation of people and betrayal. When she expresses anger at a story about an 8-year-old child celebrated because she died carrying a message — 'They just *used* her! It's disgusting!' (p. 196) — her grandfather comments, 'one of the functions of legend is to make the disgusting tolerable' (p. 196). The legend introduces an incident in which Letta's brother, Van, is badly injured in a motor-cycle accident while carrying explosives to be used in a terrorist action. Van, too, is being *used*, and embodies the vulnerability of the exile to be manipulated in the name of a cause, one more useful idiot. By the end of the novel Letta comes to a point where she sums up the history of Varina as a 'marvelous, bitter, deceitful past' (p. 251).

Border conditions as dystopias

Shadow of a Hero and *Useful Idiots* foreground how the idea of a border or border condition can signify in a variety of ways: it can describe a personality disorder ('borderline'), the effects of experiencing multiple subjectivities, a liminal space between meanings. Borders are thus also a marker of hybrid or liminal subjectivities, such as those that would be experienced by persons who negotiate among multiple cultural, linguistic, or racial, systems throughout their lives (see Brady, 2000). Borders also make space and time ambiguous, as meaning slips metonymically between the literal and the figurative. In *Shadow of a Hero*, borders serve as the container for a territorial-temporal state that cannot exist: straddling three countries, Varina is denied recognition as a nation-state by the existence of borders, although borders usually serve to define the line between one state and another. It is why they are policed.

The threat of endemic dystopia looms over the close of *Shadow of a Hero*, but tempered by the hope that memory, tradition, and human agency can make a difference (p. 252). With the future of Varina left undecided, the close, through Letta's stream of thought, sustains the conjunction of fact and fiction through a meditation on the problem of memory and tradition, juxtaposing a television report about the mayhem in the Balkans following the collapse of communism with a list of key components of threatened Varinian culture. The mayhem itself — 'smashed towns, refugees, lives that had lost their meaning' — is a product of remembering 'things that had been said and done long, long ago'. Weighed against this is the positive side of difference: 'Somehow it still had to be worth it. You can't have everybody the same. That was what Ceausescu had wanted, wasn't it? So somehow it had to be worth it' (p. 252). Dickinson here simultaneously invokes one of the key elements of a dystopia and the form of resistance to dystopia which permeates children's texts: 'dystopias acknowledge the demise of individual differences as a way of keeping order in power and power in order. Dystopias are stories that contrast the failure of the main character with the unstoppable advance of society towards totalitarianism' (Mihailescu, 1991, p. 215).

What *Shadow of a Hero* is reaching for, through the principal character's perceptions, is a sense of a relationship between subjective agency and semiotic system which recognises the connectedness of signs and the richness of their semantic dimension, in contrast to the dystopian aptitude for signs to become empty or arbitrary. The deployment in *Come Lucky April* of the term *civilised* to denote males who had been castrated, subjugated, and assigned menial social roles is one of the sharpest examples of dystopian linguistic etiolation in the bundle of texts we are considering here. Ten years after *Shadow of a Hero*, Jan Mark posed the same question about the consequences of new world orders. The power of *Shadow of a Hero* lies in its representation of the paradoxes of political exile. What is the exile's relation to the homeland? How many generations does exile span? Is the idea of a nation worth killing or dying for? What kind of truth lies within fiction? This novel is one of the less optimistic dystopian fictions, because it focuses more on how events, institutions and desires are endowed with ideological force, rather than focusing on personal development within a *bildungsroman* structure.

Authoritarianism and the pessimism of YA dystopias

Contemporary Western social ideologies condition subjects to value personal freedom, innovation, self-realisation, and self-expression, so readers are quick to discern when a society is being depicted as authoritarian and repressive. The assumption that in a dystopian world human beings must strive for a form of subjective agency pervades children's literature. While the characteristic genre is futuristic fantasy, realist, historical realist, and hybridic forms are also employed. Urban realism, for example, has been used to depict dystopian worlds since 1974, when Robert Cormier's *The Chocolate War* appeared.[9] At that time Cormier's fiction shocked the children's literature establishment because of its apparently unrelenting pessimism. Now, almost 40 years later, it seems easy to see what readers back then didn't fully grasp — that is, that almost coincident with the emergence of YA fiction, dystopian fiction had become a mode within children's literature, presenting for the first time bleak analyses of human society without promise of the euphoric ending which is usually expected in that literature.

The bleakness of YA realism is a major impediment for authors aspiring to engage with new world orders by envisaging more utopian outcomes, so strategies need to be found to enable such a perspective. A simple method, as in Joan Bauer's *Rules of the Road*, is to employ a first person narration for a highly metonymic narrative. The narrator/protagonist, Jenna Boller, from a family broken and stressed by the father's alcoholism, is suddenly promoted from her part-time job selling shoes to personal driver for the owner/manager of the franchise. The common narrative of personal growth is here imbricated with a story about American capitalism, in which 'price cutting and warehousing are the new world order of this new retail world' (p. 178), as opposed to quality and personal service. Like *Shadow of a Hero* and *Useful Idiots*, the novel warns against consent to a future grounded in a highly relative concept of culture and morality, and valorises a more traditional sense of value as a basis for self-realisation and self-expression. Thus Jenna's passionate intervention in the company's stockholder's meeting which will shape its future (she loses the vote but effects a compromise which protects quality), and her final ultimatum to her estranged father ('If you keep drinking I won't see you', p. 199) offer a broadly utopian view of agency in the capitalist ideology which seemed to be determining the global future of the world in the 1990s.

In comparison, Norma Howe's zany, even preposterous, realist narrative, *The Adventures of Blue Avenger* (1999) explores transformative utopian possibilities by interpolating into a realist narrative elements of absurdity, blurred boundaries between the fictive and experienced, and surprising juxtapositions (e.g. the hero, the eponymous Blue Avenger, at the same time finds the solution to his community's problem with hand-guns and the solution to how to bake a weepless lemon meringue pie — the recipe is included in the book). In its zany way, this novel again resists the loss of self and dystopian aptitude for signs to become empty or arbitrary that we have noted as major themes of children's texts:

> The year preceding David's metamorphosis to Blue Avenger had been a time of confusion and pessimism for him ... nothing seemed to make any sense any more. It was as though the world around him and the people inhabiting it were growing more insane every day, and he was doomed to stand and watch, unable to stem the tide. Occasionally, he would go to the movies with Mike or his other friends and observe in puzzled silence as the people around him screamed and hollered and jumped out of their seats every time someone on the screen was blasted to bits or slashed into mincemeat or impaled with a sharp stick. And real life was almost as bad.
>
> (p. 106)

The scene David/Blue focalises instantiates a process of habituation which empties signs of their meanings, and leaks out of iterated representations into actual life. So instead of continuing to draw an escapist comic book super hero named Blue Avenger, David changes his name to 'Blue Avenger' and sets out to reconnect signs and things. *The Adventures of Blue Avenger* is thus particularly interesting for its thematic concern with semiotic systems and notions of connectedness and for its foregrounding of questions of agency.

The possibility of agency is the topic of a continuing debate carried on between the two main characters of *Blue Avenger*, Blue and Omaha:

> [Blue:] 'All right then, here it is, the question of questions: *Are we truly the masters of our fate or merely actors on a stage, playing our parts in a predetermined cosmic drama over which we have no control? ......*'

> [Omaha:] 'Of course we have choices in this life! We make them every day! But — and here's the real question — do we have any choice in choosing the choice we choose?'
>
> (p. 89)

While the various incidents in which Blue plays a role, and the marvellous chains of causality underpinning them, have positive outcomes and are replete with meaning, the book resolutely resists constructing a teleology. It glances at a large range of things that constitute a civil society, mixing the international and the domestic and the serious and humorous (from 'a comprehensive and affordable healthcare plan for *all* Americans' [p. 142] to 'lemon meringue bliss to young and old of every race and creed' [p. 152]). Its lack of an overarching narrative and its arbitrary, indeterminate ending (will Blue go to sleep or turn the page of the book he is reading in bed, and thus change Omaha's life?) declare transformative utopianism to be an always unfinished business. People may, or may not, 'have any choice in choosing the choice we choose,' but the concept of agency favoured in the novel is not the hard-line Foucauldian determinism articulated by Omaha but the more voluntarist understanding enabled by the creative solutions which Blue's costumed identity enables him to instantiate (for a clear outline of creative agency see McNay, 1999, pp. 187–190).

Agency thus resides in the making of choices and taking responsibility for them, in accepting the moral imperatives which in a properly functioning civil society should determine 'the choice we choose,' and hence in processes of making signs meaningful. Although actions may presuppose routine and pre-reflexive forms of behaviour, 'the existence of values also presupposes a creative process by which values are fashioned and transmitted' (McNay, p. 189). Hence in its quite wild leaps between the private and the public *Blue Avenger* offers a perspective on choice and agency consistent with that offered by, for example, international relations expert Steve Smith:

> the future of world order depends on the choices our leaders make and the values we think they should promote. World orders always reflect dominant values, are always partial and may well hinder the search for global justice and peace. They are not given, they are not natural — they reflect our conscious or unconscious choices. That is how domestic and international debates interact, and is why an informed, questioning and diverse civil society is essential to the debate now more than ever.
>
> (http://www.ssrc.org/sept11/essays/smith.htm)

Through the dissonances and absurdities that defamiliarise the everyday world, *The Adventures of Blue Avenger* succeeds in reframing utopian possibility as an individual, achievable project. Such an outcome is more likely to be found in books for younger readers, especially in picture books dealing with environmental issues — for example, Michael Foreman's *One World* (1990) or Jeannie Baker's *Belonging* (2004; see Chapter 5, and Stephens, 2006b). Published at the very beginning of the period covered in this study, *One World* can be taken as exemplary of how transformative utopianism operates in such books.

A book which strives to transform reader attitudes towards the natural environment will tend to do so by contrasting global with local effects, on a 'think global, act local' principle, and by identifying ways in which negative social and cultural assumptions are naturalised. It will seek to define some notion of 'best practice' in terms of social formations and ecological sustainability, and will offer a form of agency as local action through which a transformation might be attained. These are the purposes of *One World*. The message offered to the book's young audience is very overt: two children at the beach find a rock pool containing pebbles, fish, and sea plants, but also some pollutants. In their play, they take things from the pool and create a micro-world in a bucket: 'The two children had made their own world. It was a new world with its own forests, its own life.' The 'world' in the bucket is a metonym of the global impact of human activity on the environment, where exploitation of natural resources leaves behind depleted and despoiled landscapes: 'but the more they added to their world, the more they took from the real world. The only things now floating in the pool were the feathers and the blob of oil'. The children then understand that their actions reproduce the destruction of ecology on a larger scale, and so they return the natural objects to the environment and remove the pollutants. They resolve that next day they will do this for other pools, and will ask other children to help.

The book represents a tension between utopian and dystopian tendencies. It is utopian in its vision of an expansion of the small action of these children to embrace the whole world. It is dystopian in its depiction of a human tendency to consume the world's natural resources and leave behind a polluted wasteland. While the book is simple, it connects with more complex social theory. Thus, the prospect of an increasingly dystopian future is a measure of the deficiency of contemporary societies, especially their temporal short-sightedness. In making its appeal to children, and — as such books generally do — placing the responsibility for the future into the hands of today's children, it implicitly exhorts them to overcome the selfishness in time and space which characterises the current adult generation. Because modern societies shun responsibility for the consequences of their actions, they reject the fact that they inhabit a temporal frame. By refusing responsibility for what lies beyond the self in time and space, they deny that selfhood must exist through relations with others and the world.

By reframing the utopian possibility as an individual, achievable project, and hence attributing a transformative power to human endeavour of a very local kind, *One World* restores meaning to human finitude. Thus the actions of an individual, or of a limited number of individuals (such as introducing pollutants to waterways) can have collective consequences of a universal and possibly irreversible nature — here extrapolated to the destruction of forests, pollution of cities, and disappearance of animal species. The reverse of this is for individuals to accept an ethical responsibility to protect the world's ecology. To be able to act — to have *agency* — also means being able to answer for our actions, to be responsible. In moving between palpable examples of local and global phenomena, the picture book also metaphorically moves between material examples and the more abstract contrast between concepts of utopia and dystopia.

Texts produced for young audiences are often self-conscious about the debt they owe to the utopian/dystopian literary tradition. For example, Monica Hughes's *The Other Place* (1999) directly alludes to Orwell's *1984* ('some ancient book — banned of course, but a book that was almost like a bible to the dissidents' [p. 151]), and an airship, the *Jenny Haniver*, which at various times is used by all of the principal characters in Philip Reeve's tetralogy, is named for a type of animal forgery and quite mischievously said to be powered by 'Jeunet Carot pods', an undoubted reference to film makers Marc Caro and Jean-Pierre Jeunet, co-directors of the 1990s cult urban dystopian films *Delicatessen* (1991) and *The City of Lost Children* (1995). On the other hand, as we remarked at the beginning of this chapter, the varied genres and strategies through which the linking of new world orders and transformative utopianism is effected are very much the familiar genres and strategies of children's literature.

The understanding by the children in *One World* that the 'new world' they had made was a parasitic diminution of the actual world clearly situates their story within the literature of warning and exhortation. As a story about the growth of awareness, the book encapsulates how a quasi-utopian closure emerges from plotting story events as a story about subjectivity. When environmental issues are thematised, as in *One World*, texts emphasise ethical responsibility as both necessary and possible: characters can have agency.

Being responsible for one's actions is also a theme of books for older readers, but now emerging new world orders are more apt to be filtered through the pessimism of YA realism. In *Shadow of a Hero, Useful Idiots,* and *The Hungry Cities Chronicles,* the efficacy of action is tempered by global political forces and conflicts, so that the capacities of individuals to make a difference is more limited. None of these novels, however, suggest that this is a reason for ennui — on the contrary, it demands a greater action, as resistance and opposition to the tendencies of the world. Difference, persistence, even eccentricity, are valorised as individuals are summoned to play whatever role they can to ensure that whatever new world order is on the horizon will not be a new dark age.

3
Masters, Slaves, and Entrepreneurs: Globalised Utopias and New World Order(ing)s

> It is Noospace, the stunning new universe. The Noos, they
> call it; the amazing creation of the global Supermind that has
> sprung into being among the cities of the New World.
>
> (Bertagna, *Exodus*, 2002, p. 245)

In Julie Bertagna's *Exodus* (2002), Noospace is superior to the old cyber-space. In Noospace young people literally jump into a new cyber world and race at frightening speed through the gleaming maze that traverses the New World, with its endless pattern of connections: 'A living world of info and data within each pattern. All of it endlessly changing and mutating and repatterning. All dying and recreating every microsecond' (Bertagna, 2002, p. 245). Welcome to global utopia: the ultimate adventure!

Like many utopias, *Exodus* relies on *topos* — a place. However, Bauman's counter-argument of a 'Utopia with no topos' (2002b) warrants consideration if we are to engage with the idea of transformation. Bauman contends that the traditional utopian model of a 'better future' is not possible for three reasons: it ties its notion of happy-ever-after to a fixed, geographically defined, immovable city; its project of social reform will inevitably result in stasis; and its future orientation does not match today's emphasis on happiness now, rather than tomorrow (pp. 239–40). For Bauman, liquid modernity, the context in which globalisation has flourished, demands mobility, rapid and sophisticated communications technologies, individualism, and the seeking of personal pleasures: 'the liquid modern equivalents of the Utopias of yore are neither about time nor about space — but about *speed* and *acceleration*' (p. 241).

Bauman's points about 'a utopia without topos' and the 'speed and acceleration' of liquid modernity can be reconsidered in the light of a correspondence between Ruth Levitas and Lucy Sargisson (2003). Levitas suggests that 'for Utopia to be transformative, it must also disrupt the structural closure of the present' (p. 16). She cites 'globalization', particularly global capitalism, as one of the material political difficulties that block the realisation of Utopia. Global capitalism has engendered worldwide divisions of labour along with a reduced and politically weakened workforce, a growing number of people in need of social services, and an information-based system that relies on systems of control, surveillance, and exploitation.

Ever since the end of the Cold War, the international has been reimagined through the processes of globalisation, a phenomenon that embodies both utopian and dystopian elements. While Francis Fukuyama hailed the triumph of capitalism and the rise of the United States as the world's only superpower in *The End of History and the Last Man* (1992), Samuel P. Huntington contested such claims in *The Clash of Civilizations and the Remaking of World Order* (1996), predicting a struggle between 'the West and the rest' (p. 33). At the heart of these debates is the notion of liberal democracy. Fukuyama argued that the end of the Cold War proved that liberal democracy is a superior form of governance, and that future modern societies would be governed within a democratic, capitalist-driven model. Huntington contested this position, arguing that that the future would continue to be marked by violence because strongly contested cultures, especially those in the developing world, do not accept globalisation and modernisation. In the context of this chapter, these viewpoints also represent the way in which utopia and dystopia form an inevitable dyad, in which norms are interrogated and hierarchies of power are resisted, repudiated, or reabsorbed.

This chapter considers the impact of globalisation on children and youth as evident in a selection of literary and filmic texts which illuminate the differing ways in which young people's subjectivities, identities, legal and ethical entitlements, and cultural and sub-cultural allegiances are continually subject to transformation on a local and a global scale. Such transformations occur across a range of cultural and political spheres and variously illustrate the agential, exploitative, and diminishing potential of globalising forces for the young protagonists.

Our discussion is organised as follows. First, we sketch the contours of the contemporary crisis of representation in the context of globalisation, technological change, and sovereignty in an age of fear, insecurity, and rampant consumerism. Second, we discuss a range of children's fictions and films which embody these conflicting representations within the context of contemporary global trends and transformations. Third, we consider the extent to which these texts continue to offer 'spaces of hope', to borrow David Harvey's (2000) term, 'aimed at producing the future we want and preventing the future we fear' (Piercy, 1994, p. 2).

As a prelude to these fictional new worlds, two books set during the Cold War era — *The Fire-Eaters* by David Almond (2003) and *The Red Shoe* by Ursula Dubosarsky (2006) — offer something of the changing social and political climate which captured the tensions and optimisms of that period. They also touch upon some of the conditions of possibility that are at the core of Fukuyama's argument. As historical fictions these books look back to some defining moments of the Cold War and implicitly involve the increasing globalisation of the era. Though set in different countries (England and Australia, respectively) each represents shifting retrospective perceptions of the Cold War.

The Fire-Eaters is set during the time of the Cuban Missile Crisis (1962) and *The Red Shoe* is set in 1954 in Australia, a time when Communism was widely regarded as the most serious threat to a democratic way of life, polio was claiming the lives of many children (or rendering them disabled), and when the defection of the former Soviet spy, Vladimir Petrov, to Australia was a hot news item. In both these fictions, the world is experiencing the uneasy tensions created by the Cold War and international politics are structured by the bipolar enmity of the two superpowers, the Soviet Union and the United States. These books convey both uncertainty and optimism.

A sense of changing times permeates *The Fire-Eaters*. The story takes place at a time when education in England was emerging as a matter of national significance because the government of the day realised that a fully industrialised and technological society needed educated and skilled workers. The desire by parents for a better life for their children was also a feature of that time, especially as many young parents had received the equivalent of a secondary education either during the war in the armed forces or in the immediate post-war years (Peterson, 1967). A further factor identified by Peterson is 'the strongly democratic tenor of articulate opinion in post-war England and the growing dissatisfaction with the degree of class-stratification in traditional English society' (1967, p. 288). Bobby Burns, the protagonist, is on the brink of change: he has won a scholarship to an elite school, and his working class parents and friends have high hopes for his future which they see as lying beyond Keely Bay, a place which newcomer Daniel says has 'had its day' (p. 37). Bobby's father expresses the optimism that many believed an education would bring: 'You can do anything. You can go anywhere. The world is yours. You're privileged and free' (p. 60). However, the school principal, Mr Grace, is sceptical of such optimism with respect to the working classes: 'The working classes,' said Grace. 'The lower orders. Perhaps it is a fantasy that they are ready for true education. What do you think, Burns?' (p. 198). The story maintains a productive dialogue between the classes by conveying an underlying societal pull which suggests the disappearance of the local (utopian) working class, and the homogenisation of society through middle class gentrification. The threat of global disaster, however, serves as a mediating presence between the classes. As the world is poised on the brink of annihilation, a new form of community emerges in Keely Bay as people united in fear find love and comfort in each other's presence. Once the crisis is averted, Bobby's friend, Ailsa, remarks, 'the world's just so amazing' (p. 249). Such optimism expresses the hyperbolic entrepreneurism which has been promoted as a central component of globalisation and its promises of a new, enhanced way of life.

In a related way, *The Red Shoe* considers the lives of ordinary people living through the uncertain political times of the 1950s, a world in which both children and adults talk of the 'H-bomb' and the 'cold war'. It was the year when Queen Elizabeth II made her inaugural visit to Australia as part of the Commonwealth's celebrations of her coronation. It was also the year of the 'Petrov affair' and the imaginations of Australians were fuelled with newsreel and newspaper stories about the defection of a former Soviet spy who was living 'in hiding' in a Sydney suburb. The fact that Australia was simultaneously host to both the Queen of England and a Soviet spy is not without irony; yet it also juxtaposes two of the main contrasting points of the Fukuyama/Huntington debate, localism and globalisation, and points to how they are inextricably bound together. The sense of a nation based on the principles of fair play and democracy that the Australian government was endeavouring to promote at that time is encapsulated in newspaper excerpt interpolated into the narrative, reporting that the Prime Minister Robert Menzies refuted the claim that Australia had kidnapped the Soviet spy: 'We don't go in for that kind of thing (kidnapping) in Australia' (p. 95). However, the defection of Petrov and the media stories that this event generated demonstrate that contact between Australia and the world was unavoidable.

Another unavoidable sign of contact with the world beyond Australia takes the form of the novel's intertextual references to Hollywood films.

The 1950s was a time when Hollywood was making its presence felt in cinemas in Australia and other parts of the Western world. In the story, the children go to a theatre in the city to see *Roman Holiday*, and while the two younger girls are unimpressed, the older sister, Elizabeth, seems to have succumbed to the romance: 'I loved it,' said Elizabeth. She closed her eyes, smiling to herself, as though she was thinking about it' (p. 118). For the youngest, Matilda, the State Theatre, where she and her sisters saw the film, is so opulent that she asks doubtfully: 'Are we allowed in?' (p. 108). In fact, Matilda spends most of the time in the 'Ladies' toilet', where she finds the luxurious surroundings far more than enjoyable than watching a film in scary darkness. Given its pre-globalisation times, this scene looks nostalgically to a more innocent and less materialistic past, which serves as a subtle contrast to the excesses and worldliness that the processes of globalisation have subsequently brought to many children in Australia and other parts of the Western world.

These texts subtly thematise the dialogic relationships which circulate across the local/national/global triad through references, images, and recordings of the past which map the contours of the British and Australian nations in the 1950s: the origins, differences, kinship relationships, and distinctiveness of these peoples, and their increasing sense of international contexts. While these texts present us with images of nations on the brink of change, other fictions engage with globalisation overtly or in ways which demonstrate its power to shape ideologies.

Crisis of representation: globalisation and its dis/contents

Globalisation is both a familiar and a contested term. Like the categories *children* and *youth* it carries its own ambiguities of definition and competing ideological viewpoints. In some respects, globalisation is a fashionable buzz-word. Yet there can be no denying that there is a political and economic investment in globalisation, and significantly for this chapter, its undoubted impact on children and youth can be understood in terms of both benefits and negative outcomes. Thus, globalisation is not a uniform or homogenous process. Similarly, children and youth are not uniform or homogenous subjects and an underlying argument throughout this book is that any attempt to universalise childhood and youth fails to acknowledge the cultural spaces in which young people are subjected to ideological, institutional, and social forces and power relations. The myths of childhood innocence that circulate in many sectors of Western societies belie the fact that childhood is 'a cultural and political category that has very practical consequences for how adults 'think about children'; and it has consequences for how children view themselves' (Giroux, 2000, p. 5). Nowhere is this more pertinent than in texts written and produced for children by adults.

As we noted in Chapter 1, we seem to be living through a constant state of crisis. With the collapse of one of the world's two superpowers in 1991, international politics changed bringing an end to the bipolar international system that had dominated since the end of the Second World War and introducing a new phenomenon — globalisation. Globalisation emerged along with the declaration of a new world order as international economy and culture were undergoing a rapid transformation that shows no signs of abating. In broad terms, globalisation refers to the compression of space and time, and thus the intensification of social and political relationships and heightened economic competition (Castells, 2000) which characterise contemporary societies. Recent forms of globalisation are marked by two distinguishing features: first, the predominance of symbolic, cultural flows as opposed to earlier material or political exchanges; second, the increasing importance of global terms, or scales of reference in imagining global-local ('glocal') connections. As we have noted, the narratives of *The Fire-Eaters* and *The Red Shoe* offer twenty-first-century analyses of emerging *glocalisation* during the Cold War. Thus, globalisation is variously defined as a set of structures and processes that are economic, social, technological, political, and cultural and that have arisen from the way in which goods are produced, consumed, and traded within an international political economy. Glocalisation, however, is a useful concept in that it reminds us that the local is now also the 'glocal', as local communities engage with globalising pressures for institutional change and social adaptation at the same time that they seek ways of preserving local identity and customs. These tensions are especially apparent in 'sites of cultural diversity and economic inequality' (Stephens and McGillis, 2006, p. 367).

The effects of globalisation have been far-reaching and are assessed in contradictory terms — homogenising or heterogenising, liberating or stratifying, standardising culture, markets, ideologies or catalysing difference on a global scale (Cooppan, 2004, p. 11). As globalisation is a complex of processes, not a single event or entity, it defies a single representation, spawning instead multiple representations; one of the most politically charged is the neoliberal vision of 'a single globalised marketplace and village' (Friedman, 2000, p. xvii), whereby technological changes make possible the global flows of goods and finances, which in turn erode state sovereignty. Other representations contest this notion of the neoliberal global village, defending the sovereign-state ideal and noting how states engage in adaptive responses to international trade, finance, and production (Weiss, 1999).

Our concern here is how these representations and others are taken up in literature and film produced for children and young people. An equally important consideration is the narrative construction of the many discourses and 'fictions' of globalisation in these texts. Globalisation has prompted sovereignty narratives such as *Exodus*, which proffers the goal of an ideal sovereignty or independent territorial space that is free of interference from the outside. Paradoxically, however, it is often the intervention of a foreigner (as in *Exodus*) that brings about a transformed society that is based on 'humanist and cosmopolitan principles' (Doucet, 2005, p. 302). Other narratives are concerned with cultural optimism and pessimism, such as celebrations of global democracy and commodity culture, and lamentations of ecological disaster and technological determinism. However, despite the totalising schemata that often operate through texts that attempt to erase cultural difference and locality, 'the nation' still persists as a critical frame through which texts are produced and received. Herein lies one of the problems associated with the widespread use of the term 'globalisation': as an all-encompassing signifier it evades charges of ethno-euro-anglocentrism. Consequently, as we examine the global forces at play in the focus texts, we are mindful of the modalities of race, gender, and ethnicity in relation to the hegemonies of Western practices and ideologies. For example, in viewing the Iranian film *Turtles Can Fly* (2005), a story about children living on the border between Iraq and Turkey prior to the invasion of Iraq in 2003, we cannot separate cultural form from geopolitics and Western hegemony. It is worth noting, however, that a totalising Western view is to see Iraq as culturally and ethnically monolithic (simply as part of the 'axis of evil'), whereas it contains substantial Arabic, Turkish, and Kurdish minorities. This text and others require us to consider the historical and cultural transformation of identities, local communities, migrations, and livelihoods that are the result of the compression of the world and the growth of a global consciousness about fear and insecurity in times of international terrorism and retaliation. While such considerations invite scepticism regarding the 'good society' of utopian dreaming, they often retain the desire that a better place must continue to be imagined as a constitutive and defining characteristic of humanity.

A further crisis of representation lies in the ways in which subjectivities are embodied and experienced in the light of global telecommunications networks. Subjectivities in the new global order are both dispersed and integrated. The intensification of worldwide social relations 'link distant localities in such a way that local happenings are shaped by events occurring many miles away...' (Giddens, 1990, p. 64). As Castells explains, this connection of the local to the global has been made possible by a range of technologies and other capacities that enable social interactions 'in real time or in chosen time, on a planetary scale' (2000, p. 101). In the satirical futuristic novel, *Feed* (Anderson, 2002), Titus and his friends rely on their 'feeds' (transmitters implanted in their brains) to tell them what to do, from socialising to accessorising (*Feed* is discussed in detail in Chapter 8). Novels such as this raise questions about the relevance of old nation-state terms such as identity, proximity, labour, and belonging, given that the citizens of nations experience life in a globalised age of fluid and hybrid subjectivities, communicative networks, and a widening digital/economic divide. However, in thinking and writing about subjectivities there is often the tendency to negate 'bodies': material bodies that live and breathe in time and space. David Harvey makes the connection between globalisation and bodies by acknowledging that 'globalization is about the socio-spatial relations between billions of individuals' (2000, p. 16). It is the ways in which globalising processes reconfigure social space, and transcend human and physical borders that distinguishes it from other universalising processes such as Westernisation and Americanisation.

In the following discussion, we attempt to trace the processes by which identity is constructed and reconstructed in relation to others (including products of technological science) and in ways that challenge and subvert existing power structures and globalising forces. Despite the achievement of utopian intersubjectivities and transformed social relations in many children's texts, the driving force behind the actions of the protagonists is often towards self-preservation. Jameson (2004) poses an interesting but fearful outcome in that the achievement of utopia may result in obliteration of the past along with all that combined to form human subjects, including the desire for self-preservation. This 'terror of obliteration' (2004, p. 51) is something that needs to remain in our thinking as we explore the prospect of total systemic change suggested by some of the texts we discuss.

Further aspects of globalisation that we consider in relation to the focus texts are those of consumerism and commodity culture. As Jameson writes, 'indeed, no society has ever been quite so addictive, quite so inseparable from the condition of addictiveness as this one, which did not invent gambling...but which did invent compulsive consumption' (2004, p. 52). In discussing M. T. Anderson's novel, *Burger Wuss* (1999), we attend to those aspects that characterise the global: mass production, mass communication, and mass consumption. In this text, the impact of the global spread of free-market capitalism in terms of profits, productivity, production, and labour is examined within the ideological unravelling of the narrative. Another text that relates to commodity culture and its imperatives is the animated Disney/Pixar film, *Monsters, Inc.* (2001). As a global purveyer of consumerist values and ideologies supportive of capitalist globalisation, Disney animations, spin-offs, and theme parks entice an international consumption of its products by children and adults in ways that are unparalleled. As our discussion will show, *Monsters, Inc.*, while ostensibly offering a utopian vision of democratic cooperation and social responsibility, has an underpinning conservative strain that reinforces notions of hyperindividualism and hierarchical social ordering. *Monsters, Inc.* perhaps lends itself most readily to the theme of 'masters, slaves, and entrepreneurs' which runs through this chapter. Cinematic entertainment for children is never innocent, and as Doucet contends in his discussion on Disney films:

> The cinematic confirmation of dominant mappings of our 'real world' offers a potentially powerful cultural pillar for the construction of hegemonic meanings of global political order. Moreover, the particular genre of these films tends to 'disneyfy' politics, both internal and external, thereby making sense of the world in the same simple and sanitized way for which the legendary global entertainment company has become famous.
>
> (Doucet, 2005, p. 291)

As we examine the following texts, we consider how they take up the theme of 'masters, slaves, and entrepreneurs' and the limitations this schematising imposes on realising a transformed world.

Masters, slaves and entrepreneurs: fictions of globalisation

In his appraisal of 'globalization as process', David Harvey contends that 'something akin to 'globalization' has a long presence within the history of capitalism' (2000, p. 54). We noted earlier with reference to the stories by Almond and Dubosarsky how the beginnings of globalisation were impacting on the lives of the characters during the 1950s and 1960s. For Harvey, capitalism constructs its own distinctive geographical landscape, which is both spatial and temporal. In terms of contemporary globalisation, this dynamic geographical landscape has a number of aspects, two of which are pertinent here: the movements of commodities and people have been largely liberated from the tyranny of distance; and the preservation and production of cultural diversities and ways of living under different religious, linguistic, and technological circumstances exist in a complex relationship with the homogenising influences of the global market.

An exploration of cultural diversities and the movement of commodities and people are offered in the following texts through their depictions of 'self-other' relations across different socio-spatial dimensions. In *Flotsam* (Wiesner, 2006) a boy finds an old-fashioned camera washed up on a beach. To his surprise it contains a roll of film which, when processed, reveals a set of photographs of strange and exotic underwater worlds: mechanical fish swim alongside real ones; a giant turtle carries a shell city on its back; an octopus reads to an audience of fish in an under-water living room. There are also images of other children from different ethnic, cultural, and historical backgrounds. Each one is embedded in a photograph of a photograph creating a *mise en abyme* effect of recurring child subjects. After the boy takes a photograph of himself, he tosses the camera back into the ocean where it is carried like flotsam across the seas until it is washed up on an island far away where another child is about to retrieve it. This picture book demonstrates for young readers the idea of the interconnectedness of people across time and space, and the possibilities that wait to be explored. The exploration of possibilities, albeit fantastic ones, is one of the defining characteristics of utopian literature for young children. Such texts typically recognise that communities and spatialities are shaped by imagination and a sense of positive self-other relations, and are in contrast to dystopian fictions for older readers which tend to highlight struggle and conflict between people and societies.

Films produced for children often embody the struggle and conflict between the forces of good and evil as a way of highlighting a hier-archical ordering which clearly delineates 'us' and 'them' in terms of a sanctioned moral authority. In *Aladdin* (1992) and *Toy Story* (1995), a different kind of self-other relations from those suggested in *Flotsam* is developed which has significance for old/new world order politics. In *Aladdin*, identity politics is given an unintentional ironic twist in that while the Arab characters are the 'other' (in contrast to a predom-inantly Western viewership), they are further divided between those light-skinned and wholesome characters who are most like 'us' (Aladdin and Princess Jasmine), and the collective dark-skinned 'them' who are variously depicted as barbarians (the guards), buffoons (Sultan), or conniving usurpers (Jafar). In simplistic terms, the story celebrates the victory of the good and the beautiful over the bad and the ugly. But given the obvious Anglicisation of the characters and the Disneyfication of the story, which is faithful to contemporary American capitalist culture and its valorisation of the search for individual happiness and the main-tenance of a stratified social order, this victory can be interpreted as providing children with a model of the kind of absolute opposites that shaped the Western imaginary during the Cold War, and more recently with the 'axis of evil' rhetoric.

In *Toy Story*, old style liberal democracy drives the ethos of the film and is embodied in Woody, a stuffed pull-string sheriff toy who is the leader of the toys who live in Andy's bedroom. Nostalgia for the past (figured in a white American cowboy politics) permeates the film. However, a more immediate past is noted by Doucet: '*Toy Story* pivots on three political spaces that are framed by the Cold War imaginary' (2005, p. 292). Doucet claims that the first of these spaces is Andy's bedroom, which ostensibly operates on the lines of liberal democratic principles but in practice sides with liberalism's suspicion of democratic power in the hands of the people: the decision-making process ultimately lies with the collective of toys, but Woody's sheriff status ensures that he is the symbolic law enforcer maintaining a hierarchical social order. The second space is Sid's bedroom, 'a dark foreign political space modelled on the totalitarian social order' (Doucet, 2005, p. 295) in which Sid (the bully who lives next door to Andy) mutilates his toys and engages in sadistic practices which ensure that these toys, unlike those living in Andy's bedroom, have no voice and live in terror of Sid's brutal regime. The outside world beyond the two bedrooms serves in global political terms, as the equivalent to the third ('international') space that exists outside of (but impacts on) the two bedrooms, which comprise rival nation states informed by opposing political orders. Doucet's Cold War analogy offers a convincing interpretation of the victory of liberal democracy over totalitarianism when Woody liberates the toys who have suffered under Sid's oppressive regime. In the context of current world politics, Woody's cowboy persona with its liberation of the innocents (toys) from the clutches of evil (Sid) not only embodies the triumph of liberal democracy that Fukuyama proclaimed (and which Doucet's thesis supports) but also anticipates the arrival on the world political stage of another 'cowboy':[1] one who has declared a 'war against terrorism' and who is committed to establishing democracy in the Middle East and Iraq.

Whereas the boys' bedrooms in *Toy Story* can be seen as sites for the staging of glocal politics, the global is given a different treatment in *The Yellow Balloon* by Charlotte Dematons (2003). This wordless picture book offers a visual display of aerial images with readers positioned to take up a commanding high vantage point above a changing global landscape. Time and space are released from historical and geographical limits so that past, present, and possible future co-exist. Double page openings offer colourful pastiches of realistic and fantastic images which convey a seemingly natural order of a mix of topographical, historical, cultural, recreational and technological elements. The contrasts between rich and poor, urban and rural, ancient and modern, old and new technologies in this book invite recognition of and response to the globalising processes that shape notions of identity, location, and interdependence. While it is easy to identify the masters, slaves, and entrepreneurs who are represented in the illustrations in *The Yellow Balloon* and in the narratives of *Aladdin*, and *Toy Story*, it is perhaps a more useful exercise to contemplate the ways in which the diverse peoples depicted in *The Yellow Balloon* across time and space might relate to and are dependent upon each other in a global economy. This kind of speculation opens up a range of utopian possibilities which do not necessarily eschew practical relevance. As Harvey notes, 'without a vision of Utopia there is no way to define that port to which we might want to sail' (2000, p. 189).

Charting a course to Utopia, however, may not be directed towards an external destination but to an inner state of self-fulfillment. In *Empire* (2000), Hardt and Negri consider how changes in economic production from Fordism to a post-Fordist model of economic organisation blur the boundaries between home and factory or nation and nation. These changes have given rise to a new organisation of capital and labour force, and to what Hardt and Negri describe as a biopolitical economic production in which labour produces affect and desire within the labouring body. These new social beings seek and achieve feelings of 'well-being, satisfaction, excitement or passion' (2000, p. 293) as products of their labour. This affective labour is epitomised in the helping professions (e.g. counselling, nursing, hairdressing) and in the importance of the entertainment industry. Together with what Hardt and Negri call 'informatization' whereby new communications networks enable the coordination of the workplace to be deterritorialised and the workforce to be reorganised, new subjectivities are formed which are hybrid, mobile, and subsumed within global capitalism. This image of labour contrasts with the stable, located, community-oriented workers of traditional or non-industrial societies. We turn now to consider how this new global order of labour and labourer are represented in the film *Monsters, Inc.* and the novel *Burger Wuss*.

Monsters, Inc. is the eponymous and anachronistic factory run and staffed entirely by fluorescent-coloured monsters. The location is presumably somewhere in 'America' but place is not important despite the oversized map of the world that hangs at the entrance to the factory. It is this very ambiguity of geographical location that makes Monstropolis a familiar Disneyfied site in that the internal narrated space (America) stands for the world. In this instance, the internal space of the factory operates as the global space — there is no world beyond its parameters. This collapse of the inside/outside division is commensurate with Hardt and Negri's contention that current world order has seen the emergence of a new global sovereign power that 'no longer follows the territorialized inside/outside cartography of the nation state' (Doucet, 2005, p. 303). There is also a contrast between the visualisation of fluid time–space compression as represented in *Flotsam* and *The Yellow Balloon,* and the more managed and delineated time and space depicted in *Monsters, Inc.* In the latter narrative, time and space are carefully constructed and controlled features of the workplace and company policy: workers 'clock in' by swiping their ID cards; sirens signal lunch break; and the parallel human world is accessible through bedroom doors that are lowered into plug-in electric slots via an overhead pulley system. The work of the monsters ('scarers') is to scare small children in order to capture their screams, funnelling them into sealed containers, which are then used to generate energy for the monster city/world of Monstropolis. The 'scarers' work together on an old-fashioned, mechanised production line. They are loyal, passive workers who have internalised corporate goals and work to maintain the corporate order. Like many utopian/dystopian spaces, control is maintained by a security team; in this instance, they are known as the Child Detection Agency (CDA). Their role is to ensure that no children contaminate the factory, and when one monster returns from a successful scaring exercise with a child's sock caught up on his fur, he is immediately decontaminated and shaved.

Another kind of production line and system of checks and controls operates in *Burger Wuss,* where the rival chains are thin disguises for the giant American food chains McDonald's and Burger King. Kermit O'Dermott is a fast-food burger place that attracts teenage-workers and predominantly youthful consumers. Just as the scarers are encouraged to be proud corporate workers, so too are O'Dermott workers — star employee, Turner, reminds the newly-employed part-timer, Anthony: 'You've got to be proud of your job, man … There's nothing more American than

48   *New World Orders in Contemporary Children's Literature*

O'Dermott's' (Anderson, 1999, p. 48). When Anthony decides on his 'Master Plan' ostensibly to bring down the O'Dermott chain, but more accurately to exact revenge on Turner for stealing his girlfriend, his accomplice Shunt, a self-styled communist, collaborates with boundless and reckless enthusiasm. In Michael Moore fashion, Shunt delivers a diatribe about 'The enfeeblement of the American mind. The corruption of the corporate structure. The commodity fetishism of the marketplace' (p. 97); his outpourings provide a telling commentary on the problems with multinationals, consumerist society, and the impact of globalisation on developing countries and the environment. His comment, 'These companies are monsters' (p. 83), provides an ironic connection with the monstrous-like activities of the scarers from *Monsters, Inc.*, who are, within the double logic of that film's narrative frame, real corporate 'monsters'.

Monstropolis operates on several levels as a dystopia. Despite the garish colours, jokes, and, paradoxically, the non-threatening looking monsters (given their job as scarers), the factory which is all we are shown of the city is a closed and sinister place whose *modus operandi* is based on terrifying small children. The factory's motto — 'We scare because we care' — is a perverse reworking of familiar Western political rhetoric regarding child protection, education, and welfare.

Baccolini and Moylan (2003b) highlight strategies to identify the literary dystopia exemplified in this text. For instance, they suggest that the dystopian story opens *in media res* within the terrible new world and 'cognitive estrangement is at first forestalled by the immediacy and normality of the location' (p. 5). As young viewers of *Monsters, Inc.* would most likely be familiar with other Disney/Pixar animations, the estrangement that would normally be experienced by seeing monsters of various shapes and sizes, and with single or multiple eyes, hair of snakes, and bodies covered in fur is lessened. Furthermore, similar monsters can be found at 'Toys R Us' and other retail outlets. But the most significant characteristic of dystopian narrative that accords with this film is the 'construction of a narrative of the hegemonic order and a counter-narrative of resistance' (Baccolini and Moylan, 2003b, p. 5). The hegemonic corporate order that is clearly evident in *Monsters, Inc.* is resisted by the most loyal of workers, Sulley, the monster who has the best scare rating. The disruption to the order occurs when a young girl (later named 'Boo' by Sulley) finds his presence in her bedroom a source of amusement and immediately engages with him, initiating a bond between the two. Through his contact with Boo, Sulley comes to realise the cruelty of scaring children and the exploitative motive behind the corporation. However, despite Sulley's victory in saving Boo from harm and his ousting of the evil company manager, he becomes another corporate boss who values individualism and competition, and maintains the hierarchical ordering between management and workers. While the company now harnesses children's laugher instead of their screams, children remain exploited for corporate profits. Lee Artz comments that Disney maintains a class-based social ordering in many television sitcoms and films it produces with the work site serving as 'the backdrop for self-centred, ego-driven protagonists modelling appropriate middle-class, entrepreneurial values and practices' (2005, p. 91).

In *Burger Wuss*, grubby entrepreneurialism and misplaced company loyalty are the motivations behind hostility between the O'Dermott and the Burger Queen workers. While Anthony and Shunt are the misfits or dissidents who can see through the shallow capitalist hype of O'Dermott's, they have different reasons for bringing down the company, employing strategies that are akin to corporate sabotage. Anthony steals the Burger Queen condiment troll and Shunt edits the script for O'Dermott's 'Dream Campaign' commercial in a way that draws attention to its toxic products ('Laced with amaranth [E123]...BHA [E320] and BHT [E321]...and hormonal growth promoters'), exploitative labour practices ('dreams of underpaid positions'), and unhealthy processing ('our meat's uncooked and still goes "Moo"') (Anderson, 2000, p. 139). However, their efforts to secure a better way of life are not for the good of the community, but for personal gain. Six months after the climactic altercation, Anthony sees Shunt dressed like a businessman. When Anthony asks Shunt whether he has sold out, Shunt reassures him that he is undertaking 'O'Dermott's management training programme' (p. 220) only as a way to infiltrate the company. However, Shunt's final comment to Anthony, 'Give me a ring sometime...We'll do lunch' (p. 231), suggests that, like Sulley, he has been absorbed into the company ethos, becoming another corporate player.

What *Burger Wuss* and *Monsters, Inc.* offer in terms of utopian discourse is that their constructed worlds-within-in a-world are designed according to a utopian political arrangement which regards the workers, not as individuals, but as a collective who work for the good of the company. In order to be good company workers they need to embody (while at work) the characteristics of Thomas More's utopians who 'in general are easygoing, cheerful, clever, and fond of leisure' (More, 1992, p. 57). When Anthony applies for a position at O'Dermott's, he takes a 'clever and cheerful-sounding' attitude in order to please the manager. His efforts are rewarded as the manager responds: ' "That's the spirit!... We work as a team here. We even play as a team"' (p. 9). (Yet, despite this team spirit, hierarchy is symbolically installed through colour: green for workers, blue for management.) Jameson sees this kind of collective depersonalisation and anonymity as 'a very fundamental part of what utopia is and how it functions' (2004, p. 40). Hence, in *Monsters, Inc.* when Sulley names the child 'Boo', who in turn calls him 'Kitty', the naming not only provides an ironic moment for viewers who realise the reversal of the monster–child hierarchy in terms of who frightens whom, but it also personalises their interaction and thereby destroys the unemotional and amoral protection that anonymity allows in this context.

While these texts offer ways of reading commodity culture and a depersonalised subjectivity of multinational employees, their implicit neoliberalism defines the societies in which their narratives occur (and which resonate with our own empirical present) through the privileging of marketing, privatisation, and consumerism. Within this market-driven perspective, there is little space for envisioning the kind of community where children and young people are considered valuable in terms that are not reductively economic. In *Monsters, Inc.* children are the raw material by which energy is produced, and in *Burger Wuss,* youth are the workers and consumers who ensure that the franchise will continue to grow and make profit.

In the film *Turtles Can Fly* (*Lakposhtha hâm parvaz mikonand*), children are subjects caught in the middle of Huntington's 'clash of civilisations'. As Kurdish refugees without a recognised homeland, they exist in a liminal space on the border between Iraq and Turkey on the eve of the US-led invasion of Iraq in 2003. What adds an extratextual dimension to this film is that the children are non-actors who have experienced the ravages of war. Many of the children and adults in the film are without limbs and exist in poverty in a makeshift camp. The view that American society has lapsed into a kind of barbarism by the 'growing refusal to pay attention to the needs of its children' (Giroux and Giroux, 2004, p. 68) is also realised in literal and metaphorical ways in this film by both Western and non-Western adults: literal, in the brutal pack rape of a young girl by Saddam Hussein's soldiers, which is shown in flashback; and metaphorical, in the false promise of a new world order by the American government. The rape is a barbarous act and means that the girl (Agrin) is forced to care, in silence and total despair, for a child she refuses to accept as her own. The film is quite unlike what Western audiences have come to expect in films focusing on young people. However, familiar elements — humour and the products of globalisation — are integral features of this film. While Western societies might well view children as 'unfit to be free agents and utterly infantilized, reduced to complete dependence on adults' (Giroux and Giroux, 2004, p. 68), the children in *Turtles Can Fly* operate alongside and, independently, of adults, who often come to rely on them for information and guidance. The dystopian landscape in which the children and adults exist is devoid of cultural markers, the absence of which almost silences its historical associations. While there are no ruined buildings to tell of past conflict or civilisations, the signs of its recent history are the remnants of the 1990–1991 Gulf War which litter the land: the bombed-out shells of armoured vehicles, barbed wire fences signifying landmine territory, a manned Turkish observation tower, numerous tents. This seemingly incongruous mix of signifiers elides issues of nationhood and cultural identity, but, paradoxically, re-enforces these issues through visual and aural representations of displacement and ethnicity. The inclusion of numerous antennae and a solitary satellite dish also acknowledges the omnipresence of globalisation. As the camera moves into closer inspection of the people who live in the camp, we can see how notions of 'home', 'community', and 'cultural allegiance' are experienced amidst the uncertainty of living in transit and with only unreliable and sporadic news reports and aeroplane leaflet drops about the impending 'liberation' by the American-led forces.

Two boys emerge as entrepreneur and prophet. Thirteen-year-old, Soran, also known as 'Satellite' because of his skill at acquiring and setting up the satellite dish and television antennae, is a Buddy Holly look-alike with large black horned rim spectacles and a charismatic presence. Satellite is a self-styled operator who wheels and deals, cons and cajoles, but manages to retain an optimism about the future and a genuine concern for the younger children who look up to him and rely on him for surviving these oppressive times. He assumes the role of leader of the children, organising the dangerous but necessary sweeping and clearing of the minefields and then haggles with the adults for trade-ins for unexploded mines. Another boy, Hengov, arrives at the camp from a neighbouring village with his sister, Agrin, and her 3-year-old blind child born as a consequence of rape. A taciturn character with no arms, Hengov's special talent is his ability to disarm undetonated mines with his teeth. He is also said to be a clairvoyant and his ability to foresee future events and predict the location of undetonated mines affords him a special respect amongst the camp's children and adults. For the children, Satellite is their big brother/protector because their biological parents are either killed or missing. When Satellite has his foot blown off after an incident in a mine field, the harsh reality of their situation means that he is given minimal medical attention and is left to suffer alone while the other children stage an agonising vigil. Adults and children are all equally inhabitants of this sinister heterotopia, a place of 'Otherness' in relation to the dominant orders that have shaped its existence. But it is a social world, nevertheless, that, like other heterotopias, has developed 'an alternative way of doing things' (Hetherington quoted in Harvey, 2000, p. 184).

Despite the facilitation of high-speed flows of information and images through sophisticated communications technologies, the people in the camp are forced to rely on discarded antennae haphazardly installed and maintained on the surrounding hillside. Video reception is highly inadequate, and the CNN reports of the American preparations confuse the adults who gather around an old television set anxious to hear the news. Since no one understands English, Satellite 'interprets' giving his own optimistic spin on the news: 'President Bush predicts rain'. Satellite has little knowledge of the United States, but he believes that they 'are the best in the world' and that their mines are top quality. He believes also that the war between America and Iraq will see the fall of Saddam Hussein and a return by the Kurds to their homeland. While the children, through Satellite, store their hopes in the Bush administration, the cruel irony is that children are among the biggest casualties of the war and of economic sanctions against Iraq.[2]

Satellite has all the sartorial markers of a global youth. He has a stock of American expressions and wears an American style baseball cap backwards, a bomber jacket, joggers, and jeans. This display of commodity consumption is the raw material for embodying an expressive subjectivity, and for the symbolic public marking of his identity for others. His pride and joy is a tricked-up bicycle. Although bicycles are common to most Western children, in the camp Satellite owns the only one and it therefore contributes to his elevated ranking in the social order. However, his utopian dream of the Americans as bearers of a better life dissolves after his accident and when he discovers that Agrin has suicided having drowned her baby. In the final scenes when the American soldiers arrive, Satellite watches as their military presence appears like spectral figures on the landscape — faceless Others jogging to a military rhythm with weapons in hand. Rather than welcome these foreigners, he turns away with a look of disillusioned detachment. The utopian promise of a better world is realised as an unlikely possibility by both Satellite and the viewing audience. However, the utopian trace is not lost as rare goldfish live in the polluted waters of the village pond signifying, in humanist terms, the ability to survive a dystopian environment.

Within the totalising logic of globalisation, it is easy to think that the world has become one big place, through the universalising processes of new communications technologies. *Turtles Can Fly* brings the local and the global together and thus exemplifies the way in which glocalisation operates in this community through satellite communications technology and international militarism. Consequently, west and east are interlinked through a politics of dependence, marginalisation, and power imbalances. The anxieties felt by the Kurds can be seen as stemming from a 'localism' that expresses a desire to settle and identify with a regional space, instead of living on the margins.

This idea that localism is associated with a geographically bounded space with its particular historical and genealogical significances related to kinship and length of residence is taken up in *Exodus*. The book is set in the future at a time when the Earth has become submerged:

> Oceans and rivers rose to drown the cities and wastelands. Earth raged with a century of storm...Imagine the vast, drowned ruin of a world washed clean. Imagine survivors scattered upon lonely peaks, clinging to the tips of skyscrapers, to bridges and treetops.
>
> (2002, u.p.)

From this global catastrophe, the narrative then moves to the isolated farming community, 'Wing', a high island somewhere in the Atlantic Ocean, in the year 2099. On the eve of a new century, hopes are high for a miracle that will save the surviving villagers as the ocean attempts yet again to devour the land. Mara Bell is the reluctant but destined hero. Like Satellite, she is also a techno-savvy youth who initially uses old technology, a 'cyberwizz', to project herself into the Weave. On one of these excursions into cyberspace she encounters the mysterious cyberfox. Like many such spaces, both inside the text and outside of it, the Weave (an embodied version of an online chatroom) provides participants with a shared social space bound up with mystery and in which identities are open to creative manipulation. Mara's use of the technology not only sets her apart from the others on the island, who appear as luddites, but it provides her with information and a vision of the New World that exists beyond her island and the Atlantic Ocean. The news of another place also surprises the cyberfox:

> 'Does the New World exist in realworld too?' Mara demands. 'Are there really giant cities that rise up above the oceans?'

'Of course,' shrugs the fox. 'It's all there is — at least I thought so. That's what we've been told. But you say you live on an island. So there are islands in the world!'

(Bertagna, 2002, p. 39)

The New World comprises towering sky-cities, one of which is 'New Mungo' located in the Eurosea. In New Mungo, those on the periphery are the revolutionary Treenesters who live in trees and archive the past through their storytelling, the refugees who are forced to survive outside the city limits in a crowded and disease-ridden boat camp, and the 'ratbashers', wild, orphaned children who live in the dark watery recesses of the Netherworld that lies under New Mungo. Like those living in the Kurdish camp in *Turtles Can Fly*, these refugees and children have little hope of a better future, existing as on the periphery of New Mungo in contrast with those city-dwellers fortunate enough to inhabit the centre. The hierarchical social order means that those on the periphery are denied access to the city's resources, including their advanced technologies.

The New World has been conceived as a utopia intended to house all the Earth's refugees after Europe was wiped out by flood, but the great wall that 'was built to protect the city from the sea soon became a fortress to keep refugees out' (p. 202). The ever-vigilant sea police guard the city gates of New Mungo with brutal dedication. Rather than a socialist utopia, the New World has become an exclusive club, a place for 'the most brilliant minds, the most technically skilled' (ibid.), a 'world full of brilliant beings, of human angels' (p. 232). When Mara manages to enter New Mungo disguised as a sky police, she discovers a world that is unfamiliar and strange. Like the exterior limits of the city, the interior is also closely controlled and monitored with access via an identi-disk, and the omnipresent guards are watchful. But unlike the squalid living conditions endured by those on the outside, the inside is beautiful: 'Its long silver tunnels gleam and its arcades are vast airy places that look as if they, like the population of lumens, are crafted purely from light. The citizens are beautiful too' (pp. 232–3). Mara discovers that the beautiful surface is underpinned by a world of commodity culture and sophisticated technology. While this world appears strange to her as she has lived an isolated farming existence up to this point, it is one with which many readers would be very familiar: electronic billboards constantly flash information about New World Trading, with a logo attached to each commodity on the Trading Index; there is Arcadia — 'arcades full of bright shops and strange entertainments' (p. 231); crowds of youth zip past her on flashing skates ('zapeedos'); fake fish swim in endless electronic circles in the Looking Pond. This is an artificial world, not unlike Disneyland, designed for fun, endless entertainment, and spectacle.

Just as Satellite's facility with old technology (*Turtles Can Fly*) enables him to process and disseminate information (albeit often inaccurate) to others, Mara soon learns that the technologically enhanced environment of New Mungo provides its citizens with an 'informatized'[3] world. However, in the seemingly information-laden and entertaining utopian social processes, they are bereft of story and the capacity for empathy. When Mara asks the Noos-station for a story, the search reveals that it is a '*Defunct word*' (p. 261). Bertagna seems to set up a dichotomous relationship here between the humanist world of the past and the posthuman world of the future that is embodied in the informatised New Mungo. The fragility of this informatised world becomes apparent when Fox creates a ghost virus using the ghosts of the past to disable New Mungo, enabling Mara to lead an escape on the supply ships. Despite technology's fragility it nevertheless provides the means by which escape is possible and as such is treated as both a master and a slave, depending on how it is employed.

Although technology has played a key part in creating the transformed social world of New Mungo, old social orderings exist. The mass of the people are cyberworkers who live in basic accommodation at the lower ends of the central towers, while the 'Ideators' who compete to come up with new ideas, and the 'Noosrunners', the cybertraders who search cyberspace for new ideas and commodities to buy and sell among the cities of the New World, live in the coveted high-top apartments. The city slaves are those who are rounded up and coerced by the police to work on the construction of sea bridges. They form the liminal group occupying a social space between others. Thus, the social ordering within New Mungo is based on degrees of privilege, talent, and success, and, inversely, the social ordering outside New Mungo is based on degrees of deprivation and genealogy. The Treenesters are the ones with knowledge of the past and the city's history, the refugees are the newcomers who are not afforded any historical or national roots, and the ratbashers are the 'sea urchins' of the New World — discarded, unwanted, ignorant, and without a recognisable language. Only Mara as 'the foreigner' is able to see the value in all three groups which form the social strata of the outsiders. As Bonnie Honig argues, narratives of democracy often employ 'the image of the foreigner as the founder of democratic community in order to manoeuvre out of the impossible scenario of self-foundation which democracy presupposes' (cited in Doucet, 2005, p. 293).

Through her foreigner's perspective, Mara views New Mungo citizens as possessing 'a terrible island mentality' where 'anyone from outside of New Mungo is a second-class citizen' (p. 257). This observation of their perceived isolationist philosophy and narrow-mindedness can also be seen as highlighting the 'glocal' paradox that attempts to retain local social practices while desiring global sophistication. The division of labour and exploitation, and the processes of exclusion that are the organising principles and practices of New Mungo are not unlike those that are promoted through neoliberal globalisation. Castells's point that the primary issue of the new information age 'is not the end of work but the condition of work' (1998, p. 148) speaks also to the conditions of New Mungo where their 'new' social orderings (though sadly familiar) are the product of its failed globalised utopia. When Mara and her followers escape New Mungo and steer a course to the future, they carry with them a utopian desire to find yet another New World in the Arctic regions of Greenland, Alaska, and northern Canada, forgetting that the founders of New Mungo also carried the same dreams.

Exodus seems to proffer the idea that a feminist utopia is possible under the guidance of Mara, a young woman who puts aside her own romantic desires to forge a new democratic community in the far north (regardless of the desires and practices of any inhabitants of those areas, as we point out in Chapter 4). However, Bertagna does not offer a convincing model of a reimagined world without patriarchy, and under Mara's leadership. Positing a female hero is not enough, especially when the text relies on familiar gender binaries, gendered language, and a masculinist quest-and-conquer narrative for the story frame. As Mara heads towards the future she is asked by one of the city slaves, 'What are you looking for, Mara?' She replies 'Miracles' (p. 343) and it would seem that she might indeed need some supernatural help as she has no plans or strategies, nor has she given any thought as to what might meet the travellers on their arrival in the new lands.

Transforming the present, transforming the future

By concluding with a discussion of *Exodus*, we have arrived back at our beginning and to Bauman's contention that a traditional model of utopia is not possible under the conditions of liquid modernity. The texts in this chapter thematise globalisation as part of their narratives, and in so doing they explore the imaginative alternatives that are a necessary part of societal transformation. Given their intended audience, the stories tend to provide a utopian gloss on globalisation in proposing a humanistic outcome or view of the world. This humanism is translated in different ways: rescue from evil (*Exodus; Monsters, Inc.; Aladdin; Toy Story*); renewed sense of community (*The Fire-Eaters; Flotsam; Exodus; Turtles can Fly; The Red Shoe*); a borderless world (*The Yellow Balloon; Flotsam*). Only *Burger Wuss* retains a cynicism towards globalisation and its negative impacts. *Flotsam* too resists the technological pull of globalisation by attributing value to a recycled, pre-digital-age object: an old box camera.

Mignolo's suggestion that 'globalization is a set of designs to manage the world while cosmopolitanism is a set of projects toward planetary conviviality' (2000, p. 721) poses an interesting paradox for children's texts. On the one hand, picture books such as *Flotsam* and *The Yellow Balloon* can be read as expressing a planetary conviviality through the mixing of cultural space, time, and peoples within a genial global landscape. On the other hand, to present the world as borderless denies racial, ethnic, religious, linguistic, and cultural differences. The consequence is that cosmopolitanism is replaced by a global homogenisation, and surface conviviality may mask fear and insecurity of the 'other'. This notion is supported by Doucet in his discussion of *Rescue Heroes,* a film about global humanitarian missions undertaken by Rescue personnel with the purpose of rescuing people in peril. Doucet draws on Hardt and Negri's argument that current world order has shifted from sovereign power of the nation-state to a global level. Doucet (2005, p. 303) contends that *Rescue Heroes* 'by scripting the world in this constant state of emergency... contributes to shaping within children a form of subjectivity'; that is, amenable to global sovereignty. In other words, by living with insecurity the need is created for a global network of rescue personnel. The parallels with the current world order are easily apparent.

In this respect the image of 'the foreigner' is problematic. In *Exodus,* Mara is the foreigner but she is also the saviour who leads people to the New World, whereas the 'foreigner' in *Turtles can Fly* is an ambiguous figure. Given this story's basis in recent and ongoing global politics, viewers are able to read the foreigner in ways that speak of both threat and liberation, depending on their (geo)political allegiance. In *The Fire-Eaters* and *The Red Shoe* communists are the foreigners who threaten world peace and democracy.

Mignolo argues that 'ethnicity became a crucial trademark after the end of the Cold War' (p. 739), and since September 11, 2001 ethnicity and religious affiliation have taken on more significance in terms of the global imagination. Consequently, while pre-September 11 films such as *Aladdin* may indeed present a convivial picture of good-hearted foreigners winning out over their evil compatriots, *Turtles can Fly* and other children's texts published since 11 September may be less amenable to 'imagining conviviality across religious and racial divides' (Mignolo, 2000, p. 740). In the case of *Aladdin*, race and ethnicity are absorbed into a moral framework which is inextricably tied to the ascribed 'whiteness' of the 'other'. In *Exodus,* ethnicity, race, and religion are erased as discursive elements of subjectivity. However, given Mara's originary home and the reworked northern European setting of the story with new world horizons to the North, current real world geopolitics which look to the South (Korean and China) as emerging superpowers are ignored. Such old world imaginings suggest that, at least in this text, there is no alternative to the hegemony of the Western world as part of any imagined utopian community.

This scenario is implicit in the superficial benevolence of the new world order of Monstropolis in *Monsters, Inc.* As monsters and children work in seeming harmony, one could imagine a convivial Cosmopolis where technology and a neoliberal management have softened the edge of child exploitation through the film's overtly benevolent discourse, which is monolithic and a literal embodiment of 'Toys R Us'. There is no binary opposite. The logic of 'only us and no them' is to reinforce for children that, like the victorious Woody and the good guys in *Toy Story*, they are part of what Doucet calls a 'moral cartography' that leaves no doubt that they are on the side of the angels, albeit at times avenging angels. If this is the future of global utopian texts for children then our schematisation of masters, slaves and entrepreneurs will continue to hold sway despite attempts to show that it is a small (convivial) world after all.

4
The Lure of the Lost Paradise: Postcolonial Utopias

> Every culture has one place it will not allow to be touched. This is ours. As long as Resthaven exists, the Heart of Africa is safe.
>
> Farmer, *The Ear, the Eye, and the Arm*, 1994, p. 148.

Contemporary children's texts in English are produced both in former colonies such as the United States, Canada, South Africa, and Australia, and also in nations which were formerly colonising powers, such as Britain (see Bradford, 2001, 2007). Moreover, modern societies (in particular the United States) have since the Second World War engaged in neocolonial processes and politics that have effected new forms of conquest, seeking to produce a world order based on international capital and Western conceptions of democratic government. Formulations of nationhood and cross-cultural relations in many children's texts are thus shaped by colonial histories and by a plethora of contemporary debates centring on colonial, postcolonial, and neocolonial politics, including the extent to which citizens of postcolonial nations should take responsibility for the consequences of past acts of invasion and violence; the ethics of the 'war on terrorism', especially in relation to its impact on the citizens of nations such as Iraq, Afghanistan, and Iran; and the projected 'clash of civilisations' which, according to Huntington, will inevitably take the form of a contest between 'the West and the rest' (Huntington, 1996, p. 33).

The texts we consider in this chapter — and the wider body of texts from which they are chosen — confirm Ralph Pordzik's argument that 'the transformation of utopian issues in postcolonial English fiction cannot be seen merely in terms of the historical development of a literary genre, but should also be interpreted as a means by which the writers have engaged actively in the politics of cultural formation and representation' (2001, p. 169). Elsewhere Pordzik notes that novels addressing postcolonial issues 'are hardly ever prescriptive in their conception of a "better" society; in fact, they leave it open to their readers to construe their own image of utopia which is not and cannot be a fixed and reliable end in itself any longer' (2001, p. 18). The openness of utopian texts addressing postcolonial issues is comparable to the open-ended, ambiguous endings which characterise critical dystopias, since both postcolonial utopias and critical dystopias maintain a space for imaginings of new world orders while engaging in self-reflexive critiques of contemporary politics. Similarly, children's texts which refer to colonial histories and contemporary postcolonial cultures are typically qualified and guarded in their projections of new world orders.

Nevertheless, it is not always the case that children's authors advert to the colonial and postcolonial implications of their narratives. For instance, Phil Cummings' *Tearaway* (2002) is a science fiction novel which tells of Earth's colonisation of other planets, basing this process on the European colonisation of Australia in the eighteenth century. Its narrative replicates Australia's colonising by Europeans as a convict settlement, and repeats the common information that many of the convicts were the victims of a dystopian society, but fails to interrogate the *terra nullius* doctrine that informed British colonialism in Australia; instead, it depicts the 'natives', as it calls them, as innocent savages, full of smiles and obliging behaviour. Hence it loses its opportunity to explore and interrogate the basis of the Australian utopia in oppression and genocide.

Another text which depicts a colonising journey while excluding reference to colonial history is Julie Bertagna's *Exodus* (2002), a refugee narrative set in post-disaster Scotland, where global warming has caused the rising oceans to cover most of the land (see Chapter 3). The novel's protagonist, Mara Bell, leads the citizens of the island of Wing on a journey to Mungo, one of the new cities which have been built far above the flooded land, only to find a vast refugee camp comprising boats which have been forbidden entry and which are kept under surveillance by New Mungo's sea police. When Mara discovers a book about the Athapaskans, the Indigenous inhabitants of territory covered by the coniferous forests which stretch across Alaska, parts of the Yukon and the Northwest Territories of Canada, she resolves to save the survivors of Wing and the other displaced people she has gathered, by sailing to the Arctic Circle and settling in 'high land in the far north of the world' (Bertagna, 2002, p. 322). In this way the novel's vision of an empty land waiting to become home to 'settlers' recapitulates the narrative directions of the many colonial texts in which the ancestral territory of Indigenous peoples is assumed to be there for the taking.[1]

In contrast with *Tearaway* and *Exodus*, which are seemingly oblivious to the colonising directions of their narratives, many children's texts manifest an anxious preoccupation with questions relating to colonial histories and their repercussions in postcolonial societies. A powerful trope in these texts is that of a utopian space inhabited by autochthonous communities whose modes of life afford models for human sociality and for relations between humans and the natural world. Representations of such utopias in texts for young people are often informed by anticipatory regret, since they are coloured by consciousness of the displacement and subjugation of Indigenous cultures and by debates about relations between Indigenous and non-Indigenous peoples, about land rights, memory, history, and nationhood in contemporary postcolonial societies. It might be expected that texts revisioning colonial histories would originate principally from former colonies such as Australia and Canada; rather, many such texts have been produced in Britain over the last few years as authors address the nation's imperial history and its neocolonial directions.

A concept germane to the texts we consider in this chapter is that of cultural identity. In his essay on Caribbean film-making, 'Cultural Identity and Diaspora', Stuart Hall compares two ways of thinking about this notion. The first, he says, 'defines "cultural identity" in terms of one shared culture, a sort of collective "one true self", hiding inside the many other, more superficial or artificially imposed "selves", which people with a shared history and ancestry hold in common' (Hall, 1996, pp. 110–11). The second view of cultural identity is characterised by the 'play of difference within identity' (Hall, 1996, p. 114), wherein subjects position themselves and are positioned by historical circumstances, by cross-cultural encounters, by the multiple, changing meanings of representational acts and processes. The term 'authentic' evokes the first of these models of cultural identity, implying a hierarchy where 'authentic' is preferred over 'inauthentic' ways of being. Referring to Indigenous peoples and cultures, it conjures up notions of primordial, unchanging traditions passed on through the generations and producing stable, transcendental identities. Historicist treatments of precolonial pasts are informed by this model, since, as Bill Ashcroft notes, 'Historicism fixes the indigenous subject at a static moment in the past, a prehistory located under the sign of the primitive; a primal innocence or barbarity. This is the static historical moment from which History, the record of civilization, begins' (Ashcroft, 2001, p. 117).

When notions of 'authentic' precolonial identities are conflated with constructions of utopian settings and elements, they imply a chasm between prehistory and history, imaged through contrasts between plenitude and loss, between the primal innocence of the utopian world and its fall into corruptibility, and between bounded, localised societies and the universal reach of global capitalism. In this chapter we focus on treatments of utopian spaces in YA texts addressing postcolonial themes and narratives,[2] and on the subject positions constructed for contemporary readers. The texts we consider address utopian desires for transformed postcolonial orders in which colonial appropriations of Indigenous territories and cultures are acknowledged and redressed, and where cultural identities are wrought, in a specifically postcolonial way, through productive engagement between the descendants of those formerly situated on either side of the colonial divide. Nevertheless, it must also be noted that in nations with colonial histories there exist diverse and often divergent views about the meanings of the past for the present; and the texts we consider manifest many of these tensions.

Utopia lost: the tragic turn

The modes of representation whereby colonisers depict their others typically rely on assumptions and stereotypes: for instance, that the colonised constitute an homogenised group, naïve, barbaric, and depraved. The texts we now consider, Frances Mary Hendry's *Atlantis* (1997) and Susan Price's *The Sterkarm Handshake* (1998), write back to colonial discourse by disrupting the binary logic on which it depends, which is expressed in oppositions between colonisers (white, civilised, educated) and colonised (black, primitive, illiterate). However, the disruptive force of these texts relies more on complicating the processes and practices whereby humans value one culture or worldview over another, than on a simple reversal of oppositions.

If utopia can be defined as 'the desire for a better way of being' (Levitas, 1990, p. 198), and given that desire is historically and culturally situated, it follows that utopias and utopian elements take on a variety of modes and forms across time and place. In *Atlantis* and *The Sterkarm Handshake*, 'desire for a better way of being' is framed by critiques of imperialism and of the hegemonic power of state and corporation in late modernity. *The Sterkarm Handshake* is set in Britain, following the development of a Time Tube which enables humans to travel from the twenty-first back to the sixteenth century. The Company, a powerful commercial conglomerate, has negotiated with the sixteenth-century English and

Scottish courts to take control of the unsettled border region, where it intends to mine coal, gold, and oil and to establish a time-travel tourist industry. In *Atlantis*, a city state exists in caverns below the Antarctic ice. Its inhabitants are descendants of Rammesak and Elonal, sole survivors (or so the Atlantans believe) of cataclysmic events which destroyed the world when its inhabitants failed to honour the gods of fire, rock, and water. However, when the young protagonist Mungith is trapped in the old gold mines of Atlantis by a roof fall, he discovers a human, 'Bil', a geologist who has been working 'Outside', in the Antarctic, and who has fallen through the ice to the mines below. In both texts, then, pre-modern societies encounter modern humans: in *Atlantis* through Bil's accidental entry into their world, and in *The Sterkarm Handshake* in the form of reconnoitring visits by geologists and Company officials as well as through the presence of an anthropologist, Andrea Mitchell, sent by the Company to investigate Sterkarm culture and language.

The depiction of the Company's project in *The Sterkarm Handshake* underlines its neocolonial purposes and colonial antecedents. Like colonised peoples across the British Empire, the Sterkarms are showered with cheaply produced gifts (here in the form of generic aspirin) which are calculated to distract them from the Company's project of occupying their land; the bureaucrats who lead the project, like those who established colonies, regard the inhabitants of Sterkarm territory as primitive, ignorant, and superstitious; and, in accordance with the colonising practices of British imperialism, land not farmed or used for profit is regarded as waste territory open to 'improvement'.[3] The Company's colonial activities are associated with an absolute conviction that the Sterkarms are barely human; that they belong to the category of uncivilised others. It is, then, only a small step to conclude that they are dispensable and their lands open to appropriation. Like other historically marginalised groups (such as the Irish), the Sterkarms are 'not quite white' or 'not white enough', an idea enforced by Windsor's references to them as 'natives' (Price, 1998, p. 159) and as 'barbarians' (p. 216).[4]

Andrea, whose work has required her to spend a lengthy period with the Sterkarms, is the principal focaliser of events. Her perspective is complicated by the fact that, in contravention of the undertaking she has made in her employment contract, that she will not 'fraternize' with the 16th-siders (Price, 1998, p. 159), she is romantically involved with Per, son of Old Toorkild, the Lord of the Sterkarm tower and its surrounding land. In the beliefs and cultural practices of the Sterkarms, Andrea sees utopian elements which answer her longing for a more 'real' way of being. The Sterkarms are expressive and demonstrative; they are intensely loyal to those they regard as family; their lives revolve around communal interests and obligations. These qualities expose the limitations of Andrea's bland, middle-class existence, with its consumerist and individualistic preoccupations.

On the other hand, Andrea is keenly conscious of dystopian aspects of sixteenth-century life. The Sterkarms, including her beloved Per, are violent, duplicitous, and ethnocentric; they die of diseases curable in the twenty-first century; and they are in constant danger because of endemic warfare among border families. This see-sawing of utopian and dystopian elements complicates the very possibility of utopia, so that Andrea's return to the twenty-first century at the end of the novel, after the Sterkarms have comprehensively routed the Company, seems reluctantly to acknowledge the futility of longing for a better way of being. Nevertheless, her decision, at the end of the novel's sequel, *A Sterkarm Kiss* (2003), to make a life with Per in the sixteenth century, enforces the idea that for all its violence and dangers, Sterkarm society is preferable to the dystopian world of Andrea's twenty-first century, where human lives are ruled by the economic order of capitalism and corporate power. Andrea's choice of Sterkarm society makes it clear that the horrors of a dystopian order in which individuals are robbed of freedom, creativity, and agency outweigh her concerns for her life and safety in the sixteenth-century setting.

The Company proposes to exploit the environmental advantages of Sterkarm territory by producing a pseudo-utopia for which, in the words of James Windsor, the project manager, 'people are going to pay big money' (2003, p. 81). Windsor regards the quiet of the Sterkarm countryside, its clear water and unpolluted skies, as assets to be improved through the judicious renovation of the built environment, since Sterkarm living conditions are, he says, 'a damned sight too authentic' (2003, p. 91). Windsor's avowal that the Company will preserve 'the essential flavour of 16th-century life' parodies those varieties of tourism which rely on nostalgic renditions of a peaceful, agrarian past while avoiding reference to the rigours of manual labour, low life expectancy, and violent conflict. The novel's strategy of switching between the sixteenth and twenty-first centuries discloses another form of concealment: Windsor's imagining of a time-travel tourism industry erases a history of colonisation, since he expects that by the time wealthy tourists enjoy time-travel tourism, the Sterkarms will have been obliterated or transformed into exemplars of an 'authentic' past, adding local colour to the tourist experience. The time-travel tourism he envisages thus accords with the variety of tourism discourse which, in the words of

C. Michael Hall and Hazel Tucker, is itself 'based on a colonial desire to fix the identity of the other in order that it remains ... distinct from tourist identity' (Hall and Tucker, 2004, p. 17), an identity made possible by the rise of transnational capital.

Those modern characters whom readers are positioned to regard as honourable and self-aware, such as Andrea and the security guard, Bryce, are depicted as experiencing a lively sense of loss and regret at what they believe to be the inevitable destruction of Sterkarm land and culture. As Bryce and Windsor enjoy the view of hills, valley and river, Bryce remarks, 'It's a shame we'll spoil it all' (2003, p. 82). Later in the narrative, after the Sterkarms have killed a party of 21st-siders and destroyed the Time Tube, Andrea attempts to warn Toorkild, Per, and their family of what is to come:

> If only the Sterkarms had known something — anything — about the elimination of the Sioux, the Nez Perce, the Cheyenne, she could have made the desperation of their position so clear to them. An invading people with superior weapons moving in unstoppably. Making deals and treaties and promises, and breaking them all. Using any resistance as an excuse for all-out war and genocide. It had happened over and over again.
>
> (2003, p. 271)

In the novel's final scenes, Windsor's retaliatory raid is thwarted by the shrewdness of the Sterkarms, who play on his firm conviction that they are stupid and trusting. Even so, the narrative ends in a profoundly ambivalent moment, when Andrea weighs the 'bland, neat landscape' of the twenty-first century, 'all pastel painted walls and smooth carpets' (2003, p. 445), against the passionate energy of Sterkarm life, and opts for safety. In the final moments of the novel, Andrea and Per stand in the same physical space, which in the sixteenth century is Sterkarm territory and by the twenty-first has become a 'heritage site', each longing for the other but now separated by five centuries. The thwarted romance of Per and Andrea is, then, metonymic of the loss of the utopian possibilities exemplified by the cultural and environmental values associated with the sixteenth-century setting. To twenty-first-century readers, Andrea's world is a near-future version of their own times, and the wider implications of the novel's closure are, first, that positive change is impossible in a world ruled by capitalist modernisation and populated by a disempowered and undereducated citizenry; and, secondly, that precolonial societies characterised by communitarian social structures, agrarian economies, and an unpolluted environment represent utopian orders irrevocably lost to contemporary industrialised societies. The novel's emphasis on the violence and uncertainty of the sixteenth-century setting interrogates conservative, touristic treatments of the past fuelled by nostalgia, even as it implies that despite these dystopian elements the Sterkarms are, unlike the inhabitants of the twenty-first century, vividly alive.

Whereas the Sterkarms occupy their territory by force of arms, engaging in sporadic skirmishes with other border families, in Hendry's *Atlantis* the 8000 inhabitants of Atlantis live in a self-contained world, a complex and ordered society which accords with Lyman Sargent's account of utopia as 'a good or significantly better society that provides a generally satisfactory and fulfilling life for most of its inhabitants' (Sargent, 2003, p. 226). In the crowded environment of the city, a system of Custom and Manners (law and protocols) has been developed in order to regulate behaviour and maintain order; those who fail to observe Custom are cast out into the furthest caves, where they experience violent lives as Wilders. The narrative follows a conventional rite-of-passage trajectory, tracing Mungith's progress as he seeks to pass the 'Trial' which will qualify him as an adult, up to the point where he discovers Bil, when the novel's focus turns to larger questions of risk, responsibility, and ethics.

Having adapted to the dim world and limitations of space under the Antarctic ice, the Atlantans have large, sensitive eyes and are small of stature, so that the human intruder Bil, perceived as a giant, is both other and potentially dangerous. However, his thoughts, memories, and emotions are accessible to those Atlantans (known as Sensers) who possess telepathic powers, such as 12-year-old Chooker, one of the novel's focalisers together with her cousin Mungith. Whereas Andrea's perspectives and reactions filter the otherness of Sterkarm culture, in *Atlantis* the strategy of focalising events through the perspectives of Chooker and Mungith achieves a defamiliarising effect, positioning readers to interrogate human behaviours and values generally accepted as givens.

It is in episodes involving divergences between the norms of Atlantan culture and Bil's perception of these norms that the novel foregrounds epistemological differences, notably in an episode in which Bil observes an act of euthanasia involving an incurably-ill baby. The Atlantans believe in reincarnation and subscribe to the view that those certain to suffer and die should be ceremonially consigned to Beliyyak the Dolphin God, in order that they may begin new and better lives.

Bil's horror at the infant's death and his attempt to prevent it is regarded as a sign of his lack of care for the baby's suffering. However, it is Bil's proposal that medical intervention should be used to correct 'faults like birthmarks and extra limbs and fingers' (Hendry, 1997, p. 87), that most affronts the Atlantans, who value and accentuate the physical differences common among them, including multicoloured skin, extra limbs and fingers, body hair, webbed feet, manes, and tails. Bil's assumption that to be human is to look like other (white) humans collides with the Atlantans' high regard for their visible differences.

Like the incursions of the twenty-first century into the sixteenth in *The Sterkarm Handshake*, Bil's advent to Atlantis rehearses colonial histories. When he wakes from unconsciousness in the mines and sees the Atlantans preparing to rescue him, his fear and panic are racialised: Chooker, sensing his thoughts, 'saw herself through its mind — fearsome little black people. The black was coal dust, of course. It was used to light' (Hendry, 1997, p. 66). This reflex reaction on Bil's part points to the cultural assumptions he holds, and which shape his view of the Atlantans as other to a normative idea of whiteness and humanness. Without intending to, Bil introduces 'floo', so that a thousand Atlantans die when exposed to a disease against which they have little resistance. And like Andrea, Bil seeks to warn the Atlantans of the destructiveness of colonising power:

Desperately, Bil warned them, *Stay away!* Giants' fires belched poisonous smoke, and they carelessly poured poison into the streams and the sea, and on to the land. Every small nation of people who had ever met Giants had suffered. Their land had been taken, by force or lies. They had been slaughtered, hunted like cockroaches, or had died of disease — sometimes deliberately spread. And there was no way to fight; Giants had gas bombs and flamethrowers that would reach to the furthest tunnels. *Stay away from Outside!*

(1997, pp. 90–1)

Following the disastrous outbreak of influenza in Atlantis, the old Queen Sullival follows Custom by determining that she must sacrifice herself to appease the gods. Before she does so she introduces a debate in the Atlantan Council: she proposes that the right course of action is to hazard the dangers of Outside and go to meet its inhabitants, while the young King Pyroonak suggests that the Atlantans should close off the tunnels leading to the Outside, so ensuring that Atlantis remains hidden from the knowledge of Outsiders. The Council's debate thus concerns itself with nothing less than the directions the city should take in order to maintain its utopian project, contrasting Pyroonak's advocacy of a politics of isolationism with Sullival's preference for conciliation and engagement with the Outsiders.

The conflict between these two positions reaches a climax when Bil attempts to thwart the Queen's sacrifice, kidnapping her and seeking to take her Outside. In defiance of the Queen's order that Bil should be spared and sent back to the Outside, he is killed by Hemminal, the King's sister, a former Wilder. The novel ends with Mungith reflecting on what has happened: 'The Giant was gone. It was all over. Atlantis was safe' (1997, p. 153). Readers following the cues provided by the text but inaccessible to Mungith — that the city's name constitutes a warning of imminent disaster, that the air over the Antarctic is becoming warmer and that the ice is melting — are positioned to understand that Atlantis is not safe, that the killing of Bil will not ensure that the city remains hidden from the Outside, and that Hemminal's action, which contravenes Custom, is a portent of further violence.

In both *The Sterkarm Handshake* and *Atlantis,* contemporary readers are positioned to consider dystopian features of their own time and to imagine better worlds located in pre-modern and precolonial societies. However, the two novels propose contrasting strategies for sustaining utopian worlds. According to the deterministic narrative direction of *The Sterkarm Handshake,* historical change inevitably leads to environmental and cultural degradation, so that the maintenance of cultural identity depends upon the extent to which societies at risk of colonisation are capable of excluding potential colonisers. In *Atlantis,* in contrast, Queen Sullival's receptiveness to the Outside is promoted as a desirable and positive direction, despite the fact that colonial histories cast a shadow over the future of Atlantis. The Queen's conviction that the Atlantans stand to benefit from exchanges with Outsiders — and that Outsiders may prove capable of learning Manners from Atlantans — argues for a radical openness to the utopian possibilities of alignments across geographical, cultural, and historical divides.

Utopia (re)discovered

Whereas the narrative trajectories of *Atlantis* and *The Sterkarm Handshake* are structured by encounters between pre-modern and modern cultures and the immediate consequences of these encounters, Nancy Farmer's *The Ear, the Eye, and the Arm* (1994), Brian Caswell's *Deucalion* (1995) and Louise Lawrence's *The Crowlings* (1999) locate events in futuristic settings which look back towards colonial histories. Utopian imaginings in these texts are thus located against a backdrop of events ranging over centuries and including the contemporary time of the novels' readers. *The Ear, the Eye, and the Arm* is set in Zimbabwe in 2194, while the settings of *Deucalion* and *The Crowlings* are planetary Earth colonies analogous to eighteenth-century and nineteenth-century settler societies.[5]

In all three novels utopian societies define themselves in relation to their connections with precolonial Indigenous cultures. In *The Ear, the Eye and the Arm*, a group of dissident traditionalists has established a village, Resthaven, which purports to 'preserve the spirit of Africa' (1994, p. 147) and which exists as an independent entity within the nation of Zimbabwe. In *Deucalion,* improved social and political orders derive from the restitution of the Indigenous Elokoi to their ancestral homelands at the end of the novel, while in *The Crowlings,* too, Indigenous people return to the territory from which they have been displaced by colonisation. However, as we will argue, the closure of *The Crowlings* envisages a utopian order that reinscribes colonial hierarchies. *The Crowlings* begins in the village of the Wolf-clan, on a colonised planet, Gamma Centauri Five, whose inhabitants' lives have been destabilised by the advent of humans, and ends, five generations later, when the Crowlings return to their territory under the protection of the karra-keel, winged mythical creatures from the precolonial past. *Deucalion* concludes with a revolution in which the Elokoi combine with first and second-generation settlers to overthrow the imperial centre and produce a utopian society.

In *The Ear, the Eye, and the Arm,* Tendai, Rita, and Kuda, the three children of General Matsika, the 'Chief of Security for the Land of Zimbabwe' (1994, p. 7), live in a palatial home replete with futuristic features such as robots and an automatic Doberman, where they are imprisoned by their father's obsessive fear that they will be kidnapped by criminals from Gondwanna, described in the novel's Glossary as 'a large country carved out of northern Africa by bloody wars in the late twenty first century' (1994, p. 392). Zimbabwean society in the novel is itself riven by disorders deriving both from the colonial past and from more recent environmental disasters when the land has been over-used and degraded: toxic chemicals have despoiled Dead Man's Vlei, a vast area of Harare which is now a rubbish dump inhabited by the dispossessed and desperate; beggars haunt the wealthy suburbs; and the Masks, a secret society composed of Gondwannan criminals, engage in kidnapping and extortion.

The children's journey, which commences when they are kidnapped and imprisoned in Dead Man's Vlei, takes them to a series of territories which evoke aspects of the nation's past. The Vlei is controlled by a purveyor of illicit alcohol known as the She Elephant, who nonetheless affords a sense of stability and home to the beggars and criminals who live in these polluted slums. Another territory, which constitutes a remnant of British imperialism, is the home of Beryl Horsepool-Worthington, where the members of the Animal Fanciers' Society maintain their quaint customs, including afternoon tea, the veneration of animals, and the consumption of large quantities of sherry for purportedly medicinal reasons. A third territory, on which we focus here, is the Valley of Resthaven, 'the Heart of Africa' (p. 100), where the children find refuge after they escape from Dead Man's Vlei.

The parodic and satirical tone of *The Ear, the Eye, and the Arm* endows it with a self-reflexivity which renders literal readings untenable and works against any simple identification with focalising characters. Accordingly, the novel's representation of Resthaven is far from an uncritical celebration of originary 'African' culture, but rather plays with notions of appearance, reality, and fantasy. Thus, Resthaven is not a remnant of the past but an invented world, having been established 200 years before the time of the novel's setting, along nativist principles — that is, as a return to a world view and style of living which existed in precolonial times. It is enough for the society outside Resthaven to know that it exists: General Matsika says that 'Every culture has one place it will not allow to be touched. This is ours. As long as Resthaven exists, the Heart of Africa is safe' (1994, p. 148). The *idea* of Resthaven, then, is that of a good place sealed off from the world around it, a utopian enclave which affords a consolatory fantasy for Africans living in the modern world.

When the children persuade the gatekeeper of Resthaven to allow them entry, 13-year-old Tendai is struck by the fact that the village is organised exactly according to the descriptions of precolonial African life with which he is familiar. The smell of wood fires evokes 'something deeply buried in Tendai, an ancestral memory of sitting by such a hearth and letting the smoke wash over him' (1994, p. 102). Later, swimming in the clear waters of a pool and scrubbing himself with the loofah he has been given, he feels that he is 'washing off the despair of Dead Man's Vlei' (ibid.). It is, however, significant that the ancestral memories evoked by these sensory experiences originate not from Tendai's ancestors but from stories told by a character known as the Mellower, the son of Beryl Horsepool-Worthington. The Mellower's function in the Matsika household is to carry out a daily ritual known as

Praise Singing, during which he reassures the members of the household of their worth and of the commanding futures which await them, interspersed with stories of traditional life: 'Sometimes it was Praise, sometimes history, and a lot of the time it was pure fantasy, but told with such authority that they all believed it' (p. 103). Just as the Mellower's mélange of fiction, fantasy, and Praise Singing reflects back to the members of the Matsika family enhanced versions of themselves which they internalise as true, so Resthaven deals in illusion: its walls comprise an enormous curving mirror which creates the impression that the world inside stretches out endlessly.

By deploying the common trope whereby strangers enter a utopian space, the text denaturalises the presuppositions and ideologies of both the inhabitants of Resthaven and of the Matsika children. The gendered nature of Tendai's and Rita's experience functions in part as an interrogation of the patriarchal order of the community. During his enforced stay in Dead Man's Vlei, Tendai has been guided by an ancestral spirit to discover an ancient *ndoro* (a talisman shaped as a spiral and made of shell), a sign which marks him as a potential Spirit Medium; he is also a gifted story-teller. For these reasons he is afforded a privileged life even by the standards of Resthaven, where boys and men are indulged, whereas 11-year-old Rita endures a miserable existence carrying out the menial tasks expected of girls and women. Nevertheless, Rita's reluctance to carry out the cleaning tasks she is allocated also draws attention to the fact that the Matsika children have been exempted by their parents' status and wealth from taking any responsibility for themselves or for their physical environment, so that the novel's critique of patriarchy runs alongside its commentary on the value of self-reliance.

The catalyst for a sequence in which the villagers turn against the children is the birth of twins, a boy and a girl, to 14-year-old Chipo, the junior wife of the Chief. When Rita realises that the baby girl is to be killed because of the villagers' belief that the birth of twins is unnatural and unlucky, she attempts to save the child, whereupon the village's Spirit Medium, resentful of Tendai's growing reputation, embarks on a witch-finding ceremony. On one hand the narrative undermines the rituals and practices of this ceremony: for instance, the chief's senior wife Myanda gives Tendai and Rita a bag of chicken-droppings which they are to eat along with the emetic drink prepared by the Spirit Medium, because Myanda suspects that he will give the children a placebo mixture in order that they will fail to vomit and so expose themselves as witches. On the other hand, the novel also proposes that there exists a world of spiritual beings who work through imperfect humans such as the

Spirit Medium. When the villagers assemble to see who will be selected to undergo the witch-finding test, the Spirit Medium looks into each face in turn. Tendai, returning the man's gaze, is surprised to find that he sees not the Spirit Medium but an ancient presence 'hovering inside the man's body.... It gazed at him from a vast distance, full of deep knowledge he couldn't begin to understand. It neither approved nor disapproved of him, but it *knew* him right down to the soles of his feet' (p. 166). The spirit inhabiting the Spirit Medium's body orders that the placebo drinks prepared for the children should be discarded to be replaced by genuine witch-finding preparations, with the result that Tendai and Rita vomit and are duly cleared of the charge of witchcraft.

The text's treatment of the witch-finding ceremony is analogous to its representation of Resthaven more broadly, in that it accepts as given the existence of a world of spirits and of the rituals whereby humans access this world, even as it foregrounds the fallibility of Resthaven's inhabitants, their machinations, and intrigues. It critiques the nativist imagining on which the village is based by exposing its patriarchal assumptions; and while it foregrounds Myanda's resourcefulness at evading and manipulating misogynist rules and practices, such subversion does not extend to a transformation of power relations. The novel ends with a proleptic account of Tendai, at 16, revisiting Resthaven Gate and listening for signs of human life. The bell goes unanswered and the entrance is never opened; but Tendai is sure that the people of Resthaven continue 'in their timeless way, farming, hunting and thatching their round huts when the season of long grass was upon them. And at night, they gathered in the *dare* to tell tales. Or so Tendai believed. Someday, when the spirit of Zimbabwe stumbled and the *mhondoro* [the spirit of the land] grew faint, the gate would open again and remind the rest of the world of what it once had been' (p. 300).

The novel achieves a distancing effect through its pervasive playfulness, realised in the mobility of its narrative (especially its shifts between narration and focalisation), its deployment of intertextual references, and its habit of irony. In this way it challenges its readers to construct subject positions of some complexity as they negotiate the novel's varying perspectives and discoursal modes. Thus, Resthaven might be understood in a number of ways: as an anti-utopia (if a reader were to regard its patriarchal and gerontocratic government as an assault on the very possibility of utopia); or as a flawed utopia in the sense that Sargent uses this term (i.e. a society which demands or expects too great a cost to achieve the good place);[6] as a conservative utopia (Wegner, 2003, pp. 172–3); or as an instance of strategic essentialism where those seeking a better future for a postcolonial society invoke valued aspects of its precolonial past. Like the postcolonial utopias described by Pordzik, *The Ear, the Eye and the Arm* deploys 'a set of disjunctive writing techniques deliberately frustrating all attempts on the reader's side to reduce the text to one single meaning, so that the world offered as radically discontinuous from the existing one always returns to confront it in some epistemological way as well' (2001, pp. 167–8). Thus, the different significations suggested by Resthaven argue against any simple formulation of postcolonialism or decolonisation.

While Resthaven is both the good place which constitutes the fixed and stable moral centre of Zimbabwe and also a no-place remote from modernity, both *The Crowlings* and *Deucalion* track processes during which colonised people recuperate space, identity, and cultural meanings. The narratives of these novels are structured by journeys undertaken by colonised groups intent on reclaiming appropriated territories after years of living on lands allocated to them by their conquerors. In *The Crowlings,* the Luppa, or Wolf-clan, whose land comprises the foothills of the mountain Skadhu, on the planet Gamma Centauri Five, are attacked by a neighbouring clan, themselves robbed of their territory by the human colonists (or starmen) who have appropriated the planet. When the Luppa village is torched and the adults killed, the children of the clan embark on a journey to a Reservation, guided by Joel Baxter, an earth colonist, who acts as their mentor.

The novel divides into three phases and traces the progress of the Luppa as they depart from their ancestral land and adopt the customs and values of humans, and then return to the mountain from which they came. At the time of the attack on the clan, Small Fry is undertaking the test (involving fasting and staying apart from the clan) which comprises his rite of passage to manhood. Against his will he has been promised to Cloud, plump and with a club foot; when he wakes from sleep during his trial, the first creatures he sees are crowlings, tiny birds which feed on carrion, so that instead of the more glamorous name for which he hopes, 'snow bear or mountain cat or luppa [wolf]' (1999, p. 11), he is obliged to take the name 'Ben Crowling'. By the novel's third section, the crowlings have mutated as a result of the organophosphates with which colonists have sprayed them, and when they begin to attack living creatures the colonists abandon Gamma Centauri Five and move on to other planets, refusing to allow the 'natives', descendants of the Luppa and other Indigenous groups, to emigrate with them.

The disintegration and recovery of the clan is plotted against its departure from, and return to, traditional practices and beliefs. By the time the narrative reaches its third phase, Linni Crowling, the descendant of Ben and Cloud, lives a frivolous and consumerist life under the disapproving gaze of her grandmother, whose stories of the old ways strike her as hopelessly outdated: 'Grandmother Rhawna lived in a time warp, clung to her nativeness and refused to change' (p. 170). Nevertheless, Linni is endowed with dreams of the karrakeel, the winged creatures which formerly defended the Luppa, and when the crowlings attack her home in the city of Jasper's Creek, she embarks on a journey to the original home of the Luppa, guided by the karrakeel. Like Ben Crowling and Cloud, she gathers around her refugee children who accompany her on the long trek to the northern mountains where the Luppa once lived.

In the first and third episodes of *The Crowlings* the female protagonists Cloud and Linni lead the way, conducting children to safety: Cloud protects them from colonisation by humans, Linni from the ravages of the crowlings. Cloud is obliged to maintain the fiction that Ben Crowling is in charge: Mikklau, her grandson, reflects that 'When Grandmother Cloud was around no one stepped out of line. She ruled the clan as she ruled her husband, except that Grandfather Ben never knew it' (p. 94). In the third episode, Linni is accompanied by Will Baxter, the descendant of Joel Baxter, the coloniser who accompanied the Wolf-clan children on their trek. In line with Hall's formulation of that version of cultural identity which is grounded in 'a mere "recovery" of the past, which is waiting to be found' (Hall, 1996, p. 112), both Linni and Will are compelled by instincts and inherited knowledge to return to the traditions of their ancestors. The utopian space to which Linni 'naturally' tends is a world defined by its difference from modern industrial life: it is 'without cities and motorways and gas stations, with no soda-light glows at night to dim the moons and stars, no sprawling estates of identical houses, no debt, no money ... just the great freedom of the land' (1999, p. 238).

If the text represents Luppa values and culture as characterised by simplicity of life, closeness to nature and access to spirit figures, these ostensibly admirable features also reinscribe notions of Indigeneity as static and as located in prehistory. Linni, explaining the history of Gamma Centauri Five to the refugee children in her charge, speculates that the karrakeel may have come from other planets; or 'maybe they had simply evolved here alongside the native population, and progressed into an advanced civilization while Linni's people remained primitive' (p. 234). The utopian space to which Linni has brought the children, then, is provided by the karrakeel, whose bio-laboratories under the mountains store 'the genetic material of everything that existed, ready to re-stock the planet' (p. 2234); and Linni and the children constitute the 'primitives' destined to occupy the lower reaches of a hierarchy of species which echoes the racial hierarchies of imperialism. Will Baxter is needed, in Linni's words, for 'the standards he set them' (p. 238) and (with a nod towards a romantic outcome projected to occur just beyond the end of the narrative) for 'the man in him that balanced the woman in her' (pp. 238–9). Depictions of utopia in *The Crowlings* thus collapse into the unexamined clichés and stereotypes of colonial discourse, recycling notions of an 'authentic' and ancient mode of life, universalised and romanticised.[7]

Brian Caswell's *Deucalion,* in comparison, proposes a utopia which addresses in very specific terms the colonial oppression and postcolonial unease of one settler society, since the novel is a somewhat transparent refashioning of the history of the settlement of Australia. The map of the continent which precedes the narrative is a squashed version of Australia, complete with the inland sea which early explorers were convinced existed; the Indigenous Elokoi represent the Aboriginal peoples, and the terms of their near genocide are readily applicable; and the utopian propaganda used to attract colonists and later settlers reflects that used for over a century to attract people to Australia. This dream is ironised early in *Deucalion,* where the lure is expressed as 'Land of your own. Full employment in a booming environment. No pollution, no ruling class. Build a new life with hard work' (p. 24). Instead, settlers drawn from an underclass swiftly find themselves returned to an underclass.

Caswell's analogy presents a very scathing presentation of Australian history and its underpinning imperialist metanarratives. The alternative is then expressed most specifically in the genetically engineered Icarus children, true genetic and cultural hybrids produced by splicing Elokoi and human genes. One of the principal characters, Jane, is one of these hybrids, but the other crucial trait attributed to her is progressive, rapid loss of memory of her life on Earth, a loss induced as a consequence of cryogenic freezing for the 50-year journey to Deucalion. This strategy enables the character to be fractured and reconstructed, and thence to perceive with new eyes and to become acutely aware of the dystopian nature of the colonialist society from which she has emerged. The fissuring of the character is also an effective aspect of Caswell's structuring of the novel as a polyfocalised text — that is, events are presented through the thoughts and perceptions of nine or ten characters — and this enables Caswell to represent processes of cultural difference, culture-contact, and paradigm shift from multiple perspectives (albeit with a unified outcome in mind).

The driving themes of *Deucalion* are individual liberty, personal, political and economic independence, and social justice, and one of the main story strands with which this is linked — the struggle of a colonised planet's Indigenous inhabitants to reoccupy their ancestral land — is patently modelled on and alludes to the situation of Aboriginal Australians and the quest for land rights. Readers would have to be thoroughly obtuse not to grasp this. It is cued by: the importance of rock paintings in Elokoi culture; the centrality of the concept of *Dream* in Elokoi tradition and everyday life; and the parallel growth of awareness in one of the main characters (Daryl) that the experience of his Aboriginal Australian ancestors as a colonised people was similar to the experience of the Elokoi.

At the beginning of the novel, the colony of Deucalion is a century old, and its citizens are about to cast votes in the inaugural election marking the transition of government from the Earth-based Ruling Council to a President and independent Congress. However, the elections are rigged by Dimitri Gaston, who engineers his own election as President as well as the assassination of his chief rival. The Elokoi, and the Icarus children who share their genetic makeup, possess telepathic abilities which enable them to read the thoughts of others. This circumstance propels Gaston into a programme of murdering the Icarus children for fear that they may expose his election and his self-serving alliance with the Deucalion Mining Corporation, a body controlled by the Ruling Council of Old Earth. At the same time, the Elokoi have received a 'True-dream' from the teller Saebi, instructing their entire population to return to their ancestral lands on the shores of the inland sea. These two narrative strands combine in a sequence which proposes a utopian politics whose culminating achievement is the restitution of their land to the Elokoi, the overthrow of Gaston's corrupt government, the election of a new President and Council, and the establishment of the republic of Deucalion.

In his introduction to *Archaeologies of the Future*, Fredric Jameson notes that 'the fundamental dynamic of any Utopian politics (or of any political Utopianism) will ... always lie in the dialectic of Identity and Difference, in the degree to which such a politics aims at imagining, and sometimes even at realising, a system radically different from this one' (2005, p. xii). Jameson goes on to point out that 'it is not only the social and historical raw materials of the Utopian construct which are of interest ...; but also the representational relations established between them – such as closure, narrative, and exclusion or inversion' (2005, p. xiii). As we have frequently observed in this book, it is through discoursal features and narrative strategies that texts construct subject positions for young readers assumed to be the decision-makers and citizens of the future.

The 'dialectic of Identity and Difference' which plays out in the final chapters of *Deucalion* addresses Australian politics following the landmark Australian High Court Mabo decision of 1992, which rejected the concept of *terra nullius*, 'uninhabited land', which had hitherto been applied to the entire country. While this decision appeared to promise land rights to Indigenous Australians and compensation for the appropriation of their ancestral lands, by the time Caswell produced *Deucalion* in 1995 little advance had been made: land rights legislation proved slow and cumbersome; and mining and pastoral interests had slowed down the legal processes whereby Indigenous groups sought access to and restitution of land. In a scene where Elokoi representatives meet Gaston to inform him of their plans to undertake a Trek across the desert to the inland sea, the narrative draws on the Elokoi capacity for telepathy to undermine Gaston's appearance of sympathy: they sense the disjunction between his smiling demeanour and his inner attitude of contempt for them. When he falls back on political and bureaucratic discourses to intimidate them, readers are thus positioned to look to his motives of greed and self-interest and to read his behaviour metaphorically, as referring to the powerful interests that opposed Aboriginal land rights in the Australian setting.

The utopian project described in *Deucalion* relies on a collective of disparate but aligned groups: Elokoi, native-born Deucalions, Icarus children, and those 'Old Earthers' who reject the colonial imperatives of the Ruling Council. That the Deucalions themselves constitute a mix of cultural and ethnic backgrounds is signalled by the names of key players: Jane Sukoma-Williams, Ricky Nguyen, Denny Woods, Amanda Kostas, in a 'multicultural' alliance which echoes the diversity of the Australian population and implicitly advocates productive cross-cultural relations. In contrast to the technophobic tendencies of many dystopian texts for young people, *Deucalion* advocates the exploitation of technology in the service of the revolution, so that when Gaston is interviewed on a news programme and questioned concerning his attempted assassination of Elena, one of the Icarus children, his guilt is proven through the activities of a computer hacker, Peter Tang, who has retrieved all the incriminating computer files deleted by Gaston, and who displays them on prime-time television. This imagining of socio-political processes which redress the wrongs of colonialism thus advocates a new alliance of Indigenous and settler citizens capable of influencing the direction of the body politic.

The final chapter and epilogue of *Deucalion* leap forward some 60 years, to what is probably the most overtly depicted utopian world in Australian children's fiction. The revolution has brought into being a prosperity evocative of 'Earth in the golden age of the twentieth century' (p. 211); the trade economy, like that of More's Utopia, is grounded on the exchange of goods, not 'paper profits' (p. 211); the Elokoi homeland — like many postcolonial utopias situated, as Pordzik (2001, p. 20) puts it, 'in the vast and impenetrable interior of a defeated continent' — is a garden reclaimed from the desert. If there is irony in this depiction of utopia, it is that Australia has not achieved the utopian dream envisaged as a possibility in Caswell's portrayal of a transformed Deucalion.

The utopian spaces represented in these texts propose a variety of strategies and political positions. What Leela Gandhi describes as 'the silences and ellipses of historical amnesia' (1998, p. 7), the tendency for nations implicated in the imperial project to engage in a strategic forgetfulness concerning the brutality and violence of colonialism, is evident in *Exodus* and *Tearaway*. In contrast, most of the texts we have considered in this chapter advocate processes of remembering, through narratives envisioning new modes of collaboration and engagement that address the dysfunctional relations of colonialism. Apart from *Deucalion*, with its overt proposal for a reconfigured Australia, these novels accord with Pordzik's description of postcolonial utopias which 'leave it open to their readers to construe their own image of utopia which is not and cannot be a fixed and reliable end in itself any longer' (2001, p. 18). Thus, the utopian spaces of *The Sterkarm Handshake, Atlantis*, and *The Eye, the Ear and the Arm* suggest transformative directions without proposing specific social and political orders. To conclude on a cautionary note: the reinscription of racialised hierarchies in the closure of *The Crowlings* demonstrates the potency of colonial discourses naturalised in habits of thought and representation.

5
Reweaving Nature and Culture: Reading Ecocritically

> Ecocriticism is essentially about the demarcation between nature and culture, its construction and reconstruction.
>
> Garrard, *Ecocriticism*, 2004, p. 179

> It's human beings that are the problem. Everything that they do pollutes and destroys.... If we are really to protect the good earth we must first cleanse it of human beings.
>
> Reeve, *A Darkling Plain*, 2006, p. 504

One of the more extreme polarities of utopian and dystopian representation appears in the relationship between nature and culture in depictions and interpretations of 'natural' environments. This is not a concern which in itself emerges as a consequence of a post-Cold War 'new world order', but the range of discourses falling under the broad titles of *ecopoiesis* and *ecocriticism* emerged slowly and sporadically in the last quarter of the twentieth century from even broader discourses about 'the (natural world) environment' or simply 'nature writing'. There were, however, some significant confluences. As an analytical discourse, ecocriticism became identified as a distinctive — albeit loosely defined — field in the first half of the 1990s. The collapse of the East–West binary also coincided with a growing acceptance across the world that global warming was a fact, not a theory. Hence, the coincidence of an identifiable critical discourse emerging at the same time as major changes in global political structures resulted in a palpable shift of emphasis, and for almost a decade until the advent of the 'war on terror' environmental issues, especially global warming, were widely perceived as the greatest threat to the continued survival of human beings. Environmental issues — habitat protection (and celebration of wilderness), ecosystem conservation, pollution prevention, resource depletion, and advocacy of harmonic balance between human subjects and natural environments (as opposed to an anthropocentric hierarchy of humans and nature) — became major social concerns.

An obvious example of a shift in global priorities and alignments is the *Kyoto Protocol*, which became legally binding upon its signatories on 16 February 2005. The protocol aspires to a 5.2 per cent cut in emissions of carbon dioxide and other greenhouse gases from the industrialised world as a whole by 2012. Over 140 countries signed the accord, which finally became possible when Russia agreed to ratify it. However, at the time of writing in early 2007, the world's largest polluter, the United States, had refused to sign and hence, along with other mavericks such as Australia,[1] occupied the position of world environmental villain. Dissenting countries argue that the changes required are too expensive, while supporters maintain that implementing the Protocol would 'stimulate the hi-tech and construction industries, create jobs, reduce health-care costs from air pollution, and help protect our ecosystems' (David Suzuki Foundation).

Global challenge and local transformation

Children's texts will not typically incorporate the full range of benefits which might flow from positive environmental policies, but rather seek to convey them by metonymy and analogy, while dystopian narratives allude to them as absence or loss. Jeannie Baker's wordless picture book *Belonging* (2004), for example, begins with a desolate urban landscape that juxtaposes images of a newborn baby with wrecked cars and wrecked lives (alcoholism, drug abuse, human isolation), and thereby implies that human beings may only survive in harmony with natural landscapes (see Stephens, 2006b). Furthermore, as this parable of urban greening transforms the landscape from dystopia to utopia, the plants that are represented — and consequently the fauna that comes with them — are all indigenous Australian flora, as if true harmony of subject and world depends on this level of authenticity. The home garden from which transformation emanates also evolves from bare and broken concrete through a lawn stage to low-growing plants not requiring to be mowed: that is, it becomes a vibrant, ecologically self-sustaining structure.

Connecting more overtly to politics and economics, Michael Morpurgo and Christina Balit's fantasy picture book *Blodin the Beast* (1995) opens with a dystopian scene that juxtaposes oil wells with a long column of displaced and enslaved people. Glimpses of Islamic architecture (domes, cupolas, repetitive geometric shapes) and women wearing head-scarves, in conjunction with a monstrous beast which is a murderous tyrant, suggest that the book might be read as a post-Gulf War (1990–1991) narrative, an analogy with the tyrannical rule and defeat of Saddam Hussein, and hence implicitly imbricated with President Bush's announcement of a new world order in his famous speech to Congress of 6 March 1991.[2] Habitat destruction and pollution are explicitly linked in this picture book with a destructive human activity depicted as having a reach far beyond local setting (the main character, Hosea, whose name is Hebrew, travels through a central African forest in his flight from Blodin). The narrative concludes with the destruction of Blodin and Hosea's entry into an ecological utopia, or *ecotopia*:[3]

> he could see flowery meadows and golden corn swaying under a golden sun. There were men and women working together in the fields, and laughing children ran towards him. They took him by the hand and led him up into a land of plenty and peace.
>
> (1995, n.p.)

This ecotopia, however, does not merely depict people living in a harmonious state with each other and with nature but is already a clichéd pastoral idyll, both in components described and the language of description. The overworded sequence 'flowery meadows...golden corn...golden sun' together with the conjunction of 'men and women working together' with 'laughing children' is both nostalgic for an Edenic world and an erasure of the realities of labour. The final sentence evokes an inclusive society, but the extraordinary resort to a favourite cliché of religious and nationalistic discourses as a conclusion to the text – 'a land of plenty and peace' – foregrounds a dual difficulty for ecopoiesis in children's texts: first, the challenge to imagine and represent utopian ecologies at all, and second, the challenge to communicate the complex social, political, and economic factors that impact upon human relationships with natural environments.

Ecopoeisis in children's literature

Early developments in ecocriticism, especially derived from deep ecology or ecofeminism, perceived an endemic disjuncture between human subjects and natural environments because humanity's anthropocentric assumptions privileged culture over nature. Such ecocritics consequently aspired to develop a criticism that would overturn this hierarchy.

However, the ecopoietic children's literature of the past 15 years has not sought to address anthropocentrism, apart from a few exceptions: Isabel Allende's mystical, magical realist *City of the Beasts* (2002); Justin D'Ath's fantasy about nature-culture reweaving, *Shædow Master* (2003); and the satirical representations of androcentrism in Anthony Browne's picture book, *Zoo* (1992), and of what Deane Curtin defines as 'the lunatic-fringe misanthropy that hovers at the edges, and threatens to discredit, some of the more radical schools of ecological thought' (Curtin, 1999, pp. 19–20) in Philip Reeve's *Hungry Cities* tetralogy, especially in the final volume, *A Darkling Plain* (2006).[4]

In *Zoo*, representation of the caged animals develops a metonymic function informed by psychological, political, and philosophical concerns. Through a brilliant rendering of the haecceitas of the non-human, the illustrations place viewers in an affective and empathetic position, and then viewer subject position is further shaped both through an empathetic reciprocal gaze with the mother of the depicted family and through a withdrawal of any empathy from its males.

The challenge to androcentrism is twofold. First, the principal human male characters are depicted in a pictorial modality lower than the modality of the mother, and much lower than the animals: in as much as the males are thereby coded as 'less real', they are seen as alienated from the natural world. Second, the males are entirely incapable of ascribing a point of view either to the animals, which indeed hold little interest for them, or to the wife/mother of the family. The failure to transcend solipsism is all the more evident because the story is narrated by the older of the two boys. The mother, in contrast, is attributed with moral authority because she is consistently depicted in a higher modality than her family and can empathise with the captive animals — *Zoo* indeed reproduces a grounding perspective of ecofeminism, namely that the domination of women and the domination of nature are fundamentally connected. In augmenting the illustrations with temporality and narrative point of view, the text of *Zoo* also contributes powerfully to the book's effects:

> Then we saw the tigers. One of them was just walking along the wall of the cage, then turning round and walking all the way back. Then it would start again.
> 'Poor thing,' said Mum.
> 'You wouldn't say that if it was chasing you,' snorted Dad. 'Look at those nasty teeth!'
>
> (*Zoo*, n.p.)

The narrator is precisely describing an example of stereotypy which frequently afflicts animals in captivity: stereotypic behaviour is repetitive and invariant, spatially restricted, and apparently functionless. In carnivores and large mammals this commonly takes the form of stereotyped pacing (in *Zoo* stereotyped pacing is also attributed to the rhinoceros and polar bear). It is a 'behavioural disorder', developed in stress situations or in cages without external stimuli. It is believed to be used as a coping strategy for a 'suboptimal' environment (see Jenny and Schmid, p. 574).

There is a complex irony at work in this scene. Most obviously, the child, unlike his mother, fails to recognise what he describes, whereas her simple comment, 'Poor thing', foregrounds that the tiger's behaviour has degenerated from 'natural' to 'unnatural'. In describing the tiger as 'just walking', the child registers not only his boredom but his inability to see the tiger in and for itself. Of course, as the accompanying illustration shows, a tiger decontextualised in a bare enclosure, between a steel mesh fence and a flat grey wall behind, has been reduced to a simulacrum of a tiger. The father's invocation of 'nasty teeth' and the man-eaters of hunting stories is no better. The zoo itself functions as a metonymy for the alienation of humans from nature, but for the male members of this family that alienation lies even deeper. *Zoo*, finally, is an attack on the subordination of nature to culture which underpins the kind of zoo depicted (if not all zoos) and the kind of family depicted. It is also an attack on the androcentrism which would validate that subordination. Readers may like to compare *Zoo* with Browne's earlier *Piggybook* (1986), in which Mrs Piggott's behaviour is similarly stereotypic before she rebels.

Ecocriticisms and ecofeminism

The principles underpinning ecofeminism underwent modification in the decade after the publication of *Zoo* to place more emphasis on intersubjective relations with others. This should give ecofeminist criticism a wider purchase in children's literature, enabling it to work with other ecocriticisms to engage constructively with texts that are principally anthropocentric. Jonathan Levin's broadly inclusive definition of ecocriticism as 'an interdisciplinary approach to the study of nature, environment, and culture' (2002, p. 171) is thus a useful starting point, encapsulating the invariably cited definitions from Cheryll Glotfelty's 'Introduction' to *The Ecocriticism Reader* (1996). Glotfelty there defined ecocriticism as a critical method and an ethical discourse that 'takes as its subject the interconnections between nature and culture, specifically the cultural artefacts of language and literature' (Glotfelty, p. xix); a 'study of the relationship between literature and the physical environment,' it 'negotiates between the human and the nonhuman' (Glotfelty, pp. xviii–xix).

The tendency in deep ecology to see anthropocentrism as the primary cause of dystopian conditions was quietly sidelined by Glotfelty's essay, although the collection did include Glen Love's 1990 attack on anthropocentrism, 'Revaluing Nature: Toward an Ecological Criticism'. By the end of the decade, there was a sense that after a brief initial period of ecocritical consensus the field had already moved on and diversified (as early as 1999, Dana Philips had remarked that the Glotfelty and Fromm collection contained 'a representative sample of early work' (1999, n. 4)). While the desire to critique anthropocentrism has not disappeared, more recent thinking takes a wider view of the relations between environmental practice and humankind. The predominant concerns of cultural studies — race, class, and gender — are taken up by social ecologists in imagining communities grounded in participatory democracy and sustainable life modes. They are also central to the concerns of ecofeminism, although in recent years ideas about embodiment and the materiality of social life have moved beyond this social constructionist formula. In addition, ideas about natural environments are informed by elements associated with postmodernism, such as globalisation, technologies of the posthuman, and new communications media, which we have considered in other contexts elsewhere in this book.

A focus on issues of race, class, and gender and their intrication with embodiment and materiality brings us to a different possibility. While our primary source examples here, as in other chapters in the book, are drawn from works in which the thematic concerns of the chapter are conscious or foregrounded, ecocritical approaches also enable readings against the grain of foregrounded interests, a mode of reading which Robert Kern describes as 'designed to expose and facilitate analysis of a text's orientation both to the world it imagines and to the world in which it takes shape, along with the conditions and contexts that affect that orientation' (2003, p. 260).

Ecofeminism, in particular, is apt to perceive the world as always already a dystopia. Arising from the fusion of feminist and ecological thinking in the early 1970s, it proposed that the social assumptions that underpin the domination and oppression of women are the same assumptions that bring about the abuse of the environment.

It aims, therefore, to find ways of understanding both humans and the natural environment that are not male-biased. It draws from feminism the understanding that Western patriarchal thinking is based on binarisms, that is, opposed pairs of concepts organised hierarchically: mind over body, spirit over matter, male over female, culture over nature, reason over emotion. The *eco* element of ecofeminism demands an interrogation of the nature/culture binary as a step towards dismantling the other binarisms and for creating an environmentally aware society in which often discounted values (friendship, nurturance, love, trust) shape human subjectivity. Contemporary ecofeminism has evolved beyond an essentialist notion of oppression to a position which valorises intersubjective relations with others — human others, other creatures, natural environments — as the ground for possible, not yet existing, new world orders.

Ecofeminism is, however, a third-wave feminism (see Mack-Canty, 2004), whereas the feminist criticism in children's literature is predominantly second-wave and has thus made little reference to ecofeminism. Likewise, the primary texts thematising environmental issues do not reflect ecofeminist thought. In their introduction to *Wild Things: Children's Culture and Ecocriticism*, Dobrin and Kidd affirm that, 'it is critical to recognise that any ecocritical look at children's literature must include ecofeminist perspectives' (2004, p. 10), but only one of the 16 essays in the collection does this — Marion W. Copeland's attempt to retrospectively reclaim Beatrix Potter and Gene Stratton-Porter as ecofeminists. A wide integration of ecofeminism is yet to come, although we envisage that it will eventually play an oppositional, interrogative role in the field, with a potential to reshape the nature and direction of environmental advocacy in children's texts and to disclose the operation of the culture/nature duality in a text's orientation towards the material environment.

Ecofeminist criticism as an interrogative mode

The interrogative potential of ecofeminist criticism can be demonstrated by applying it to Charles Butler's dystopian fantasy *Calypso Dreaming* (2002). Set on Sweetholm, an imaginary island in England's Bristol Channel, this novel draws heavily on place and landscape without foregrounding them as environmental issues, while its male-biased assumptions in the use of its setting and its evocation of a female power that increases in destructive force as it becomes embodied look back to British fantasy of the 1960s and 1970s, before the emergence of discourses such as ecofeminism.

Working from the familiar assumption that physical places are sources of metaphors for social constructions of reality (see Sheldrake, 2001, p. 45), *Calypso Dreaming* posits the island as 'a place where the world's fabric has rubbed... thin' (p. 48) and hence a portal through which demons may enter the world — in other words, the social construction attains actual embodiment. The paradox that evil is both a social construction and an immanent force that awaits a human agent to give it form and embodiment underpins Alan Garner's *The Owl Service* (1967), Susan Cooper's *Dark is Rising* series (1965–1977), and Penclope Lively's *The Whispering Knights* (1971), among others.

Both Sweetholm itself and the evil power that is its embodiment are female. This is initially suggested obliquely in an early description of the island's littoral:

> The Haven was the island's one harbour. Elsewhere, the land plummeted in stark cliffs or was skirted with lavish margins of mud. The undredged quicksands were an asylum for wading birds. The sand and mud squirmed with life, but had also sucked down sheep, dogs, even (the guidebook said) occasional unwary humans. A party of Edwardian nuns had made their last pilgrimage to the site of St Brigan's ancient chapel and been swallowed, a hundred years before.
>
> (p. 13)

Rod Giblett (1996) has observed that, 'Wetlands have almost invariably been represented in the patriarchal western tradition in metaphors of despair and despondency in an overworking... of the lower echelons of the pathetic fallacy in which the psychological is projected on to the geographical' (p. 8). A very obvious example appears in Anne Isaacs and Paul Zelinsky's tall tale, *Swamp Angel* (1994), where negative constructions of wetlands are accepted as a given: 'When she was twelve, a wagon train got mired in Dejection Swamp. The settlers had abandoned their covered wagons and nearly all hope besides' (n.p.). The passage from *Calypso Dreaming* contains, and is feminised by, a significant prolepsis, marked only by the space allocated to it: the sea cave that lies beneath the site of the chapel was itself a shrine dedicated to the more ancient Celtic goddess Brigan (the place is a savage version of the holy wells still maintained in St Brigid's honour in parts of Ireland). One of the local inhabitants, Davey Jones, has found the shrine, carved and adorned an effigy of Brigan within it, and dedicated it with a human sacrifice. In this way he has embodied evil in a female form.

This initial mention of Brigan links her with the wetland and death, not with the positive qualities of creativity and healing usually associated with Brigan/Brigid (both as goddess and later saint). Rather than existing as an unmarked natural environment, the wetland is an uncivilised and hostile space, as denoted by the extended lexical sequence, 'skirted with lavish margins...undredged quicksands...asylum for wading birds...squirmed with life...sucked down...swallowed'. The assumption of culture's superiority over nature is especially evident in the negative formulation 'undredged', which implies that in a proper order of things the wetlands would be drained. The horror associated with 'quicksand' — that is, nature in its destructive aspect — is underlined by the contrast between the site as an 'asylum' for birds but a threat to humans, and by the implicit horror of female bodily excess ('skirted with lavish margins'). As ecofeminist criticism would argue, the privileging of nature over culture instantiates associated hierarchical dualities: mind over body, spirit over matter, male over female, reason over emotion. This hierarchy is reinforced by the conventional association of wetlands with despair, horror and gloom.

Ecofeminism argues that male conceptions of freedom and happiness depend on 'an ongoing process of emancipation from nature, both human embodiment and the natural environment' (Mack-Canty, p. 156), whereas future human well-being will need to reweave the culture/nature duality by incorporating embodiment and nonhuman nature. Embodiment is a charged term here: on the principle that existence is physically enframed, the concept is concerned with how 'subjectivity and identity emerge not from disembodied consciousness, but from the experience of acting through — and on — the physical, visceral and mortal vehicle of the body' (Bakker and Bridge, 2006, p. 15). Attention over the past decade to the materiality of social life has taken criticism beyond earlier social constructionist notions of 'situated knowledges' to an understanding of how bodies may function in the construction of socialities — places, spaces, and processes of all kinds, whether cultural, political, or economic — in conjunction with the natural world.

These issues seem remarkably pertinent to *Calypso Dreaming*, which involves a configuration of male and female characters premised on a different understanding of embodiment. The novel is set in a not too distant future, where the familiar world continues but has also developed substantial dystopian elements caused by 'the floods, the poison algae, the triple plagues' (p. 39). Other familiar post-disaster tropes constitute frames within which characters are situated: 'All over the world sleeping powers begin to stir: old beliefs find willing minds to lodge in. Dabblers in magic are shocked to find their spells taking hold with a new and horrifying potency. Unheard-of diseases spring up, insidious and always deforming. As if in recompense, certain people discover gifts of healing in themselves' (p. 22). The novel contains ordinary people: Tansy, a teenage girl oppressed by guilt because she had dabbled in magic and thought she had harmed people with it; her parents, Geoff and Hilary, on the brink of divorce because of Geoff's involvement with another woman; Harper, a boy about Tansy's age, who lives with his mother in a commune on the island; and some minor characters. The extraordinary people are Dominic, a healer, and his sister Sophie's 4-year-old daughter, Calypso. Because Calypso's father was a selkie her appearance is not entirely human, and she has enormous, uncontrolled magical powers. Her wild magic is highly dangerous, both because it transforms her feelings into acts of carnage and because it makes her a potential conduit for Brigan's embodiment in flesh. Dominic's power to heal, on the other hand, cannot match the female power of Brigan when flowing through Calypso: he tries to kill his niece, but she transforms him into a heron and he is attacked and killed by gulls.

These components of the novel's convoluted plot grow out of the culture/nature dichotomy we discussed above. In an explicatory conversation with Harper, Dominic explains why the world is sinking into deeper crisis:

> 'Beneath each rational mind lies another: deeper, darker, older. That is where the nightmare demons live. Our precious reason is just a side-effect — and so easily overthrown!' ... 'What only the theologians know is that the World too has a mind. Its conscious thoughts are time, space, gravity — the laws of physics. They seem to be everywhere we look, regular and predictable. But the dreams of the World Soul too are demon-haunted. And, as with human minds, the demons may escape into waking life.'
>
> (pp. 98–9)

A tendency to hybridise genres seems evident here, in that Dominic's distinctly archaic worldview owes as much to gothic horror narratives as to British fantasy of the 1960s. However, this is not merely the perspective of a character who, slated for death, should not attract reader empathy. Dominic's earlier attempts to articulate a similar view were peremptorily dismissed by other characters, but subsequent events in the novel confirm the rightness of his understanding. Only the intervention of Calypso's selkie father, who destroys the idol of Brigan, prevents the goddess from becoming the island and devouring its inhabitants. The close of the novel slips several years into the future when Harper, now an adult, uses web news to try to keep track of Calypso. He thinks he recognises her presence in an incident which mirrors the events on Sweetholm and culminates in the destruction by means of a severe weather event of a small West Indian island community — but this time 'there were no survivors left to speak of it' (p. 191).

Fantasy fiction can, of course, draw on conventional motifs, but an ecofeminist criticism must also take an interest in fiction which identifies woman with nature (as early ecofeminist discourses themselves did) but then asserts that the loss of masculine rationality entails the irruption of a 'deeper, darker, older' mentality 'where the nightmare demons live' and in turn identifies this mentality as female. Calypso wants to resist Brigan, but each is an emanation of nature's irrationality. The identities that emerge 'from the experience of acting through — and on — the physical, visceral and mortal vehicle of the body' are thus not conducive to a reweaving of the culture/nature duality because it hinges on a false embodiment and a subjugation of nature.

Positive and informed interventions

An environmental scientist might object that the future dystopia will arrive not because of floods, poison algae, and plagues brought about because demons have invaded the dreams of the 'World Soul' envisaged by Plato, but by climate change caused by intolerable global warming, the burning of fossil fuels, and destruction of wild habitats, and consequently by severe weather events and rising sea-levels. This is precisely the scenario imagined in, for example, Julie Bertagna's *Exodus* (2002). In his most recent book, *The Revenge of Gaia* (2006), James Lovelock — the original proponent of the Gaia hypothesis[5] — has argued that, unless humans greatly alter their lifestyles, within only a few decades the Earth will be largely uninhabitable:

> The prospects are grim, and even if we act successfully in amelioration, there will still be hard times, as in any war, that will stretch us to the limit. We are tough and it would take more than the predicted climate catastrophe to eliminate all breeding pairs of humans; what is at risk is civilization. As individual animals we

are not so special, and in some ways the human species is like a planetary disease, but through civilization we redeem ourselves and have become a precious asset for the Earth.

(p. 10)

As the assumption that human beings are basically just another animal underlines, Lovelock's depiction of civilisation as a kind of ecosystem here doesn't entirely revert to an anthropocentric mode of thinking, although the conditions for a possible survival of humanity are the focus of his book, which proposes a large, and often controversial, raft of necessary actions. Lovelock is often scathing about 'green' lobbies and some of the changes they have brought about, and deeply sceptical of many 'green' solutions for the future. Herein lies a dilemma for children's literature, which has an abundance of texts advocating positive action to manage an endangered environment, but is seldom in a position to convey deeply informed information. The primary purpose of environmental texts is to shape attitudes by contrasting utopian and dystopian possibilities. Books for younger audiences are apt to focus on a single issue, presumably on the premise that a bundle of such books will encompass a range of issues, and hence a larger picture of habitat destruction, say, will consequently emerge.

Ecowarriors in liminal spaces

As we have pointed out in earlier chapters, the devastations caused by pollution and habitat destruction have become a primary catalyst for new world (dis-)order in the post-disaster narratives which have taken the place of the nuclear holocausts of Cold War-era fiction, and in such narratives ecopoiesis is grounded in dystopian settings and themes. At the same time, there has also emerged a mode of realist fiction, such as Tim Winton's *Lockie Leonard, Scumbuster* (1993, Australia) or Carl Hiaasen's *Flush* (2005, USA), in which young eco-warriors battle evil polluters. After US President George W Bush abandoned any participation in the Kyoto Protocol as soon as he took office in 2001, any representations of US environmental pollution, such as *Flush*, will be read under the shadow of rogue market capitalism's assertion that clean industry is too expensive.

Realist fictions such as *Lockie Leonard, Scumbuster* and *Flush* are versions of distinctly anthropocentric environmental literature. Problems are caused by human greed and disregard for the natural world, and are solved by human intervention. In contrast, ecocriticism at its inception had often looked to the deep ecology precepts of Arne Naess (see, e.g. Garrard, pp. 21–2), especially his distinction between nature-centred ('deep') ecology, which aspires to alter the norms of modernity's anthropocentrism, and human-centred ('shallow') environmentalism, which aims to change socioeconomic practices without changing the anthropocentric premises of modernity (see, e.g. Zimmerman, 1994, p. 20). *Lockie Leonard, Scumbuster* and *Flush* would thus be character-ised as 'shallow environmentalism'. In that they represent a norm-ative position for children's literature and related discourses, they have significant implications for any would-be ecocritic of children's literature. In children's studies both the literature and the critical discourse will remain 'environmentally informed' rather than 'ecocrit-ical' if ecocriticism is assumed to preclude all forms of anthropocentrism. Children's texts remain constrained by the intrinsic commitment to maturation narratives — narrative structures posited on stories of indi-vidual development of subjective agency, or of bildungsroman. This tends to ensure that any environmental literature remains anthropo-centric in emphasis, rather than engaging with the biocentrism of 'deep ecology'.

By focusing on liminal spaces, such as forests or the littorals of *Lockie Leonard, Scumbuster* and *Flush*, texts implicitly or overtly evoke a version of being-in-the-world which corresponds to Victor Turner's well-known rite of passage narrative structure: separation, liminality, reintegration into society. The ecological crisis of both novels centres on industrial pollution of waterways. Although such dumping of effluent has been a practice of industry since the Industrial Revolution, littoral spaces, where land and water meet on an ever-shifting boundary, are symbolic and figure forms of liminality, including intricate relationships between ecological well-being and human subjectivity. Representations of subjectivity in children's literature 'are intrinsic to narratives of personal growth or maturation, to stories about relationships between the self and others, and to explorations of relationships between indi-viduals and the world, society or the past' (McCallum, 1999, p. 3), and hence the rite of passage frame is an apt underpinning for eco-warrior narratives.

The moral and political orientation of personal development becomes intensified when linked to actions informed by ecocritical perceptions, that is, by perceptions that nature, the environment, earth itself, are endangered and in need of appropriate management. Thus the life of 13-year-old Lockie Leonard revolves around his family, surfing, friends, and girlfriends. While kayaking with a new friend, a recent arrival in town, Lockie discovers the point at which effluent enters the town's harbour, 'a huge pipe that spewed into the waterway':

> On the algae-choked bank lay dead crabs and fish all snagged in the weed so thick you could almost walk on it
> 'Whew,' said Egg, 'what a nostril thrasher. This is sputagenous olfactorizing.'
> 'Eh?'
> 'It stinks to the max. On a scale of one-to-ten it's a — '
> 'Fifteen,' said Lockie. 'Who would do this? This is terrible.'
> 'Anyone who could get away with it.'
> They looked at the steaming gunk that fell from the pipe and behind them the whole of Angelus Harbour lay rancid and still, choking on algae and poison.
>
> (Winton, 1993, pp. 34–5)

As it reveals the enormity of what the two boys have found the passage skilfully positions readers: an appropriate revulsion from effect and hence cause is educed by the slipping between narrator perception (first and last clauses) and character focalisation ('you could almost walk on it'; 'They looked at the steaming gunk'), and the corresponding narrator and character registers, and by the incorporation of the boys' dialogue as they respond to what they see and smell. The tight cohesion of the dialogue also points to the close affinity developing through the boys' interrelationships. The counterpointing of environmental and personal narratives is accentuated when their success as eco-guerrillas in exposing the town's most powerful politician as the polluter is dampened by the unrelated decision of Egg's parents to move away again. In a parallel action, Lockie's developing friendship with an attractive new girlfriend is suddenly ended, but his former (and first) girlfriend steps up to help in the operation that exposes the waste dumpers. Through this multi-stranding the personal, the political, and the environmental are closely interwoven.

Despite the realist mode of these texts, the ecowarrior may actually be a fantasy hero. As indicated by Neal Stephenson's adult novel, *Zodiac* (1988), the ur-text for representing eco-guerrilla action in a littoral space, the genre is classified as speculative fiction. The new world order it imagines — a world where corporations and their supporters in governments can be called to account for their pollution of environments and destruction of natural habitats — still predominantly lies somewhere in the future.

Books for younger readers: making a difference

The realist fictions we have just discussed are symptomatic of ecological literature for children in their concentration of attention on a local area and their emphasis on the responsibility and agency of individuals. In literature for younger readers, two principal textual focuses are narratives about large-scale destruction of pristine wilderness, such as destruction of areas of the Amazon forest, and ecological relationships in small-scale communities — a beach or rock pool in natural environments, or home, street, or suburb in urban environments (see Stephens, 2006b). If Lovelock, for example, is correct in his predictions, then such books cannot make any timely difference, other than influencing ideas and expectations about quality of life and offering a sense of individual agency in making a contribution to that quality of life. They might thus have more to do with conserving civilisation, in small ways, than conserving natural environments.

A clear example of an attempt to imagine the birth of a civilisation from a fusion of nature and culture in a small-scale community can be seen in the emerging ecotopia in Monica Hughes's *The Other Place* (1999). Exiled from a dystopian Earth, where a new world order has been instantiated as a World Government, and where dissent is equated with subversion and its proponents simply 'disappear', a group of dissenters' children become colonists of another planet. Their presence there is a social experiment, designed by another dissenter, with the purpose of establishing a utopian society 'based on cooperation and consensus' (p. 160). With no prior experience of uncultivated wilderness, and with minimal adult guidance, the group's survival will depend on weaving nature and culture into a seamless unity. By the novel's close, the oldest children — Alison (the novel's narrator) and Kristin — have envisaged what appears to be the groundwork for a kind of ecofeminist civilisation, especially once the 'Big Brother' surveillance of the colony's founder has been permanently withdrawn. Thus, articulating principles such as 'make sure that anything new [is] also good, both for the community and the planet itself', 'discoveries and ideas [must] not come only from us, but from everybody' and 'No ruined environment' (p. 150), the girls begin envisaging the accoutrements of culture: almanacs, writing materials, star charts for navigation, stories, poems and story telling, practical architecture, and eventually philosophy. Knowing nothing about the planet, Alison embraces the prospect that 'every day we might search for meaning and order in the mysteries around us' (p. 148). Hence because the world is beginning anew, the children can begin with ecofeminist principles, creating an environmentally aware society in which human subjectivity is shaped by mutuality, trust and nurturance.

The Other Place can model an ecotopia because it is an 'other place', nowhere, the utopia implied by the title. We will have more to say about this when we come back to this novel in our next chapter. Everyday humans don't have the opportunity to return to a beginning, but need to apply such a model in a more constrained context. A place evoked in literary text and/or pictures has an implied observer and usually a narrative component which tracks the movement from utopian to dystopian state, or vice-versa. What is presented to the observer is not unmediated nature, but an interpretation of nature, through language, in terms of socially and culturally grounded categories.

One of the favourite metonymies for threatened pristine nature is 'rainforest', which, as Candace Slater has shown, is a modern cultural category that emerged in popular usage as a term with marked positive connotations at the same time as environmentalism emerged as a political and social movement, and in the last two decades of the twentieth century 'acquired…ever stronger Edenic overtones' (1996, p. 125). Adjectival uses of the compound form *rainforest* or *rain forest* are apt to carry even stronger positive/emotive connotations. In such usages, the binary opposite of the highly charged term *rain forest* is *environmental dystopia*.

Lynne Cherry's picture book about the destruction of Amazon habitat, *The Great Kapok Tree* (1990), makes extensive use of *rain forest* in precisely this way. The book tells how a logger, employed to cut down the kapok tree, falls asleep and while sleeping is educated and appealed to by various inhabitants of the forest, and leaves without cutting down the tree. The implication, of course, is that a single individual can make a difference. The opening words of the text — 'Two men walked into the rain forest' — establishes setting by invoking the special term. That it is more than simple scene setting becomes clear when compared with the book's closing words — 'Then he dropped the ax and walked out of the rain forest' — in which 'rain' is denotatively redundant, but connotatively indicates that Eden/eutopia still survives. After the first opening, 'rain forest' occurs again in the fourth, sixth, seventh, tenth, eleventh, twelfth and fourteenth (final) openings, and this high frequency ensures that the heightened signification is further suggested in the text's four occurrences of simple, unmarked 'forest'.

'Rain forest' is positively collocated with the interdependence of living things in an ecosystem, and its destruction collocates with the replacement of 'life and beauty' by 'smouldering ruins' and desertification, disappearance of species, loss of beauty from the world, and displacement of nature-associated peoples — here specifically 'a child from the Yanomamo tribe'. In redescribing this child as 'the rain forest child', the text elides any need to gloss 'Yanomamo', even though this is potentially controversial: at the end of the 1980s, the Yanomami peoples were popularly perceived as the world's most 'primitive' people and attributed with living in harmony with the natural environment to a degree unmatched elsewhere. On the other hand, Brazilian anthropologist Alcida R. Ramos has dismissed such representation as '[a] rhetoric of conservation that clings to the romantic idea that a good Indian is a naked, isolated Indian' (1987, p. 301).[6]

Any temptation for ecofeminism to present nature-associated peoples as superior examples of organic embeddedness, and hence less subject to the nature-culture dualism, must be treated with caution and not simply taken as a given, as in *The Great Kapok Tree*. Future children's books might therefore be expected to be wary about enlisting 'nature-associated people' in such a naïve way: in this example, a glitch in syntactic sequencing even effectively includes 'the rain forest child' amongst the 'wondrous and rare animals' that surround the woodcutter.

The rhetorical strategy of *The Great Kapok Tree* is for each opening to contrast an Edenic present with a dystopian possibility. Each illustration depicts the creature which speaks, set in a close-up, lush setting of abundant flora and related fauna. Each opening offers a micro-scale story: monkeys, for example, argue that, 'You chop down one tree, then come back for another and another. The roots of these great trees will wither and die, and there will be nothing left to hold the earth in place. When the heavy rains come, the soil will be washed away and the forest will become a desert.' Such direct processes of cause and effect convey a persuasive message about a massive ecological issue. But what is the projected role of the audience? The peritextual material frames the rather mystical text as an information book: a map shows the world's rain forests; a preface defines 'canopy' and 'understory', and the type of creatures that inhabit them; and a 'hand-written' letter from author to readers as part of the back matter explains the author's intention in writing the book and urges readers, 'I hope that after reading this book you will help save the rain forests.' But how is this almost absurdly utopian demand on children to be realised? How much weight can be carried by a story of an individual who drops his axe and walks out of the forest?

Small-scale community narratives and practical action

The positioning of children as audience for an appeal to 'help save the rain forests' is rather meaningless in itself, apart from whatever consciousness-raising effect it might have. As Glen A. Love has suggested, literature is an activity 'which adapts us better to the world' and may possibly play a role in 'the welfare and survival of mankind' through '[the] insight it offers into human relationships with other species and with the world around us' (1996, p. 228). Small-scale community narratives demonstrate this more materially, as they can both raise consciousness and offer avenues for practical action available to children as well as adults. In other words, the positive and negative impacts on environment caused by ways of inhabiting it can be very transparent in small-scale ecologies, and hence people can be motivated to reweave culture and nature by means of sound ecological decisions. Such actions won't save the planet, but are a local example of how civilisation can be upheld.

Good examples of small-scale community narratives such as Baker's *Belonging* offer attainable visions. The utopian model of environmental concern depicted in *Belonging* envisages an ordinary urban life in which human subjectivity becomes shaped and enriched by the development of a local ecosystem that produces a harmonic balance between human subjects and natural environment. Symbiosis between a healthy environment and individual subjective agency is modelled through the principal character's growth from a baby to a young adult as shaped by her developing ecological awareness and steadily increasing capacity to change her local environment from dystopia to utopia. The good practices she evolves are also learnt by childhood friends and her future partner. Human subjectivity is central to this process, but constructed as an intersubjectivity with an environment that includes flora and fauna as well as other humans. In other words, to borrow a formulation from N. Katherine Hayles, 'civilization and wilderness coproduce each other' (1999b, p. 676).

The process depicted in *Belonging* and its outcome accord with contemporary ecofeminist aspirations. In depicting the greening of an inner city environment as a cooperative act that unites generations, peers, and individuals with diverse interests, *Belonging* demonstrates how human activities and communities inform a bioregional sensibility, and how emotional bonds — parent and child, friend and friend, lover and lover — grow in conjunction with the development of a feeling for place (cf. Armbruster, 2000). The burgeoning of insect and bird life in

Tracy's garden also implies that emotional bonds with animals are part of this feeling. The book further shows that material bodies are implicated not only in the construction of social places and spaces but also in political processes, illustrated here by an implied agreement between the immediate community and local government to restrict the street to pedestrian traffic and extend the green space into the public area.

The attempt to extend the wordless picture book to embrace political concerns also reveals a limitation in such a text, however: the large political issue of reconciliation between indigenous Australians and the white community becomes decontextualised and co-opted into the book's vision of greening the inner city in a banal and simplistic way. Token black figures are incorporated into the utopian space, and the word 'Sorry' appears written in the sky, evoking Australia's National Sorry Days (1998–2004) held to acknowledge and apologise for the history of forcible removal of Aboriginal and Torres Strait Islander children from their families. Potentially the most problematic appropriation, however, is a piece of graffiti on a wall opposite Tracy's window, which reads, 'From little things big things grow'. The utterance is the title and refrain of a 1992 song written by Paul Kelly and Kev Carmody commemorating the seven year struggle (1966–1973) of the Gurindji people for land rights, which constituted both the nascence of the reconciliation movement and a turning point for Australian society. In *Belonging* the words are the culmination of a vector running from Tracy through a neighbour: because the two figures are isomorphic, each squatting while transferring a plant from a pot to the ground, the metaphorical import of the words is shifted, so that the literal sense of the vehicle of the metaphor ('a tree grows from a seed') is foregrounded, and the tenor is thereby given a specific environmental import ('local environmental action changes the world'). An astute adult may attempt to tease out the reference to the Gurindji, and explore how environmental politics embraces areas such as indigenous land rights, but it seems more probable that, like any piece of random graffiti, the allusion has been rendered peripheral.

Beyond anthropocentrism

As we remarked earlier, there is a small group of texts which have directly addressed the question of anthropocentrism. These employ either fantastic dystopias as setting for environmental concerns (*Shædow Master; A Darkling Plain*), or fuse fantasy with magical realism, as in Isabel Allende's *City of the Beasts*. Each of these books deals in some way with the key environmental concerns of children's texts, especially habitat protection and the consequences of its destruction, ecosystem conservation, and the quest to reweave nature and culture through a harmonic balance between human subjects and natural environments. Each concludes by evoking a new world order which has arisen as a consequence of events portrayed in the narrative.

City of the Beasts achieves a deep ecology perspective, even though it charts the development of subjective agency of its 15-year-old male principal character, from whose point of view the story is principally narrated, and concludes with a large environmental vision of establishing a foundation to guarantee the integrity of an Amazon region unspoiled by 'civilisation'. The novel's thematisation of aspects of language, for example, explores how change in relationships with the natural world can be negotiated; and its depiction of an indigenous Amazonian people living as an integral part of an ecosystem dismantles the anthropocentric orientation to the natural world and offers a glimpse of alternative modes of thinking and feeling.

At the heart of *City of the Beasts* is the city of the title, the fabled realm of *El Dorado*. However, Allende doesn't depict this as the El Dorado of legend, the quintessence of culture, fabulously wealthy in gold and precious stones, but as 'a group of natural geometric formations' (p. 262), whose golden colour came from mica and pyrite ('fool's gold'). It is the dwelling of the 'beasts', huge sloth-like creatures with intelligence and speech, survivors from some other era, who live in a symbiotic relationship with the local Indians, the 'People of the Mist'. These Indians, who have lived in the forest for 20,000 years, are a version of the Yanomami, once again represented as a nature-associated people characterised by their utopian organic embeddedness — 'They had lived in harmony with nature for thousands of years, like Adam and Eve in Paradise' (p. 398) — although the novel also satirises, in the character of an arrogant and inept anthropologist, Ludovic Leblanc, Napoleon Chagnon's widely disseminated description of the Yanomami as the world's most violent people:[7] 'these natives are the proof that man is no more than a murderous ape' (p. 56).

The central plot of *City of the Beasts* — a scheme to infect the tribe with measles under the pretence of vaccinating them, with the purpose of gaining control of their land's mineral wealth — seems loosely based on an incident which also forms a central plank in Patrick Tierney's *Darkness in El Dorado* (2000). Tierney accuses prominent anthropologists of mistreating and misrepresenting the Yanomami, and maintains that a measles vaccination program initiated in 1968 used an unsafe, live-virus vaccine to determine whether the Yanomami's close to nature lifestyle equipped them with more robust immune systems. Hundreds of Indians died. The 'foundation' proposed at the close of the novel seems also to reflect a campaign brought to fruition in 1991, and spearheaded by a private group, the Commission for the Creation of a Yanomami Park, which, according to a New York Times Report (19 November 1991, would enable the Yanomami 'to roam freely over 68,331 square miles of Amazon wilderness, an area the size of Missouri' (cited in Slater, 1996, pp. 119–21).

In evoking these events from recent history, and linking them with the novel's fantastic, magical realist elements, *City of the Beasts* sets up an extended contrast between utopian imaginings and dystopian possibilities. Through this dialogue, it has begun to show how it might be possible for children's literature to imagine alternative futures in which anthropocentric modes of looking at humankind and its relation to the world might be creatively transformed. It does this by drawing on an ecologically informed position which has affinities with deep ecology: intrinsic value is ascribed to all living beings, and human beings are not attributed with any kind of privileged status.

The novel also deploys an element in deep ecology that aspires to the production of an animistic, or shamanistic, language which might enable the silenced world of nature to rediscover a voice while erasing human presence. Here it pursues a common strategy of looking to indigenous cultures and their nature-associated stories as models. Allende does this in myriad ways: Alexander's mystical exchange with a jaguar, that indicates his own totemic animal is a jaguar; the communications from the shaman of the People of the Mist, Walimai; the closeness to nature of Nadia, Alexander's age companion on the journey, who speaks with the Indians, and with animals, and maintains that 'we [women] get our strength from the earth. We *are* nature' (p. 109). An ideal deep ecology text might entirely efface a human presence, as with the ability of the People of the Mist to become invisible, or with the multiple negations that are Nadia's being:

> 'Walimai says that I don't belong anywhere, that I'm not an Indian and not a foreigner, not a woman and not a spirit.'
> 'What are you then?' asked Jaguar [Alexander]
> 'I just *am*.' The girl replied.

In practice, effacement of the human is impossible, and the most that can be expected is an uncentered, unhumanised perspective, as ecocritics concede. Kate Rigby expresses the position precisely: 'An acknowledgement of the centrality of the human actant, however contingent, contextualised, and decentered she might be in herself, is also a necessary condition for there to be such a thing as literature' (2004: 427).

Justin D'Ath's *Shædow Master*, arguably the first novel for YA readers to achieve a highly successful combination of ecological and postcolonial perspectives, strives to decentre the human actant through a unique transformation of the maturation narrative. On the day of her fifteenth birthday, Aqua-Ora — the novel's principal (and only focalising) character — is positioned to become queen of her country, and has developed the wisdom and maturity to tackle the racial divide between a ruling settler culture ('Folavians') and a dominated 'indigenous' people ('Guests'). The Folavians had arrived two and a half centuries earlier, and had appropriated the land because the nature-associated Guests 'weren't running it like a country' (p. 40) — one of the standard reasons for colonial domination of indigenous peoples. This history loosely reflects Australian history (and in the lake around which the story revolves Australians might recognise the mythical inland sea which lured early European explorers), but, as in some other recent fantasies dealing with race, history is defamiliarised by inverting race stereotypes: the subjected Guests are blond and blue-eyed, while the Folavians have dark hair and brown eyes. On the day of her coronation Aqua-Ora not only renounces the throne (and abolishes it), but also surrenders her human form, accepting instead that her fate is to become the Shædow Master, or Dalfen, a dolphin-like spirit which embodies and sustains the country's ecosystem.

Shædow Master thus brings together discourses in a way not commonly found in YA fantasy: characters who possess paranormal powers and take part in paranormal events evolve through some of the normative assumptions in children's literature concerning personal growth and development, but do so in relation to discourses about environmental degradation, perceived aboriginal relationships with environment, colonisation, and race relations.

Shædow Master is a utopian narrative which begins with a dystopian world afflicted by racial tensions, rulers divided by internecine conflict, and above all ecological catastrophe (drought; the destruction of the trees which balance the environment and bring rain; the 'poisoning' of the lake on which the economy had depended), and ends with a utopian vision. By transforming Aqua-Ora into a semi-mythic, non-human, but transcendentally sentient entity the novel also transforms the natural world into an ecotopia, offering a fantastic version of how our own world might be transformed. An Epilogue, set 44 years after the events narrated in the body of the novel, instantiates a schema for an ecotopia — a good society grounded in sound ecological norms and principles, and in harmony between human beings and the natural environment, and hence democratic and free of race consciousness.

The novel's dialogue between an imagined environmental crisis and a postcolonial situation pivots on a struggle for social and ecological justice. While the society depicted, like the majority of societies in fantasy, lacks basic technology, and the processes of cause and effect are fantastical, the novel's structures signify symbolically. The imagined future is thus not a literal model of how the world might become — although more realistic fictions, such as Louise Lawrence's *The Disinherited* (1994), do imagine a future utopia as a pastoral community with minimal technology — but an expression of hope that the relationship of human subjects with the Earth and with their 'others' might be creatively transformed.

Because Aqua-Ora is represented as being of mixed race, the novel thematises the important issue of who speaks and for whom as, at various times, each race insists she is ethnically or culturally the other, rather than a hybrid who might speak for both. Once she has taken on the mantle of Shædow Master she speaks to and for both races, affirming both an ethical commitment to intercultural reconciliation and the more general principle that culture and environment are primarily local issues. D'Ath here anticipates Lovelock's subsequent argument that individual countries will need to resolve ecological problems by acting from their own self-interest to 'act locally over global change,' rather than hoping for global agreement and action (2006, p. 13).

Perhaps the most remarkable ecotopian sequence in children's literature of the past 15 years appears as the concluding six pages of *A Darkling Plain*, the final volume in Philip Reeve's great dystopian series that began with *Mortal Engines* (2001). The series is set in a post-disaster world, devastated a thousand years earlier by a nuclear holocaust known as 'The Sixty Minute War'.[8] The new world order that has arisen from the wreckage is particularly relevant to this chapter because it revolves around warfare between the Municipal Darwinists of the traction cities and the dystopian deep ecology of the Green Storm, the military wing of the 'Anti-Traction League', whose credo is 'we shall make the world green again' (p. 423). Municipal Darwinism is a satirical representation of extreme modern capitalism: it consumes what others produce, but does not produce anything itself; it simply moves commodities around for the sake of profit; its workforce consists of slaves; it is incapable of altruism. As such, it is also an extreme version of the alienation of culture from nature and a profound threat to the continuation of human civilisation.

Reeve further explores key binaries of experience through an unusual linking of environmental issues with the posthuman. Two of the main characters of the series, Shrike and (Anna) Fang, are 'Stalkers', cyborgs of great physical power constructed out of and around the bodies of dead humans, but with an often unstable interface between the human brain and the 'gimcrack Engineer-built part of [the] brain' (p. 528). The longer they exist, the more susceptible they become to human memories and emotions. The principal story strand of *A Darkling Plain* reflects post-Cold War fears that weapons of mass destruction will fall into the hands of fanatical and eccentric terrorist groups: the Stalker Fang plans to find and implement the access codes for Orbital Defence Initiative (ODIN) an enormously powerful weapon orbiting the Earth since before the Sixty Minute War: 'It was part of the American Empire's last, furious arms-race with Greater China' (p. 378). Stalker Fang was elevated to become leader of the Green Storm, but her mechanistic brain took some deep ecology principles to a logical, nonhuman conclusion: the power of ODIN was 'the power to make the world green again. Where the Storm has failed, ODIN will succeed' (p. 222).

One of the principles of the original Deep Ecology Platform is, 'The flourishing of human life and cultures is compatible with a substantially smaller human population. The flourishing of nonhuman life *requires* a smaller human population' (in Zimmerman, 1994, p. 24). Ecologists who subscribe to this envisage a reduction of the Earth's population by up to a billion people (over a long period of time, and by 'humane and just' methods). In the Stalker Fang's logic, this becomes a determination to eradicate all humanity from the Earth, and she plans to use ODIN to create the kind of cataclysm readers will recognise as replicating the best explanation for the extinction of the dinosaurs. Her logic is simple:

> You have to take the long view, Tom. It isn't only traction cities which poison the air and tear up the earth. All cities do that, static or mobile. It's human beings that are the problem. Everything that they do pollutes and destroys. The Green Storm would never have understood that, which is why I didn't tell them my plans for ODIN. If we are really to protect the good earth we must first cleanse it of human beings.
>
> (504)

Fortunately for the Earth, soon after Stalker Fang has devastated the world's cities, both traction and static, effectively destroying all military capabilities, her brain 'malfunctions' so that the human side takes control and she chooses instead to order ODIN to self-destruct. In the next new world order, power passes to moderate ecologists.

The book, and tetralogy, reaches closure in a chapter of intense lyrical beauty focusing on the end of two human characters, Tom Natsworthy and Hester Shaw. The comings and goings of Tom and Hester are a key part of the tetralogy's structural fabric: lovers, combatants, husband and wife, parents, between them they embody a profound sense of what it is to be human — to enquire, to remember, to love, to hate, to forgive, to feel at one with, or alienated from, the natural world. Just after ODIN is destroyed (and the Stalker Fang is herself destroyed by an opportunistic adventurer), Tom's weak heart gives out and Hester suicides to remain with him. They are found by the Stalker Shrike (whose human component has become deeply cathexed with Hester); he carefully lays them out 'at the head of the valley where a river tumbled down in white cataracts past a rocky outcrop; where a stunted oak tree grew' (p. 529), cuts away the clothing 'they would no longer need', and sits himself down in a nearby shallow cave to watch and wait. Through a superb — and quite self-conscious — piece of nature writing, the description of the decomposition of the two bodies under Shrike's gaze is a remarkable transformation of the horror of human decay into an ecologically acute evocation of the final unity of culture and nature. The disintegration of the physical body becomes a contribution to an ecosystem:

> In the fitful sunlight Tom and Hester began to swell and darken beneath their shroud of flies. Worms and beetles fed on them, and birds flew down to take their eyes and tongues. Soon their smell attracted small mammals, who had been going hungry in that cheerless summer.

> Shrike did not move. He shut down his systems one by one until only his eyes and his mind were awake. He watched the graceful architecture of Tom and Hester's skeletons emerge, their bare skulls leaning together like two eggs in a nest of wet hair. Winter heaped snow over them; the rains of spring washed them clean. Next summer's grass grew thick and green beneath them, and an oak sapling sprouted in the white basket of Hester's ribs.

(pp. 529–30)

The description continues, evoking cycles of growth and decay which, by implication, originate with these bodies, this grass, this oak sapling.[9] The travesty that was Municipal Darwinism — 'the simple, beautiful act which should lie at the heart of our civilization: a great city chasing and eating a lesser one' (p. 155) — has given way to the relocation of the human within a functioning ecosystem.

Reeve does not leave it there, however. Centuries later, Shrike reawakens to find himself in an ecotopia, in an apparently simple, nature-associated, pre-modern society. There are vestiges of a forgotten past world — the 'ancient metal walls' of their town 'were made from the tracks of a mobile city' (p. 532), and the surprising futuristic technology visible in the engines that powered 'delicate airborne ships of wood and glass' is an outgrowth of the last technological achievement recorded in *A Darkling Plain* (and testimony to its survival). In this epilogue, the conflicted world described throughout the four volumes has been replaced by a small ecotopian community: humanity has prevailed, but in a new world order in which the bond between nature and culture has at last been rewoven. Perhaps.

To the extent that 'ecocriticism' is a critical method and ethical discourse that considers the interconnections between nature and culture (and hence between actual environments and textual representations of them), it is highly pertinent to the imagining of various new world orders in children's texts, their pervasive concern with social issues, and the critical assessment of them. Ecocriticism offers not only a welcome return to activism and social responsibility in literary and cultural criticism, but also usable propositions and a language for discussing the relationships between nature and culture. The primary concerns of environment-focused texts — habitat protection, ecosystem conservation, pollution prevention, on the one hand, and celebration of wilderness and of a harmonic balance between human subjects and natural environment on the other — move readily between the possibilities of eutopia/Eden and the dystopias brought about by human greed, negligence, or ignorance. As determinedly activist texts, they share a strong desire to bring about a new world order in which nature and culture are rewoven and the world is made green again.

6

'Radiant with Possibility': Communities and Utopianism

> The dream [of utopia] becomes vision only when hope is invested in an agency capable of transformation.
>
> Levitas, *The Concept of Utopia*, 1990, p. 200

When, in 1987, Margaret Thatcher made her now-infamous pronouncement 'There is no such thing as society', she was enunciating an idea which has been formative in the development of neoliberal politics — that individuals are solely responsible for their lives and that they have (or ought to have) the capacity to be and do what they most desire. In line with this principle, the political directions of many Western nations during the 1990s were characterised by assaults on social welfare systems, the privileging of corporations and an emphasis on market forces. Writing *The End of History* (1992) soon after the disintegration of the USSR, Francis Fukuyama proclaimed euphorically that 'as we reach the 1990s, the world as a whole has not revealed new evils, but has gotten *better* in certain distinct ways' (1992, p. 12), chief among them the collapse of communism and of totalitarian forms of government. Fukuyama promoted capitalism as 'the world's only viable economic system' (p. 90), the indispensable condition of modernisation and of the 'worldwide liberal revolution' (p. 39) which he believed would result in the spread of democracy.[1]

According to Fukuyama, a liberalism founded on capitalism is inevitably associated with a weakening of community, since he believes that the core liberal values of liberty and equality are to some degree at odds with forms of community life based on shared religious or philosophical values (1992, pp. 322–7). Thatcher's claim as to the non-existence of society is grounded in a similar ideological framework, leading her to the position that: 'There are individual men and women, and there are families.' As we have noted elsewhere,[2] in modern Western cultures as well as in social analysis produced by the new right, families are frequently regarded as the building-blocks of nationhood; the emotional, physical and economic well-being of families as a litmus test of the nation's health.[3] In contrast, utopian traditions, whether liberal-humanist or Marxist, have consistently looked beyond families to locate the 'good place' within communities and societies. If, as Ruth Levitas argues, the principal function of utopia is 'the education of desire' (1990, p. 122), then a crucial component of utopian desire is 'the pursuit of a society in which unalienated experience will be possible' (p. 131).

Darko Suvin defines utopia as the construction of a community where sociopolitical institutions, norms, and relationships between people are organised according to *radically different principles* from those of the author's community, and by extension, the reader's community (2003, p. 188). While Suvin disagrees with the logic behind traditional definitions of utopia, which assume that relationships between people are organised according to a radically more *perfect* or *better* principle than the society that the contemporary reader/author knows, he views dystopias as 'radically less perfect' (2003, p. 189) than the society of the reader or author. Further, the difference between the society of an author or reader and a utopian or dystopian society is judged 'from the point of view and within the value system of a discontented social class or congerie of classes, as refracted through the writer' (p. 189). We would argue that such 'refractions' in fiction for children do not merely originate in the imagination of the discontented writer, but are complicated both by the socialising agendas of children's texts, and by the ways in which cultural values and discourses are embedded in narratives and language.

Another approach to utopian notions of communities is proposed by Leela Gandhi in her essay 'Friendship and Postmodern Utopianism', which considers the connections between utopianism and 'ideas of community, communication, sociability, *conatus*' (2003, p. 12). Gandhi considers how the Aristotelian model of *philia,* or friendship, insists on a *homophilic* bond which centres upon the *polis,* the State, so that the ideal of human sociality privileges those bound together as citizens, sharing ties of blood, friendship, similarity, homogeneity. In contrast, the Epicurean conception of friendship rests on notions of *philoxenia,* a love for 'guests, strangers, foreigners' (p. 18) and manifests an impatience or even a distaste for the sameness and predictability, which derive from 'the racial exclusivity of the *polis'* (p. 18). As Gandhi puts it,

Aristotelian and Epicurean conceptions of friendship clearly demand competing types of loyalty, which in turn produce mutually contradictory effects. *Homophilic* loyalties are enlisted as a source of security (for the State, community, citizen/ethical subject). Conversely, ... *philoxenic* solidarities introduce the disruptive category of risk.... friendships towards strangers or foreigners, in particular, carry exceptional risks as their fulfilment may at any time 'constitute a felony *contra patriem.'*

(p. 18)

Gandhi's discussion bears upon the conflict in contemporary Western cultures between *homophilic* loyalties and those more problematic *philoxenic* (or *xenophilic*) allegiances which encourage citizens to transgress notions of safety and solidarity by offering comfort to strangers and refugees, thereby leaving themselves open to the accusation of being 'unpatriotic' — for instance, un-American, un-Australian or un-British.

In children's literature since 1990, utopian imaginings have been largely supplanted by dystopian visions of dysfunctional, regressive, and often violent communities. Responding to geopolitical circumstances such as the outbreak of civil war in Bosnia in 1992; the Rwandan Genocide of 1994; tensions between citizens and guest-workers in Germany, the Netherlands and Scandinavia; and anti-refugee sentiments across Western nations, children's texts of the last 15 years have foregrounded the propensity of communities founded on common identities, beliefs, and projects to exclude and punish those outside them. Such dystopian texts commonly advocate utopian ideals either through negative examples, or by proposing models of oppositional alliances. In this chapter we consider the extent to which dystopian discourses propose transformative agendas, focusing first on texts in which individuals or groups seek to escape from or to subvert the norms of despotic and repressive social orders. Secondly, we consider some examples of the smaller category of texts whose narratives trace the formation of utopian communities.

Memory and community

Lois Lowry's trilogy comprising *The Giver* (1993), *Gathering Blue* (2000), and *Messenger* (2004) affords a striking instance of how contemporary children's literature responds to global (and, in these texts, US) politics in their constructions of community. The communities of these novels manifest a contrast between homophilic and xenophilic social orders.

In *The Giver*, a totalitarian régime drawing on Cold War rhetorics conditions inhabitants to believe that they live in a utopia where conflict, disease, and poverty are banned. Rather, they are trapped in an anti-utopia which denies the possibility that humans can aspire to utopian ideals. *Gathering Blue,* echoing the ethnic and civil wars of the 1990s, is set in a period characterised by a violent, squalid, and hand-to-mouth existence following the ecological and political disasters known as 'the Ruin, the end of the civilization of the ancestors' (2002, p. 21). The society referred to as 'Village' in *Messenger* is the xenophilic 'Elsewhere' which Jonas sought in *The Giver,* a community where those cast out by communities like that of *The Giver* are welcomed and where difference is valued. Jonas, twelve at the end of *The Giver*, is the Leader of Village in *Messenger,* ruling Village together with two other wise men, Mentor and Seer. However, the utopian social order of the community is undermined by the selfish and acquisitive impulses of its citizens, who eventually resolve to close their community to the refugees who seek a 'good place' where pluralism and agency are valued.

The communities of *The Giver* and *Gathering Blue* are, in effect, two sides of the one coin, in that ruling groups in both societies maintain their power through the repression and control of their members, whose lives are confined to a narrow range of possibilities: in *The Giver* through the myriad regulations which determine every detail of existence; in *Gathering Blue* by rituals imposed by the Council of Guardians and by the exigencies of survival. The trilogy does not trace the formation of an ideal community: in *The Giver* and *Gathering Blue,* such communities are desired but not attained by protagonists; while in *Messenger* the utopian state of Village is represented analeptically, since from the first chapter the community is at risk of destruction. Utopian communities are thus imagined, desired and (in *Messenger*) nostalgically recalled by the novels' protagonists, but are not represented as evolving and developing systems.

Jonas's vision of 'Elsewhere' at the end of *The Giver* epitomises Lowry's version of utopia. Exhausted and starving, Jonas finds a sled at the top of a hill and with Gabriel, the baby he has saved from certain death, proceeds to 'the place that he had always felt was waiting' (1993, p. 179). He sees lights flickering before him and recognises that they are the 'red, blue, and yellow lights that twinkled from trees in places where families created and kept memories, where they celebrated love' (ibid.). That the trees Jonas glimpses are transparently Christmas trees, that they are associated with family celebrations, and that the inhabitants of these homes are waiting not only for him but for the advent of 'the baby', locates the utopian community firmly within a Western imaginary where Christianity is naturalised as foundational to symbolic and ideological formations and where the nuclear family is the basis of community.

Lowry's insistence on the central importance of memory relates to the fact that in *The Giver* citizens are prohibited from access to cultural memory, from the knowledge of a past time when citizens experienced fear, sorrow, pride, and other emotions. Jonas, who unlike other children in the community possesses the capacity to see colour, is allocated the role of Receiver of Memory, which requires that he re-experience the past on behalf of the community, absorbing the positive and negative emotions associated with past events, and thus protecting other citizens from such emotions. When Jonas and his mentor the Giver decide that Jonas will exile himself from the community, the consequence is that the memories Jonas has received will return to its citizens, enforcing a painful but regenerative remembering.

Gathering Blue is rather more concerned than *The Giver* with recovery of a personal history, which then becomes metonymic of the ways in which collective history is shaped by the Council of Guardians. Kira, the novel's protagonist, has always been told that her father, a gifted hunter, was 'taken by beasts' before she was born. Like Jonas, Kira is singled out from others by the rulers of her community — as he is chosen to experience memories in order to prevent the disorder of affect, so she is set to weave stories which will determine what the members of her community believe and desire. In fact, during the course of her training she discovers that her father was attacked and left for dead by Jamison, who has become her guardian and mentor. Kira's discovery of the history of her family enables her to understand how she is to be exploited by the Council of Guardians, who intend to use her abilities at making stories out of colours and fabric in order to force her and other gifted children to 'describe the future they wanted, not the one that could be' (2002, p. 212).

Just as the narratives of *The Giver* and *Gathering Blue* are organised by sequences involving the recuperation of memory, so conversely in *Messenger* the disintegration of the utopian community is plotted onto a forgetting of individual and communal histories. Prompted by their desire for possessions and happiness, the villagers trade away their traditions of acceptance and healing and close their community to refugees, a process symbolised by the thickening of Forest, the wooded region which surrounds Village. Lowry's treatment of memory as foundational to community accords with theorists of utopianism such as Raffaella

Baccolini and Tom Moylan, who argue that 'whatever bad times are upon us have been produced by systemic conditions and human choices that preceded the present moment' and that 'such conditions can be changed only by remembering that process and then organizing against it' (2003a, p. 241). The erasure of historical memory thus precludes the transformation of negative social and political practices. Throughout the trilogy, the qualities which distinguish Village as a utopian community echo national mythologies of the United States as a haven for those from dysfunctional and impoverished communities. It follows, then, that in *Messenger* the decision of Village's citizens to erect a wall which will shut out strangers and refugees can be seen to symbolise a shift away from the values inscribed in Emma Lazarus's 'give me your tired, your poor, your huddled masses', and towards a fearful and distrustful attitude towards those figured as Other.

Nevertheless, Lowry's constructions of community in the three novels are arguably more conservative than transformative. Just as Jonas's vision of the ideal community at the end of *The Giver* is built on the image of the nuclear family engaged in a Christmas celebration of memories and of love, so the tableau with which *Messenger* concludes — where the partnering of Kira and Jonas presages the formation of a new family — proposes that the rebuilding of Village depends upon traditional family structures. And even when the community of Village returns to its founding values, abandoning the building of the wall and again welcoming strangers, its government reinscribes a patriarchal order, consolidated in the triumvirate of Leader, Mentor, and Seer. Thus, while Lowry's representation of Village reinvokes utopian imaginings of an America embracing those who seek refuge, it also proposes as normal a political economy ruled by those privileged by race, class, and gender.

In all three novels the catalysts for change are young characters constructed as focalisers — in *The Giver*, Jonas; in *Gathering Blue*, Kira; in *Messenger*, Matty, whose struggle with the 'tangled knot of fears and deceits and dark struggles for power' (2004, p. 168) symbolised by the thickening of Forest, results in his heroic death. In their emphasis on gifted individuals these texts downplay the significance of collective action and imply on the one hand that the transformation of dystopian communities depends upon individuals who possess qualities which set them apart from their fellow-citizens; and on the other, that such people are largely immune from any negative effects of power. Lowry's depiction of exceptional individuals destined to act as catalysts for reform is mapped onto humanist ideas concerning an essential human nature which exists outside social and cultural formations and which is capable of withstanding negative forms of socialisation and control. In this way these texts play out an uneasy dialogue between humanist conceptions of the individual, and utopian ideals which promote communitarian action; similarly, the novels hover between hierarchical distinctions (for instance, between gifted and less gifted) and imagined communities built on new forms of social organisation.

Discourses of inclusion and exclusion

A narrative trigger common in dystopian texts is the impending death of a character deemed by a community or political system to be so different from its inhabitants as to represent a threat or liability. In *The Giver*, Jonas is impelled to flee the community when the toddler Gabriel, who is fractious and disturbs the sleep of his carers, is marked for 'release'; in *Gathering Blue*, Kira's neighbour Vandara, who hankers after the plot of land Kira and her mother have occupied, asks the Council of Guardians to consign Kira to death on the grounds that she is disabled. Similar sequences, involving the imminent death of aged, infirm, or disabled individuals, occur in many other texts, including Rachel Anderson's *The Scavenger's Tale* (1998), Nina Bawden's *Off the Road* (1998), Claire Carmichael's *Incognito* (2000) and Glenda Millard's *Bringing Reuben Home* (2004).

Such narratives turn on concepts and values around community, since practices of rejection and exclusion are embedded in social and political systems. All four novels are set in near future dystopian societies where powerful groups have established authoritarian régimes with eugenicist and neo-darwinist regulations concerning who is to live and die. In *Off the Road* and *Bringing Reuben Home*, protagonists are faced with situations where beloved grandparents face death by euthanasia; in *The Scavenger's Tale*, aged citizens and those with physical or intellectual disabilities are culled and their bodies used to provide organ transplant procedures for wealthy and unwell individuals. In *Incognito*, the protagonist, Karr Robinson, is declared an 'oblit' — someone with no identity, rights, or access to social services — when his father is arrested as an enemy of the state. These narratives of exclusion and culling can be read in the light of contemporary unease about ageism, genetic engineering, and the quest for bodily perfection in Western cultures.

It is easy enough to extrapolate from the dystopian settings of these novels what they propose about ideal models of community. For instance, sequences where powerful groups cast out aged, disabled, or sickly members interrogate the assumptions underlying these processes, advocating relations of respect and mutuality between individuals and within communities. Similarly, interactions where protagonists are prohibited from questioning the norms and customs of their communities gesture towards values such as the rights of citizens to interrogate, criticise, and oppose authoritarian rule. Again, the limitations of choice experienced by the protagonists of these novels — for instance, in regard to occupations and sexual partners — argue for individual agency. Our emphasis here is on the extent to which these narratives advocate resistance to those 'radically less perfect' (Suvin, 2003, p. 189) features of dystopian societies which refer to negative characteristics of contemporary societies.

In *The Scavenger's Tale* the protagonist, Bedford, lives in London City Sector One with his surrogate mother, Ma Peddle, and his family of Dysfuncs (categorised as Dysfunctionals because of their physical or intellectual disabilities). The Sector's rulers, greedy for profit, step up their programme of culling, so that Bedford, as well as other family-members, is at increased risk. Ma Peddle, who is elderly and almost blind, is herself a Dysfunc; nevertheless, she offers unconditional love and the scanty resources available to her to the abandoned 'Low-Caste' children whom she has rescued. In the derelict dwelling where she raises her family she produces a haven, a community built on principles of equality: 'Our Ma Peddle reckoned that Dysfunctionals and Abs ["Abnormals"] had the same basic right to education, food, justice, as every other citizen. Some hope' (Anderson, 1999, p. 3). The downside of her style of resistance is her unrealistic and pathetic loyalty to a cruel and voracious system. As Bedford's 'Some hope' indicates, she is powerless against institutional might, and one by one the members of her household fall prey to the euphemistically named Community Health and Welfare Monitors (CHAWMs), who abduct those targeted for organ transplants.

If Ma Peddle's alternative community is incapable of resisting the harsh régime of London City Sector One, *The Scavenger's Tale* suggests that traditional forms of community such as those based on religious belief are no more effective in opposing totalitarianism. When Bedford is on the run from the CHAWMs, he seeks refuge in an old church where he is befriended by a priest, Father Gregory, who rescues the discarded children of the Sectors, selling his own blood to buy food for his charges. Father Gregory's self-sacrifice is, however, as futile as Ma Peddle's attempts to save her family, and when he dies his band of 'Dysfuncs' seek refuge in 'Mother Church', a monastery-like institution across the Thames from Sector One. However, the Tribunal of Mother

Church refuses the children asylum because of 'the menace they are to visiting foreigners, the threat they post to hygiene, the air of degeneracy and misery they create' (p. 125), and instead they are licensed as official beggars and set to gather money to fund the building of an institution where they will be housed. Bedford, recognising that to place his trust in Mother Church is merely to 'exchange one kind of Low-Caste misery for another' (p. 129), leaves Mother Church in search of a better world, in company with a blind boy whom he has befriended.

Despite the controls and regulations which have circumscribed his life, Bedford has learned both from Ma Peddle's stories and from his encounters with other travellers that there exist places of hope and plenty. In the final moments of the narrative he speculates about alternative futures:

> I don't know where we're going. Will we find a way back across the river, head north ...? Or will we walk over to the west, to find one of the New Age settlements that's willing to take us in? Or perhaps misfits like us can't ever belong anywhere and have to keep roaming forever, till the end of our days.
>
> (p. 131)

A crucial element of Bedford's sense of self is his sense that he is a social being, 'we' rather than 'I', and that his best prospects lie in incorporating himself within a community which offers escape and a better life. Nevertheless, these visions of utopian communities are literally and metaphorically on the horizon of Bedford's vision, and readers are thus positioned to hope that he and the unnamed blind boy (who metonymically represents those who inhabit the margins of dystopian communities) will discover a better world.

Like *The Scavenger's Tale,* the other novels we discuss here provide explanations for the dysfunctionality of the societies in which their narratives are set. However, their responses to these dystopian social orders support Tom Moylan's observation that the dystopian genre 'has always worked along a contested continuum between utopian and anti-utopian positions: between texts that are emancipatory, militant, open, and "critical" and those that are compensatory, resigned, and quite "anti-critical" ' (2000, p. 188). In Claire Carmichael's *Incognito,* members of Incognito, an underground resistance group, have infiltrated the government and are working to transform the social organisation into one which restores the rights of the individual. The tenet underpinning Incognito's philosophy is 'Every individual has sacred rights to privacy, including the right to have secrets and the right to hold back information' (Carmichael, 2000, p. 29). This utopian enclave functions as an oppositional culture within and against the hegemonic social order of the community. Through his contact with Incognito and his part in the overthrow of the corrupt data lord, Karr is transformed into a subject who is able to critique his society and retain his right to resist. By the end of the novel, Karr has had his obliteration revoked and he is once more a legal member of the society, but he and his Incognito ally, Brenna, agree to remain rebels beneath their surface appearance of conformity. The romantic closure of the narrative, in which Karr and Brenna anticipate a shared future as dissidents, jostles against its more sceptical treatment of the effects of political resistance, suggested proleptically by the fact that Incognito has won a 'grudging official acknowledgement as a legal protest group' (p. 194).

A somewhat similar outcome is evident in *Bringing Reuben Home,* where the technologically sophisticated built environment of New Carradon serves as the material evidence of the dramatic transformations wrought by historical change. The citizens of New Carradon live a sheltered and controlled existence in a city that is encased by a huge transparent dome, which eliminates environmental change and sensation, but casts rainbows and a rosy hue over the interior. The government's policies of ensuring a healthier society are enforced through genetic mapping of all infants at birth. The G Code is imprinted on every citizen's ID card; only couples with compatible G codes are allowed to marry or have children, those who marry without GC Certification are punished by incarceration or cessation, and children born of unapproved liaisons are tattooed with the Omega sign, 'symbolic of the end' (Millard, 2004, p. 17). Old Carradon, a derelict, outer-urban space which functions as the urban space's other, comes to stand for the past and old ways, and is inhabited by refugees and resistance groups.

Reuben's resistance to the requirement that he should be 'cessated' when he turns eighty is the event that changes the lives of his granddaughter Cinnabar, her friend, Judah, and her mother Claire. In their efforts to help Reuben achieve his goal of returning to Old Carradon, Cinnabar and Judah learn of the history of resistant groups who continue to oppose the government. For Claire, the event is the catalyst for her resumption of her past revolutionary spirit. However, at the end of the story when the rulers of New Carradon are planning a referendum to make changes to the Charter of Rights and Freedoms in order to improve the lives of its inhabitants, the protagonists decide to remain in Old Carradon, reflecting that 'this was what [the rulers of New

Carradon] said the last time' (p. 240). The story of Cinnabar and Judah's radicalisation in *Bringing Reuben Home* is intertwined with the trajectory of their romantic and sexual relationship, and the novel ends with the birth of their son, named after their friend, JC, who sacrifices himself so that they will survive. This outcome, strikingly reminiscent of Lowry's *Messenger*, proposes that the family is the core of communal life and survival. JC is an outsider and wanderer, and following his death the new community, comprising the four generations of Cinnabar's family, reinstitutes its homophilic and conservative shape, settling down to a life of simple living and subsistence farming in the heterotopic space of Old Carradon.

Of the texts we consider in this section of the chapter, Nina Bawden's *Off the Road* offers the most anti-critical perspective of a totalitarian social order. Tom, the novel's protagonist, is the only child of parents living in Urb Seven, a vast urban conglomerate in a mechanised and controlled society where 'everyone had all they wanted or needed, which were exactly the same things as everyone else' (Bawden, 1998, pp. 46–7). On the other side of the Wall, an enormous barrier beyond which citizens of the Urbs cannot pass, exists a society constructed as other to the Urbs: the Wild, which the children of the Urbs are taught to regard as a dangerous space full of lawless and deformed creatures. When Tom's parents are driving his grandfather Gandy to the Memory Theme Park where he is to be 'gently and permanently cared for' (p. 27), Gandy makes the excuse of visiting a lavatory to escape through the Wall. Tom follows him, believing his grandfather needs rescuing, and once he is on the other side is unable to return because of the vigilance of the Rangers who guard the Wall on the other side.

Like Bedford in *The Scavenger's Tale*, Cinnabar in *Bringing Reuben Home* and Karr in *Incognito*, Tom's enforced departure from the society in which he has grown up provides him with the critical distance to interrogate its values. However, the liberatory possibilities of his encounter with the Outside world are limited by the social and political conservatism of this culture, which comprises former citizens of the Urbs, who either chose to leave or were forced to leave when the Wall was erected, including his grandfather's brother Jack, and the large family he has gathered around him during his years Outside. The world over the Wall is a pre-industrial agricultural society which accords with the tenets of communitarian politics, in that it is based on 'the traditional family' — that is, a social order in which power is exercised by men, with women responsible for domestic and child-rearing duties, and where children are expected to obey adults unquestioningly.

By positioning readers to align themselves with Tom, the narrative constructs as admirable a society which offers him new freedoms and pleasures, and where Tom learns the rewards of physical labour, enjoys eating farm-produced food, and finds himself part of a large extended family in which roles and responsibilities are clearly delineated. Compared with the highly mechanised world of the Urbs, where parents are prohibited from having more than one child, and every detail of life is ordered and controlled, the Outside appears to offer a 'natural' world in which Tom is part of a cohesive community. Nevertheless, systems of control and surveillance exclude the underclass of the Outside, the 'Dropouts' who live in the Wild beyond the farms; and Tom is eventually tracked down by the Rangers as an unauthorised visitor or Illegal. The extent of state control is signalled in an exchange between the Rangers and Tom's great-uncle, Jack Jacobs, when one of the Rangers outlines the dangers of infiltration across the Wall:

> 'Let me explain, Mr. Jacobs. Think what would happen if we let in too many! They would swamp us. They would have to be fed. They would want jobs and land. Or they might join up with our Dropouts and become even more of a nuisance.' He lowered his voice as if what he was about to say was the worst thing of all. 'If they haven't already been sterilized, they will start to breed.'
>
> (pp. 181–2)

The language of this warning, so reminiscent of the xenophobic anti-refugee discourses of contemporary Western nations, does not function simply as a criticism of such discourses, since Jack Jacobs persuades the Rangers to allow Tom to stay, demonstrating that some refugees (in Tom's case, because of his family connections) are more acceptable to the society of the Outside than others. The novel's model of community thus adheres to the Aristotelian privileging of homophilic loyalties which treats difference as a cause of disquiet and anxiety.

At the end of *Off the Road,* Tom and his cousin Lizzie return to the Urbs — Lizzie because she wishes for a life free from domestic and child-minding chores, and Tom because he intends to alert the citizens of the Urbs to 'the lies we've been told' (p. 184) about the superiority of life in the Urbs and the dangers of the Outside. In fact, the world of the Outside, with its romanticised and idealised representation of pre-industrial society, embodies another version of totalitarian rule where a conservative patriarchal past is reinstated. The Outside is, in effect, constructed as an anti-utopia where humans are denied agency and autonomy and where human happiness depends on the maintenance of past structures and habits.

Communities and religious fundamentalisms

A significant number of dystopian texts for young adults feature protagonists who are members of, are drawn into, or are on the fringes of, communities organised around religious beliefs and practices. Although the discourses of the 'war on terrorism' have invited an unprecedented focus on 'Islamic fundamentalism' since September 11, 2001, many texts for adolescents and young adults during the 1990s interrogate Western fundamentalisms, generally by representing individual and collective resistance to conservative and patriarchal power structures. The secularisation of Western cultures — except in the United States, where discourses of Christianity maintain a powerful hold on conceptions of national identity and on political processes — allied with the disaffection with humanist metanarratives characteristic of postmodernism, and the influence of various feminisms from the 1960s, have reduced the influence of institutional religions, which despite the conceptual advances of feminist theologies, have failed to throw off the patriarchal power-structures which they have inherited. Small wonder, then, that children's texts involving communities organised around religious beliefs are solidly dystopian, representing such societies as antithetical to individual agency, progressive gender relations and egalitarian social practices — that is, as cults or sects, communities gone wrong. Symptomatic texts include Libby Hathorn's *Rift* (1998), Robert Swindells' *Abomination* (1998), Kerry Greenwood's *Cave Rats* (1997), Catherine Jinks's *The Rapture* (2001), Gary Crew's *No Such Country* (1991), Fleur Beale's *I Am Not Esther* (1998), and Jane Yolen and Bruce Coville's *Armageddon Summer* (1998).

The narratives of such novels, especially those built on millennial themes, evoke historical events including the Jonestown Massacre of 1978 and the Waco Siege of 1993, so that the potential for such catastrophic events as mass suicide and violent death is always present as a plot outcome. However, children's and YA texts tend to focus on personal development and questions of human agency rather than on wider questions of religious belief, so that even in *Armageddon Summer*, which ends with the death of 20 of the Believers who have gathered to wait for the end of the world, the focus is on the two protagonists, Marina and Jed, and on the ideological implications of their actions and judgements.

A common narrative strategy in these texts is to set insider perspectives of dystopian religious communities against the views of an outsider or an unwilling member. For instance, in *Armageddon Summer*, events are recounted in alternate chapters by Marina, who complies with the doctrines and rules of the community, and Jed, who resists them; in *The Rapture*, one of the narrators is Jarom, son of Heber Woodruff, the elderly leader of a break-away Mormon community living in a remote forest setting in Tasmania, while the other narrator is 19-year-old Aldo Frewin, who lives in what he thinks of as 'Mormon Central' (Jinks, 2001, p. 12), Salt Lake City. Jarom is a believer — indeed, he is led to expect that he has been chosen to follow Heber Woodruff as his 'ordained successor' (p. 130) at the End Time; Aldo, in contrast, is an unbeliever and lives much of his life in virtual reality (the setting is 2087), attending virtual mode (VM) parties and studying journalism at the University of Utah. In Beale's *I Am Not Esther*, the first-person narration is focalised by Kirby Greenland, abandoned by her mother and renamed as Esther when she is adopted into her uncle's family. In all three texts, plot outcomes involve the delivery or escape of protagonists from fundamentalist communities. The effect of this narrative trajectory is to enforce a sense that liberation from communities organised along fundamentalist lines will always bring positive consequences for those so liberated. Focusing on the narrative outcomes of *I Am Not Esther*, *The Rapture*, and *Armageddon Summer*, we examine how these texts construct as dystopian the fundamentalist communities they describe, and what they propose as alternatives to these communities.

In their discussion of 'movement narratives', the collective stories developed by fundamentalist groups to situate themselves historically and to locate members within a common ideational framework, Joshua Yates and James Hunter point to common features of such narratives across religious traditions:

> [The movement narrative] begins with the deep and worrisome belief that history has gone awry, demonstrates that what 'went wrong' with history is modernity in its various guises, and leads to the ines- capable conclusion that the calling of the fundamentalist is to make history 'right' again.
>
> (2002, p. 130)

The fundamentalist communities of the three texts have in common their conviction that modernity — associated with individualism, consumerism, and feminism — has indeed perverted a 'true' or 'original' cosmic order, and that their members belong to a select group of saved individuals and families. In *Armageddon Summer*, Jed and Marina join the Believers, led by Reverend Beelson, who gather on the side of Mount Weeupcut in Western Massachusetts to wait for the end of the world, when the Believers will comprise a transformed nation. In *The Rapture*, Heber Woodruff's followers at Nauvoo[4] regard themselves as inheritors of 'authentic' Mormon traditions, including the polygamy practised by Brigham Young, the founder of Salt Lake City; and in *I Am Not Esther* the Children of the Faith, a community living in the North Island of New Zealand, resolve to move to a more remote region in order to 'live apart from the iniquities of the world' (Beale, 1998, p. 158).

Strategies of exclusion are crucial to the communities which feature in these novels, based as they are on distinctions between the saved and the damned. One such strategy involves redefining spatiality so as to encode hierarchies of value — thus, in *The Rapture*, Heber Woodruff establishes a farming community in Nauvoo, a remote area near Cradle Mountain in Tasmania. A prolonged period of drought has meant that crops have failed and water is in short supply, and it has been necessary for some of the younger women in the community to work in the tourist resort at Yarumbin; however, they are prohibited from developing friendships with anyone at the resort, and are obliged to surrender their wages to the community. Heber Woodruff distinguishes between Nauvoo and Yarumbin in terms of godly and ungodly spaces: Nauvoo is the wilderness into which the godly have been called to await the End Time; Yarumbin, on the other hand, is inhabited by unbelievers and marked for annihilation. Similarly, in *Armageddon Summer* the public space of Mount Weeupcut is redefined, its log cabin renamed the Temple and its perimeter protected by an electrified fence, and by the 'Angels', the armed guards who patrol the borders once the symbolic number of 144 has been reached.[5]

In all three texts, dystopian communities are characterised by practices of surveillance which ensure that the movements and thoughts of members are monitored for adherence to the systems of rules by which power is maintained. Episodes when characters escape such surveillance — for instance, when Jed in *Armageddon Summer* uses his prohibited laptop to access local radio — foreground the mismatch between views of events inside and outside the community. In *The Rapture*, Heber Woodruff has established a ritual, known as the Profession of Faults, where members of the community profess their own failings or report on the misdemeanours of others, receiving punishment or praise. When Kirby/Esther attends a local high school in *I Am Not Esther*, her movements are monitored and reported to her uncle and other authority figures by Beulah, one of the girls from the community, who attends the same school.

It is a given in narratives involving dystopian religious communities that they are marked by regressive patriarchal systems of power. Heber Woodruff's insistence on the authenticity of Mormon practice at Nauvoo in *The Rapture* is merely a cover for his own lechery and violence; and the ritual practices which structure the lives of the community at Nauvoo are centred on masculine authority, with women denied autonomy and relegated to the domestic sphere. In *Armageddon Summer*, Reverend Beelson's allocation of roles in the camp of Believers is similar to the distinction between women's and men's spheres of activity at Nauvoo. Talking with one of the adult men in the camp, Jed learns that Beelson intends to select girls of 16 and over to provide sexual partners for the male Believers in order to ensure that the group's population will be renewed following Armageddon. To be female in this setting is, then, to be valued for one's childbearing potential and to be subjected to the will of the father, since girls are to be denied any choice of partners. Marina, reflecting on the possibility that she might be allocated to one of the older men in the community, considers that 'dying in flames [would be] preferable' (Yolen and Coville, 1998, p. 148) to such enforced partnering. Again, in *I Am Not Esther* girls are betrothed at the age of 14 and married at 16 following negotiations conducted by the men of the community.

Each of the three narratives concludes with an episode where a crisis occurs during which protagonists escape from or are excluded from fundamentalist communities and restored or introduced to mainstream society. At the end of *Armageddon Summer*, a violent struggle develops between the Believers and those too late to join the 144 saved. Marina and Jed are freed from Reverend Beelson's totalitarian rule and from the burden of resisting it, at the cost of the death of Jed's father and 19 other Believers. Like *Incognito* and *Bringing Reuben Home*, *Armageddon Summer* relies for closure on the establishment of a romantic liaison between protagonists. Jed's email to Marina, formulating what he believes, sets out what the novel proposes as desirable:

- I believe there's something inside us that you can't kill, that lives on afterward.
- I believe no one has a lock on the truth. Or the Truth, for that matter.
- I believe people spend too much time fussing about details and not enough time looking at the big picture.

- I believe you have to connect, with people, with the world, to be really alive.
- I believe you are the best thing that ever happened to me. (p. 265)

With its reference to a transcendent reality 'bigger than us' and its insistence on some form of personal survival after death, Jed's list of beliefs gestures towards a version of contemporary secular humanism in which Christianity is naturalised as foundational to ideologies and practices. His formulation rejects institutional religion for forms of community based on common goals and aims — 'looking at the big picture' — and which are capable of bringing people together without requiring them to submerge individual agency within totalising systems of belief. Jed's relationship with Marina is treated both as affording purpose and meaning, and as metonymic of positive relations between people more generally.

At the end of *The Rapture,* the community of Nauvoo collapses following the death of Heber Woodruff and the ensuing struggle for power by rival groups. Jarom, placed in the care of his natural grandmother, embarks on a process of establishing new family relationships and of relearning systems of thought and values. The psychological and conceptual progress of the novel's two protagonists is encoded in their enhanced openness to interpersonal relations and to ideas; thus, Aldo discovers that real relationships are preferable to virtual experience; and Jarom realises that 'there's more than one way of reading the Bible' (Jinks, 2001, p. 409). The principles promoted here are similar to those advocated through Jed's statement at the end of *Armageddon Summer* in that they revalue human relationships based on trust, equality, and empathy, and advocate plurality of beliefs. A strikingly similar pattern of closure is evident in *I Am Not Esther,* in that when Kirby/Esther and her cousin Daniel are expelled from the Children of the Faith they form new allegiances with members of their families who have previously departed the community and who now induct them into mainstream society. Kirby is reunited with her mother, who was herself expelled from the community as a pregnant 16-year-old. Utopian outcomes in these three novels focus, then, more on individual and familial relations than on communitarian possibilities, implying that the restoration of personal agency and mutually supportive relationships will inform larger social and political formations.

In his *Theology of Liberation* (1974), the Latin American writer Gustavo Gutierrez notes that utopian thought incorporates both *denunciation* — the rejection of an existing order — and *annunciation*, the 'forecast of a different order of things' (p. 233). In *Armageddon Summer, The Rapture,* and *I Am Not Esther,* denunciation wins out over annunciation. These texts denounce the founding narratives of fundamentalism, with their claims to orthodoxy, their literalism in interpreting sacred texts, their distrust of science. By representing the psychological and psychic progress of protagonists in terms of their escape or liberation from fundamentalist communities, they embrace instead the narrative of modernity, built on Enlightenment principles of secularism, pluralism and rationalism.

In the texts we have discussed so far in this chapter, child protagonists are central both to representations of resistance and opposition, and also to narrative processes which position readers to critique contemporary societies. As our analysis has shown, fiction concerning itself with the disorders and fractures of modern communities tends to propose better futures indirectly, by extrapolation from undesirable and negative forms of society. Texts representing utopian enclaves within dystopian societies, such as Ma Peddle's community of marginalised children in *The Scavenger's Tale* and Incognito, the eponymous resistance group which features in Claire Carmichael's novel, foreground the resistant activities of such groups as well as their vulnerability to the power of the state. And in some texts, such as *Bringing Reuben Home* and *Off the Road,* communities constructed as alternatives to dystopian systems are based on nostalgic imaginings of idealised pre-industrial arcadias. During the remainder of this chapter we turn to texts which deal directly with the development and progress of utopian communities, and with the subject-formation of young people engaged in building such communities.

Communities in the making

Feminist principles and concepts inform many of the texts we discuss, through narratives which identify gender-inflected oppression and advocate social orders characterised by equality and reciprocity. While feminist visions of a better future have produced many utopian and dystopian texts for adults, relatively few fictions for children and adolescents situate narratives within matriarchal communities. A notable exception is Jean Ure's *Come Lucky April* (1992), set in Croydon Community, a post-apocalyptic settlement where the continuation of the population is ensured by artificial insemination, and where boys are castrated at the age of 12 and taken away for 'training', returning to the community as 'civilised' members, suited to minor roles and responsibilities. At the time of the novel's setting, Croydon Community has been established for a century, and the narrative involves the sequence of events which occur when an intact young man, Daniel, is brought into the community (see Chapter 2).

Daniel's presence opens up old tensions and arguments about the norms which structure the community's practices and ideologies, in particular its members' assumptions about sexual difference. The women and girls of the Croydon community are taught from an early age about men's aggressive and violent natures and when Daniel arrives in their community they fear that he will rape a woman if she is left alone in his company; further, the castrated males who carry out routine tasks within the community are affronted by his presence, which reminds them of how they might have been. April, one of the two girls who discover Daniel when he is injured, experiences a guilty pleasure after she kisses him and imagines sexual relations with a man.

For his part, Daniel is a product of his patriarchal community, and misrecognises the women's rejection of heterosexuality as a sign that they are sexless, having discarded opportunities for passion and pleasure. The novel's construction of an implied lesbian sexuality can be read in naïve terms as implying the absence of sexuality, which is how Daniel reads the women's relationships; to him, it is inconceivable that a woman could desire another woman. However, the text leaves it to readers to judge whether the women gain significant pleasure through their relationships with one another, which may be sexual as well as emotional. Rather than positing a lesbian utopia inhabited by lesbian desiring subjects, Ure constructs a narrative that is based on, but does not interrogate, binary oppositions — that is, between male and female; and (implicitly) between heterosexual and lesbian identities.

The social organisation of the Croydon Community is based on a feminist politics of democracy and emotional support whose flipside is the chauvinistic conviction of its members that they inhabit the best of all possible worlds, evidenced by their use of the term 'primitive' to describe other communities, and 'advanced' to characterise their own. Like the fundamentalist communities which feature in *I Am Not Esther*, *The Rapture*, and *Armageddon Summer*, the Croydon Community refuses to invest its effort in technological development (apart from its deployment of artificial insemination), and in this sense it rejects modernity, which assumes that the quality of human life can be indefinitely improved by technological advancement. In contrast to fundamentalist groups, however, the community's sense of itself as 'socially advanced' (Ure, 1992, p. 107) incorporates a commitment to gender equality — Willow, one of the community's leaders, tells Daniel that 'every man or woman has an equal right to have her say in the running of the community' (p. 118).

Nevertheless, the *realpolitik* of the community is more complex than Willow acknowledges. In April's more cynical account of community decision-making, general meetings called to consider contentious issues merely afford an appearance of democracy: 'And everybody talks and in the end they all do what [Willow] wants them to do' (p. 160). One such issue is that of male castration, brought into sharp relief because Daniel's presence in the community coincides with the return of David, April's childhood friend, after an absence of five years during which he has been castrated. David, conscious that April is sexually attracted to Daniel, resents the fact that he has been denied choice and agency, and proposes that he should bring the question up at the next community debate.

That the community is thoroughly subjected by strategies of control and surveillance is clear when Willow explains to Daniel that while the question of male castration has been raised at community debates, proposals for its cessation have been defeated 'largely by the men themselves. I think if you were to ask them you would find them perfectly content with the way things are. You must appreciate that things have been this way for very nearly a hundred years. It seems to them quite natural' (p. 119). Deploying the strategy of estrangement, Ure ascribes to Willow an argument common in historical and contemporary anti-feminist thought — that 'most women' are 'perfectly content' with patriarchal orders which deny them independence and agency. In this way readers are positioned to recognise the argument but at the same time (applied to castrated boys) to experience it as unfamiliar, and are thus enabled to take a distanced, but fresh view of the ideas involved, engaging critically both with the imagined world of the community and with the real world of the reader and the author. Later in the novel, when Daniel addresses a community meeting and is questioned as to how many members of the governing council of his society are women, he falls back on precisely the same argument: 'women prefer to occupy themselves with domestic matters. It's their own choice entirely' (p. 176).

To most members of the community Daniel represents contamination and disorder, and his departure re-establishes social harmony. However, April's obligation to choose between leaving with Daniel and remaining to support David entails a fracturing of subjectivity, and when she decides to stay in the community, the narrative positions readers to interrogate the notion that she enjoys untrammelled freedom of choice. Even as Willow reminds David that April 'never does anything she doesn't choose to do' (p. 200), this bland reassurance is problematised by the episode which has preceded it, where the community's hostility to Daniel and to David's proposals for change have been all too evident. On the one hand, April's decision to remain reasserts the law of the mother and not the law of the father and as such embodies another form of repression; on the other hand, this closure evokes the possibility of positive change in the Croydon Community.

If *Come Lucky April* depicts a matriarchal community which tends towards totalitarianism, Jackie French's short story 'The Lady of the Unicorn', published in *The Book of Unicorns* (1997), thematises a process whereby women effect positive change by adopting principles of feminine solidarity and refusal of violence. The setting is an Australian post-apocalyptic community whose titular head, the Lady of the Unicorn, is a young girl, Ethel. The community is bound together first by the interdependence of a self-sufficient rural economy (with its miller, baker, barrel-maker, pig-keeper, weaver, tanners, and farmers) and also by loyalty to the Lady of the Unicorn. But this is no utopia of peace and harmony, since the warlike T'manians, flooded out of their own island homes, raid the countryside killing and capturing people for slaves and, when the story begins, seeking land. The unspecified disasters of the past have left a legacy of birth defects and deformities of body and mind and those who grow into these observable differences are excluded from the life of the community. Ethel finds that her position marks her also with an unwanted difference, constricting her behaviour and setting her apart from her peers.

Through Ethel's meetings with the giant Alice and with Alice's friends the 'forest people', who inhabit territories beyond the Hall and its surrounding farmlands, as well as through Ethel's confrontation with the invading T'manians, the narrative interrogates concepts of inclusion and exclusion, of difference, of community, of identity, and of child/adult relations. As in *Come Lucky April*, the narrative uses the strategy of estrangement to open up a space for speculation — specifically, around the politics of difference. Ethel's encounter with the giant Alice, in her hidden hut on the hill above the village, marks the beginning of this process. The representation of the giant as female challenges the Western folktale schema in which giants are male, even when they are not malevolent. In *Contemporary Women's Fiction and the Fantastic* (1999), Lucie Armitt suggests that the figure of a female giant, in a society which all too often treats women as 'little girls', may create 'not a terrifying Gorgon, but an empowering utopian possibility' (1999, p. 14). In 'The Lady of the Unicorns' Alice acts as Ethel's mentor, leading her to interrogate the homophilic and exclusionary attitudes of her community.

In contrast with the village and farms whose inhabitants feel themselves to be privileged by their proximity to the Hall, Alice and her friends have forged a heterotopic community of choice, bringing together those who have experienced exclusion from the mainstream community, and it is through Ethel's encounters with the forest people that she is impelled to interrogate the ideologies of her community. Thus, on catching sight of one member of the group, whose face has been horribly deformed by fire, illness or an attack by an animal, her first reaction is one of horror: 'This was a ... monster, monster, monster shrieked Ethel's mind. But it can't be a monster whispered another part of her. This is M'um Alice's friend...' (French, 1997, p. 135). Thinking beyond the deformities of the forest people, Ethel realises that they have created a community of care characterised by interdependence and respect.

A crucial aspect of Ethel's subject-formation is that she occupies quite different positions in the two communities. With Alice and the forest people she is a child negotiating relationships of trust and friendship with the forest people; in her role as Lady of the Unicorn she is potentially powerful and influential, although she has resisted taking on the duties associated with this role. M'um Margot, the steward of the Hall, has trained Ethel as to her duties, which include tedious tasks such as conducting an inventory of supplies. In one sense, then, Ethel's assumption of her role as Lady follows the common narrative trajectory whereby a child takes on responsibilities which usher her into adulthood. However, 'The Lady of the Unicorns' traces the formation of community as well as of individual identity, and Ethel comes to see that it is precisely by adopting multiple subject positions that she can help effect change.

When the T'manians invade the mainland and march towards the Hall, the cowardly Grand Marshal Kevin absconds with his guard. Ethel is obliged to take charge, gathering the inhabitants of the village and planning defensive tactics. As Ethel gives the order to advance, Alice and the forest people descend from the hills where they live; Alice orders attackers and defenders to lay down their arms; and the T'manians flee, terrified by the 'monsters'. At the end of the story, Ethel allows one of the T'manians, wounded in the battle, to make his home in the village. The utopian order whose development is modelled in this story is characterised by the rejection of violence and war; a philoxenic insistence on welcoming difference (the 'monsters' and the T'manian); and the valorisation of women's power and agency as Ethel, Alice and Margot collaborate in the process of forming community.

In this community, then, children are not merely beings in transition between dependence and autonomy, but connections and intersubjectivities between children and adults constitute a mode of overcoming boundaries and separation. The difference between friend and enemy is exposed as a matter of positioning: to the villagers, Alice and the forest people are monsters, while to Ethel they are rescuers; to Margot the wounded T'manian is someone to be cared for, while to Ethel he is the enemy before being incorporated into the habitus of the Hall. The story does not, however, conclude with a sense that acceptance of difference is simple. At the end, Ethel reflects that 'The world had seemed so simple when enemies were simply enemies, and giants sucked their victim's bones. The world was more confusing now ... Things had changed in the past. Maybe tolerance could come once more' (p. 178). By extrapolating from attitudes to difference in contemporary Western societies, the narrative offers a critique and an indication of the ways change might be imagined. Its lack of closure marks the narrative not as a blueprint for an ideal society but one where social change is in process.

Similarly, Monica Hughes's novel *The Other Place* (1999) represents a utopian community in the process of formation — in the tradition of utopian texts, located in a place and time which distinguish it from our own, a planet in another solar system and with a temporal system different from that of earth. Raffaella Baccolini points out that 'Utopia ... offers an alternative to the problems of a specific time and space' (2003, p. 114), and accordingly the inhabitants of 'the other place' seek to address the propensity for contemporary nations and groups to deal with conflict either by violence or through totalitarian rule. The protagonists, Alison and Gordie Fairweather, are sentenced along with their parents to transportation in a penal colony, Habitat W Correctional Facility, because their father, a journalist, has produced internet material attacking the totalitarian World Government.

Habitat W is a white windowless dome filled with supplies for the 5-year term to which the family is sentenced. First Gordie and then Alison escape, breaking through the force field surrounding Habitat W and discovering a utopian community inhabited by children who have similarly escaped the penal colonies where they have been sent with their parents. Alison, at 16, is older than the other children, who are initially reluctant to allow her to remain on the grounds that she will seek to control them. To all appearances, the children's community (referred to as 'Xanadu' by Gordie) is the 'good place' of eutopia: its practices are environmentally sound; power is vested in collective decision-making; and it is relatively self-sufficient for food and supplies. However, as Alison quickly realises, the processes and practices of the community are stage-managed by an adult, the mysterious Jay, who appears at intervals to monitor the children's activities and to supply them with game which they cook together with the vegetables they themselves produce.

Hughes's emphasis on environmentalist values is folded into an idealistic and romantic vision of a pre-industrial past which has much in common with the anti-utopia of Bawden's *Off the Road*, especially in the comparisons both texts make between technological and 'natural' production of food. Just as Tom's first experience of eating meat in *Off the Road* is represented as a moment of ecstatic insight, so Alison's introduction to roast meat is described in language loaded with sensory and sensual detail: 'The outside was crackly and brown, and beneath was a layer of creamy fat that melted softly, while the meat itself filled my mouth with juice' (Hughes, 1999, pp. 65–6). In both texts, the consumption of meat metonymically promotes a pastoral vision of utopian plenty, set against a technologically advanced social order characterised as arid and unsatisfying.[6]

Nevertheless, it is precisely through technological means that the utopian community of *The Other Place* has been established and maintained, as Alison and her friend Kristin realise when they access Jay's computer files. Here they discover that the World Government Council designed the settlement as an experiment to determine whether a colony of children (referred to as 'Project Botany Bay') could survive and prosper as a cooperative group. To this end, the children of dissidents have been removed from their parents, conditioned and trained, provided with an initial supply of clothing, bedding and tools, and their progress monitored by Jay, a psychologist employed by the World Government. At the end of the novel, Jay destroys the World Government's computer system and the access route to the colony before departing for earth. He will, he promises Alison and Kirsten, report to the Security Council of the World Government that the experiment has failed, having resulted in the death of parents and children; but in reality the children's parents, now held in detention and treated with drug therapy to render them docile, will join their children to be retrained by them as community members.

Even as the utopian community of *The Other Place* turns out to have been formed through manipulation and social engineering, the text justifies these processes by pointing to the children's success as young colonists. As Krishan Kumar notes, utopia is 'a way of looking at the world that has its own history and character' (1991, p. 3), and in its curious way *The Other Place* draws on those traditions of adventure novels in which children are ostensibly outside adult control, but where in fact their activities are contained within a more or less invisible network of adult authority and power. When the children decide on the name they will call their community, they select a name — 'Jay's World' — which underlines the extent to which their collective identity has been shaped by Jay's desires and ambitions.

To examine utopian tropes in contemporary children's literature is to acknowledge the preponderance of dystopian over utopian narratives. Yet as a whole both utopian and dystopian narratives propose that even the most destructively totalitarian systems can be transformed. This potential is symbolised in *Messenger* by Matty's recognition that while the thickening of Forest signifies 'a tangled knot of fears and deceits and dark struggles for power', Village is capable of transformation into a 'good place': 'Now it was unfolding, like a flower coming into bloom, radiant with possibility' (Lowry, 2004, p. 168). The epigraph to this chapter, from Ruth Levitas, suggests that transformation is contingent upon agency. Utopian and dystopian texts are far from uniform in their treatment of questions of sexuality, gender, child-adult relations, and politics, and as we have suggested throughout this discussion they are frequently riddled with inconsistencies and ambiguity. However, they position readers to hope in the possibility of 'agency capable of transformation' by representing young characters possessing intelligence, compassion, and resourcefulness in their dealings with others and in the political action they take. It is, therefore, within the narrated spaces that constitute these various subjective and intersubjective experiences and responses, that young readers are positioned to recognise the interaction between their own understandings of the world as it is now and the vision of what it might become.

7
Ties that Bind: Reconceptualising Home and Family

> We have to go where we most need to be, to follow our hearts to where they take us. Perhaps we travel there in fear and in unknown darkness, yet maybe we journey towards the light.
>
> Shearer, *The Speed of the Dark*, 2003, p. 280

The subject of 'families' has long been a dominant topic of children's literature and films. While literary and filmic representations of families are impossible to catalogue, they invariably align with other contemporary social and political discourses which position the institution of 'the family' as both a problematic and an ideal social construction: *problematic* in that 'the family' is not a fixed, known entity, but a formation that is always in the process of construction; and *ideal* in that families carry the burden of the utopian promises of a better future promulgated by governments, nations, and religious idealists. Thus, family is often metonymic of the State and other forms of governmentality in that it stands for the collective desires, dreams, and political visions of a new social order of the future.

Representations of families are always discursively shaped by class, culture, and historical moment. The Industrial Revolution of the late eighteenth and early nineteenth centuries initiated significant changes to the nature, structure, and form of families in Western societies across Europe and the United States. As a market economy replaced a subsistence economy, the family as consumer rather than producer meant a change in social positioning from the private sphere to the public sphere (Berebitsky, 2000, p. 21). However, the emergence of the 'modern family', particularly amongst the bourgeoisie or middle classes, brought with it new forms of romantic and parental love, authority, and strict sex-role divisions within the domestic household that generated a new emotional structure and approach to child-rearing practices which were different from earlier aristocracy and peasantry. Directions for further changes to families have occurred in Western societies in the period of late modernity due to the growth of capitalism, democratic political institutions, and cultural secularisation. These changes include changes to family law regarding adoption, increased diversity of family forms (sole parent and gay/lesbian family), the rise and decline of the nuclear family, and the public exposure of the private lives of families through reality TV, talk shows, and tabloid press. The latter opens up for public consumption and scrutiny the contrast between appearance and reality, between masquerade and truth. This point is captured in the satirical television series *The Simpsons* when Homer, seeking to impress his boss Mr Burns at the company picnic, reminds his children: 'Remember as far as anyone knows, we're a nice normal family' (1990). However, 'going public' on the family is symptomatic of a more general trend in late modernity where moral dilemmas, taboos, and uncertainties previously silenced and obscured by convention and codes of behaviour are exposed and debated.

A fundamental tenet of modern societies has been an implicit and explicit responsibility to children, a responsibility that sees an investment in young people as the embodiment of future dreams and possibilities. The political translation of this tenet has been the provision by governments of resources and services, including education and social welfare, to ensure that young people are materially and legally cared for. This was modernity's social and moral contract and it was based on adult commitment and intergenerational support for children and youth (Giroux, 2000). In the public sphere, the family has been promoted as the most fundamental form of social capital, offering the individual resources, support, and networks for meeting mutual interests and needs. When the family becomes fragmented or its members separated or alienated from the collective, the individual must function independently of familial structures and support. In these instances, individuals seek or desire other forms of associations or networks providing a shared and collective level of economic, emotional, and functional security. These substitute families or alternative homes replace kin-based networks and blood ties with other intimate (or coercive) relations with their own networks, norms, and social practices.

It seems that despite these changes, which conservatives often view as having led to the phenomenon of 'family breakdown', families still matter in what has been described as 'an age of individualisation' or times of 'Do It Yourself' identity formation where past roles and categories no longer serve as the framework for individual behaviour or societal beliefs and practices (Bauman, 2002b). While previous modes of behaviour, expectations, and familial ties may have been disembedded from society, Beck and Beck-Gernsheim (2002) provide an optimistic note in suggesting that we are in the process of 're-embedding'. Such re-embedding invites both reformulating old ways and developing new ways of being and belonging.

By locating literary and filmic representations of families within the political and social discourses of the late stages of modernity, we attempt in this chapter to critique the ways a selection of texts reconceptualise home and family as fictional families (like their real-life counterparts) struggle with now near-obsolent but lingering traces of 'the modern family'. In examining the ties that bind families, the chapter evaluates the different configurations that these texts offer. Unlike traditional utopian narratives where the subject lives in a harmonious familial or communal space, some of the children's texts in this chapter provide imagined accounts depicting an antagonistic relation between subject and society, in which individualisation, power, and control replace, or are in competition with, more conservative familial structures and relationships. Other texts depict the ways in which conflict and other disruptions have split families, causing children to become independent survivors seeking new support and emotional networks. Despite these hardships, the utopian impulse remains a powerful desire in these texts for restoring subjectivity and identity within a transformed familial/social space. Before providing detailed analyses of the focus texts, we briefly sketch the conditions which have given rise to the current crises and hardships experienced by many children and families today, and foreground the part played by children's utopian texts in reflecting and responding to these changing times.

Honey, we've lost the kids! changing notions of family and childhood

Beginning in the 1950s, the new post-war phenomenon of the suburban nuclear family with clearly delineated sex-roles was promoted as the domestic ideal. For many politicians, members of the public, the media, and social commentators of that time, suburbia was regarded as a means to ensure a 'bulwark against communism and class conflict' (May, 1988, p. 20). The narrativisation of the domestic ideal through books, film, and television served to strengthen in the minds of many the possibility of the American/Australian dream. However, dreams are never as they seem and by the 1960s challenges to this ideal and its restrictive social roles and codes were being openly challenged as youth, race, and gender revolutions attempted to expose the hypocrisies, inequalities, and restrictions behind the masquerade.

In more recent years, other kinds of families that are more representative of complex societies of late modernity have emerged, often in spite of governmental agendas and laws. These new configurations are reflected in both literature and film from many Western and non-Western countries, thus serving as privileged sites/sights of cultural change. However, it is our contention in this chapter that despite the diversity of families that are narrativised in children's texts, there remains for the main part a conservative strain which works against the stories' utopian enterprise. For instance, the (heterosexual) marriage norm remains a highly valued social arrangement, and fictional families remain tied to societal notions of 'normality', even when they attempt to subvert constructions of conventionality and 'normal' familial relations ('The Simpsons' is a case in point). Consequently, despite the many attempts to promote diversity and difference there is a strong tendency in texts produced for young people to delimit the political agendas of their narratives by refusing to consider how the utopian impulse is implicated in and produced by existing conditions. In other words, the utopian rhetoric espoused in many cultural texts mimics the liberal democratic rhetoric of assimilation, equality, and freedom despite legislative, social, and homophobic actions which are hostile to this rhetoric.

Commenting on recent efforts in various countries to promote lesbian and gay marriage, Judith Butler argues that matters of kinship are invariably tied to family and marriage: 'efforts to establish bonds of kinship that are not based on a marriage tie become nearly illegible and unviable when marriage sets the terms for kinship, and kinship itself is collapsed into "family"' (2004, p. 4). Children's books have attempted to show alternatives to the heterosexual family life. However, these texts are often at pains to point out how alternative gay families are different but in many ways just the same as heterosexual families. This eliding of sexual difference through an accommodating sameness appears in Nancy Garden and Sharon Wooding's picture book *Molly's Family* (Garden and Wooding, 2004). The book's utopian impulse can be seen as founded on difference, since the phrase 'all kinds of families' is repeated throughout the book, and the book's cover blurb states in part: 'even if a family is different from others, it can still be a happy, loving — and *real* — family' (emphasis in original). The story's implicit double bind emerges here in that the wording provides an explicit, sanctioned endorsement of same-sex families as legitimate (as real and as loving) as heterosexual families, yet at the same time it diffuses lesbian sexuality's potential for subverting those power relations which exist as part of society's ideal: the patriarchal family.

Other books produced for young adults which attempt to expose rather than cover up the gap between utopian and contemporary social discourses throw into sharp relief the contradictions and hypocrisies that often characterise accounts of happy families. To this end, the novel *Come Lucky April* (Ure, 1992) employs the notion of estrangement to explain how representations of imagined communities such as the matriarchal 'Croydon' depicted in this novel allow readers to recognise its subject but at the same time make it seem unfamiliar. Such cognitive estrangement allows readers to take a distanced, but fresh view of both the text's reality and their own. Thus, the alternative Croydon community has its own reality yet it stands in a critical relationship with the real world of the readers. In a related way, Lois Lowry's trilogy — *The Giver* (1993), *Gathering Blue* (2000), and *Messenger* (2004) — raises issues concerning pluralistic family and community structures that offer alternatives given the political and cultural debates and changes in the post Cold War era. However, unlike *Come Lucky April*, these texts, despite their reformist agendas, fail to offer an alternative to patriarchy, and the teleology of the trilogy resolves into a traditional romance outcome (Mallan et al., 2005). Other novels, such as *Girl Walking Backwards* (Williams, 1998) and *Twilight* (Meyer, 2005) posit a queer reality which calls into question norms and conventions that restrict the conditions under which people exist, both inside and outside the text. The explorations of dysfunction and normality[1] in these novels invite considerations on the part of readers of the ways in which discourses of social transformation can promote as well as deny individual subjectivity and agency according to the extent to which writers utilise the utopian impulse for conservative or emancipatory purposes.

Another concern of this chapter is the way in which families no longer provide a source of emotional and financial support for many young people. With the emergence of the so-called 'risk society' alternative forms of kinship and networks are sought and made by young people as traditional allegiances and practices are either abandoned or destroyed. For Giroux (2000) the situation in which many contemporary youth find themselves typifies how adult society has abrogated its social responsibility, thus severing 'the social bonds that once existed between adults and children' (p. 19). Furthermore, as we have argued previously, the move from a culture of dependency to an age of 'post-emotionalism', in which people are largely indifferent to the needs of welfare of others and committed primarily to their own personal concerns and well-being, has implications for families with their associated notions of trust and reciprocity. These implications emerge as key concerns both in the literature and in society (Mallan et al., 2005, p. 8).

While family displacement and child abandonment are not recent phenomena as outcomes of war, terrorism, natural disaster, or poverty, what concerns us here is not that these phenomena continue, but that the utopian enterprise endeavours to shake readers from their media-induced complacency by challenging them to see the world (past, present, and future) from a new or different perspective. In many of these texts, there are no adult saviours, no guaranteed system of fair play, and no recourse to divine intervention. As our discussion in Chapter 3 highlighted, global conflicts and changing political agendas have destroyed many families and altered the life course and choices of countless children as they are set adrift in hostile spaces to fend for themselves and keep alive a hope of a better future. Other children are victims of other kinds of atrocities — poverty, kidnapping, slavery, and prostitution. In these dystopian worlds, children require not only resilience but a determination to survive against the odds. Sometimes resilience and determination are not enough as many children do not survive, or if they do, they remain psychologically damaged and traumatised.

In *The Garbage King* (Laird, 2003), the horrors of a long civil war, extended famine, and poverty in Ethiopia provide the historical context for this story of a group of street children who forge an alliance borne from their individual and collective experiences of abuse, exploitation, and abjection. However, despite the extreme harshness of their life on the streets, the utopian impulse remains and is reinforced in the Afterword by a (supposedly) former street child who directly addresses two kinds of implied readers: 'children who want to run away' from home, and children who are already living on the streets. For the former, he admonishes them to 'think about your life, and be happy with it', while he urges the latter to 'be brave' and to know that 'the power of God will come some day to visit you' (p. 330). By incorporating the utopian discourse into the Afterword, this paratextual strategy attempts to strengthen the subjective point of view of the narrative (as told by the adult author) and affirmed (by the 'real' child author of the Afterword), thus giving a sense of truth and legitimacy to the text and its (double) utopian promise of a better world to come. However, despite the naïveté and goodwill of the paratext, it nevertheless registers an ironic note in that the sweet nostalgia for a home and family as the ideal grounded space, disguises the bitter reality that for many children home and family are dangerous sites, and homelessness might offer an emancipatory alternative. This suggestion runs counter to modernity's democratic desire to conflate the discourse of the nation-state with the discourse of the home whereby both home and nation function as metaphors for order, security, and a united *polis* (Manning, 2003).

The following discussion examines the above themes more closely as they emerge in a selection of texts written and produced for children and young people. By attending to strategic and necessary affiliations with and between different imaginary families and kinship groupings based on either blood or choice, we consider how the experience of a single universalising notion of family is given legitimacy or replaced by alliances from alternative sources. As a way of organising the discussion in this chapter, the focus texts have been grouped according to their differential treatment of identity in relation to blood ties and as a process towards social subjectivity.

Travelling in the unknown darkness

The texts discussed in this section share a common element in that they all deal with children who have become separated from their parents and each raises questions about the presumed certainty of blood ties for securing family cohesiveness. Left to their own devices, the child protagonists struggle to gain agency and subjectivity in hostile or alien spaces, while for the most part seeking reunion with their parents. Part of the utopian tradition in many stories written for children is that the dichotomy between good and bad is often spatially schematised: internal (good) domestic space versus external (bad) societal space. Fairy tales more often than not illustrate this reification between domestic and societal spaces. However, some tales, such as 'Hansel and Gretel' expose the home as a site of the uncanny: a notion that runs counter to the desire to see home as offering security and belonging. In *The True Story of Hansel and Gretel* (Murphy, 2003) the familiar fairy tale is reworked inverting stereotypes and spatial dichotomies, resulting in an even more sinister account than the original. In this story, two Jewish children are left by their father and stepmother to seek safety in a dense forest in the last months of Nazi occupation of Poland. Their stepmother gives them the names of the German fairy tale characters as a means to disguise their Jewish origins. However, the uncanny domestic spaces of the fairy tale are refigured in this story, especially the Witch's cottage which becomes a refuge for the children. In the animé *Spirited Away*, a young girl 'Chihiro' inadvertently enters a strange world inhabited by ancient and unusual spirits and gods and must find inner resources to help restore her parents to their human form after they are turned into pigs because they gorged on food from the spirit world. The horror of seeing her parents transformed into animals speaks to the way in which the familiar can become strange and frightening when external forces subvert the discourse of security that comes with utopian notions of family. In her quest to save her parents, Chihiro grows as an individual and is thereby enabled to face the changed world entailed in her family's move to a new city.

In *Bloodtide* (Burgess, 1999), children are the ones who suffer the consequences of family feuds. In this reworking of the first part of the Icelandic Volsunga saga, warring gangland families (the Volsons and the Conors) vie for absolute control of a dystopian futuristic London which is set apart from the technologically advanced world by a waste-land populated by halfmen who eat anything that comes within their reach. Here Freud's account of the home as the place where the *Unheimlich* resides is given full treatment.[2] Furthermore, the family functions as a metonym of the state as a contested site of power, surveillance, and control. A similar disruption to the utopian tradition of the home-as-haven occurs in *The Speed of the Dark* (Shearer, 2003). This story of obsession and familial love speaks to the deep psychological fear of separation that haunts many children. When Christopher's father and his girlfriend become imprisoned inside a snow dome through a mini-aturisation process carried out by the jealous Eckmann, they learn to adapt to the spatial confines of their new world; however, Christopher remains an external witness to the unfolding spectacle of life inside the dome. In a related way, the children who form part of Shade's family in *Shade's children* (Nix, 1997) have been removed from their families during the period known as 'the Change' but unlike Christopher they have no knowledge of their parents and life before the Change. Thus, this family while ultimately upholding the utopian ideal of the patri-archal family explores the limitations and strengths of other 'family' configurations that are not based on blood ties. The following discussion examines these children's texts in close detail to consider the extent to which utopian desire informs notions of home and family.

In her discussion of child abandonment in both history and story, Melissa Gross (1999) posits economic factors as the primary reason for parents abandoning their children: 'Children are abandoned or killed because of a condition of poverty, lack of food, or some other kind of scarcity situation' (p. 103). In the traditional story of 'Hansel and Gretel' a combination of economic necessity and jealousy is the driving motivation for the stepmother's insistence on the abandonment of the children in the woods. In *The True Story of Hansel and Gretel*, Louise Murphy attempts to rewrite the original fairy tale and its abandonment motif by exploring the notion of (biological and step) parents' abandonment of their children out of love and a need for mutual survival. Just as postmodern analysis has questioned authority and reliability with respect to philosophy, history, and narrative's relationship to truth, this story also questions the memory of tradition, whereby past 'truths' are scrutinised and reimagined in ways that break with stereotypical representations. The children in this story are abandoned near a wood by their father and his new wife and told that they must call themselves 'Hansel and Gretel' and find refuge while their parents speed off on their motorcycle becoming 'the lure that would lead the hunters away from the children' (p. 5). The stepmother is not cast as the evil woman, thereby defying the legacy of evil fairytale stepmothers. The witch figure also given new meaning in the form of the kindly Magda who takes in the children giving them food, shelter, and security.

In as much as *The True Story of Hansel and Gretel* is about memory and history (key elements to a knowable family genealogy) it is also about remembering and the need to know when to remember and when to forget. The children are told to forget their Jewish names, language, and traditions so that they may survive. Yet their bodies and minds bear the signs and traces of their past and refuse to be lost to oblivion. When Gretel is raped by two men, she is so traumatised by their actions that fragmented memories of a happier past attempt to break through the grimness of the aftermath, yet she struggles to remember her real name:

'I can't remember my name. It's gone.'
Magda turned and saw the girl's face. 'Now, dear one. It's all right. You're safe now.'
'I want it,' Gretel spoke loudly. 'I want it.'

(p. 146).

In a related way, Chihiro in *Spirited Away* must struggle to remember her name after Yubaba the witch literally takes possession of it, grasping the *kanji* from the contract she forces Chihiro to sign, leaving Chihiro only one piece of her original two character name. Her new half name in isolation is pronounced 'Sen'. The mysterious boy, 'Haku' (who has forgotten his true name), warns Chihiro of the importance of not forgetting her full name and to keep the farewell card written by her friends when she and her family departed for a new home in a different city as a reminder of who she is. When Chihiro's body begins to become transparent, Haku offers her spirit food which prevents her from vanishing. By contrast, in Murphy's text, Hansel needs his body to be transformed as his dark hair and eyes make him look Romany. While Gretel has blonde hair, Hansel's dark curly hair must be dyed with peroxide and shaved short so that he looks Polish. This transformation of the head provides the superficial change but his circumcised penis is his traitorous body part that must never be revealed. This struggle by the three characters in these texts to remain true to their original embodied selves underscores their quest to survive and to restore their identity. Here identity has its roots in knowledge of the past — history, memory, family, and specifically blood ties.

Both these texts (like others in this chapter) can be said to fall into category of critical dystopia in that they do not give up on hope despite the dystopian worlds they depict. As Baccolini notes, critical dystopias promote 'historical consciousness' because 'history is central and necessary for the development of resistance and the maintenance of hope, even when it is a dystopian history that is remembered' (2003, p. 116). In *The True Story of Hansel and Gretel*, the Jewish holocaust is the dystopian history that is recounted through the microcosm of the village of Piaski near the Bialowieza Forest. *Spirited Away* does not recall a dystopian history, but situates its story in the parallel worlds of old and new Japan. The dystopian features of the imaginary ancient world, nevertheless, inscribe a space for agency and intersubjective relations, and for being at one with nature. Both stories offer critical accounts of the circumstances which cause people to act in evil (and good) ways and of the relationship between humans and their natural environment. Despite their different historical and cultural contexts, they retain a utopian trace and as such each can be read as redemptive tales.

Spirited Away begins and ends in the contemporary world of modern Japan, but the action occurs in an ancient spirit world, specifically the spirit bathhouse where the spirits and gods, drawn from the Shinto religion, go to relax and bathe. The beliefs of Shintoism provide the causal framework for understanding the narrative resolution and the characters' motivations. As Shinto is an optimistic faith, there are no absolutes. Thus, 'evil' characters are essentially good or they are made evil because of evil spirits and it is only through purification (at the bathhouse) and offerings to the *kami* (gods) that evil spirits can be kept away. The 'evil' witch Yubaba has her 'good' side in the form of her identical twin Zeniba. This duality is also present within Yubaba:

she might steal Chihiro's name and plot her demise, but she is a loving, albeit over-indulgent mother to her giant baby boy ('Boh'). Similarly, the monstrous spirit 'No Face' whose rapacious appetite and destructive actions are appeased by offerings by the bathhouse workers, responds to Chihiro's kindness and ultimately finds a home with 'call me Granny' Zeniba. As Chihiro becomes part of the Bath House community (a temporary family substitute while her parents are changed into pigs), she also matures because she develops intersubjective relationships outside her real family. In a related way, when Boh journeys away from home with Chihiro and her band of followers, he reproduces Chihiro's own process of growth by having intersubjective experiences away from the stifling maternal domestic space, and at his return places Chihiro's well-being above his mother's desire. What the film valorises is community and an extended family, which is supported by Zeniba's willingness to take in No Face. In contrast, Yubaba's relationship with Baby is bad parenting: she smothers him (symbolised by the way he is buried under a vast heap of cushions) and his mode of communicating is by means of threats and tantrums. Consequently, *Spirited Away* conveys hope by insisting on the fundamental goodness of humans and the enduring need to belong in a family (nuclear or extended) and to be loved.

Chihiro and her band of loyal companions form a family of necessity (similar to the street family in *The Garbage Kings*) as they care for one another and provide collective support. When the final challenge is issued to her by Yubaba to recognise her parents (in their porcine form) from amongst numerous identical-looking pigs, her intuitive knowledge of her parents aids her in making the right decision and she is reunited with her parents in their human form. As the family leaves the spirit world via the tunnel that served as the portal into the alternative time/space dimension, their memories of what had happened are seemingly erased and only the leaf litter and dirt on the family car are an indication that time has passed. However, a hair band given to Chihiro in the spirit world is a memento that may offer her some remembrance of things past.[3]

Hansel and Gretel too are reunited with their father by the end of *The True Story of Hansel and Gretel* (the stepmother has died). While the children's experiences in the village threaten to erase their memory of their former life, their father reassures them that he will help them to remember and he begins this long journey back to the past by speaking their real names:

He spoke each name slowly, quietly, the crowd of workers that had gathered around the three catching up the sounds and echoing the names in whispers. He spoke their names over and over, and watched these gifts brought out of the darkness, these bits of flesh, this blood of his blood and bone of his bone, his children, begin to smile as they became, once again themselves.

(p. 296)

The human capacity for goodness and narrative resolutions pivoting on family reunion are explicit elements in both tales. Yet, while Murphy attempts to rewrite the evil witch motif of fairy stories through the kind and brave Magda, and shows other characters (such as Nazi officer Major Frankel) as humanly flawed, she offers an ambivalent account of her depiction of the evil Oberführer in 'A Penguin readers guide' to the story presented as part of the paratext: 'No humanizing can explain and forgive such evil. Men like the Oberführer appear when historical events give them permission to use this dark side of the human imagination' (p. 6). The linguistic choices and syntax in these sentences seem to be working in such a way as to abrogate human agency and responsibility for action. By conflating Oberführer with other (evil) men ('Men like the Oberführer'), he is erased as a man with the capacity to make moral choices. Further abrogation is afforded by blaming history as the reason and explanation for evil actions.

Evil people live among us in the real world, and they often appear ordinary, almost indistinguishable. The notion of what makes ordinary people do cruel things is also explored in *The Speed of the Dark*, here through the character named 'Mr Eckmann':

Everyone called him Mr Eckmann. ('Probably even his mother,' Poppea had said once.) He dressed formally in two or three piece suits, not the way you would expect, not for an artist. His home was in one of the old Regency houses, where the crescent curved above the park. But he didn't spend much time there. He was usually in his studio above the gallery, way up in the attic, alone there with his working tools, his microscopes and his telescopes and lenses.

(Shearer, 2003, p. 25)

This surface of ordinariness complicates recognition and detection, and in these current times of terrorist alert, citizens in Western countries are told to be ever watchful of 'others' who might do extraordinary things with cataclysmic consequences. Hence, the discourse of the other loses its smug certainty and exclusivity when the other is inscribed in an already existing discourse, and may or may not be 'just like us'.

Eckmann is just like us in the sense that he blends into a crowd, but he is also 'other' in many ways. He is a genius, but taunted for being 'funny looking', 'a garden gnome' (p. 30). His physical appearance causes him pain and is the presumed reason for his enjoyment of his god-like presence, watching from the attic of his home 'the world in miniature' projected on a to large bowl from his *camera obscura*:

> It was as if the tiny figures were his creations, their destinies were in his hands, and he was like some divine being, high up in an ivory tower. Here he was no longer small and overweight and unattractive, nor waddled when he walked.
>
> (p. 25)

The passing parade projected through the *camera obscura* encapsulates Eckmann's desire to create a world in miniature, one where he is not the smallest, most ridiculous-looking inhabitant. His skill in developing miniaturising technology is evident in the displays of the tiny objects he has created and which are admired by the tourists who pass through his gallery: an exact replica of the Taj Mahal, a camel passing through the eye of a needle, all no bigger than a grain of sand. It is when he begins to miniaturise real things and eventually people that his obsession turns sinister. When Christopher befriends Eckmann he, like everyone else, is amazed by the skill of the miniature scenes which are encapsulated in glass domes, but detectable only through a microscope. Christopher finds in Eckmann someone who is like himself, someone 'not normal': 'At school they're normal. Me, my dad's an artist, and Poppea is a living statue. I don't know anyone normal' (p. 83). These words unwittingly carry a portentous irony as Eckmann's jealousy for Christopher's 'normal' family and his unrequited love for the beautiful Poppea drive him to miniaturise Christopher's father and Poppea, trapping them forever inside a miniature dome city. 'Normality' becomes an absent referent for something that no longer exists.

For some time Christopher does not know what has happened to his father and Poppea, and Eckmann assumes the role of the boy's guardian; he is also God the Father, controlling the daily lives of the trapped couple in the dome, regulating night and day with a switch of a lightbulb, providing sustenance, water, and all manner of material supplies. For Eckmann now has the family he has always desired: 'For he had a son now. He was a man with family, with responsibilities, of all shapes and sizes' (p. 192). Just as war brings out the worst (and the best) in people, so too Eckmann finds that watching the helplessness of the couple and the father's loss of his son ignites a desire for cruelty: 'The ability to deal out cruelty without having to be answerable for it somehow aroused the desire to inflict it' (p. 191). Yet he also becomes the omnipotent and omniscient patriarch, watching, responding to their needs, becoming 'Uncle Ernst' to baby Maria who is born to the couple. When Eckmann dies from a heart attack Christopher discovers the awful truth about the mysterious disappearance of his father and Poppea. However, Christopher never gives up hope that one day he will be reunited with his father, Poppea, and his half sister. After years of trying unsuccessfully to create a 'decelerator' that will reverse the miniaturising process, Christopher makes the ultimate decision to miniaturise himself and join his family in the dome, such is the strength of the ties to his family.

Accompanying hope in the three texts discussed to this point is physical and psychological displacement. This loss of subjectivity (either permanent or recoverable) can be seen as symptomatic of critical dystopias, as the protagonists caught up in dystopian worlds experience disorienting spaces that render illusory all fixed concepts of identity. The dome city (*The Speed of the Dark*) is the ultimate postmodern space, a simulacrum whereby technology has taken mimicry and imitation to the extreme. The abandoned theme park (*Spirited Away*) that Chihiro and her parents first encounter in the spirit world is also a simulacrum but one that has lost its referent. In *The True Story of Hansel and Gretel,* as a way of offering 'proof' of the children's Catholic background, Hansel and Gretel are photographed and the images of their heads are pasted onto an old photograph of two children on their first communion day. The photographed children (both the original communion pair and Hansel and Gretel) become objects shaped by the photographers' vision or imagination. Poststructuralism's 'death of a subject' is literally enacted in this instance. This small incident in the story is nevertheless representative of the narrative's exploration of lost identity and displaced/substituted subjectivity as the photograph affects notions of who the children are and how they see themselves. When the children are shown the completed framed photograph, Hansel admires the boy's body that is situated below his face: a boy fatter than Hansel dressed in a black suit, clean white socks and shiny shoes. For Hansel, the simulacrum is the reality. He remarks:

'My shoes are beautiful.'
'Those aren't your shoes.' Gretel was angry.
'Yes they are.' Hansel was complacent. 'I remember them.'

> Gretel stared at the picture of the girl. It was her but it wasn't her....
> 'I was never like that.' Gretel frowned.
> 'Yes, you were. I remember.' Hansel picked up his picture and cradled
> it in his arms.
>
> (p. 47)

Consequently, the photograph, like the dome city and the theme park, changes the shape of reality, replacing real time and space with a substituted or parallel time–space dimension that is a simulacrum of the original.

Bloodtide and *Shade's Children* continue with the theme of children being separated from their families, but complicate the issue of blood ties. Despite their dystopian projection of societies where 'family' has become a warped signifier, the narratives, nevertheless, can be read as redolent of many current configurations of families in contemporary society. They, paradoxically, expose the myth of the 'traditional' harmonious family, but inevitably draw upon that myth as part of the utopian impulse for restoring intersubjectivity and family ties within a transformed social space. It is this rootedness in the present that marks utopian/dystopian literature's ability to engage with concerns of contemporary society through a hypothetical unfolding of some possibilities (both redemptive and apocalyptic) inherent in the present condition.

Both *Bloodtide* and *Shade's Children* proffer fascist narratives of social domination, fear, and exploitation, in ways that fit what Tom Moylan (2003) terms 'the dystopian imaginary'. According to Moylan, such literary works dispense with the state as the centre of social control and replace it with 'the totalizing political-economic machinery of the hegemonic system (and not simply the state, party, corporation, religion, or other undemocratic power) that brings exploitation, terror, and misery to society' (2003, p. 136). In dispensing with the state as the locus of social control, both *Bloodtide* and *Shade's children* relocate that power in the hegemonic masculine subject: Conor, the ruthless megalomaniacal ganglord (*Bloodtide*), and Shade, the self-appointed messianic 'electronic reality' (p. 80) father figure (*Shade's Children*). In both *Bloodtide* and *Shade's Children* traditional allegiances to family are either long-forgotten or in the process of breaking down and as such they are symptomatic of societies that no longer take responsibility for children. Whereas families have traditionally been viewed as the idealised model of social capital, two possible scenarios are played out in these stories. One is that the allegiance to family can become so strong that it weakens ties of community, so that trust and reciprocity are not extended beyond the bounds of the family. This is a characterising feature of the warring gangland families in *Bloodtide* where the Volsons and the Conors are unable to trust those outside the family, and yet ultimately trust within the families is also destroyed. The other scenario is that if the ties within family are weakened then this could lead to an increase in social ties outside the family. In *Shade's children,* there are no biological families left after 'the Change'. During the period of the Change, all people over the age of 14 were removed from their families and homes leaving only babies and children to be taken into the Dorms where they were educated to keep their brains developing and later sent to the Meat Factory where their brains were inserted into other artificially-generated creatures known as Wingers and Overlords. Consequently, young people who have been rescued by the computer-generated Shade are euphemistically his children but in reality they are a community of young people brought together through circumstance, rather than through blood. Together they work towards the defeat of the Overlords, and although they have been denied childhoods and the nurturing that families traditionally offer children, they nevertheless learn to love and care for one another. By extension, this book signifies an alternative to those theories of social capital being measured by the strength of relations between parents and children and open up the possibilities for considering alternative family structures and networks beyond normative familial relations.

The heroic narrative of destiny and conquest underpins both stories and as such they fall into a Freudian Oedipal narration with their accounts of 'fatherhood' and patriarchal succession as the only viable means for progression towards identity formation and the continuity of culture. In the Oedipal tale, the originary violence of culture is masculine, and social reproduction and subjectivity are achieved by a repetition that re-enacts the trauma of that violence. Crucial to the line of succession from father to son is the repudiation of the mother, seen as inhibiting separation and subjectivity and as providing a dangerous image of women that must be encountered by a masterful man in what may be called heroic Oedipal resolution. In *Bloodtide*, mothers are either dead (dying in childbirth as in the case of the mother of twins Siggy and Signy), or missing without mention (we know nothing of Conor's mother). When a mother substitute is needed as a nurturing presence, she appears in the form of an old, deformed Pig with a compassionate heart and the incongruously sweet name of Melanie. Despite the twins Siggy and Signy being cast as a reversal of traditional gender representations in that Siggy is the soft masculine subject, while his sister Signy is the dangerous feminine subject, Signy is eliminated leaving open the way for a heroic repetition of the authorising myth of patriarchy. However, when Siggy emerges as the destined heroic figure (he is the chosen one of the god Odin), he appears disillusioned and lacks confidence in his leadership ability: 'I'm ... no ... hero' (p. 293) ... 'I'm just dead meat walking' (p. 295).

In *Shade's children*, the dangerous woman who needs to be eliminated is Silver Star, the Overlord who 'was responsible for destroying 98 percent of the human race, someone who now preyed upon captive children' (p. 290). When the female heroic subject, Ella, is killed it is left to the besotted couple, Gold Eye and Ninde, to emerge from the climactic battle destined to live the domestic fantasy of pre-Change times that will soon be possible. In an archival discussion session recorded as no. 24768, Gold Eye who was a survivor of the Change but escaped the Dorms expresses in his elliptical style his desire for home and family:

> I like trees ... grass ... only birds in sky. People walking safe. Family.
> No creatures. Sleep at night safe. Walk under the sun in own place.
> Grow plants. Build.
> Be father with mother. Have children. A place like Petar told me. Home.
> After Change goes back ...
> I want home.
>
> (p. 157)

Gold Eye's desire for home and family is realised in the final scene of the book when in some future time, he and Ninde are married and have two children named after their dead friends Ella and Drum. The romance of the nuclear family that Gold Eye expressed as a boy of 14 becomes his adult reality. In the final words of the story, Ninde calls their children while unwittingly recalling the Oedipal return to the father: 'Ella! Drum! Daddy's here! Said Ninde. 'It's time to go home' (p. 302). In this short exhortation, both identification and loss are acknowledged in a mininarrative that plots the beginning of a family's history.

As we discussed in the opening of this chapter with respect to gay marriages, the matter of social capital takes a different turn when queer families and communities based on either non-sexual or sexual ties become part of the broader social and economic discourse. Although *Bloodtide* signals in its title the paradox of the tidal ebb and flow of blood relations, it also entertains the possible triumph that chosen ties can achieve. When the halfman resistance group led by Dag Haggerman enlists Siggy as a joint leader the shared goal to overthrow the Conors is given impetus. This new impure collective of hybrid animal and human creatures is a queer alternative to the pure genetic breeding that characterises the dominant gangland families. Metaphorically this queer community offers transformative spaces of belonging that cross racial, sexual, biological, gender, and geographical lines. Ironically, it is the breaking of trust in both novels that triggers the downfall of family unity and the rise of a new social order. When Signy tricks her twin brother into an incestuous act it is just one of the many deceptions she carries out between her brother and her husband. Notions of traditional family relations, maternal love, and matrimonial loyalty are queered by the birth of Siggy and Signy's child Vincent and the accelerated growth of its clone Styr. In a similar way, deceit and betrayal by Shade destroy his adoptive family enterprise and the end of this 'family' gives rise to a collective of young people that are able to function effectively without a parental figure. Consequently, both books canvas new forms of identity and belonging that emerge out of risk societies where original bloodties might be severed, but new productive allegiances are forged.

Journeying towards the light

As the above discussion illustrates there is a hopefulness in the texts that governs what is possible under the rubric of 'family'. In some instances, there appears an inclusiveness that becomes the condition for the recognition of a separate configuration of collective support and affection, which is an 'Other' that is neither repudiated nor incorporated into the dominant ideal. However, the conditions which create these alternative 'families' are extremely harsh and they raise questions about what are the implications for the self in relation to identity. In the following texts, we consider how the self is understood or comes to be understood as having an identity of belonging within a family. It seems that in the previous texts, with the exception of *Bloodtide*, the individual undergoes a familiar *Bildung*, travelling through darkness in order to find light in the form of a family reunion or a new family at the journey's end. The texts that we turn to now can be seen as complementary to this notion of travelling through darkness towards light, but they focus more on the dynamics of family life within contemporary societies and how this impacts on identity and subjectivity, particularly as the individual moves towards a sense of social subjectivity. In *Coraline*

(Gaiman, 2002), family is given a gothic treatment by creating a feeling of homelessness for the eponymous Coraline even though she remains at home throughout the story. Here home and family become alienating spaces and her home is inhabited by *döppelgangers* who conspire to deprive her of her identity. The animated film, *The Incredibles* (2004), provides a comic take on the nostalgia of the 1950s, a time when good and evil were supposedly clearly identifiable and known, when happy families were mythically portrayed as the norm, and superheroes saved the day. This film's satirical comment on contemporary society provides a subtle critique of the liberal subject-citizen, institutional sets of practices, beliefs and binding norms relating groups of people, and societal expectations for family conformity and 'normality'. Finally, *Tribes* (Slade, 2002) traces Percival Montmount's process of acceptance of the breakdown of his family and his father's departure. Assuming his 'dead' father's identity provides Percy with a means to live out his father quest and to develop a father–son bond that he is unable to experience in his real world.

Fredric Jameson's (1991) argument that postmodern space is unmappable, transcending the individual body's ability to locate itself or perceptually organise its immediate surroundings, is evident in the previous discussion of *The Speed of the Dark* where the fictional hyperspace created by Eckmann's technology circumvents the laws of physics. In *Coraline* we find a similar kind of parallel world, one which is an exact replica of Coraline's home and surroundings. This un/familiar world confuses notions of subjectivity. Although this new space is familiar, perhaps even mappable, Coraline nevertheless experiences an inability to situate herself that Jameson describes. When Coraline explores the empty flat that is part of the large house in which she now lives with her family, she discovers a different kind of familial space:

> She wondered what the empty flat would be like — if that was where the corridor led. Coraline walked down the corridor uneasily. There was something very familiar about it. The carpet beneath her feet was the same carpet they had in their flat. The wallpaper was the same wallpaper they had. The picture hanging in the hall was the same that they had hanging in their hallway at home.
> She knew where she was: she was in her own home.
> She hadn't left.
> She shook her head, confused.
>
> (Gaiman, 2002, p. 37)

Coraline discovers that the woman who has shiny black buttons for eyes, looks but does not look like her mother: she is her 'Other mother'. Similarly, the man with button eyes is her other father, and her neighbours are the other neighbours. This other world erases the boundaries between reality and representation, time and space engendering a loss of subjectivity for Coraline. Mirrored rooms, repetitive art, and familiar people and objects all conspire to deprive Coraline of any sense of a solid identity. Only her cat who can talk in the other world refuses to be anything other than itself. When Coraline asks the cat: 'You must be the other cat.' It shakes its head and replies: 'No' ... 'I'm not the other anything. I'm me.' (p. 47). Despite its nod to Descartesian logic ('I think, therefore I am') as a way of explaining its existence, the cat speaks, therefore it is not itself. When Coraline insists on befriending the cat she tells it her name and enquires about its name, but is told that cats don't have names, only people have names and 'That's because you don't know who you are. We know who we are, so we don't need names' (p. 48). Of course, what the cat doesn't realise is that naming is inextricably part of the process of recognition — to name is to identify, to be known. Thus, while Coraline struggles with an alienated subjectivity, her name provides her with the lasting remnant of her former identity in much the same way that Chihiro (*Spirited Away*) needed to remember her name so that she could return to the real world.

For a short time, life in the other world is interesting, and her other parents are affectionate towards her and seem interested in her (feelings that seem to be not forthcoming from her real parents). However, to stay in their world Coraline must have buttons sewn onto her eyes: perhaps as a perverse means of marking 'family' resemblance. The button eyes are emblematic of the Other and as such are effective markers of difference and non-belonging, just as they are markers of sameness and belonging. Coraline's own 'otherness' is apparent before her encounter with the other parents: she is in a constant state of boredom, feeling ignored and unloved by her parents. However, in the other world, she is also Other but encounters alterity in this counterfeit familial space: replicas of people and animals who live in the flats in her house; dead children whose souls have been hidden; her other parents; her real parents trapped in a snow city dome. By recognising others' desires, Coraline comes to desire life as it was: a desire that is based not on the utopian ideal, but on the limitations of what is possible. Nevertheless, traces of the utopian narrative are evident. For instance, by the conclusion, family and home become the figures of utopian social unity: harmony has been restored (family are reunited), conflict has been resolved (the souls of the dead children are released), and contamination from external threat (the other mother) has been eliminated. Coraline, too, is representative of the individual utopian body as the narrative maps her transition from solipsism to social subjectivity through the processes of loss, identification, and courage. In restoring social harmony, she also realises the value of her family and the extended family of neighbours who inhabit the large house that is now home.

Otherness and true identity are given a twist in The *Incredibles* as the Parr family comprising Bob Parr, his wife Helen, and their three children Violet, Dash, and Jack Jack who live the conventional American middle-class life in the suburbs, but are secretly 'retired' superheroes. With the exception of baby Jack Jack, each of the Parr family has a special talent: Bob used to be Mr Incredible, one of the greatest and strongest superheroes; Helen was formerly Elastigirl; Dash is super-fast and super-confident; and Violet, who wants to be a normal teenager, is able to turn invisible. Bob yearns for the good old days and is unhappy working as an insurance clerk for a company that is only interested in making profits from human suffering. While Helen works to maintain normality by becoming a housewife and a stay-at-home Mum, her decision nevertheless suggests the failed utopian promise of second-wave feminism just as 1950s superheroes seem an anachronism in a world that has become increasingly greedy and individualism has replaced a sense of community. Both 'nuclear family' and 'superheroes' were foundational social and political concepts of the 1950s as they were a response to Cold War fears and an attempt at nation building. However, lawsuits seeking damages for unsolicited deeds (Bob once saved a suicide jumper and was served with a wrongful-non-death suit) by ungrateful people they had saved forced the Supers into retirement and government-funded anonymity through the Superhero Relocation Program. It is the dilemma of representing a powerful utopian desire for 'truth, justice, and the American way' and at the same time representing a thoroughgoing scepticism concerning the possibility of its fulfilment that is the basis of the film's critique of modern American liberalism and the importance placed on uniformity, normality, and civil action. As Bob laments: 'They keep finding new ways to celebrate mediocrity'. The change in contemporary American society from 'the innocence' of the 1950s is captured in a scene where the family rally to support Bob who has reverted back to his Mr Incredible role.

[Helen hands two masks to Violet and Dash]
Helen: 'Put these on. Your identity is your most valuable possession.

Protect it. And if anything goes wrong, use your powers.'
Violet: 'But you said never to use ...'
Helen: 'I know what I said.'
[sighing]
Helen: 'Remember the bad guys on the shows you used to watch
on Saturday mornings? Well, these guys aren't like those guys. They
won't exercise restraint because you are children. They will kill you
if they get the chance. Do not give them that chance.'

(*The Incredibles*, 2004)

The mask is a signifier of comic book fantasies about superheroes,
where true identity is always what lies beneath the mask. Furthermore,
to ensure that their real identity is not discovered, the Parrs engage
in a double form of cross-dressing which complicates social codes of
normality: wearing 'abnormal' clothes in their everyday lives as the
Parr family, and dressing 'normally' when on superhero business. This
confusion is illustrated in the way that Bob Parr's muscled body, albeit
now overweight and with an expanded waistline, feels more at home
in the flexible body-hugging material of his Mr Incredible suit than
when it is squeezed into his normal work clothes, bulging in resistance
to the restrictions of conventionally sized shirts and trousers made for
mere normal male bodies. Despite the overtly parodic scene when 'E'
(the humorous intertextual reference to James Bond's gadget master,
'Q') lectures on the dangers of capes, the Parr family's cross-dressing
as superheroes exceeds a mere performance of parody if read within a
utopian framework. As superheroes, the utopian body is one of excess as
it needs its excessive strength, skills, and abilities to overcome the forces
of evil that threaten the harmony of the ideal metropolis. However, if
we draw on Foucauldian theorising, there is a double utopian logic at
work in the text. The Parr family, as disguised superheroes are subjected
to the disciplinary (societal) gaze that is part of traditional utopian oper-
ations necessary to stabilise the harmonious social space. Thus, their
bodies must be disciplined and exist in a state of oppressive restraint.
However, the perceived harmonious space is an illusion as crime, corruption, and a disgruntled, self-serving citizenry are endemic. Whereas the
Parrs conform to the social practices that define the 'politics of everyday
life' (Foucault, 1977, 112), as the Incredibles they have a vision of a
transformed society (one that is crime and corruption free) and actively
use their powers in coercive ways to defeat the forces of evil. Ironically,
it is the problem with all superheroes that their true identities need
to be removed from their (super) bodies in order for them to continue

with their heroics. Similarly, their re-located identities are only possible through the (normal) individual's immersion into the community and the necessary social relations it demands.

Identity and processes of identification underpin *Tribes*. Rather than face the reality of his father's departure from the family home to forge a relationship with another woman, Percival Montmount invents an elaborate story about his anthropologist father having died after been bitten by a tsetse fly while living with a tribe of blue-skinned pygmies during one of his field trips. This explanation for his sudden departure is further narrativised through Percy's adoption of his father's anthropological identity whereby he chronicles in a field journal his observations of the daily interactions and rituals of his fellow students whom he classifies according to tribes — The Born-Again Tribe; The Lipstick/Hairspray Tribe; The Logo Tribe; The Digerati Tribe; and so on. The identity is so complete that not only does Percy share the same aquamarine-coloured eyes as his father, but he claims:

> I have my father's eyes. The night he died, Dad materialized at my bedside, extended a ghost arm, and opened his fingers to reveal a pair of glowing spirit eyes. He gently held the back of my head and inserted the magical orbs into my sockets.
>
> (Slade, 2002, p. 3)

His father's departure is compounded by the suicide of Percy's best friend, Willard. The double impact on Percy is described by his friend, Elissa, after a failed romantic moment between the two of them: 'You don't live, do you, Percy. You just record' (p. 103). In reading the desired utopia of Percy's imagined world of a 'dead' (but loyal) father and the dystopia of an alive (but estranged) father we draw on Jennifer Burwell's notion that utopia is not a space, 'but rather the narration of a space' (1997, p. 203). As Burwell suggests, by describing the social space the utopian vision is realised in terms of its relation between oppression and transformation, and as such provides the means for visualising 'the problematics of moving back and forth between' (p. 203). Percy has developed a utopian space which provides him with respite from the hurt and anger he feels towards his father. In this space, which is articulated through his anthropological jottings and witty observations, he is able to accept the absence of his father while keeping alive the memory of his work and the limited time they shared together. This imagined utopian space like other such spaces discussed in this chapter is an illusion that offers a suspension of reality and a respite from the non-utopian conditions of daily life.

When Christopher's father turns up for his high school graduation ceremony, his father's physical presence and the vacant chair left to honour the dead Willard combine to take him out of his denial and the memory of the real reason for his father's leaving of his family and the knowledge that Willard has not been forgotten by his fellow students and teachers. The intensity of this dual realisation is such that he faints and falls from the stage. As he drifts in and out of consciousness he asks his father:

> 'Want your eyes back?' I whispered.
> 'Whu-what?'
> 'Taking? Your eyes back now?'
> Then blackness.

> (p. 123)

No longer reliant on his father's 'magic' eyes, Percy comes to the realisation that it is time to move on and become himself, not an imitation of his father. However, he continues to draw on his Darwinian knowledge to illustrate how the past continues to inform the future: 'Things change. They evolve. One has to adapt to these changes' (p. 129).

This chapter has explored the various conceptions of family across a range of texts that draw on utopian and dystopian tropes. In examining the various ways in which family ties are broken and restored or irretrievably severed, we note that there is a reluctance by the writers of these texts to propose or endorse an alternative familial arrangement to those that are conventionally experienced in society. Consequently, there remains a strong utopian impulse in all the texts to restore a collective destiny as a 'family' unit, regardless of the numerical combination of parents and children that comprise that unit. In the majority of the texts there is tendency to plot individuals on a path towards social subjectivity, in that the individual's actions and interactions outside the family provide a space for working through processes of identification and loss. It appears that at least within this chapter's sampling of critical dystopian narratives, family is represented as a social construct and a necessity, and as such it continues to function as an institutional site with differential power and emotional relations. Consequently, the utopian impulse remains strong, for when the individual moves away from the family and embarks on a journey that may be undertaken 'in fear and in unknown darkness', it invariably becomes a 'journey towards the light'.

8
The Struggle to be Human in a Posthuman World

Without relation, existence (if it is conceivable at all) would be a mean and miserable thing. We do not exist in order to relate; rather, we relate in order that we may exist as fully realized human beings.

N. Katherine Hayles, 'Flesh and Metal', 2002, p. 320

We live in a very peculiar time, in which more media circulate more information to more people than ever before, and yet when the phenomenon of 'disconnection' has never been more dramatically evident.

W. T. J. Mitchell, 'The Work of Art in the Age of Biocybernetic Reproduction', 2003, p. 490

Over the preceding chapters, we have discussed many possibilities for new world orders, some utopian but more often dystopian. One of the possibilities facing the world at the beginning of the twenty-first century is the prospect that we are entering a posthuman era in which many of the binary concepts used to make sense of experience in the past will no longer function. Western culture, dominated as it has been by liberal humanist principles, has traditionally been underpinned ideologically by binary oppositions between concepts such as natural and artificial, organic and technological, subject and object, body and mind, body and embodiment, real and virtual, presence and absence, and so on. Such binarisms have been increasingly critiqued, first by postmodernist deconstruction of how they function within Western culture as strategies of inclusion and exclusion, and second, through posthumanist reconceptualisations of the oppositional boundaries underpinning dominant conceptual paradigms. Thus, during the last few years a new range of concepts has begun increasingly to enter children's literature — the cyborg, virtual reality, technoculture, cloning, and genetic engineering. In short, children's books and films have begun responding to the posthuman, the focus of this chapter.

In children's literature so far, the prospect of a posthuman future is invariably aligned with notions of dystopia, shaped by a humanistic hesitation about or suspicion of the far-reaching ideological and social implications of those developments within information theory and cybernetics which have been driving 'posthumanism' since the 1940s. Such developments have impacted on how we think about the world, how we make sense of our experience, and, most significantly perhaps, what it means to be human in a world in which traditional conceptualisations of being 'human' have been increasingly problematised and rendered inadequate. Some commentators, recognising that human beings have been a relatively short-lived phenomenon in the Earth's history and seem intent on making that earth uninhabitable for themselves along with a vast number of other species, accept that humans are destined to be replaced by other more complex forms. From this perspective, the idea of a posthuman future is to be embraced and celebrated for the possibilities it opens up. For others, such a future is to be regarded with scepticism and fear, and the prospect of becoming 'posthuman' evokes antihuman and apocalyptic visions of the future (Hayles, 1999a, p. 283).

Clearly, the idea of a posthuman future has utopian and dystopian potentialities. Responses to such a future, both imagined and 'real', within popular culture, the media and academic and scientific discourses have canvassed both possibilities. The focus of this chapter is on narrative fictions for children and young people which engage with posthumanist visions of the human subject through the use of ideas and motifs derived from either imagined or real advances in informational technology, cybernetics, and biological and genetic manipulation, and use these ideas to imagine both utopian and dystopian futures. Such motifs have occurred in (adult) fantasy and futurist fictions since at least the 1940s, and gained increased popularity throughout the 1960s, 1970s and 1980s in mainstream adult and popular culture. Their penetration of children's genres, however, has been more recent — although there are some significant precursors, for example, Tanith Lee's *Silver Metal Lover* (1981) and Monica Hughes' *Devil on my Back* (1984). For many authors of narratives directed at young readers, the prospect of a posthuman future represents a dystopian state, and the possibility evokes technophobia. In general, such futurist texts then seek to determine what value might be posited against a metanarrative grounded in the end of human subjectivity, and that value is usually some (positive) sense of being human. This chapter will begin by mapping out some key posthumanist ideas and concepts, drawing principally upon Katherine Hayles' work (1999a), and will then go on to show how these relate to some key texts. Of particular interest are the ideological implications of these ideas, especially in relation to humanism and postmodernism and the pervasive way in which they have entered fictions and films for young people.

Posthumanism and humanism

Recent developments within informational technology have obviously changed radically the ways in which we experience and live in the world. Following Baudrillard, Bukatman defines the information age as 'an era in which the subject has become a "terminal of multiple networks"' (1993, p. 2), and borrowing from William Burroughs, he calls this new subjectivity 'terminal identity': 'an unmistakably doubled articulation in which we find both the end of the subject and a new subjectivity constructed at the computer station or television screen' (p. 8). While the term posthumanism encompasses much more than just computer technology, the computer terminal — and the multiple networks it comprises and is part of — has become a key symbolic image of posthumanism. As Hayles elaborates, the implicit doubleness in the concept of 'terminal identity' signals 'the end of traditional concepts of identity even as it points towards the cybernetic loop that generates a new kind of subjectivity' (1999a, p. 115). Hence, as with the antihumanist bent of postmodernism, posthumanism spells the 'end of the (humanist) subject'; at the same time, however, it also points towards renewal as it (re)conceives of a subjectivity utterly entwined with technology.

Hayles suggests that posthumanism is characterised by four assumptions. First, informational pattern is viewed as more significant than material instantiation (1999a, p. 2). An important, and quite old, distinction here is that between information as pattern or code and information as content or message. Cybernetics defines information as 'a theoretical entity' (1999a, p. 50), that is, as pattern 'defined by the probability distribution of the coding elements composing the message' (1999a, p. 25), rather than the presence, or absence, of content or meaning. Such a conceptualisation clearly privileges form and pattern over meaning, and the abstract and general over the concrete, material or particular, and it has implications for theories of language and human subjectivity, as well as life, the universe, and everything. In viewing pattern as more significant than material instantiation, information is 'conceptualised as an entity separate from the material forms in which it is thought to be embedded' (1999a, p. 2). In this sense, 'Information is given the dominant position' and embodiment is seen as 'the supplement to be purged, an accident of evolution' (1999a, p. 12). Thus, Hayles speaks of information as having 'lost its body' (1999a, p. 2). Cybernetics seeks to understand phenomena, including human beings, animals, and machines, as sets of informational processes, emphasising the underlying codes and patterns of information constituting human beings, for example the conceptualisation of neural structures as flows of information or individuals as strands of DNA code. Human beings are 'to be seen as ... information-processing entities', whose 'embodiment in a biological substrate is as an accident of history rather than an inevitability of life' (1999a, p. 2).

These kinds of ideas are played out in various ways in many contemporary texts. For example, in *Feed* (Anderson, 2002), a futuristic YA novel, an internet/television hybrid, or 'feed', is directly hardwired into people's brains, becoming the means by which information, especially advertising, is 'fed' directly to passive consumers whose subjectivity is thus utterly interpellated by technology in a way which clearly echoes Bukatman' image of 'terminal identity'. The 'feed', which has replaced both written and verbal forms of communication, that is, the material signifiers of language, further figures the disembodiment of information described by Hayles. Similarly, in *The House of the Scorpion* (Farmer, 2002), Matteo Alacran, the central protagonist, is valued for his status as a clone, and hence for the DNA coding which makes him a storehouse for the harvesting of future organs for his 'father', El Patron, of whom he is a facsimile. Ideas derived from information theory are also incorporated as structural devices and strategies within texts. The idea of a 'universal informational code underlying the structure of matter, energy and space-time' (Hayles, 1999a, p. 11) sees the world as a 'set of informationally closed systems' (p. 10), an image which has obvious possibilities for the conceptualisation of imaginary worlds and narratives as virtual realities which parallel and intersect with the 'real'.

A second assumption characterising the posthuman perspective is that consciousness is to be regarded as an 'epiphenomenon', a late development within the evolutionary process (Hayles, 1999a, pp. 2–3). Liberal humanism, grounded in Cartesian concepts of subjectivity, has traditionally considered consciousness as the seat of human identity. The humanist subject is characterised by an ideology of the self (and hence individual consciousness) as being essential and unique, and thereby possessing agency. In contrast, the posthuman subject is viewed as 'an amalgam, a collection of heterogenous components, a material-informational entity whose boundaries undergo continuous construction and reconstruction' (Hayles, 1999a, p. 3). In general, posthuman subjectivity is represented as fragmented, decentred, tenuous, constructed, hybridised, and enacted or performed.

There are obvious affinities and intersections between the posthuman deconstruction of the humanist subject and that performed by feminism, postcolonialism, and postmodernism (Hayles, 1999a, p. 4; Simon, 2003, p. 3). The image of the posthuman subject as an 'amalgam of heterogenous components' echoes the fragmented and dispersed postmodern subject. Both approaches also problematise the notions of agency intrinsic to humanist ideologies. However, as Hayles argues, 'embodiment has been systematically downplayed or erased within the cybernetic construction of the posthuman in ways that have not occurred in other critiques of the liberal humanist subject' (1999a, p. 4). And it is this feature, the erasure of embodiment and concomitant privileging of cognition, which gives the posthuman its specifically *posthumanist* turn, precisely because it is a feature common to both posthumanism and humanism, the latter having enacted a split between mind and body by identifying subjectivity with consciousness (and hence cognition). Both humanism and posthumanism share an emphasis on cognition, but posthumanist conceptualisations of the subject problematise the link between cognition and agency that underpins humanist notions of agential subjectivity. A key problem, then, is how to define and articulate notions of agency within a posthuman context (Hayles, 1999a, p. 5). Such a problematic has an explicitly ethical dimension as concepts such as human judgement and responsibility hinge on the possibility of conscious agency. Hence posthumanism raises questions about human responsibility, especially in the context of underlying fears about technology and science 'taking over' and human beings 'losing control' through either abdication of responsibility or irresponsible uses of science and technology. Again, such ideas are played out in many contemporary fictions and films. Questions about human responsibility are central to all of the texts to be discussed later in this chapter: *Feed* (Anderson, 2002), *Eager* (Fox, 2003), *Ferren and the Angel* (Harland, 2000), *Artificial Intelligence: A.I.* (Spielberg, 2001), *Only You Can Save Mankind* (Pratchett, 1992), *Virtual War* (Skurzynski, 1997), *Virtual Sexual Reality* (Rayban, 1994) and *Noah and Saskia* (Anastassiades et al., 2004).

The critique of modernism enabled by postmodern discourses was also inherently a critique of humanism, especially the humanist subject. The ideological dimension of posthumanism represents a convergence of that critique with the social and cultural implications of developments within informational technology. In a sense, then, posthumanism signals a shift of focus onto what was really at stake in postmodern discussions of 'the end of the subject', and hence a much larger paradigm shift which has ethical, as well as ideological, implications. As Ihab Hassan suggested, 'five hundred years of humanism may be coming to an end as humanism transforms itself into something we must helplessly call the posthuman' (1977, p. 212). Such a transformation signals a shift in the dominant Western metaethic from liberal humanism to something which can only be called 'posthumanism', a cultural paradigm which 'comes after', engages with, and potentially recuperates and reinstates humanism while at the same time enabling a reconceptualisation of what that concept entails. Thus, as many posthuman theorists have argued, posthumanism has an ethical imperative, which, while not lacking in postmodernist discourses, was not always acknowledged. Hence the idea of 'critical posthumanism', defined as 'a general critical space in which the techno-cultural forces which both produce and undermine the stability of the categories of "human" and "nonhuman", can be investigated' (Waldby, 2000, p. 43), has recently emerged and offers a useful addition to the concept of transformative utopianism. Donna Haraway (1991) has further argued that the posthuman constitutes a unique type of politics, challenging the ways in which the relationships between human and nonhumans, and biology and technology, are all regulated. Such ethical concerns are the context for posthumanist ideas articulated in fiction for young people, a literature inextricably grounded by ethical considerations in its engagement with social practice. This does not necessarily mean that such texts are any more conservative than others, but the more overt ethical concerns of a novel such as *Eager*, for example, does give the fiction a critical dimension which in general precludes both the uncritical embracing of posthuman utopias, and the equally uncritical condemnation of posthuman dystopias, pointing instead towards visions of a reconceptualised and transformed (post)human world.

A third assumption characterising the posthuman perspective, and which follows from the idea that human beings are 'information-processing devices', is that the body is to be thought of 'as the original prosthesis we all learn to manipulate, so that extending or replacing the body with other prostheses becomes a continuation of a process that began before birth' (Hayles, 1999a, p. 3). The epitome of such cyborg beings appears in Reeve's 'Hungry Cities' tetralogy, whose most intelligent Stalkers link to the fourth, and final, assumption — the view which 'configures human being so that it can be seamlessly articulated with intelligent machines' (Hayles, 1999a, p. 3). As 'information processing entities', human beings are seen as '*essentially* similar to intelligent machines' (p. 7). Thus, 'in the posthuman there are no essential differences or absolute demarcations between bodily existence and computer simulation, cybernetic mechanism and biological organism, robot teleology and human goals' (p. 3). The implications of these ideas are wide-ranging, and they are articulated in literary and popular culture especially through cyborg, robot and android figures, and self-evolving computer programs.

Key texts which utilise posthuman ideas and motifs fall broadly into three groups according to thematic and story motifs: narratives about robotics and artificial intelligence; narratives about genetic engineering, cloning, and cybernetics; and (to date, the smallest group) virtual reality narratives. Needless to say, however, there are common thematic and ideological concerns and narrative strategies which cut across the three groups.

Artificial intelligence and robotics — *Eager* and *artificial intelligence*

Narratives about robotics and artificial intelligence, such as Spielberg's *Artificial Intelligence* (*A.I.*) and Fox's *Eager*, raise questions about what might constitute human subjectivity, as the shape of a world to come is narrated in the context of key metanarratives which seek to scrutinise what it is to be human through representations of mechanoid experience and perceptions. Such representations offer a hypothetical position of outsidedness and hence otherness from which to examine and re-evaluate the known and familiar human world. Both texts centre on, and are substantially focalised by, mechanoid 'child' figures who have been programmed with 'human' characteristics — David, the protagonist of *A.I.*, has been programmed with the capacity for 'love', while Eager has been programmed with the ability to learn. Both are essentially modelled on concepts of the human child: 'love' as it is defined within the narrative of *A.I.* is conceived as the unconditional love a young child has for, and expects from, his/her parent; the capacity for learning in *Eager* is modelled on a conception of child-learning which sees the child as actively and responsively learning through language and through engagement with the physical world within a familial social environment. Such conceptions of the human child shape the central mechanoid characters and give each narrative its peculiar ideological bent. As always in narratives about artificial intelligence, however, notions of cognition and consciousness are central to conceptions of 'the human' and, hence, of the possibilities for artificial intelligence and life. Being is always in some way equated with consciousness and perception (both physical and emotional).

A.I. tells the story of David, a mechanoid 'child' who has been programmed with human sentience, specifically, the capacity to feel love. David is abandoned by his adoptive human 'mother', Monica, and wanders a dystopian, environmentally, and socially decaying Earth in search of 'home' and 'mother'. His quest to be a 'real' boy, and for his mother's love, is overtly unfolded as a replay of the stories of both Pinocchio and Frankenstein. After escaping destruction at a 'Flesh Fair' — a fair at which Mechanoids are ritualistically destroyed for the entertainment of humans — David sets off in search of (Pinocchio's) Blue Fairy, whom he finds in Coney Island in a now submerged 'Manhattan, the lost ciy at the end of the world where the lions weep ... and dreams are born'. Like *Frankenstein*, the film closes in an arctic wasteland setting, with David's quest only partially resolved. At the close of the film, after being frozen in ice for 2000 years, he is reactivated in a world in which humans have been replaced by mechanoids possessing a range of extraordinary powers, but not the power to create life. David can never become a real boy and his 'mother' can only be brought back to life for a day, but he does at least finally receive her unconditional love for that last day of her life. The ending of the film enacts a paradigm shift described by Hayles, from an 'artificial intelligence' paradigm — which in aiming to build a consciousness comparable to human consciousness within a machine (such as David) uses human subjectivity and consciousness as a measure — to an 'artificial life' paradigm — which in aiming to evolve intelligence within a machine (such as the mechanoids at the close of *A.I.*) reconfigures human intelligence so that the machine becomes the model for understanding the human (see Hayles, 1999a, pp. 238–9). Indeed, the film itself enacts a kind of thought experiment in which the story of a machine becomes a way of exploring notions of human subjectivity and love.

The love which David is programmed to give is more than just imitation or replication of human sensory response, but a capacity for affective response towards another being. There are two significant characteristics about the way in which love is defined here. First, it is modelled explicitly on the unconditional love a child feels for its parents, and, more implicitly, that which a parent feels for his/her child. Significantly, as the film unfolds, both types of love are disclosed as being solipsistic in nature, and, ultimately, in Lacanian terms, as unfulfilled desire and absence: both are loves which 'will never end' precisely because they have their roots in the pre-oedipal, pre-mirror stage parent/child bond and hence can never be regained or, in David's case, fulfilled. The problem for David is that he is created to be a child. He will live and remain a child forever; hence, he will never 'grow up', but remain forever driven by this need to compensate for the loss he experiences when Monica abandons him. For his surrogate parents, Professor Hobby and Monica, he is a copy, a simulacrum, of a child they have lost; hence their motives in creating and adopting him are grounded in the desire to regain that arrested pre-oedipal child/parent bond. That David's 'love' for Monica is at its heart solipsistic is made clearest in the final moments of the film when she has been brought to life again to exist entirely for him: 'all the problems seemed to have disappeared from his mummy's mind. There was no Henry, no Martin. There was no grief. There was only David'.

A second feature of love in the film is that it is conceived of as 'the key' by which, in the words of Dr. Hobby, David's creator, a mechanoid can 'acquire a subconscious, an inner world of metaphor, of intuition, of self-motivated reasoning, of dreams'.[1] It is 'love' that motivates David's desire to find the blue fairy or, in other words, to desire, again in the Lacanian sense, the unattainable, and to believe in a dream, that is, a fiction. Desire and belief are 'flaws' because they can not be achieved, but at the same time 'gifts' because they enable dreams and the capacity for subconscious thought. And it is this capacity for desire and belief, and hence the subconscious, which ultimately the film defines as being essentially 'human'.

A key difference between 'robots' as they are imagined in *A.I.* and in *Eager* is their relationship with human beings and the purposes for which they have been designed. A central source of conflict propelling the narrative in the first half of *A.I.* is the threat that robots as a 'species' pose to the human race in a dystopian world of rapidly diminishing resources — by the close of the film this threat has been fulfilled with the extinction of humans. The potential for robot, android, and cyborg figures to express cultural anxieties and beliefs about technology and to disrupt and blur traditional binarisms, such as human and machine, animate and inanimate, has been remarked upon by many writers about mainstream popular and adult science fiction literature and film (for example, see Haraway, 1991). One effect of placing viewers in a position from which the world is perceived from the point of view of a robot who seems uncannily 'real' in appearance, behaviour, and perception is that the human audience is consistently asked to identify against itself throughout the film. If, as Scott suggests, 'we fall for David, and ... side with his mechanical brethren against their human oppressors, are we affirming our humanity or have we been irrevocably alienated from it?' (2001, p. 2; see also W. J. T. Mitchell, 2003). Robot figures, especially when they function as focalising characters within a narrative, destabilise boundaries between self, other, and world, and hence raise questions about 'humanness' and human subjectivity. And *A.I.* also uses the common strategy of depicting such figures as more feeling (or 'human') than their human counterparts, and human characters as more unfeeling (and hence 'mechanical' or inhuman) than robots. A key effect of sequences structured around differences between David and other 'human' characters is to contrast David's childlike vulnerability and incomprehension of the adult/human world with human characters' inhumanity and lack of compassion or altruism.

The conflict between humans and robots in *Eager* is more diffuse. As in *A.I.*, robots have been designed and built to perform tasks otherwise performed by humans, but the society of *Eager* is only really beginning to imagine the possibility of a new world order in which robots might replicate and replace human beings. Like *A.I.*, *Eager* invokes the story of Frankenstein's 'monster' in its contrast between different types of robot (p. 270). Robots like Grumps, the Bell family's Butler robot, represent the 'old-fashioned' type of robot: they can move, talk, think, reason, and learn, but have been designed and produced to perform particular tasks, such as cleaning, preparing meals, and babysitting, as in Grumps' case. There are two new types of robot: the prototype robot, Eager, who has been programmed to learn as a child does through imitation, experience, language, and understanding, and to feel emotion; and the BDC4 series who have been programmed with actual human memories and hence understand humans because they have memories of human life. Both types of robot have been freed from science fiction writer Isaac Asimov's 'three laws of robotics which stipulate that robots cannot harm or deceive people,[2] but the implications for each are quite different. The two types of new robot, Eager and the BDC4s, actually narrativise the so-called Turing and Morevec tests. In the Turing test the responses from two computer terminals are used to decide which of two entities in another room is human and which is machine — Eager's construction within the narrative as a thinking, feeling, perceiving being ascribes him with a subjectivity comparable to, if not indistinguishable in nature from, that of his human counterparts. The Morevec Test, which toyed with the possibility that human consciousness could be downloaded into a computer and hence that machines could be the repository of human consciousness, underpins the idea of transferring human memory into a robot. Eager has been designed to learn for himself, as a child does, from his experiences, and make his own decisions. In modelling artificial life on such a fundamentally humanist ethic, Eager exemplifies that artificial life may still be life *as we know it*. In contrast, the assumption in designing the BDC4s was that the learning process could be circumvented — if actual human memory networks were simply transferred into a robot's brain then such robots would also understand human life without having to be programmed, and hence share human understanding of right and wrong. The assumption of the Morevec test that consciousness and subjectivity could exist, unchanged, independently of material lived bodily experience also informs the scientists' actions in the novel, and, here, proves incorrect. The BDC4s are 'neither humans nor robots... only machines replaying human memories, memories that were no longer part of them' (p. 287), and they are eventually driven insane by those memories. The negative example of the BDC4s thus reinscribes the link between consciousness and subjectivity and embodiment.

Point of view strategies used in *Eager* and *A.I.*, whereby the narrative is significantly focalised by a mechanoid character, serve to highlight both ethical and philosophical issues. These are touched on in the opening scene of *A.I.* where, following Professor Hobby's proposal to build a robot who can love, one of the other scientists responds: 'But isn't the real conundrum, can you get a human to love them [robots] back? If a robot can genuinely love a human being, what responsibility does that person hold towards that Mecha in return?'. The question, of course, presupposes a love that is not self-serving or solipsistic, but instead one that is altruistic and dynamic, and it is a question which remains implicit and ultimately unanswered throughout the film. Ethical questions about the responsibility which human beings might have towards their own creations are treated much more overtly in *Eager*, as are philosophical questions about the nature of being. Strategies used to imply point of view in prose narrative highlight the extent to which Eager is a thinking, feeling, 'real' being. The narrative presents him as if he were a human being and, as the distinction between the human and nonhuman begins to dissolve, what we imagine as 'natural' feelings are attributed to the machine. The question remains, however, as to whether Eager is incipiently human or whether his programming constructs a monologue of perceptions which create the illusion of a coherent and unified self.

Strictly speaking, the BDC4s are cyborgs, not robots: that is, they are hybrid beings which are an amalgam of cybernetic and organic components. On the whole, such hybrid forms of being are treated in YA fiction and film negatively, usually as aberrations, and social commentary tends to be much fiercer and more satirical in tone.

Cybernetics and biological engineering

Narratives about cybernetics, biological and genetic engineering, and cloning depict the merging of organic material with either mechanical or scientifically and/or genetically engineered components. In general, such narratives have a concern with social responsibility in the wake of scientific advances in biotechnology and genetics. Up to the present time, children's fictions have rarely taken a utopian or positive view of cybernetic or genetic engineering. Where these motifs occur in fiction they are normally in conjunction with dystopian worlds, which, through parallels with contemporary culture, function as critiques of that culture. Most fictions of this type have positive closures, pointing towards the possibility of a renewed, transformed world to emerge from the dystopian images of the future through the opportunities afforded by personal relationships and dialogic exchange.

Norbert Weiner's visions for the cybernetic subject are pertinent here. Weiner 'scripted' the cybernetic subject into a cosmological drama of chaos and order, in which the 'good' cybernetic machine, envisioned in the image of the humanistic self, reinforced the autonomous liberal humanist subject, and the 'evil' cybernetic machine undermined and destroyed the autonomy of that subject (see Hayles, 1999a, pp. 86, 100). As Hayles explains, Weiner's script is underpinned by the second Law of Thermodynamics, which states that entropy tends to increase in a closed system. Thus closed systems, such as the universe, tend to move from order to randomness. These ideas have, of course, informed many imagined social formations, which, as closed systems, are depicted as being subject to decay as entropy increases — for example, *Castrovalva*, a 1980s episode of *Dr. Who*. For Weiner, 'the dominance of the machine presupposes a society in the last stages of increasing entropy' (qtd. in Hayles, 1999a, p. 105); as Hayles suggests, Weiner's 'nightmare was the human reduced to a cog in a rigid machine' (1999a, p. 140), a vision which has been replicated and embellished by many science fiction and film writers.

Feed and *Ferren and the Angel* focus on cybernetic and technological engineering. Both novels examine how identity is constituted within futuristic dystopian societies where the human body is routinely assimilated with technological and cybernetic components, and both are quite savage indictments of societies which develop an irresponsible attitude towards the use of technology in ways which reduce human beings to resources, products, or consumers. *Feed* is an ironic satire on consumer culture and, like *Eager*, this novel expresses a cynicism towards corporate and media dominated culture. The 'feed' with which most people in this future new world order are equipped constantly bombards individuals with an array of advertisements specifically tailored to their demographic, and is controlled by large corporations which, aiming to create a society of homogenous consumers, seek to deny individual subjectivity. In this way, individuals are quite explicitly interpellated by technology as passive consumers of global capitalism. *Ferren and the Angel* pivots on choice and agency, and its thematic focus on debates about subjectivity and the rise of the posthuman reflects the 'culture wars' of the late twentieth century. It is a post-disaster novel set in the year 3000 CE in a radically dystopian Earth populated by cyborgs, or 'Humen', who are engaged in an on-going war with Heaven, and Residuals (i.e. remaining human beings), who live in scattered small tribes in a primitive and ignorant state, and are subject to the tyranny of the Humen. The Humen are constructed as inherently evil and cruel, and as distinctly 'inhuman'. This is illustrated most clearly by their cannibalistic habit of injecting themselves with the brain matter of unfortunate Residuals who on displaying intellect or imagination are marked out as 'different' and 'selected' by the Humen for 'military service'; remaining tissue and organs are then used in the creation of 'Plasmatics', or hybrid organic machines. Extrapolating forward to a world rendered largely uninhabitable as a consequence of the ideology, economics, and practices of a materialistic society, the narrative seeks a dialogical relationship between spirit and flesh, as the angel of the novel's title, Miriael, takes on the physical being and concerns of humanity, while Ferren, a Residual human and the 'thinker' in his brutalised tribe, recuperates humanity and agency through an archetypal heroic quest narrative.

In both novels, language plays a pivotal role in the depiction of a dystopian posthuman society. In each, metonymies for a dying, or degenerate, world are figured verbally by a representation of the death, or degeneration, of language. The decay of language in *Ferren and the Angel* is represented as symptomatic of the decay of civilisation and culture, and the loss of subjective agency. The treatment of language in *Feed* is perhaps more subtle. The novel opens with a quotation from Auden's 'Anthem for St. Cecilia's Day' — 'O dear white children casual as birds, Playing among the ruined languages' — and in its lament for the decay of language it strangely echoes Hayles' discussion of the function of language for post-war cybernetic theorists:

If what is exactly stated can be done by a machine, the residue of the uniquely human becomes coextensive with the linguistic qualities that interfere with precise specification — ambiguity, metaphoric play, multiple encoding, and allusive exchanges between one symbol system and another. The uniqueness of human behaviour thus becomes assimilated to the ineffability of language, and the common ground that humans and machines share is identified with the univocality of an instrumental language that has banished ambiguity from its lexicon (1999a, p. 67).

The idea that the 'residue of the uniquely human' might be correlated with 'the ineffability of language' underpins the behaviour of the father of one of the central characters, a college professor who teaches the 'dead language' of print culture and 'tries to speak entirely in weird words and irony, so no one can simplify anything he says' (p. 151). In this future society, advances in communication technology have actually disabled communication, producing a society disempowered by inarticulacy. Extending the contemporary abuse of SMS and email, few people talk out loud because everyone 'chats' over the 'feednets', and reading and writing have become redundant. Language here has become not merely 'univocal and instrumental', but nonfunctional — as Violet's father recognises, the only way to say anything complex is to reinstate ambiguity and irony.

Feed also engages with and critiques the posthuman concept of subjectivity as fragmented and tenuous. A destabilised sense of identity is a normalised part of life with teenage protagonists willing to surrender their individuality for the sake of marketing trends and fashions communicated through the feed. For example, because cultural status is measured by consumer goods, Marty obtains a Nike 'speech tattoo' (p. 291) which forces him to say the word 'Nike' in every sentence he utters, thus epitomising the extent to which subjectivity is interpellated by technology in this society. Not only do individuals willingly submit to identity lobotomies which render them inarticulate and a walking product endorsement, but they are happy to pay for the privilege. Further, the encroaching role of technology is correlated with a blurring of distinctions between nature and artifice — air is produced in factories (trees being too inefficient) (p. 139), meat is artificially grown on 'steak farms' (p. 156) and whales are laminated in order for them to survive in polluted oceans (p. 294).

Feed closes with the death of Violet, one of the main protagonists, and as she dies her boyfriend, Titus, merely gazes solipsistically at his own reflection in her eyes; unlike most heroes in YA novels, he has failed to mature or learn anything from his experiences. Thematically, the novel echoes Weiner's vision of the 'evil' cybernetic machine: the society of *Feed* is in the latter stages of increasing entropy and cybernetics has destroyed the autonomy of the human subject. In contrast *Ferren and the Angel* develops a more positive response to the prospect of a posthuman subjectivity. This novel depicts a future Earth that has been devastated and, for the most part, laid waste by war. The war waged by the Humen with Heaven is essentially a battle between science (as represented by the Humen and the Doctors who have created them) and religion (as personified by the Angels), and as the story is dual-focalised by the 'fallen' angel Miriael and the Residual Ferren, reader alignment is firmly situated against not just the cyborgs, but also the higher Angels of Heaven, who abandon Miriael to her earthly and material fate. While the Angels are portrayed as spiritual beings, the Heaven of this future cosmos is one lacking conventional (Christian) notions of spirituality. Heaven has, in a sense, been corrupted through Earth's invasion and war, and there is no sense in the novel of traditional (Christian humanist) religious concepts of forgiveness or redemption — instead, this is a heaven of the Old Testament, intent on moral justice.

The dynamic of Miriael and Ferren's relationship is complex. On the one hand, it mediates the hostility with which the concept of biotechnology is presented by complicating the more usual (binary) conflict between human being (the Residuals) and machine (the Humen). The war with Heaven incorporates a spiritual dimension into the human/machine binarism which blurs the boundaries between what is 'natural' and 'artificial'. As disembodied consciousness, Miriael, the fallen angel, parallels the posthuman subject as it is figured by the cyborg, that is, as consciousness transferred to, or re-embodied within, a machine. On the other hand, the developing intersubjectivity of Ferren and Miriael also reconfigures Cartesian mind/body and spirit/flesh dualisms. Just as his 'naturalness' (and hence humanity) contrasts with the Humen's artificiality (and lack of humanity), Ferren's material bodily existence initially suggests a contrast with Miriael's supernatural incorporeal existence. The conventional mind/body dualisms implied are undercut, however, partially through the characterisation of Ferren as

the intellectual in his tribe, but also through Miriael's gradual material-
isation and physical embodiment. Ferren is clearly differentiated from
his peers as being imaginative, intelligent, thoughtful, and as having
regard for others — in a move utterly conventional of the YA novel,
Ferren is represented as the 'sensitive new man' in contrast to his
more 'macho' male peers, who spend their evenings drinking fermented
sunflower liquor and brawling.

Miriael's transformation in the novel is dramatic, serving to revalue
key humanist concepts, in particular the capacity for altruism or regard
for others, a sense of the materiality of lived bodily experience, with
an emphasis on sensual experience, and agential subjectivity. Alienated
from Heaven and hence rendered abject, Miriael must reconstruct her
subjectivity, a reconstruction which proceeds along a trajectory from
self-centredness to altruism. Initially, she is appalled by her physical
transformation. However, as she takes on a physical being or form, she
also takes on the concerns of humanity, expressing a compassion and
feeling for others which her fellow angels seem to either lack or to have
lost. She finds herself compelled to know more about the Residuals, the
human race, and its war with Heaven. That knowledge, while intended
to convince her of the wickedness of Earth and hence encourage her
to 'lift [her] thoughts to the goodness of Heaven', actually deepens her
sympathy for the Residuals and drags her back to Earth (pp. 248–9),
implying a correlation between the assumption of a physical body and
lived bodily experience, and a sense of altruism and benevolence. In
order to truly understand human beings such as Ferren, she needs to
experience what it is like to be embodied, what it means to be human,
and, as in *Feed*, embodiment and lived experience is presented as having
intrinsic value, and as an essential part of being human.

Further, and perhaps most significantly, Miriael's transformation
involves a positive revaluation of agential subjectivity. Initially, she
attempts to regain spiritual transcendence through fasting, prayer, and
meditation, but realises that she is simply going to die as a physical being
rather than change back into a spiritual being, and so decides to break
her fast and remain on earth as a materialised angel (pp. 261–2). As the
Archangel Uriel explains to Miriael, while Heaven has good reasons for
destroying her at this point (because her mind contains secret strategies
which will endanger Heaven), Heaven is still bound by ethical laws
which forbid the destruction of the innocent (p. 263). Thus, a great
battle is planned by Heaven, which will make Miriael's information of
no further importance (p. 264). Having been told this by Uriel, Miriael
asks, '[a]nd what becomes of me?', and is told in reply, 'Whatever you

make happen. Your fate is in your hands now...You have chosen your form of existence. You must no longer look for help from Heaven' (p. 264). Thus, in a moment of secular humanist assertion, Miriael is cast adrift from Heaven and, like humanity of the 'first fall', left with only her own desire and capacity for subjective agency, the capacity to make decisions based on a sense of moral reason and to act on them. Accordingly, the novel closes with Miriael and Ferren persuading the rest of the People to transcend their subjected and dehumanised state, rise up against their oppressors, and live autonomously once more. The relationship between Ferren and Miriael, in its positive revaluation of both spirituality and bodily experience, alongside traditional humanist concepts such as agency, imagination, altruism, and so on, implies a vision of a transformed human world, a reconceptualisation of what it means to be human, which incorporates aspects of liberal humanism but also moves beyond them.

The positive possibility of a transformed world to emerge from dystopian images of the future is also common to narratives which incorporate forms of biological engineering, such as *The House of the Scorpion* and *Virtual War*. In general, children's texts of the late twentieth and early twenty-first centuries have been more comfortable with the creation of artificial intelligence than with the possibility of genetically modified human beings. Where the latter appears in fiction it is normally within a representation of a dystopian world, as in *Virtual War* and *The House of the Scorpion* (see Stephens, 2006a), although in these cases point of view is rendered more complex because both novels centre on and are narrated from the viewpoint of characters who are the products of cloning and genetic engineering. Matt, the principal character in *The House of the Scorpion* is a clone, whose purpose, as he eventually discovers, is to be a reservoir of body parts, especially his heart, for El Patron, his 'original', who is also the ruler of Opium, a country that lies between the United States and Aztlan, formerly Mexico. Matt is regarded by other characters as 'livestock', not 'human'; the novel opens with a description of his production from frozen cells, presenting this process not as the creation of a human being, although human attributes are invoked, but as a production line. Corgan, the principal character in *Virtual War*, is a 14-year-old test-tube baby, who has been genetically engineered with the sole purpose of fighting an eight-hour scientifically controlled 'virtual war'. Set in 2080 CE, *Virtual War* envisages a world rendered largely uninhabitable by nuclear war, 'the next two Chernobyl accidents' (p. 15) and multiple diseases, where remnant population lives in domed cities within three political federations, the

Western Hemisphere, the Eurasian Alliance, and the Pan Pacific Coalition. The 'war' is to be fought with virtual soldiers over possession of the Central Pacific Isles of Hiva (formerly the Marquesas) which have been declared decontaminated and safe for occupation, and Corgan, alongside two other genetically engineered characters, represents the Western Hemisphere. Like *Feed* and *Ferren and the Angel*, both novels focus on questions of the social implications of such technological advances, especially the reduction of human life to a product or resource. And in both, the way forward towards negotiating a 'new world order' lies in the revaluation of the cognitive and affective domains of experience. The fact that Matt, for example, is a copy, a simulacrum of another human being, does not diminish his own experience of being in the world and hence his humanity. *Virtual War* is also exemplary of a third group of posthuman texts, that is, virtual reality narratives, which we consider in the last section of this chapter.

Information technologies and virtual reality narratives

To date, virtual reality narratives are the smallest group of posthuman texts for children, although as computer technology becomes progressively more innovative and pervasive within everyday life, narratives incorporating themes and motifs associated with imagined and real information technologies are becoming increasingly popular.[3] Such narratives utilise the potential for computer technology to construct virtual realities which parallel, simulate, intersect with or constitute an alternative to 'real' lived experience, and thus function as utopian or dystopian heterotopias. As Kraus and Auer (2000) suggest, 'ever more sophisticated information technologies based on the computer as *the* simulacrum par excellence have offered us powerful new means of manipulating data — consequently, means of editing, "hacking" and inventing "reality"' (p. 1). Insofar as the virtual exists as informational code, a form of life (Hayles, 1999a, p. 11), it is also both a simulated model of the real and a simulacrum, that is, a 'hyperreal', an image which has 'no relation to any reality whatsoever... [and] is its own pure simulacrum' (Baudrillard, p. 6). Most children's texts dealing with virtual realities contextualise them within a recognisable representation of a 'real' world, but by breaching the boundaries between the virtual and the real they raise questions about the relationships between the lived embodied, or materially instantiated, world of experience and the virtual reality of information. Such questions have implications for the representation of subjectivity and of the place and function of information technology in society in general. The television series *Noah and Saskia* and Terry Pratchett's novel *Only You Can Save Mankind* (1992) are very different kinds of texts, but both are playful, comic, and irreverent explorations of ethical questions which the use of computer technologies in contemporary society raises. In *Noah and Saskia*, the central characters communicate from opposite sides of the world through avatars in an internet chatroom. Both construct online personas for themselves, but representation of the real and the virtual is further complicated by the multiplication of diegetic levels of narrative and by their own constructions of each other; despite its playfulness, the series ultimately has a serious concern with ethical issues arising from the construction of virtual and real identities. *Only You Can Save Mankind* is a fantasy novel which also uses multiple diegetic levels to narrativise some of the implications of the use of computer simulation in the military and entertainment industries. Set during the 1991 Gulf War, the novel centres on the efforts of Johnny Maxwell to help a group of aliens in a computer game out of game space before they are all destroyed by other players, and in representing humanity from the (alien) viewpoint of the other, the novel also explores complex philosophical questions relating to what it might mean to be a human being in a world in which humans are still waging wars and doing so in increasingly dehumanised ways.

Breaches of the boundaries between the materiality of lived experience and the illusion of virtual reality have ambivalent implications for subjectivity: the 'subject that can occupy or intersect with the cyberspaces of contemporary existence' (Bukatman, p. 8) can figure both a dystopian dissolution or disembodiment of the subject within the virtual, the 'death of the subject' and a utopian vision of the self as 'distributed cognition', a new subjectivity (Hayles, pp. 290–1). As many commentators have suggested, in the disembodied world of cyberspace identity can be ambiguous. The absence of geographical borders and restrictions characterising the Internet enables the construction of virtual identities at least less dependent on conventional markers of class, gender, and sexuality; hence, online identity can be shifting, fragmentary, a construction, and, potentially, a deception, as the central characters in *Noah and Saskia* find. An ACTF production set in Melbourne and London, the series brings the two characters together via the Internet. In Australia, Saskia, a musician who can't perform in front of an audience, posts one of her songs on a website in the hope of getting feedback. The song is stolen by an 'internet geek called "Max Hammer"' who has used it as the soundtrack for his web-based comic and Saskia sets out to find his identity by gaining entry to the 'invitation only' Max Hammer site. Once in the virtual cyberspace reality of Webweave, Saskia, having created an avatar for herself called Indy, meets Max and promptly falls for him when he offers to use her music in his comic. Max Hammer is of course Noah, a teenage English boy. The series proceeds by alternating between the two physical settings, with each alternate episode focusing on each character, and is centrally concerned with notions of identity and subjectivity and how these might be problematised by the apparent freedom offered by the Internet to 'be whoever you want to be'.

The series uses a range of mixed media and representational strategies which play with and blur the boundaries between the 'real', the 'virtual', and the 'imagined'. It combines live action and computer generated animation, ranging from the comic book style animation of Noah's 'Hammer's Heroes' to the use of computer simulated graphics alongside a 'real' football game (Episode 2), complete with 'player profiles' and simulated analysis accompanied by commentary by Martin Taylor and Andy Green (voiced by Martin Tyler and Andy Gray, actual English and Scottish football commentators). The live action footage also combines conventional realist film techniques with strategies which disrupt the illusion of realism, such as montage, rapid cutting between scenes, jerky handheld camera styles, and direct address to camera. The narrative structure is also complicated by the construction of multiple diegetic levels, or alternative realities. These comprise: the 'real' worlds of London and Melbourne; webweave (an online environment comprising various sites); Noah's comic (itself based on Noah's 'real life' family); and the fantasy worlds of Noah and Saskia. Both characters create an avatar represented visually as a cartoon-image. While chatting online in private, however, both are depicted by real-life actors, but the actors playing each character vary depending on which character is the focus of the episode (and is by implication the primary focaliser for that episode), as does the physical setting. In episodes centreing on Saskia, Max is played by Cameron Nugent, a young Australian actor, and the setting is contemporary Melbourne; Noah in London, however, is played by Jack Blumeneu. Likewise, Saskia is played by Hannah Greenwood, but in episodes centering on Noah where she appears as Indy, the actress is Maria Papas. Furthermore, the conversations between Indy and Noah take place in the concentration camp like setting of Noah's comic world, behind barbed wire fences against a red sky. An implication of this switching between different actors is that the 'real' life actors playing Indy and Max are each Noah and Saskia's imagined construction of the other, an implication given impetus by the ways in which Nugent and Papas are dressed and overact their characters: Max (Nugent) is the almost archetypal tall, blonde, suntanned Australian youth, who peers over the his sunglasses as he flirts with Saskia; Indy (Papas) is tall, slim, dark-haired and like Max, very sexy and flirtatious and the series constantly contrasts the artificial sophistication of Max and Indy with Noah and Saskia's more 'realistic' ordinariness. In this way, each of the two central characters has three visual images upon which to hang ideas about who that character is, none of which correspond exactly. The multiplication of identity clearly problematises the issue of subjectivity within real, virtual, or imagined worlds.

This kind of play with the possibilities virtual realities offer for multiplying and problematising identity also occurs in Chloe Rayban's *Virtual Sexual Reality*, a comic fantasy novel which explores the relation between identity and gender constructions through the fantastic possibilities that computer simulation potentially offers. Justine enters an 'alternative reality' booth at a Virtual Reality Exhibition where she constructs a new male image of herself, and having selected the 'Copy', 'Keep', and 'Switch' options at the end of the session, exits the booth as 'Jake', her male counterpart. In a slightly predictable way, much of the narrative is then taken up with Justine/Jake's learning and reflecting on appropriate 'male' social behaviours, but the novel has an added plot complication whereby Justine's identity is doubled. Justine doesn't just become Jake; her female self still exists (though the narration is by Jake) and when the two selves meet, Justine narcissistically falls for her 'virtual' male self.

On the surface, *Noah and Saskia*, with its use of mixed media, strategies which destabilise audience positioning, engagement with contemporary technology and the issues it raises, and playful mockery of British and Australian myths of identity, stereotypes, and imperialist ideologies enabled by the dual geographical and social settings, appears quite a radical children's television text. At the same time, however, the series centres on child/adult and self/other relationships, and there emerges out of its playful, irreverent treatment of conventional notions of nationalism, gender, class and power a concern with many of those (humanist) issues central to children's texts in general — notions of identity and subjectivity, the central role and place of the family within society, the need for children to move out of solipsism, the value of democratic forms of social organisation, and ethical issues such the idea of being true to oneself. The series makes its (humanist) concerns with identity quite overt through the lyrics of the theme song 'Be who you want to be', with its refrain 'Show me, if you know me, that you see who

I want to be'. As the website blurb for the program puts it: 'Noah and *Saskia* is about a little lie that leads to a bigger truth — that who you are is usually who you want to be'. Ostensibly, the blurb implies that individuals are free to carve out what ever kind of image of themselves they feel like; there is, however, a humanist metaethic underpinning this metanarrative which asserts, at least implicitly, that 'what I want to be' is 'who I (really) am' and, furthermore, is governed by basic principles of honesty.

Responses to information technology in general within popular, intellectual, and political discourses have tended to oscillate between two extremes, with representations of cyberspace and the Internet as 'utopian spaces' in the popular media (Silvio, 1999, p. 54) and popular films and fictions depicting some of the more negative dystopian possibilities of a virtual world of simulation (e.g. *The Matrix* and *Terminator 2*). Responses within intellectual and academic discourses are equally disparate, with cultural commentators such as Francis Fukuyama declaring that the technological revolution of the late twentieth century has lead to 'technologies of freedom' (p. 14). For Fukuyama, '[the] collapse of totalitarian empires and the emergence of the personal computer, as well as other forms of inexpensive information techno-logy...are not unrelated' (p. 4): computer technology has enabled 'the democratization of access to information and the decentralization of politics' (p. 4), leading to 'many social benefits' (p. 11) and the emergence of 'liberal democracy...as the only viable and legitimate polit-ical system for modern societies' (p. 14). John Pilger is less positive about both the political ramifications of information technology and the media age which it has spawned, and what he terms the 'new imperialism'. Qualifying the use of the term 'new' in the title of his collection of essays, *The New Rulers of the World* (2003), Pilger suggests that the narrative underpinning his collection is 'the legacy of the "old" imperialism and its return to respectability as "globalisation" and the "war on terror"' (p. 4), or, another euphemism for imperialism, 'civilisation' (p. 112).[4] As Pilger argues, the 'most potent weapon in this "war" is pseudo-information' (p. 1), a claim borne out potently in his, and many other commentators', discussions of media coverage of the 1991 Gulf War, coverage which took the form of 'censorship by omission in the "free" press' (p. 125). While 'the central thesis of Baudrillard's [Gulf War] essays appears to be directly contradicted by the facts' (p. 1) as Paul Patton suggests in the introduction to his translation of *The Gulf War Did Not Take Place* (Baudrillard, 1995), Baudrillard's analysis of the media coverage of the Gulf War as 'a media event' in which 'war' becomes 'a simulacrum of war, a virtual event which is less the representation of real war than a spectacle which serves a variety of political and strategic purposes on all sides' (p. 10), was certainly pertinent and astute. And Baudrillard's theories of simulation and the simulacrum have had a crucial informative function for narrative fictions, as well as for theoretical discussions of the possibilities of VR, and informational technology more broadly.

Terry Pratchett's *Only You Can Save Mankind* engages with these kinds of ideas, especially Baudrillard's concept of the simulacrum, on a number of levels. Set in England during the Gulf War, the novel has multiple narrative strands, each occurring on different diegetic levels, which map onto Baudrillard's successive phases of the image. The primary narrative, in which Johnny goes to school and plays video games, is a representation, a 'reflection of a profound reality' (Baudrillard, p. 6); the world of the computer game (whereby he converses and engages interactively with the aliens) is a simulation in which signs denature and 'mask the absence of a profound reality' (Baudrillard, p. 6); the world of dreams, in which Johnny and Kirsty/Sigourney fly the alien spaceship and help the aliens 'across the border' of Game Space to safety, collapses 'the distance between the real and the imaginary' (p. 6) and is an (apparent) simulacrum with 'no relation to any reality whatsoever' (Baudrillard, p. 6); and lastly there is the world of the television which runs endless coverage of the Gulf War. The war is mostly only referred to obliquely, as something happening on the television, for example, 'There was a film on the News showing some missiles streaking over some city. It was good' (Pratchett, 1992, p. 22). The confusion of genres ('film... News') in part conveys the child's viewpoint, but also echoes descriptions of the war as a television event (Schiller, Mowlana and Gerbner; Taylor). A second reference to the war on the television occurs shortly after Johnny's first dream of being in Game Space, in which as he is fired at and killed; he tells himself, 'It's all a game... just things happening on a screen somewhere.... It's not real. There's no arms and feet spinning away through the wreckage. It's all a game' (pp. 25–6). He wakes up and watches the television where: 'There were some more pictures of missiles and bullets streaking over a city. They looked pretty much the same as the ones he'd seen last night, but were probably back by popular demand. He felt sick' (p. 26).

In this way, oblique connections are made between the war and the video game through the discourse of the narrative: both are things 'happening on a screen somewhere' and can be endlessly repeated or 'played again'. The absence of 'arms and feet spinning away through the wreckage' also echoes the portrayal of the Gulf War as 'clean, blood-less' war enacted with surgical precision (Pilger, 2003, p. 125) and 'virtually no combat' (Chomsky, 2003, p. 51) but Johnny's feeling 'sick' can be read as a response to both the dream and what he sees on the television. In creating parallels between the war and the game, Pratchett is also alluding to comparisons made between simulated video games, 'the "video-game" type images' dominating television footage (Taylor, p. 48), and the use of computer simulation and 'smart' weaponry in the actual Gulf War, as well as interrogating the notion of war as a game. On a few rare occasions Johnny and his friends do discuss the war, but in tellingly clichéd language, using phrases such as 'kicking some butt' and 'We'll give them the 'Mother-in-law of All Battles' (p. 43), language which distances and objectifies the events of war in a similar way to television.

Pratchett's incorporation of the war into the narrative echoes Baudril-lard's analysis of the war as a media spectacle: At the same time, however, Pratchett's narrative also interrogates Baudrillard's model through the manner in which each narrative strand interpenetrates the others, disrupting the diegetic levels and blurring the boundaries between the 'real', the 'virtual' and the 'imaginary'. At times this is done play-fully, for example when Bigmac, Wobbler and Yo-less discuss their own reality in Johnny's dream (p. 76); in other episodes it has more serious overtones, for example when Bigmac creates a fiction about his and Johnny's involvement in a car crash which kills two of his friends. Within game space, however, this blurring also raises crucial questions about the potential for agency in a posthuman world of hyperreality 'inundated with images and signs that no longer have referential value' (Kraus and Auer, p. 2), questions which impact from the virtual reality of game space back onto the 'real' through the connections discussed earlier between the virtual world of the computer screen and the 'real' world of the television screen. As Johnny and Kirsty find, inside game space the virtual is in fact 'real' — aliens really do die. At the same time, because both characters are dreaming the same dream, but differ-ently, the narrative blurs the distinctions between that reality and their imagined dreaming — Johnny dreams the interior of the spaceship as 'grey metal, only interesting if you really liked looking at nuts and bolts' whereas once Kirsty/Sigourney joins him it becomes 'darker, with more curves; the walls glistened, and dripped menace. Dripped some-thing, anyway' (p. 138). Likewise the Captain changes too from 'an intelligent person who just happened to be an eight-legged crocodile' to 'an eight-legged crocodile who just happened to be intelligent'

(p. 138). Focalised narration stresses the physical sensory reality of game space, the smell, heat, and feel of a spaceship (pp. 9, 22, 36), but once Kirsty joins Johnny in the dream, that reality changes, as Kirsty, 'who dream[s] of being Sigourney and forgot she was trying to be someone who was acting' (p. 172), dreams it differently — in typically Pratchett irony Kirsty has adopted the name of the actress rather than the film character (Ripley) she emulates, a character who is killed and brought back to life at least once, and who discovers in the fourth *Alien* film that she is actually a clone, a simulacrum. Kirsty/Sigourney's appropriation of science fiction film genres to dream an alien spacecraft and as a source of behaviour codes for action is, however, no less valid than Johnny's resources — indeed, she dreams the escape capsule, unknown to the ScreeWee Captain, which she and Johnny find 'right down under the ship' (p. 156) where it should be, with the paint not yet dry (p. 158). The novel opens with the opening credits of the game Johnny is playing, 'Only you can save mankind' in which he, the player, is to be 'the Saviour of Civilisation'. While playing the game, this means defending himself (and the rest of humanity) from an alien invasion. Once within game space, however, he is not just saviour of an alien civilization, but of the concept of 'civilisation' itself, as the actions he must take imply an assertion of fundamental humanistic and altruistic values.

Conclusion

Hayles (1999a, pp. 283–5) identifies three ideological responses to posthumanism. The first sees posthumanism as antihumanist and apocalyptic, that is, as marking the end of human beings and/or humanism, the prospect of which evokes either terror or excitement. Such a response informs and shapes both radically utopian and dystopian visions of the future, and would seem to inform the very negative vision of a posthuman future depicted in *Feed*. The second response is to use posthumanist discourses as a way of recuperating the liberal humanist subject. And the third involves a reconceptualisation of the 'human' subject and a rethinking of what 'being human' means, especially problematising conventional humanist mind/body dualisms and representation of dialogic interplay between cognition and the body.

As Hayles argues, posthumanism does not really mean the end of humanity (1999a, p. 286), though apocalyptic 'doomsday' visions of the future, are certainly prevalent in both fiction and film texts, as evidenced by discussions of *Feed* and *A.I.* Posthumanism can potentially, however, mean the end of a certain conception of the human (p. 286), a response often borne out by the manner in which posthuman narratives are resolved, especially in narratives for YA audiences where there is a common impulse to offer at least some elements of optimism for the future. Generally, then, Hayles' first response is usually resolved though a shift to either the second or third ideological position. Recuperative forms of posthumanism are usually formulated as a response to either antihumanist visions or to more radical and socially revisionist aspects of a textual world. Typically, the posthuman is 'graft[ed] ... onto a liberal humanist view of the self' (Hayles, 1999a, p. 286), through the common emphasis within humanism and posthumanism on cognition, and down-playing of embodiment. Such an ideological move is implicit for example in Hans Morevec's idea of downloading human consciousness into a computer, an idea which, as we have suggested, is played out in Fox's *Eager*. Potentially, this idea represents a way of gaining immortality, of freeing the subject from the material body. The assumption, on the part of both Morevec and Fox's fictional scientists, that consciousness and subjectivity can exist independently of material lived bodily exper-ience 'expands the prerogatives of the autonomous liberal self into the realm of the posthuman' (Hayles, 1999a, p. 286) and subverts the radical potential of the posthuman. The emphasis on form and pattern (over content and presence) privileges mind over body, and hence implicitly reinstates and recuperates humanist visions of the subject. The impulse to reinscribe humanism within the posthuman is noted more generally by Goodall (1997) in her account of automatism and the fear of losing agency associated with developments in automatic machinery. Silvio presents a similar argument, claiming that there is an 'element of seduction at work, whereby information technology often presents itself to us as poten-tially liberating when in fact our actual interaction with it often rein-forces conventional social structures of domination' (1999, p. 55), as it does in negative depictions of the cybernetic subject in *Feed*, *Eager* (the BDC4s), and *Ferren and the Angel* (the Humen). W. J. T. Mitchell also questions 'the notion that our time is adequately described as the "age of information"', suggesting instead that it 'might be better called the age of mis- or dis-information, and [that] the era of cybernetic control is ... more like an epoch of loss of control' (p. 484). Mitchell suggests that the new era of what he terms 'biocybernetics' is characterised 'by an erosion of the event, and a vertiginous deepening of the relevant past, [which] produces a peculiar sense of 'accelerated stasis' in our sense of history', arguing further that at 'this moment of accelerated stasis in history ... we feel caught between the utopian fantasies of biocybernetics and the dystopian realities of biopolitics, between the rhetoric of the posthuman and the real urgency of universal human rights' (p. 498). Claims such as these of Goodall, Silvio and Mitchell have important implications for the analysis of posthuman narratives. To what extent do such narratives represent an ideological move away from dominant conceptual paradigms? To what extent do they use posthuman motifs to simply reinscribe and recuperate a humanist metaethic? As Bukatman argues of film, 'there *is* a utopia to be found in the science fiction film, a utopia that lies in *being human*, . . . [and] the numberless aliens, androids and evil computers . . . are the barbarians storming the gates of humanity' (p. 16).

The third possible response to posthumanism, a rethinking and reconceptualisation of what being human means, is perhaps the most positive, leading to visions of a transformed human world, as in the endings of *Ferren and the Angel* and *Eager*. Such re-visions depict the relation between cognition and the body as dialogical rather than as a simple dualism or binary opposition characteristic of liberal humanist discourses. As Hayles asserts, posthumanism does not need to be either antihuman, apocalyptic, or recuperative. Instead, she suggests seeing the human as 'part of a distributed system' in which 'human function-ality expands because the parameters of the cognitive system it inhabits expands' (1999a, p. 288). A central premise here is the Bourdieusian notion of the body as defining, through its interactions with the environment, the parameters within which the cogitating mind can arrive at certainties — a revaluation, in other words, of the Cartesian mind/body dualism which conceived of conscious agency as the essence of human identity (see Hayles, 1999a, p. 202). Positive revaluations of 'human' attributes, espe-cially within the domains of cognitive and affective experience, with which many of the texts discussed here close, affirm such dialogical recon-figurations of cognition, affect, and the body, and open a dialogue between posthumanism and humanism.

While we have considered texts within three distinct groupings in this chapter, there are common thematic and ideological concerns and narrative strategies which cut across the three groups. A striking feature of many posthuman texts is the preponderance of narratives featuring alienated 'child' figures. Characters such as David, the child android in Spielberg's *A.I*, Eager, the new breed of robot in *Eager*, Ferren, the central human character in Harland's *Ferren and the Angel*, all of the teenage characters in *Feed*, Matt, the child-clone in *The House of the Scorpion*, and Johnny in *Only You Can Save Mankind* are all, in different ways, isolated and radically alienated from the worlds around them through being excluded, through their own lack of understanding and incomprehension of the adult, human,[3] and posthuman worlds they inhabit, and/or through the alienating nature of such worlds.

Clearly such features have implications for the representation of relations between self and world, and hence conceptualisations of subjectivity. The 'children' produced in these fictions challenge our concepts of humanity and posthumanity: if a 'child', such as David in *A.I.* or the robot Eager in *Eager*, performs childhood, and that performativity embodies subjective agency, why is s/he/it not a child? The attempts to define a future version of humanity we find in such texts accords better with an alternative view that the posthuman does not necessitate either an evolution or devolution of the human. Rather it means that difference and identity are being redistributed. Ideas of humanity — that is, 'the human' — naturalise and hierarchise difference within the human and make absolute distinctions between the human and nonhuman. Ideas of the posthuman question what we consider to be 'natural', and create possibilities for the emergence of new relationships between human and machine, biology and technology.

Conclusion: The Future: What are Our Prospects?

Sleepers, wake! The watchman on the heights is calling ...
(J. S. Bach, Cantata no. 140, *Wachet auf*)

We face an uncertain future and calls for change tug at our consciousness. As the preceding chapters have argued, change is occurring at an unprecedented rate and on a global scale. Many of the texts we have discussed not only reflect current societal, environmental, and political changes, but extrapolate the impact of change to an unknown and unimaginable future. While change is an inevitable constituent of civilisation as we have known it, in the past few decades the world has been transforming at a bewildering pace: we have witnessed the demise of the bipolar arrangement of global politics of the Cold War era; the emergence of a global marketplace; mass migration, displacement, and relocation; the dissolution of nation states; new forms of family and community; an information explosion; rapid technological advancement; and increased global warming. These changes engender insecurities and fears, as well as offering new opportunities and ambiguities. In particular, the rapidity and intensity of new technologies and globalisation present enormous challenges in terms of posthumanism, ecological sustainability, and the utopian goal of a stable and just world order.

Utopian texts produced for children invariably construct child protagonists as the ones who must take responsibility for the future, and, as we argued in Chapter 2, these narratives implicitly exhort children to overcome the problems the adult generation has created. A feature of these texts is a generally optimistic faith in children to be able to make the right decisions, to choose the right path, and not to succumb to the burden of responsibility and oppression. To this end, young protagonists are commonly shown to respond to the ambiguities and challenges of current phenomena with creative and clear-headed actions. The attribution of resilience and ingenuity to the young in these texts often implies or thematises a sense that members of the adult generation have abandoned their youthful idealism during the course of their own life journeys. In this sense, there appears a narrative move away from more conventional archetypes such as the wise elder who counsels the young acolyte towards maturity and wisdom. Perhaps this shift is also indicative of the pace of change and the sense of urgency that underpins life in Western nations where time is a commodity and decisions need to be made without delay and with limited explanation: such is the nature of an instant communication and an information-now world. However, placing the burden of responsibility on to young shoulders is a fragile means for ensuring a better future because it assumes not only that young people share the same desires as those of social reformists, but also that the process of becoming which constitutes 'youth' is malleable in constant and predictable ways. Rather, as the best of utopian writing suggests, it is the dialogic exchange across age, race, gender, nature, and culture that proffers hope for evolving broad policies and social practices that might avoid the tyranny of the powerful over the impotent and disenfranchised.

Throughout this book we have engaged with a paradox inherent to utopian narratives, that in positing a better future they must engage with the consequences of that future as well as the obstacles that prevent its realisation. This dual imagining is evident in our discussion of the posthuman (Chapter 8) where we noted that narrative fictions which engage with posthumanist visions of the human subject draw on either imagined or real advances in information technology, cybernetics, and biological and genetic manipulation to imagine both utopian and dystopian futures. While the focus on the posthuman is a relatively recent phenomenon in children's and YA fiction, writers appear reluctant to envision a utopian state; rather, as we have argued, the prospect of a posthuman future represents a dystopian state, and the possibility evokes technophobia. While artificial intelligence and cybersurveillance exacerbate the fears of a brave new world to new heights of paranoia and human rights violation, the more worrying concern is the fatalistic acceptance of technological determinism. To hold the belief that nothing can be done to moderate or monitor technology's impact on the social and political will is to deny human subjects agency and the capacity for individual and collective ingenuity and adaptability in times of need. It is this desire for subjective agency and intersubjectivity that remains a persistent and optimistic element of utopian fiction for young people.

From our research spanning 20 years of utopian children's literature and film in English, it appears that unlike many writers of adult utopian fiction (e.g. Margaret Atwood, Marge Piercy, Philip K. Dick) writers for children and young people are less inclined to be daring in their imaginings of radically different futures. Such conservatism is due in part to the age of the implied audience of these texts and the pressures from publishing houses for writers to conform to market expectations; it is also attributable to the propensity for authors to operate within ideological frameworks accepted as normal in dominant social groups. Similarly, the restrictions of studio control and the return-on-investment imperative of the film industry often curtail the potential of a film to shake the foundations of the hegemonic order. As our discussion of postcolonial utopian fictions (Chapter 4) suggested, children's texts which refer to colonial histories and contemporary postcolonial cultures are typically qualified and guarded in their projections of new world orders, often failing to interrogate past atrocities and mistakes as they promote utopian visions. However, those writers and producers of children's texts who dare to speak a different world order into existence often achieve it by implicit means such as through symbolism and a seductive aesthetics. We demonstrated how environmental dystopian texts (Chapter 5) seek to convey the beneficial possibilities of a transformed ecological awareness through metonymy and analogy or incorporate them into the narratives as absence or loss. In speaking these possibilities into existence, these texts intend to open young readers' minds to alternative ways of being and becoming in order to create a better world for the future. As our discussion of children's film and picture books has suggested, the visual (and aural) characteristics of these media are an ideal means for utilising a seductive aesthetics for maximum effect and to produce affect.

In many ways utopian texts for children are no different from other texts produced for this age range in that writers tend to employ narrative strategies and plot trajectories which hinge on themes of individual subjectivities and intersubjective relations. However, one of the defining elements of these texts is that their broader political implications sometimes go beyond the politics of representation that invariably shape writing for young people. One of the most effective narrative strategies for achieving political effects is in the way readers are positioned by texts to take up certain attitudes and alignments that emerge through their engagement with the stories. The ideal outcome is the awakening of readers in the hope that they will extrapolate from the world of the text to their actual social realities and to grapple with the struggles, tensions, and problems that are inherent to the 'real world'. It is this potential for transformation both within and outside of the text that forms the core of our discussions.

New World Orders is founded in the belief that there is hope for the future and the survival of the planet. Throughout this book we have demonstrated how children's texts generally refuse to give in to despair and nihilism. The various utopias, critical utopias and dystopias we have discussed invariably offer closures that remain at best optimistic and at worst uncertain or open. We have refused to accept the texts at face value. Rather, we have probed their language and their verbal and visual narratives, not merely to highlight their structural weaknesses, but as genuine attempts to explore their political and ethical dimensions and to expose the layers of meaning that constitute notions of nationhood, globalisation, citizenship, family, community, environment, and new technologies. These are political and ethical categories and their incorporation into texts for young people does not mean that they carry any less weight because of the ages of their intended audience. On the contrary, we contend that they carry more weight as they are shaped and packaged according to the ideological and political orientations of their adult creators and presented to readers and viewers who for the most part are still coming to terms with their own 'subjectivity-in-process' (Manning, 2003, p. 151) and are therefore vulnerable to prevailing ideologies and politics. As Manning notes, 'reading is not just a tranquil act of deciphering, but an exposition of the irreducibility of the other (as text, as world, as human being). Reading is politics-in-the-making' (p. 151). The argument that children's texts are not 'innocent' has long been made; what *New World Orders* argues is that utopian texts for children do 'serious political work' (Weber, in Doucet, 2005, p. 290). In our consideration of how texts engage with the process of transformation, we offer adults who might not normally read or study children's texts an invitation to transform their own reading choices and take these works seriously. After all, the phenomenal success of Harry Potter proves that children's books have an appeal that transcends conceptual divisions between writing for adults and for children. It is our desire that our investigation of utopianism and children's literatures will lead to increased awareness of and critical interest in a body of texts which, in proposing new world orders to child readers, has the potential to shape the future.

Notes

2 Children's texts, new world orders and transformative possibilities

1. Lawrence's earlier *Children of the Dust* (1985) was one of the best known examples in children's literature of the nuclear holocaust dystopia, and was widely used in schools despite the controversy inspired by such elements as its graphic depiction of a major character dying of radiation sickness. Its depiction of a government which abandons its citizens looks forward to the more overt engagement with politics in *The Disinherited*.
2. The actual firing of ODIN is reminiscent of the firing of the Orbital Ion Cannon in one of the *United Nations Global Defense Initiative (UNGDI)* strategy video games episodes (http://en.wikipedia.org/wiki/Global_Defense_ Initiative).
3. John Winthrop (1630): 'men shall say of succeeding plantacions: the lord make it like that of New England: for wee must Consider that wee shall be as a Citty upon a Hill, the eies of all people are uppon us'. The metaphor has been invoked by most American presidents since John F. Kennedy. Particularly notable for our purposes here is George Bush's collocation of the metaphor — in the form of his recurrent phrase, 'the illumination of a thousand points of light' — with another repeated concept, 'a new world order, where diverse nations are drawn together in common cause to achieve the universal aspirations of mankind: peace and security, freedom, and the rule of law' (George H. W. Bush, State of the Union Address, 29 January 1991).
4. Although children's fiction to date has principally identified CCTV, ATMs, online communication, and microchipping as instruments of surveillance, the list noted by Felix Stalder (2003) indicates a greater range of possibilities (often affecting adults, but now extending to young people):

> The creation, collection and processing of personal data is nearly a ubiquitous phenomenon. Every time we use a loyalty card at a retailer, our names are correlated with our purchases and entered into giant databases. Every time we pass an electronic toll booth on the highway, every time we use a cell phone or a credit card, our locations are being recorded, analyzed and stored. Every time we go to see a doctor, submit an insurance claim, pay our utility bills, interact with the government, or go online, the picture gleaned from our actions and states grows finer and fatter.

5. Although, as Lianos points out, 'the Foucauldian model of control, and consequently its explanatory power, *refers to the past* and is not concerned with the emergence of the contemporary postindustrial subject' (2003, p. 413), the notion of the panopticon and self-surveillance has wide currency in contemporary discourses. This position is almost certainly attributable to the

continuing influence on children's literature of George Orwell's depiction of surveillance in *1984* — as O'Har puts it, 'Huxley and Orwell...expose the fatal flaw in the utopian impulse: the drive for order at the expense of freedom' (482).

6. *Useful Idiots* is a pejorative political term which characterizes people as naïve objects of manipulation by a political movement, terrorist group, or the like, so that they unwittingly give moral and material support to a cause detrimental to their own interests. It has been most commonly used by conservative forces to disparage liberals. Although erroneously attributed to Vladimir Lenin, the term appears to be a product of Cold War discourse, directed at Soviet sympathisers. It is currently widely used in rhetoric on either end of the political spectrum, especially in references to the 'War on Terror'.

7. In *Surveillance Society* (2001), Lyon argues that 'compliance with surveillance systems can be seen as participation in a kind of social orchestration. For those who are not for some reason marginalized or excluded, social participation generally means active involvement in the mechanisms that keep track of and monitor their everyday lives' (7). Lyon is careful to balance the advantages and disadvantages of surveillance within the social contract, but dystopian fictions remain attuned to an Orwellian view, even though Orwell could not have imagined how pervasive surveillance had become by the end of the twentieth century.

8. Mark is using (with some variations in the first two stanzas) the version of *Nottamun Town* collected in Cecil Sharp's *Eighty English Folk Songs from the Southern Appalachians*, p. 89. When Merrick had earlier recalled a garbled fragment of the song (p. 397), he had substituted the name 'Nottingham', which is undoubtedly the original form. Having been lost in England, the song again became current through, for example, a version (also garbled) recorded by the folk-rock band Fairport Convention in 1969.

9. J. D. Salinger's *The Catcher in the Rye* (1951) is commonly seen as a precursor of YA fiction, because the main character is an adolescent who narrates his own story, but it is also a precursor of the dystopian theme in that literature.

3   Masters, slaves, and entrepreneurs: globalised utopias and new world order(ing)s

1. President George W. Bush has often likened himself to a 'cowboy' and has included frontier and wild west rhetoric in describing his international political intentions. For example, he has been quoted as saying that he'll 'ride herd' over Middle Eastern governments and 'smoke out' enemies in wild mountain passes. He branded Saddam Hussein's Iraq as 'an outlaw regime' and took the defeated dictator's gun as a trophy. In speaking about his desire to capture Osama bin Laden, he used the old western poster 'Wanted: Dead or Alive' as his modus operandi.
Source: Erik Baard, 'George W. Bush Ain't No Cowboy', *The Village Voice*, 28 September 2004 10:10 AM. *http://www.villagevoice.com/news/0439,baard, 57117,1.html*, Accessed 12 December 2006.

2. A report published prior to the US occupation of Iraq, claims that 13 million children under the age of 18 are 'at grave risk of starvation, disease, death and

psychological trauma' and that they were worse off now than they were before the outbreak of war in 1991 (quoted in Giroux and Giroux, 2004, pp. 70–1).

3. Hardt and Negri use the term 'informatization' to refer to the way in which postmodernity has evolved a global system that has transformed the economic paradigm of modernity. The new global system is capable of 'providing services and manipulating information' whereby information produces and dominates not only economic production, but also social relations (Hardt and Negri, 2000, p. 280).

4   The lure of the lost paradise: postcolonial utopias

1. See Bradford (2007) for a discussion of the concepts of place and space which dominated British imperialism: practices of mapping and cataloguing places; the development of the discipline of geography; surveillance of colonised peoples; hierarchies of value which distinguished 'waste' land from that which might be put to profitable use.

2. Children's texts explicitly drawing upon colonial events and tropes are more likely to be found among fiction for adolescent and YA readers than for younger readers, since they generally imply an historical sense and a consciousness of the consequences of imperialism.

3. In *American Pentimento: The Invention of Indians and the Pursuit of Riches* (2001), the Canadian scholar Patricia Seed distinguishes between the colonising vision of England and that of Spain. The English, she says, 'had conquered property, categorically denying the natives' true ownership of their land. Spaniards, on the other hand, had conquered people, allowing sedentary natives to retain their terrain in exchange for social humiliation. Thus regaining soil comes first on the agenda in aboriginal communities once dominated by England, whereas seeking human respect is central to contemporary aboriginal struggles in regions once controlled by Spain' (Seed, 2001, p. 2).

4. As Alistair Bonnett (2000) and Ghassan Hage (2003) have pointed out, the emergence of the idea that the state of being white is associated with status and power coincided with the spread of European colonialism, so that whiteness was constructed, as Ghassan Hage says, 'into a racial category. It involved both a European monopolisation of "civilised humanity" and a parallel monopolisation of Whiteness as its marker' (Hage, 2003, p. 50). Hierarchies of class and of ethnicities were incorporated into notions of whiteness, with non-Anglo and working-class populations relegated to the lower echelons of whiteness.

5. See Bradford, *Unsettling Narratives*, 2007, Chapter 8, for a discussion of postcolonial allegories for children, that is, texts which treat historical and contemporary socio-political processes and outcomes by way of metaphor and allegory.

6. See Lyman Tower Sargent, 'The Problem of the "Flawed Utopia"', in *Dark Horizons: Science Fiction and the Dystopian Imagination*, ed. R. Baccolini and T. Moylan (New York: Routledge, 2003), pp. 225–31.

7. The universalising and romanticising discourses evident in *The Crowlings* remain highly influential in retellings by non-Indigenous authors of Indigenous narratives, as well as in critical work dealing with 'traditional'

narratives. For a discussion of some of the issues around retellings of Indigenous narratives, see Bradford, 2003a.

5 Reweaving nature and culture: reading ecocritically

1. A poll conducted by Roy Morgan (International) for the 2006 Future Summit and published in *The Australian* newspaper, April 2006, found that, 'An overwhelming majority of Australians (71 per cent up 4 per cent from 67 per cent in November 2005) think that if we don't act now, it will be too late to address the consequences of global warming' (http://www.roymorgan.com/news/polls/2006/4013/). This level of concern might not in itself prompt the Australian electorate to vote to change its Government, but it has elicited signs that even that recalcitrant Government is beginning to reconsider its position.
2. 'Now, we can see a new world coming into view. A world in which there is the very real prospect of a new world order. In the words of Winston Churchill, a "world order" in which "the principles of justice and fair play...protect the weak against the strong..." A world where the United Nations, freed from Cold War stalemate, is poised to fulfil the historic vision of its founders. A world in which freedom and respect for human rights find a home among all nations.'
3. The term ecotopia, referring to the notion of an ecological utopia, entered 'green' discourses from Ernest Callenbach's 1975 novel, *Ecotopia*, in which Ecotopia is a somewhat reclusive country formed when Oregon, Washington, and Northern California seceded from the United States. Callenbach's utopian vision sought to combine the best environmental practices with selected elements of high technology.
4. The entry of ecocriticism into the critical discourses of children's literature was formally marked by two journals publishing special issues dedicated to children and ecology: 'Ecology and the Child,' a special issue of the *Children's Literature Association Quarterly* 19 (1994–1995), and 'Green Worlds: Nature and Ecology', *The Lion and the Unicorn* 19 (1995). Now, several years into the twenty-first century, it would be an exaggeration to claim either that ecocriticism constitutes an established strand within the critical discourses of children's literature or that the literature itself is generally informed by ecological awareness. There has been at least one collection of essays specifically claiming an ecocritical basis (Dobrin and Kidd, 2004), but such work has seldom focused on what is being written in the contemporary world, preferring to follow the American ecocritical practice of 're-reading' the texts of the past from a loosely-defined 'ecocritical' perspective.
5. Gaia is not a personification, but a principle, now widely referred to as 'Earth system science': 'The Earth displays a stunning capacity for emergent self-regulation arising out of the tightly coupled feedbacks between the sum total of all the planet's living beings and the atmosphere, rocks and water that they have so intimately interacted with over the course of geological time.' See Stephan Harding's 'Review of *The Revenge of Gaia. Why the Earth is Fighting Back — and How We Can Still Save Humanity*' (2006), *International Microbiology* 9 (2006) 143–45.

6. By 1990 the anthropological representations of the Yanomami peoples were already controversial, although they did not become the subject of the greatest scandal in the history of the discipline of anthropology until after the publication of Patrick Tierney's, *Darkness in El Dorado: How Scientists and Journalists Devastated the Amazon* (2000). Alcida R. Ramos had already written in 1987 that the Yanomami were living in a state of extreme vulnerability and insecurity, and a great struggle was taking place to guarantee their rights to land, health care, and cultural autonomy. She continued: 'Rather than being the epitome of primitive animality, the Yanomami have become a symbol of pristine good life endangered by the brutality of capitalist expansionism. Thus a different stereotype has been created; side by side with important and committed efforts to protect the land and freedom of choice of the Yanomami, there is a whole rhetoric of conservation that clings to the romantic idea that a good Indian is a naked, isolated Indian' (1987, p. 301).
7. See, for example, Chagnon's *Yanomamo – A Fierce People* (1968).
8. We remarked in Chapter 2 that in post-disaster narratives ecological catastrophe had mostly replaced nuclear war as the cause of global destruction. In retaining the older catalyst, Reeve has been able to incorporate the same effects as attributed to an ecological disaster and also keep in tune with, for example, the Bulletin of the Atomic Scientists (BAS), which has continued to maintain that nuclear warfare remains the greatest threat to human survival. On 17 January 2007 the BAS moved the hands of its 'Doomsday Clock' two minutes closer to midnight, now for the first time including climate change as a key factor: 'In a statement supporting the decision to move the hand of the Doomsday Clock, the BAS Board focused on two major sources of catastrophe: the perils of 27,000 nuclear weapons, 2000 of them ready to launch within minutes; and the destruction of human habitats from climate change' (http://www.thebulletin.org/mediacenter/announcements/20070117.html). Media reports of this announcement, however, focused primarily on climate change.
9. Reeve's self-consciousness about how he is using various conventions in this passage is perhaps most obvious in the mention of the oak sapling amongst the ribs — a plant growing from the heart of a faithful lover is a common motif in traditional ballads.

6   'Radiant with possibility': communities and utopianism

1. The high cost of the Iraq war had, by 2006, caused Fukuyama to revise his early enthusiasm for American policies of spreading democracy through regime change. His most recent work, *America at the Crossroads: Democracy, Power and the Neoconservative Legacy* (2006), while critical of the prosecution of the Iraq war, proposes that American foreign policy should be grounded in a *'realistic* Wilsonianism that recognizes the importance to world order of what goes on *inside* states and that better matches the available tools to the achievement of democratic ends' (p. 184). That is, those 'democratic ends' deemed desirable in the United States are assumed to be universally desirable.
2. See Mallan *et al.* (2005), 'New Social Orders: Reconceptualising Family and Community in Utopian Fiction'.

3. See Elizabeth Frazer, *The Problems of Communitarian Politics: Unity and Conflict*, Oxford University Press, Oxford and London, pp. 173–202, for a discussion of tensions and inconsistencies in political communitarianism.
4. The name 'Nauvoo' refers to Nauvoo, Illinois, where Joseph Smith established the Church of Latterday Saints in the early 1840s.
5. The figure of 144 represents the Twelve Apostles squared. The significance ascribed to multiples of the number four across fundamentalist Christian groups derives from its deployment as a symbolic number in *Revelations* 7:1–8.
6. Inhabitants of the feminist utopia of *Come Lucky April*, in comparison, regard meat-eating, in a sternly self-righteous manner, as disgusting and brutish.

7   Ties that bind: reconceptualising home and family

1. In *Girl Walking Backwards* home and family are queered in that the relations between mothers and daughters are unorthodox and uncanny and the text resists the Oedipal complex by focusing on how difference and desire exist between the women (for a more detailed analysis refer to Mallan, 2004, pp. 345–57). *Twilight* deals with the dangerous love between a young woman and a vampire. In dealing with this unconventional love, the story raises questions about desire and the utopian impulse to transcend difference, in this case, at all costs.
2. Freud defines *unheimlich* (strange, unfamiliar, uncanny) as the negation of *heimlich* (domestic, familiar, intimate). The paradoxical meaning of the uncanny lies in the fact that it is something frightening, not because it is unfamiliar, but because what used to be familiar has become strange. This relates to the psychoanalytic notion of repression.
3. However, Miyazake's text needs to be considered within the context of its cross-cultural production-reception, as the English dubbed version shifts social forms and ideologies into Western modes. Notoriously, the final line of *Spirited Away* in the English version – Chihiro's 'I can handle it', which affirms her completion of her rite of passage – does not occur in the original Japanese, which thereby offers a much more open ending by closing with her father's reference to the scariness of a new home and new school.

8   The struggle to be human in a posthuman world

1. The script of *Artificial Intelligence* is available at: http://www.comeawayohumanchild.net/AIdialogue.htm.
2. Isaac Asimov's 'Three laws of Robotics' (first formulated in his 1942 short story 'Runaround'):

   1. A robot may not injure a human being, or, through inaction, allow a human being to come to harm.
   2. A robot must obey the orders given it by human beings except where such orders would conflict with the First Law.
   3. A robot must protect its own existence as long as such protection does not conflict with the First or Second Law.

3. VR narratives, and narratives in which computer technology has an agential function, have been popular in science fiction films and novels for quite some time, and some significant precursors to the texts discussed here might be: *2001, A Space Odyssey* (1968); *Enders Game* (Card, 1977); *The Hitchhikers Guide to the Galaxy* (multiple media productions between 1978 and 2005); *The Matrix* (1993); *Ghost in the Shell* (1995); and *The Terminator* films (1984, 1991, 2003) amongst others.

4. Pilger's account of the new imperialism is echoed in Noam Chomsky's discussion of the 1990s as 'the decade of humanitarian intervention' (2003, p. 22) and the emergence of a 'new era of enlightenment' (p. 51) which sees it as 'the mission' of 'civilised' or 'enlightened' states 'to bring to the rest of the world the principles of order, freedom and justice to which "postmodern" societies are dedicated', a mission necessitating a return to nineteenth century colonialism (pp. 62–3). Likewise, Baudrillard's (2004) discussion of 'globalisation' as a form of colonialism 'pitched as the endpoint of the Enlightenment, the solution to all contradictions [which] in reality ... transforms everything into a negotiable, quantifiable exchange value' is underpinned by a contrast between 'universals' (i.e. universal values as defined by humanism and the Enlightenment, such as freedom, democracy and human rights) and 'the global' (i.e. 'an operational system of total trade and exchange').

References

Primary

Aladdin. Dir. Ron Clements and John Muskar (Disney, 1992).

Allende, Isabel. *City of the Beasts* (London: HarperCollins Publishers, 2002).

Almond, David. *The Fire-Eaters* (London: Hodder Children's Books, 2003).

Anderson, M. T. *Burger Wuss* (Cambridge, MS: Candlewick Press, 1999).

——. *Feed* (Cambridge, MS: Candlewick Press, 2002).

Anderson, Rachel. *The Scavenger's Tale* (Oxford: Oxford University Press, 1998).

Artificial Intelligence: A. I. Dir. Steven Spielberg (Warner Bros, 2001).

Asimov, Isaac. 'Runaround' (1942), reprinted in *The Complete Robot* (London: HarperCollins, 1995), pp. 33–51.

Baker, Jeannie. *Belonging* (London: Walker Books, 2004).

Bauer, Joan. *Rules of the Road* (New York: G P Putnam's Sons, 1998).

Bawden, Nina. *Off the Road* (New York: Clarion Books, 1998).

Beale, Fleur. *I Am Not Esther* (Dunedin: Longacre Press, 1998).

Bertagna, Julie. *Exodus* (London: Macmillan, 2002).

Browne, Anthony. *Zoo* (London: Julia MacRae Books, 1992).

Burgess, Melvin. *The Baby and Fly Pie* (Harmondsworth: Puffin Books, 1992).

——. *Bloodtide* (London: Penguin, 1999).

Butler, Charles. *Calypso Dreaming* (London: HarperCollins Publishers, 2002).

Callenbach, Ernest. *Ecotopia: The Notebooks and Reports of William Weston* (New York: Bantam Books, 1990) [1975].

Carmichael, Claire. *Incognito* (Sydney: Random House, 2000).

Caswell, Brian. *Deucalion* (St. Lucia, Queensland: University of Queensland Press, 1995).

Cherry, Lynne. *The Great Kapok Tree: A Tale of the Amazon Rain Forest* (New York: Harcourt Brace Jovanovich, 1990).

Christopher, John. *The Tripods* (London: Simon & Schuster, 1988) [1967–1968].

Cooper, Susan. *The Dark Is Rising* sequence (New York: Aladdin, 1999–2000): *Over Sea, Under Stone* (1965); *The Dark Is Rising* (1973); *Greenwitch* (1974); *The Grey King* (1975); *Silver on the Tree* (1977).

Cormier, Robert. *The Chocolate War* (New York: Pantheon, 1974).

Crew, Gary. *No Such Country* (Port Melbourne: Heinemman, 1991).

Cummings, Phil. *Tearaway* (Sydney: Random House, 2002).

D'Ath, Justin. *Shædow Master* (Crows Nest, Aust.: Allen and Unwin, 2003).

Dematons, Charlotte. *The Yellow Balloon* (Asheville, NC: Front Street & Lemniscaat, 2003).

Dickinson, Peter. *Shadow of a Hero* (London: Victor Gollancz, 1994).

Dubosarsky, Ursula. *The Red Shoe* (Crows Nest, NSW: Allen & Unwin, 2006).

Farmer, Nancy. *The Ear, the Eye, and the Arm* (New York: Penguin, 1994).

——. *The House of the Scorpion* (New York: Simon & Schuster, 2002).

Foreman, Michael. *One World* (London: Andersen Press Ltd., 1990).

Fox, Helen. *Eager* (London: Hodder, 2003).

French, Jackie. 'The Lady of the Unicorns', *The Book of Unicorns* (Sydney: Angus & Robertson, 1997), pp. 79–178.

Gaiman, Neil. *Coraline* (London: Bloomsbury, 2002).

Garden, Nancy and Sharon Wooding. *Molly's Family* (New York: Farrar Straus Giroux, 2004).

Garner, Alan. *The Owl Service* (London: CollinsVoyager, 2002 [1967]).

Greenwood, Kerry. *Cave Rats* (Sydney: Hodder, 1997).

Harland, Richard. *Ferren and the Angel* (Ringwood, Victoria: Penguin, 2000).

Hathorn, Libby. *Rift* (Sydney: Hodder, 1998).

Hendry, Frances Mary. *Atlantis* (Oxford: Oxford University Press, 1997).

Hiaasen, Carl. *Flush* (New York: Alfred A. Knopf, 2005).

Howe, Norma. *The Adventures of Blue Avenger* (New York: HarperCollins, 1999).

Hughes, Monica. *Devil on My Back* (New York: Atheneum, 1985).

——. *The Other Place* (Toronto: HarperCollins, 1999).

Isaacs, Anne and Paul O. Zelinsky. *Swamp Angel* (New York: Dutton Children's Books, 1994).

Jinks, Catherine. *The Rapture* (Sydney: Pan Macmillan, 2001).

Laird, Elizabeth. *The Garbage King* (London: Macmillan Children's Books, 2003).

Lawrence, Louise. *The Disinherited* (London: The Bodley Head, 1994).

——. *The Crowlings* (London: Collins, 1999).

Le Carré, John. *The Constant Gardener* (Riverside, NJ: Scribner, 2000).

Lee, Tanith. *The Silver Metal Lover* (London: Unwin, 1986) [1981].

Lively, Penelope. *The Whispering Knights* (Harmondsworth: Penguin, 1987).

Lowry, Lois. *The Giver* (Boston: Houghton Mifflin, 1993).

——. *Gathering Blue* (New York: Houghton Mifflin, 2000).

——. *Messenger* (New York: Houghton Mifflin, 2004).

Mark, Jan. *Useful Idiots* (Oxford and New York: David Fickling Books, 2004).

Meyer, Stephenie. *Twilight* (London: Atom, 2005).

Millard, Glenda. *Bringing Reuben Home* (Sydney: ABC Books, 2004).

Monsters, Inc. Dir. Peter Doctor, David Silverman and Lee Unkrick (Disney/Pixar, 2001).

Morpurgo, Michael and Christina Balit. *Blodin the Beast* (Golden, CO: Fulcrum Publishing, 1995).

Murphy, Louise. *The True Story of Hansel and Gretel* (London: Penguin, 2003).

Nicholson, William. *The Wind Singer* (London: Egmont Books Ltd, 2000).

Nix, Garth. *Shade's Children* (New York: HarperCollins, 1997).

Noah and Saskia. Dir. Pino Amenta, written by Chris Anastassiades and Sam Carroll (Sydney: Australian Broadcasting Corporation, 2004).

Pratchett, Terry. *Only You Can Save Mankind* (London: Double Day Press, 1992).

Price, Susan. *The Sterkarm Handshake* (London: Scholastic, 1998).

——. *A Sterkarm Kiss* (London: Scholastic, 2003).

Rayban, Chloe. *Virtual Sexual Reality* (London: The Bodley Head, 1994).

Reeve, Philip. *Mortal Engines* (London: Scholastic Press, 2001).

——. *The Hungry Cities* tetralogy [*Mortal Engines; Predator's Gold; Infernal Devices; A Darkling Plain*] (London: Scholastic Press, 2001–2006).

——. *Predator's Gold* (London: Scholastic Press, 2003).

——. *A Darkling Plain* (London: Scholastic Press, 2006).

Rescue Heroes. Dir. Ron Pitts (Nelvana, 2003).

Salinger, J. D. *The Catcher in the Rye* (New York: Back Bay Books, 2001 [1951]).

Shearer, Alex. *The Speed of the Dark* (London: Macmillan Children's Books, 2003).

Skurzynski, Gloria. *Virtual War* (New York: Simon and Schuster, 1997).

Slade, Arthur. *Tribes* (Toronto: HarperCollins, 2002).

Spirited Away. Dir. Hayao Miyazaki (Ghibli, 2002).

Stephenson, Neal. *Zodiac. The Eco-thriller* (New York: Bantam Spectra, 1995) [1988].

Swindells, Robert. *Abomination* (London: Random House, 1998).

Tan, Shaun. *The Lost Thing* (Port Melbourne, Vic: Lothian, 2000).

The Incredibles. Dir. Brad Bird (Disney/Pixar, 2004).

'The Rise of the Cybermen', *Doctor Who*, Second Series (BBC, 2006).

The Simpsons 'There's no disgrace like home' (1990) episode 4: season 1.

Toy Story. Dir. John Lasseter (Disney/Pixar, 1995).

Turtles Can Fly. Dir. Bahman Ghobadi (IFC Films, 2005).

Ure, Jean. *Plague 99* (London: Methuen, 1989).

———. *Come Lucky April* (London: Methuen, 1992).

Whelan, Gloria. *Fruitlands: Louisa May Alcott Made Perfect* (New York: Harper-Collins, 2002).

Wiesner, David. *Flotsam* (New York: Clarion Books, 2006).

Williams, Bett. *Girl Walking Backwards* (New York: St Martins Griffin, 1998).

Winton, Tim. *Lockie Leonard, Scumbuster* (Sydney: Pan Macmillan, 1993).

Yolen, Jane and Bruce Coville. *Armageddon Summer* (New York: Harcourt Brace & Co., 1998).

Secondary

'About *Noah and Saskia*', Australian Broadcasting Corporation, http://www.abc.net.au/rollercoaster/noahandsaskia/behind_the_scenes/default.htm (accessed 17 February 2007).

Armbruster, Karla. 'Bringing Nature Writing Home: Josephine Johnson's *The Inland Island* as Bioregional Narrative', in John Tallmadge and Henry Harrington (eds) *Reading Under the Sign of Nature: New Essays in Ecocriticism* (Salt Lake City: University of Utah Press, 2000), pp. 3–18.

Armitt, Lucie. *Contemporary Women's Fiction and the Fantastic* (Basingstoke: Macmillan, 1999).

Artz, Lee. 'Monarchs, Monsters, and Multiculturalism: Disney's Menu for Global Hierarchy', in Mike Budd and Max H. Kirsch (eds) *Rethinking Disney: Private Control, Public Dimensions* (Middletown, CT: Wesleyan University Press, 2005), pp. 75–98.

Ashcroft, Bill. *Post-Colonial Transformation* (London: Routledge, 2001).

Baard, Eric. 'George W. Bush Ain't No Cowboy', *The Village Voice* 28 September 2004, 10:10 AM. http://www.villagevoice.com/news/0439,baard,57117,1.html (accessed 12 December 2006).

Baccolini, Raffaella. ' "A Useful Knowledge of the Present is Rooted in the Past": Memory and Historical Reconciliation in Ursula K. Le Guin's *The Telling*', in Raffaella Baccolini and Tom Moylan (eds) *Dark Horizons: Science Fiction and the Dystopian Imagination* (New York and London: Routledge, 2003), pp. 113–34.

Baccolini, Raffaella and Tom Moylan. 'Conclusion: Critical Dystopia and Possibilities', in Raffaella Baccolini and Tom Moylan (eds) *Dark Horizons: Science*

Fiction and the Dystopian Imagination (New York and London: Routledge, 2003a), pp. 233–49.

Baccolini, Raffaella and Tom Moylan. 'Introduction: Dystopia and Histories', in Raffaella Baccolini and Tom Moylan (eds) *Dark Horizons: Science Fiction and the Dystopian Imagination* (New York: Routledge, 2003b), pp. 1–12.

Bakker, Karen and Gavin Bridge. 'Material Worlds? Resource Geographies and the "Matter of Nature" ', *Progress in Human Geography* 30: 1 (2006) 5–27.

Bartowski, Frances. *Feminist Utopias* (Nebraska: Lincoln, 1989).

Baudrillard, Jean, trans. Paul Patton. *The Gulf War Did Not Take Place* (Bloomington, IN: Indiana University Press, 1995).

——. 'This is the Fourth World War: The *Der Spiegel* Interview with Jean Baudrillard', trans. Damir Gandesha, *International Journal of Baudrillard Studies* 1: 1 (2004), http://www.ubishops.ca/BaudrillardStudies/spiegel.htm (accessed 12 December 2006).

Bauman, Zygmunt. 'Individually Together. Foreword', in Ulrich Beck and Elizabeth Beck-Gernsheim (eds) *Individualization: Institutionalized Individualism and its Social and Political Consequences* (London: Sage, 2002a), pp. xiv–xix.

——. *Society under Siege* (Cambridge: Polity Press, 2002b).

Beauchamp, Gorman. 'Changing Times in Utopia', *Philosophy and Literature* 22: 1 (1998) 219–30.

Beck, Ulrich and Beck-Gernsheim, Elizabeth (eds). *Individualization: Institutionalized Individualism and its Social and Political Consequences* (London: Sage, 2002).

Berebitsky, Julie. *Like Our Very Own: Adoption and the Changing Culture of Motherhood, 1851–1950* (Lawrence, KS: University of Kansas Press, 2000).

Bonnett, Alastair. *White Identities: Historical and International Perspectives* (Harlow: Prentice Hall, 2000).

Bradford, Clare. *Reading Race: Aboriginality in Australian Children's Literature* (Carlton, Vic: Melbourne University Press, 2001).

——. ' "Oh How Different!": Regimes of Knowledge in Aboriginal Texts for Children', *The Lion and the Unicorn* 27: 2 (2003a) 199–217.

——. 'The Sky is Falling: Children as Environmental Subjects in Contemporary Picture Books', in Roderick McGillis (ed.) *Children's Literature and the Fin de Siècle* (New York: Praeger Publishers, 2003b), pp. 111–20.

——. *Unsettling Narratives: Postcolonial Readings of Children's Literature* (Waterloo, ON: Wilfrid Laurier University Press, 2007).

Brady, Mary Pat. 'The Fungibility of Borders', *Nepantla: Views from South* 1: 1 (2000) 171–90.

Braithwaite, Elizabeth. ' "When I Was a Child I Thought as a Child": The Importance of Memory in Constructions of Childhood and Social Order in a Selection of Post-Disaster Fictions', *Papers: Explorations into Children's Literature* 15: 2 (2005) 50–7.

Buell, Frederick. 'Nationalist Postnationalism: Globalist Discourse in Contemporary American Culture', *American Quarterly* 50: 3 (1998) 548–91.

Bukatman, Scott. *Terminal Identity: The Virtual Subject in Postmodern Science Fiction* (Durham and London: Duke University Press, 1993).

Burwell, Jennifer. *Notes on Nowhere: Feminism, Utopian Logic, and Social Transformation* (Minneapolis: University of Minnesota Press, 1997).

Butler, Judith. *Undoing Gender* (New York: Routledge, 2004).

Castells, Manuel. *The Power of Identity* (Malden, MA: Blackwell, 1998).

———. *The Rise and Fall of the Network Society* (Malden, MA: Blackwell, 2000).

Chagnon, Napoleon A. *Yanomamo: A Fierce People* (New York: Holt, Rinehart and Winston, 1968).

Chomsky, Noam. *Hegemony or Survival: America's Quest for Global Dominance* (Crows Nest NSW: Allen & Unwin, 2003).

Cooppan, Vilashini. 'Ghosts in the Disciplinary Machine', *Comparative Literature Studies* 41: 1 (2004) 10–36.

Curtin, Deane. *Chinnagounder's Challenge: The Question of Ecological Citizenship* (Bloomington: Indiana University Press, 1999).

Dobrin, Sidney I. and Kenneth Byron Kidd (eds). *Wild Things: Children's Culture and Ecocriticism* (Detroit: Wayne State University Press, 2004).

Doucet, Marc G. 'The Political Imaginary of International Relations and Contemporary Popular Children's Films', *Global Society* 19: 3 (2005) 289–306.

Dudek, Debra. 'Desiring Perception: Finding Utopian Impulses in Shaun Tan's *The Lost Thing*', *Papers: Explorations into Children's Literature* 15: 2 (2005) 58–66.

Foucault, Michel. *Discipline and Punish: The Birth of the Prison*. Trans. A. Sheridan (New York: Pantheon, 1977).

———. *Discipline & Punish: The Birth of the Prison*, trans. Alan Sheridan (New York: Vintage Books, 1995) [1975].

Free, Anna. 'Moonlit Revelations: The Discourse of the End in Gina B. Nahai's *Moonlight on the Avenue of Faith*', *Papers: Explorations into Children's Literature* 16: 2 (2006) 35–9.

Friedman, Thomas L. *The Lexus and the Olive Tree* (New York: Anchor Books, 2000).

Fukuyama, Francis. *The End of History and the Last Man* (New York: Macmillan, 1992).

———. *America at the Crossroads: Democracy, Power, and the Neoconservative Legacy* (New Haven: Yale University Press, 2006).

Gamma Ray. *No World Order* (Sanctuary Records, 2001).

Gandhi, Leela. *Postcolonial Theory: A Critical Introduction* (St Leonards NSW: Allen & Unwin, 1998).

———. 'Friendship and Postmodern Utopianism.' *Cultural Studies Review* 9: 1 (2003) 12–22.

Garrard, Greg. *Ecocriticism* (London: Routledge, 2004).

Giblett, Rod. *Postmodern Wetlands* (Edinburgh: Edinburgh University Press, 1996).

Giddens, Anthony. *The Consequences of Modernity* (Stanford, CA: Stanford University Press, 1990).

Giroux, Henry A. *Stealing Innocence: Corporate Culture's War on Children* (New York: Palgrave, 2000).

Giroux, Henry A. and Susan Searls Giroux. *Take Back Higher Education* (New York: Palgrave Macmillan, 2004).

Goodall, Jane. 'Transferred Agencies: Performance and the Fear of Automatism', *Theatre Journal* 49: 4 (1997) 441–53.

Gross, Melissa. '*The Giver* and *Shade's Children*: Future Views of Child Abandonment and Murder' *Children's Literature in Education* 30: 2 (1999) 103–17.

Gutierrez, Gustavo. *A Theology of Liberation: History, Politics and Salvation* (London: S.C.M. Press, 1974).

Hage, Ghassan. *Against Paranoid Nationalism: Searching for Hope in a Shrinking Society* (Sydney: Pluto Press, 2003).

Hall, C. Michael and Hazel Tucker. 'Tourism and Postcolonialism: An Introduction', in C. Michael Hall and Hazel Tucker (eds) *Tourism and Postcolonialism: Contested Discourses, Identities and Representations* (London: Routledge, 2004), pp. 1–24.

Hall, Stuart. 'Cultural Identity and Diaspora', in Padmini Mongia (ed.) *Contemporary Postcolonial Theory: A Reader* (London: Hodder, 1996), pp. 110–11.

Haraway, Donna J. *Simians, Cyborgs, and Women: The Reinvention of Nature* (London: Free Association Books, 1991).

Harding, Stephan. 'Review of *The Revenge of Gaia. Why the Earth is Fighting Back — and How We Can Still Save Humanity*', *International Microbiology* 9: 2 (2006) 143–5.

Hardt, Michael and Antonio Negri. *Empire* (Cambridge, MA: Harvard University Press, 2000).

Harvey, David. *Spaces of Hope* (Berkeley, LA: University of California Press, 2000).

Hassan, Ihab. 'Prometheus as Performer: Towards a Posthumanist Culture?', in Michael Benamon and Charles Caramella (eds) *Performance in Postmodern Culture* (Madison, Wisconsin: Coda Press, 1977), pp. 201–17.

Hayles, N. Katherine. *How We Became Posthuman: Virtual Bodies in Cybernetics, Literature, and Informatics* (Chicago: University of Chicago Press, 1999a).

——. 'The Illusion of Autonomy and the Fact of Recursivity: Virtual Ecologies, Entertainment, and Infinite Jest', *New Literary History* 30: 3 (1999b) 675–97.

——. 'Flesh and Metal: Reconfiguring the Mindbody in Virtual Environments', *Configurations* 10: 2 (2002) 297–320.

Huntington, Samuel. *The Clash of Civilizations and the Remaking of World Order* (New York: Simon & Schuster, 1996).

Jameson, Fredric. *Postmodernism, or, The Cultural Logic of Late Capitalism* (Durham, N.C.: Duke University Press, 1991).

——. 'The Politics of Utopia', *New Left Review* (Jan/Feb 2004) 35–54.

——. *Archaeologies of the Future: The Desire Called Utopia and Other Science Fictions* (London: Verso, 2005).

Jenny, Saskia and Hans Schmid. 'Effect of Feeding Boxes on the Behavior of Stereotyping Amur Tigers (*Panthera tigris altaica*) in the Zurich Zoo, Zurich, Switzerland', *Zoo Biology* 21 (2002) 573–84.

Kammen, Michael G. 'The Problem of American Exceptionalism: A Reconsideration', *American Quarterly* 45: 1 (1993) 1–43.

Kern, Robert. 'Ecocriticism: What Is It Good For?', in Michael P. Branch and Scott Slovic (eds) *The ISLE Reader: Ecocriticism, 1993–2003* (Athens and London: The University of Georgia Press, 2003), pp. 258–81.

Kraus, Elisabeth and Carolin Auer (eds). *Simulacrum America: The USA and the Popular Media* (Rochester, NY: Camden House, 2000).

Kumar, Krishan. *Utopianism* (Milton Keynes: Open University Press, 1991).

'Kyoto Protocol', David Suzuki Foundation, http://www.davidsuzuki.org/ Climate_Change/Kyoto/ (accessed 12 January 2007).

Levin, Jonathan. 'Beyond Nature? Recent Work in Ecocriticism', *Contemporary Literature* 43: 1 (2002) 172–186.

Levitas, Ruth. *The Concept of Utopia* (Hemel Hempstead: Philip Allen, 1990).

Levitas, Ruth and Lucy Sargisson. 'Utopia in Dark Times: Optimism/Pessimism and Utopia/Dystopia', in Raffaella Baccolini and Tom Moylan (eds) *Dark Horizons: Science Fiction and the Dystopian Imagination* (New York: Routledge, 2003), pp. 13–28.

Lianos, Michalis. 'Social Control after Foucault', *Surveillance & Society* 1: 3 (2003) 412–30.

Love, Glen A. 'Revaluing Nature: Toward an Ecological Criticism', in Cheryll Glotfelty and Harold Fromm (eds), *The Ecocriticism Reader* (Athens and London: The University of Georgia Press, 1996), pp. 225–40.

Lovelock, James. *The Revenge of Gaia: Why the Earth Is Fighting Back – and How We Can Still Save Humanity* (London: Allen Lane, 2006).

Lyon, David. *Surveillance Society: Monitoring Everyday Life* (Buckingham and Philadelphia: Open University Press, 2001).

Mack-Canty, Colleen. 'Third-Wave Feminism and the Need to Reweave the Nature/Culture Duality', *NWSA Journal* 16: 3 (2004) 154–79.

Mallan, Kerry. 'No place like ...: Home and School as Contested Spaces in *Little Soldier* and *Idiot Pride*', *Papers: Explorations into Children's Literature* 11: 2 (2001) 7–16.

——. '(M)other Love: Constructing Queer Families in *Girl Walking Backwards* and *Obsession*', *Children's Literature Association Quarterly* 29: 4 (2004) 345–58.

Mallan, Kerry, Clare Bradford and John Stephens. 'New Social Orders: Reconceptualising Family and Community in Utopian Fiction', *Papers: Explorations into Children's Literature* 15: 2 (2005) 6–21.

Manning, Erin. *Ephemeral Territories: Representing Nation, Home, and Identity in Canada* (Minneapolis: University of Minnesota Press, 2003).

May, Elaine Tyler. *Homeward Bound: American Families in the Cold War Era* (New York: Basic Books, 1988).

McCallum, Robyn. *Ideologies of Identity in Adolescent Fiction* (New York and London: Garland Publishing, 1999).

——. 'Young Adult Literature', in Jack Zipes (ed.), *The Oxford Encyclopedia of Children's Literature* (New York: Oxford University Press, 2006), Vol. 4, pp. 214–19.

McNay, Lois. 'Subject, Psyche and Agency: The Work of Judith Butler', *Theory, Culture and Society* 16: 2 (1999) 175–93.

Mignolo, Walter. 'The Many Faces of Cosmo-polis: Border Thinking and Critical Cosmopolitanism', *Public Culture* 12: 3 (2000) 721–48.

Mihailescu, Calin-Andrei. 'Mind the gap: Dystopia as fiction', *Style* 25: 2 (1991) 211–22.

Mills, Claudia. 'Utopia Explored: Three Recent Fictionalizations of Fruitlands for Young Readers', *Children's Literature in Education* 36: 3 (2005) 255–67.

Mitchell, W. J. T. 'The Work of Art in the Age of Biocybernetic Reproduction', *Modernism/modernity* 10: 3 (2003) 481–500.

More, Thomas. *Utopia* 2nd edn, trans. and R. M. Adams (ed.). (New York: Norton, 1992).

Moylan, Tom. *Demand the Impossible: Science Fiction and the Utopian Imagination* (New York: Methuen, 1986).

——. *Scraps of the Untainted Sky: Science Fiction, Utopia, Dystopia* (Boulder: Westview, 2000).

——. ' "The moment is here ... and it's important": State, Agency, and Dystopia in Kim Stanley Robinson's *Antarctica* and Ursula K. Le Guin's *The Telling*', in Raffaella Baccolini and Tom Moylan (eds) *Dark Horizons: Science Fiction and the Dystopian Imagination* (New York: Routledge, 2003), pp. 135–54.

O'Har, George. 'Technology and Its Discontents', *Technology and Culture* 45: 2 (2004) 479–85.

Parrinder, Patrick (ed.). *Learning from Other Worlds: Estrangement, Cognition, and the Politics of Science Fiction and Utopia* (Durham, NC: Duke University Press, 2001).

Peterson, A. D. C. 'Ten Years of European Education Review, 1956–1966' *Comparative Education Review* 11: 3 (1967) 288–99.

Phillips, Dana. 'Ecocriticism, Literary Theory, and the Truth of Ecology', *New Literary History* 30: 3 (1999) 577–600.

Piercy, Marge. 'Telling Stories about Stories', *Utopian Studies* 5 (1994) 1–3.

Pilger, John. *The New Rulers of the World* (London: Verso, 2003).

Pordzik, Ralph. *The Quest for Postcolonial Utopia* (New York: Peter Lang, 2001).

Ramos, Alcida R. 'Reflecting on the Yanomami: Ethnographic Images and the Pursuit of the Exotic', *Cultural Anthropology* 2: 3 (1987) 284–304.

Rigby, Kate. 'Earth, World, Text: On the (Im)possibility of Ecopoiesis', *New Literary History* 35: 3 (2004) 427–442.

Rorty, Richard. *Contingency, Irony, and Solidarity* (New York: Cambridge, 1989).

Sargent, Lyman Tower. 'The Three Faces of Utopianism Revisited', *Utopian Studies* 5: 1 (1994) 1–37.

———. 'The Problem of the "Flawed Utopia": A Note on the Costs of Eutopia', in *Dark Horizons: Science Fiction and the Dystopian Imagination* (New York: Routledge, 2003), pp. 225–32.

Schiller, Herbert I., Hamid Mowlana and George Gerbner. *Invisible Crises: What Conglomerate Control of Media Means for America and the World* (Colorado: Westview Press, 1996).

Scott, A. O. 2001. 'Film Review: Do Androids Long for Mum?', *The New York Times Movies: New York Times Review*, http://moviesz.nytime.com/mom/movies/review.html(accessed 4 May 2004).

Seed, Patricia. *American Pentimento: The Invention of Indians and the Pursuit of Riches* (Minneapolis: University of Minnesota Press, 2001).

Sharp, Cecil J. *Eighty English Folk Songs from the Southern Appalachians* (Cambridge, Mass: MIT Press, 1968).

Sheldrake, Philip. 'Human Identity and the Particularity of Place', *Spiritus: A Journal of Christian Spirituality* 1: 1 (2001) 43–64.

Silvio, Carl. 'Refiguring the Radical Cyborg in Mamoru Oshii's *Ghost in the Shell*', *Science Fiction Studies* 26 (1999) 54–72.

Simon, Bart. 'Introduction: Toward a Critique of Posthuman Futures', *Cultural Critique* 53 (2003) 1–9.

Slater, Candace. 'Amazonia as Edenic Narrative', in William Cronin (ed.) *Uncommon Ground: Rethinking the Human Place in Nature* (New York: W. W. Norton, 1996), pp. 114–31.

Smith, Steve. 'The End of the Unipolar Moment: September 11 and the Future of World Order', http://www.ssrc.org/sept11/essays/smith.htm (accessed 27 March 2005).

Stalder, Felix. 'Opinion. Privacy is not the Antidote to Surveillance', *Surveillance & Society* 1: 1 (2003) 120–24.

Stephens, John. *Language and Ideology in Children's Fiction* (London and New York: Longman, 1992a).

———. 'Post-Disaster Fiction: The Problematics of a Genre', *Papers:Explorations into Children's Literature* 3: 3 (1992b) 126–30.

———. 'Children's Literature, Text and Theory: What Are We Interested in Now?', *Papers: Explorations into Children's Literature* 10: 2 (2000) 12–21.

———. 'Performativity and the Child Who May Not be a Child' *Papers: Explorations into Children's Literature* 16: 1 (2006a) 5–13.

———. 'From Eden to Suburbia: Perspectives on the Natural World in Children's Literature', *Papers: Explorations into Children's Literature* 16: 2 (2006b) 40–5.

Stephens, John and Roderick McGillis. 'Critical Approaches to Children's Literature', in Jack Zipes (ed.) *The Oxford Encyclopedia of Children's Literature* (Oxford and New York: Oxford University Press, 2006), Vol. 1, pp. 364–67.

Suvin, Darko. 'Theses on Dystopia', in Raffaella Baccolini and Tom Moylan (eds) *Dark Horizons: Science Fiction and the Dystopian Imagination* (New York and London: Routledge, 2003), pp. 187–201.

Taylor, Philip M. *War and the Media: Propaganda and Persuasion in the Gulf War* (Manchester and New York: Manchester University Press, 1992).

Tierney, Patrick. *Darkness in El Dorado: How Scientists and Journalists Devastated the Amazon* (New York: Norton, 2000).

Waldby, Catherine. *The Visible Human Project: Informatic Bodies and Posthuman Medicine* (London: Routledge, 2000).

Wegner, Phillip. 'Where the Prospective Horizon is Omitted: Naturalism and Dystopia in *Fight Club* and *Ghost Dog*', in Raffaella Baccolini and Tom Moylan (eds) *Dark Horizons: Science Fiction and the Dystopian Imagination* (New York and London: Routledge, 2003), pp. 167–186.

Weiss, Linda. 'Globalization and National Governance: Antinomy or Interdependence?', *Review of International Studies* 25 (1999) 61.

White, Hayden. *The Content of the Form: Narrative Discourse and Historical Representation* (Baltimore: Johns Hopkins University Press, 1987).

Yates, Joshua J. and James Davison Hunter. 'Fundamentalism: When History Goes Awry', in Joseph Davies (ed.) *Stories of Change: Narrative and Social Movements* (Albany: State University of New York Press, 2002), pp. 123–48.

Zimmerman, Michael E. *Contesting Earth's Future: Radical Ecology and Postmodernity* (Berkeley: University of California Press, 1994).

Index

abandoned children, 137–8
adolescent fiction, 12, 14, 17, 29–34
  see also coming of age narratives
agency, 16–21, 26, 28–33, 93, 96, 121,
    129, 136, 141, 158, 166, 167, 169,
    170, 177, 180, 183–4
  see also subjectivity
Aladdin, 44–5, 58
Allende, Isabel, *City of the Beasts*, 82,
    98–9
Almond, David, *The Fire-Eaters*, 37–8
Anderson, M. T., *Burger Wuss*, 43,
    47–8, 49–50, 57
  Feed, 42, 157, 166, 167–8
Anderson, Rachel, *The Scavenge's Tale*,
    111–14
anthropocentrism, 81, 91, 97
anti-utopians, *see* utopianism
Armitt, Lucie, 125–6
artificial intelligence, 160, 161
Artz, Lee, 49
Ashcroft, Bill, 61
Asimov, Isaac
  three laws of robotics, 163, 191 n.2
Auer, Carolin, 171

Baccolini, Raffaella, 48, 110, 127, 139
Baker, Jeannie, *Belonging*, 80, 96–7
Bakker, Karen, 87
Balit, Christina, *Blodin the Beast*, 80–1
Bartowski, Frances, 6
Baudrillard, Jean, 171, 175–6, 192 n.4
Bauer, Joan, *Rules of the Road*, 17, 29
Bauman, Zygmont, 2, 35, 56
Bawden, Nina, *Off the Road*, 115–17
Beale, Fleur, *I Am Not Esther*, 118
Beauchamp, Gorman, 4
Beck-Gernsheim, Elizabeth, 132
Beck, Ulrich, 132
Berebitsky, Julie, 130
Bertagna, Julie, *Exodus*, 35, 41, 53–6,
    60–1, 89

bildungsroman, 9, 29
  see also coming of age narratives
biological engineering, 165, 170
Bonnett, Alistair, 188 n.4
border conditions, 27–8
Bradford, Clare, 7, 59, 188 n.1, n.5
Brady, Mary Pat, 27
Braithwaite, Elizabeth, 7
Bridge, Gavin, 87
Browne, Anthony, *Zoo*, 82–3
Buell, Frederick, 22
Bukatman, Scott, 156, 172, 180
Burgess, Melvin, *The Baby and Fly
    Pie*, 16
  Bloodtide, 137, 144–7
Burwell, Jennifer, 152
Bush, George W., 1, 7, 11, 187 n.1
Butler, Charles, *Calypso Dreaming*,
    85–9
Butler, Judith, 133

Callenbach, Ernest, 189 n.3
capitalism, 13, 14, 15, 29, 36, 42–4,
    46–8, 50, 101, 105, 166
Carmichael, Claire, *Incognito*, 113–14
Castells, Manuel, 40, 42, 56
Caswell, Brian, *Deucalion*, 68–9, 73,
    75–8
Chagnon, Napoleon, 98
Cherry, Lynne, *The Great Kapok Tree*,
    94–5
Chomsky, Noam, 177, 192 n.4
Christopher, John, 13
'clash of civilisations' doctrine, 1, 7,
    16, 50, 59
  see also Huntington, Samuel P.
cloning, 165
closure, 12, 14, 17, 29
  refusal of, 3, 13
Cold War, 6, 12, 13, 15, 16, 25, 36,
    37, 45, 90, 108, 150, 182, 187 n.6
colonialism, *see* postcolonialism

202